A KILLING MOON

By Steven Dunne

The Reaper
The Disciple
Deity
The Unquiet Grave
A Killing Moon

www.stevendunne.co.uk

A KILLING MOON

STEVEN DUNNE

headline

First published in 2015 by
HEADLINE PUBLISHING GROUP

1

Cataloguing in Publication Data is available from the British Library

ISBN (HB) 978 1 4722 1492 8
ISBN (TPB) 978 1 4722 1491 1

Typeset in Hoefler by Avon DataSet Ltd, Bidford-on-Avon, Warwickshire

Printed and bound in Great Britain by Clays Ltd, St Ives plc

HEADLINE PUBLISHING GROUP
An Hachette UK Company
Carmelite House
50 Victoria Embankment
London EC4Y 0DZ

www.headline.co.uk
www.hachette.co.uk

In loving memory
Vincent 'Vinny' McKenna
A fan, a friend, a brother

Acknowledgements

Love and thanks to my wife Carmel for her support and encouragement. To my sister Susan for the same. Jeff Fountain for his editorial comments that are always to the point and insightful.

My vast team at Headline – too numerous to mention – whose skills have contributed so much to the DI Brook series, chiefly my indispensible editor Vicki Mellor and publicity bod (her words) Elizabeth Masters.

Thanks to my agent, David Grossman, for continuing to believe in me and using his expertise to promote the series around the world. Also Joseph McDonald for his keen insights into modern policing procedure in addition to his excellent batting and fielding for The Weekenders.

Finally a warm hug to my favourite book chain Waterstone's for the passionate and knowledgeable people who comprise the staff who have welcomed me through their doors on many occasions to peddle my wares. A special mention for my local stores in Derby, Burton-on-Trent, Loughborough, Chesterfield and Nottingham.

One

20 March

CAITLIN DOWNED THE SHOT, SLAMMED the glass on the counter and followed it with an urgent sip of ice-cold Guinness to dissipate the heat burning a path to an empty stomach. She revelled in the unfamiliar buzz of alcohol and grinned across at her disapproving friend.

'What?' she shouted above the pulse of the band thrashing out their unsubtle rhythm from the stage. 'Another one over here, Jack.' She waggled a hand at the barman to flag up her empty glass.

After a brief hesitation to assess her condition, the barman swept up the glass for a refill and pointed at the name tag on the breast of his shirt. 'I'll serve you if you can read this.'

Caitlin peered myopically at the badge. 'Jake.' The barman nodded and moved over to the optics.

'Going at it a bit hard, aren't you, Kitty?' hissed Laurie.

'Celebratin',' slurred Caitlin in return.

'It's something you celebrate, is it?'

'I'm Oirish,' giggled Caitlin. 'I missed the craic on St Patrick's so I'm making up for it.'

'You know what I mean.'

Caitlin sighed. 'Laurie, it's Friday night, I'm having a drink. Tomorrow I'm away home to Belfast. That means I don't have to endure another lecture for three weeks, and that includes yours.'

'You don't wanna talk about it,' nodded Laurie. 'I get that. But you don't fool me.'

'Meaning?'

'Meaning I know what it cost you,' replied Laurie, her eyes burning into her friend's. 'So if you want to talk about it, I'm here.'

Caitlin looked at the floor to find the words, then, wishing she hadn't, managed to relocate Laurie's face in the murk of the bar. 'Look, it's in the past. I'm grand now . . .'

'But you—'

'No more lectures, okay.' Caitlin smiled. 'I'm a free agent again – happy days.' She took another long draught of Guinness.

Laurie relented with her own smile. 'Okay. And as a bonus, I suppose you found out what a shit Rollo is.'

'Don't think there was ever much doubt about that, was there?' Caitlin hiccuped and threw a hand to her mouth, feeling the first peep of vomit at the back of her throat.

'You okay, Kitty?'

'Never better,' mumbled Caitlin, trying to persuade herself. No, she wasn't okay. She hadn't had a serious drink in weeks and now the alcohol was biting back hard. The room was beginning to sway and her head felt like it was bobbing around on a stick.

Suddenly, instead of enveloping her in a hubbub of dark contentment, the pub began to crowd in on Caitlin and details began to grate – the music, the crush of bodies, the sudden heat in her chest and the dots of sweat appearing on her forehead. She splashed her pint glass on to the bar and pushed through bodies for the exit. 'Toilet,' she garbled over her shoulder.

A moment later she slithered out into the cold Derby night as the first rush of vomit heaved its way out of her mouth and on to trampled snow on the pavement. She groaned with self-loathing and propped her hands on her knees to wait for more. After a second expulsion, she was finally able to stand upright and wipe her watering eyes, feeling better now the poison was out of her system. She took a few deep breaths, enjoying the bite of winter after the dank perspiration of the pub. About her, snow was falling in fists, throwing its gentle veil over the city's customary bustle.

Recovered, she pushed at the black and white door of the Flowerpot, but hesitated at the wall of bodies in front of her, all nodding to the rudimentary music crashing over them from the stage. After a moment's hesitation, she pulled out her phone and thumbed out a message to Laurie.

I'm done. Heading off. Coming?

Caitlin walked briskly along King Street, feeling the cold leave her bones as her strong young legs bounced her along, crunching through the snow. At Five Lamps, she turned on to Kedleston Road, heading towards the university and, half a mile beyond that, the small down-at-heel bungalow she rented with Laurie. Although it was a Friday night, the hum of the city was numbed by the curtain of snow falling across her vision. Only the occasional crescendo of cars tearing past on the A38 ahead and the buzz of approaching and receding street lights broke the silence. The harsh weather had deterred all but the hardiest travellers.

Her phone vibrated. *Where R U?*
On Ked. Halfway home.
U OK?

Caitlin stopped on the bridge over the A38, tapped out a smiley face. She leaned on the rail to get her breath. A passing white van slowed as it approached the bridge, and she turned disinterestedly towards it. Having worked out which road to take, the van driver sped past her, spraying slush on to her shins.

'Asshole,' she shouted after it.

She let out a quick laugh and returned her gaze to the four lanes below, feeling a glow of anticipation. People going places. It raised her spirits. She felt tranquil for the first time in weeks. She'd be on the train to Liverpool tomorrow, then the boat to Belfast to see her sister, Mairead. Travel was good. It soothed her, gave her time to think, time to stare out of the window or down at the timeless water to mull over her life.

She stood upright. Well, her life was going just fine again, and now she wanted to get on with it. Another text from Laurie. *Tommo's here, getting a cab to his. Sure U R OK?*

Caitlin sent a final reassuring message – *Never better* – and continued on her way, tramping through the snow, which squeaked underfoot, enjoying the solitude and the pale light of the leaden sky. She glanced to the university buildings looming large up the hill on her right, and at the shadows of Markeaton Park on her left.

She'd walked a further hundred yards down the road when she became aware of a sudden movement and rustling of leaves in the bushes to her left.

Something crashing around the park in this weather? Must be a stray.

She cocked an ear for subsequent noise, but heard nothing.

No barking, no panting. 'Here, boy,' she called. No reaction. A second later she resumed her journey but almost immediately came to a halt, her head snapping round at the low voice calling from the blackness of the park.

'Kit-ty!'

Frozen in shock, she stared towards the dark holly bush from where the voice had seemed to emanate. Was that a human shape crouched in the foliage? Snow fell in her eyes and she blinked furiously to keep her vision clear. She stared on, aware only of the falling snow, her beating heart, and the vapour exhaled from her mouth.

The darkness in the bush didn't move. If it was a human shadow, it was incredibly still. Embarrassment invaded her features and she turned to move away.

'Guinness and vodka,' she muttered, falling into step once more. 'Lethal combo.'

'Kit-ty!' The voice again, muffled yet urgent, demanding attention.

Caitlin swivelled, all her senses supercharged. Her heart pounded in her chest and she flushed with heat in spite of the sub-zero temperatures. 'Who's there?'

'Here, Kitty, Kitty, Kitty.'

A tingle ran down Caitlin's spine and she picked up her pace again. *Don't run! Don't panic! Walk quickly but calmly.* She'd learned that in her women's self-defence group. Self-control was everything. Fear was an aphrodisiac to some of the perverts out there.

'Don't turn round,' she told herself as she walked briskly without breaking into a run. 'Someone's lost their cat, is all.' But when she heard the crashing of undergrowth behind her, she broke into a trot.

'Kit-ty!' The voice was louder now, panting, on the move. She turned to look but, seeing nothing, kept moving.

'Whoever the fuck this is, it's not funny,' she barked over her shoulder, without slowing.

'Kit-ty!'

Caitlin slithered to a halt and turned. *Who would know my nickname, if not a friend?* She gazed intently behind her, raising a hand against the flakes blurring her vision.

'Rollo? Is that you?' No reply. No movement and nothing to be seen. She was about to retrace her steps when, through the white curtain, she saw a burly figure appear some twenty feet away, standing perfectly still, breath steaming in the air, looming large. 'If that's you, Rollo, then say something, you stupid fecker. You've got a bloody nerve after what—'

'Kit-ty!' cried the voice, growling now, using her name like an accusation, the voice mournful but with an edge of hate.

Caitlin wanted to run but was transfixed, staring through the blinding flurries for a clue to her tormentor's identity. The snow confined her, cut her off from all but the distant lights of houses, the occupants safe and warm. She looked about for the comfort of other pedestrians, a car even, but there was no one to answer an appeal.

'Jesus, this is *so* not funny. I mean it!'

'Kitty.' The voice was harsh and rasping, exuding aggression, confidence. 'Here, puss-puss. Come to Daddy.'

Finally Caitlin turned from the voice and broke into a sprint, keeping her eyes firmly on the path ahead but all the time listening for noise of pursuit behind her.

'Here, Kitty, Kitty, Kitty!'

Again she slithered to a halt. The voice was in front of her now. The same voice? No, different. A higher pitch. Someone younger? A boy? Hard to be sure. What she couldn't mistake was the malevolence, the mocking tone, taunting her. She hesitated before deciding to cross the road and make a run for it to the university. As she retreated, she saw another form emerge from the shadows ahead of her, and, letting out an involuntary whimper, she pivoted to run in the opposite direction.

In the split second of consciousness remaining to her, Caitlin registered the large form with which she collided, as well as the crackle of electricity. There followed a searing pain that jolted through her body, robbing her muscles of function, and she collapsed to the ground with a crunch.

TWO

ETECTIVE SERGEANT JOHN NOBLE WALKED back through the light rain to his car and drove the short distance from the campus to Derby Constabulary Headquarters at St Mary's Wharf. After parking his car, he lingered a while in the darkness, pulling out his cigarettes. He produced his notebook to peruse the few facts he'd gleaned from Caitlin Kinnear's ex-boyfriend, a second-year undergraduate, recalling the scorn with which he'd been treated.

With a pen he wrote *Cocky slimeball* next to the name Roland Davison. He would have liked to write something more abusive, but DI Brook might see his notes, and Noble imagined his response. *Swearing is a symptom of a mind that's not under control, John,* he'd say, before adding, *and control is what they pay us for.*

'I bet *your* self-control would've taken a pasting, dealing with that . . .' Noble halted in mid-sentence and lit up. If there was ever a time he'd needed Brook to cut a witness down to size, today was it. A few puffs later, equilibrium returned and

Noble threw away his butt to head for the smoked-glass entrance, feeling calmer after his tobacco hit.

'Do the paperwork and pass it on to the Northern Irish police. The PSNI can handle their own missing persons.'

He pushed through into the light and warmth. Seeing DI Frank Ford enjoying a joke with Sergeant Hendrickson at the reception desk brought him up short as they both turned towards him, their grins downgraded into mocking smiles. After a tough day, Noble needed to think, and hankered after the comfort of his office. But he knew from experience that Brook, the socially awkward outsider, scuttled away from these encounters, and Noble was determined not to feel uncomfortable in his own house.

'John,' said Ford, hailing him like a long-lost friend.

'Sir,' replied Noble, lingering to see if either of Brook's most voluble critics had anything to impart besides abuse.

'How's life without the organ-grinder?' grinned Ford, glancing at Hendrickson to register the desk sergeant's approval.

Noble smiled mechanically. 'Are you calling me a monkey, sir?'

'More of a gopher, I'd say,' said Ford. Hendrickson laughed at this.

'Here to serve,' retorted Noble cheerily. Deciding this was sufficient banter, he angled his frame towards the stairs.

'Seriously, though,' said Ford quickly, 'when are you going to stop letting that oddball hold back your career?'

'Sir?' enquired Noble.

'Got passed over for DI last time, didn't you?'

'In favour of someone else on DI Brook's team,' retorted Noble, his polite smile dimming at each of Ford's barbs. 'Sir.'

Ford's eyes narrowed, the implication not lost on him. 'Where is he? On the sick again?'

Noble stared at Ford and Hendrickson, their grins churning his stomach. Ford was referring to Brook's mental breakdown while serving in the Met over twenty years ago. 'Holiday,' he managed to wrench out, though the smile was no more. 'Back on Monday.'

'I didn't think Brook did holidays.'

'He takes a week at Easter to walk around the Peaks, blow the winter cobwebs off.'

'Does he?' nodded Ford, composing his next witticism. 'Yeah, I've always thought Brook was a bit of a walker.' He winked at Hendrickson, who laughed again.

'Yeah,' said Noble, heading for the stairs. 'He reckons it helps him think.' He held the door, considering his two smirking colleagues. 'Seems to work, judging by the number of cold cases he cleared last year.'

He let the door swing behind him and bolted up the stairs. He didn't need to see Ford's face to relish the sudden anger that would have distorted his features. Nor had he needed to add, *Most of them yours!*

Still grinning, Noble booted up his computer to check his inbox and flicked on the kettle. Sipping hot coffee, he read an email about an impending court case that had been moved forward to Monday morning. He was required to give evidence and made a note of the time in his phone diary. That was next week up in smoke.

On the positive side, he was pleased to see a couple of prompt responses to his enquiry about Caitlin Kinnear. One, from a DS in the PSNI, carried Caitlin's name in the subject line. The other, from a friend in Merseyside CID, referred simply to *Missing Irish girl*. Noble read carefully through both emails before pulling his notebook towards him and flipping to a new page to write down a checklist for the morning.

- Photo from uni admin
- Follow up with PSNI
- Midland Mainline CCTV and ticketing
- Local taxis
- Friends, tutors, etc.
- Bar staff at Flowerpot
- Border control (if any)

After a few more notes, he flipped back to the previous page, located Roland Davison's name and wrote Check alibi, triple-underlining it before draining his coffee. He blinked wearily at the monitor, his gaze held. Something nagged at him. 'Missing Irish girl,' he mumbled, as though trying to work out its meaning. Repeating the phrase, he loaded the PNC database and typed it into the search engine, adding *Derby* to the tagline.

'Jane,' said Noble, pushing open the door to DI Gadd's office.

A slim woman the same age as Noble looked up from her monitor. Smiling at first, she adopted an air of perplexity. 'Sorry, who do you want?'

Noble sighed. '*Detective Inspector* Gadd.'

'Inspector Gadd?' She grinned at him. 'Oh, that's me.'

Noble laughed. 'Not over the novelty yet?'

'Not even close. What can I do you for?'

'Bernadette Murphy. Disappeared three years ago. Staying at her aunt's place in Darley Abbey. You picked it up.'

'Remind me.'

'Irish girl from Dublin. Staying with Mr and Mrs Finnegan on Bank View Road.'

'Got it,' said Gadd, nodding. 'What about it?'

'I picked up another missing Irish girl,' explained Noble, feeling silly voicing it.

'Caitlin Kinnear,' said Gadd. 'I saw it in the paper. Bit tenuous.'

'I know,' conceded Noble. 'Humour me.'

'As far as I can remember, it was a routine enquiry from the Garda after Bernadette failed to return to Dublin at the end of August. She left her aunt's taking all her stuff with her.'

'That would be early July three years ago.'

'If you say so. She was on holiday, travelling around, so natural enough. The aunt thought she might have gone to London. I did a risk assessment and a twenty-eight-day review, but as far as I could tell, it was out-of-area and the Garda owned it. End of story. Still missing as far as I know. If there ever was a trail, which I doubt, it was stone cold by the time I came on board.'

'So not worth me going round to interview the aunt.'

'To Bank View, no,' said Gadd. 'By the time I got involved, the aunt and uncle had separated and she'd already moved out.'

'Oh? Know why?'

'If you're thinking they broke up because Bernadette and the uncle were having it off, forget it,' said Gadd. 'He was on an oil rig in the North Sea.'

Noble shrugged. 'Just a thought.'

'Though there was something in the aunt's manner that sent the wrong signal when I interviewed her.'

'What?'

'I'm not sure, but I suspect she and her niece might have had a falling-out, probably why Bernadette left. The aunt didn't want to elaborate and I had no reason to go hard at it. Never heard another thing.'

'Maybe the aunt killed her and buried her in the back garden.'

'Not with her physique,' said Gadd. 'Or her stone-flagged garden. I can look up the file and email the aunt's new address if you want to waste your time.'

'I'd appreciate it. Inspector.'

Gadd grinned again. 'Call me Jane.'

Two days later, Noble knew his testimony backwards. He closed the file for the impending court case and tossed it on to his desk. A mess of other papers was displaced by the file, some to the floor, and Noble picked them up. One was an enlarged photograph of Caitlin Kinnear, posing for her student union card. She had a nice face, short blond hair, green eyes. Full of the promise of a youth that was a distant memory to Noble, only just the wrong side of thirty.

For something to do, he pinned the portrait on to the corkboard and stared at it, then glanced at the file on his desk and pulled out his mobile. He began to dial Brook's number, but stopped, realising the late hour; with Caitlin's trail cold for nearly a month, he wasn't even sure it was worth it. He thumbed out a text. *In court Monday. Need a favour. Speak tomorrow?*

'Prepare to get laughed at,' said Noble. He logged off and pulled on his jacket. A second later, the theme from *The Rockford Files* blasted out from his phone.

'What's up, John?' said Brook.

Three

20 April

DETECTIVE INSPECTOR DAMEN BROOK PLACED the
tray on the freshly wiped plastic table, gazing about
the bright food hall of Derby University, its various
outlets barely open for business at ten in the morning. The hall
was heavily populated, though most of the students were using
it as a common area, sitting around without purpose, not
drinking or eating, not even talking that much. Some nodded
to unknown music feeding through headphones; others stared
hypnotically at iPhones, thumbs scrolling furiously at the
tablet for conversational titbits.

'You're that detective who looked for those missing
students,' said Brook's nervous companion, sitting across from
him.

Brook returned his attention to the first-year undergraduate,
five years younger than his daughter. Laurie Teague was wide-
eyed, with mid-length brown hair, slim and petite. Brook
pushed her paper cup, half filled with froth, across the table,
slid on to the opposite bench and took a sip of his watery tea.

'That's right.'

'Is that why you get to look for Caitlin?' she said. 'You're some kind of expert.'

'On missing students?' replied Brook. 'No. I'm just a detective . . .'

'Laurie,' said the girl, staring through an external glass wall towards a covered courtyard beyond. Her fingers fiddled with a cigarette, but unable to light up, she caressed it in her fingers.

'Laurie,' repeated Brook, his smile awkward. Noble usually prompted him with the names he habitually forgot.

'What happened to DS Noble?'

'He's busy.'

'I see.'

'I didn't mean it like that,' said Brook. 'He had to go to court and didn't want you thinking he wasn't taking it seriously, so he asked me to speak to you.'

'You're his boss.'

'Yes.'

She nodded. 'Thought you'd found a body when I saw your ID.'

'Don't worry, we haven't.'

'I realise that, or there'd be a junior officer along to do the hand-holding when I go all girlie. At least that's how it works on the telly. And it's always a sow.' Brook raised an eyebrow and Laurie lowered her head, her apology to her sex unspoken. 'What's happened to Caitlin, Inspector?'

'There's no proof *anything's* happened to your friend.'

'Something has,' insisted Laurie. 'She's dead in a ditch somewhere.'

Brook considered her. She was nervous, affecting a worldliness she didn't possess. 'If so, her body would've been discovered by now. After all, it's been nearly a month.'

'And I only reported her missing last week. I explained that to Sergeant Noble. We're just back from Easter recess.'

'Which lasts two weeks,' said Brook. 'According to DS Noble, you haven't seen Caitlin since the week *before* the holiday. March twentieth.'

'We had a reading week,' explained Laurie. 'That's when we read books for our courses.'

There was a slight emphasis on *read books*, and for some reason Brook had to stifle his indignation. As a policeman on a university campus, he should've known to expect such jibes, but this morning he was unprepared. 'I know what a reading week is,' he said quietly. 'You said Caitlin was going home to Belfast.'

'She has a sister in Belfast – Mairead. She took the train to Liverpool the next morning and then the ferry.'

'Saturday the twenty-first,' said Brook, darting an eye at Noble's notebook.

'Yes.'

'For which she bought an advance train ticket.'

'It's cheaper,' said Laurie.

'But she never arrived at her sister's house,' said Brook, watching her reaction carefully.

'So Sergeant Noble said.'

'But you weren't aware of that.'

'No.'

'Mairead didn't call you.'

'Why would she call me?'

'Oh, I don't know,' said Brook, his tone betraying the opposite. 'To ask why Caitlin hadn't arrived, maybe.'

Laurie looked coldly back. 'I don't think Mairead even knows I exist. I've never spoken to her.'

'What about Caitlin's other friends?'

'I'm her best friend,' said Laurie. 'If she gave Mairead any number to call it would have been mine. But she didn't.'

'That strikes me as odd,' said Brook. 'Sergeant Noble thought so too.'

Laurie stared enviously at two students lighting up in the courtyard. 'Caitlin kept things separate, in compartments, so she could handle them more easily. That's the way she was. It's a Catholic thing apparently.'

As a lapsed Catholic, Brook's interest stirred. He knew the impulse. A different face for home. 'So she never got in touch during the holidays.'

'Never. If she was in Derby she'd text. If she wasn't . . .' She shrugged the rest.

'Not even a text from the train. Or to say she'd arrived safely in Belfast.'

'Not a text, not a call, not an email,' insisted Laurie. 'It wasn't Kitty's way.'

'Odd.' Remembering his own reluctance to use his mobile phone unless he had to, Brook added, 'For someone of your generation, I mean.'

'No argument here,' said Laurie. 'I've known Kitty since September and at first it drove me mad. I'd text her over Christmas or half term and never get a reply, even at New Year. She said that when she was at home, she needed all her powers of concentration to slot back in; that if she divided her mind thinking about her life in Derby, she lost focus.'

'On what?'

'On behaving the way that was expected of her.'

'Her family were very traditional.'

'So she said,' said Laurie.

'And Caitlin didn't want them to think she'd changed.'

'If her parents got an inkling of how she lived in Derby, it might have caused problems, so when she went home she was . . .'

'Playing a role.'

Laurie pointed a finger at him to confirm.

'And in that way any binge drinking or casual sex couldn't become an issue,' probed Brook.

'Don't judge people like that.'

'I'm not,' said Brook. 'It's common for people who relocate from their home town to behave differently. The past is another country . . .'

'. . . they do things differently there,' said Laurie. 'Yeah, I know.'

Brook smiled. Poetry-lovers were thin on the ground amongst his limited circle of acquaintances, most of them coppers. 'So for instance, I'm willing to bet she never once went to church in Derby, but in spite of her pathological opposition to organised religion went willingly with her family in Ireland, am I right?'

'Actually, you are.'

'And,' continued Brook, 'leaving home gave her the freedom she craved, the chance to live the life she wanted.'

'You sound like you know her,' said Laurie.

Brook took a sip of tea. 'She started losing her accent as well, didn't she?'

'As a matter of fact, yes,' said Laurie, impressed. 'It came back when she drank, though.'

'The return of the unconscious self,' said Brook. 'What else did she say about her family?'

'Nothing. She never mentioned them except to tell me

Mairead's name. That was all the detail she ever gave me. Except that her parents didn't want her coming to university in England so Caitlin had to lie to them. She would have felt stifled living at home so she turned down an offer from Belfast but told her parents she'd been refused a place.'

'So when exactly *did* you expect to hear from her?'

'When she arrived back in England she usually sent a text. She should have been in touch the Sunday before summer term started. That's when she was due back.'

'April twelfth?'

Laurie nodded. 'When she hadn't turned up by Monday, I began to worry, started texting and ringing her, but her phone was dead. It still is.'

'We know,' confirmed Brook.

'See, that's suspicious, isn't it?'

Brook didn't argue. 'So the last time you saw her was the night before she was supposed to leave.'

'We were in the pub – the Flowerpot. There was a gig by a local band we wanted to see.'

'And you were there for a couple of hours,' said Brook, reading from Noble's notes, 'before Caitlin left.'

'She'd been going at it pretty hard. She'd been off the booze for a spell and I think she was feeling it. She headed off to the toilet with a hand over her mouth like she was going to spew. The next thing I know, she texts me to say she's walking home.' Laurie's lip began to wobble. 'I haven't seen her since.'

Brook hurtled into the next question. Dealing with the tearful was not the strongest part of his repertoire. 'What's she studying?' he asked, careful to use the present tense.

'International relations. She wanted . . . wants to travel.'

'Anywhere in particular?' said Brook.

'Everywhere,' answered Laurie. 'She loved new places.' She smiled at a memory.

'What?'

'I say she liked new places, but oddly, the thing she always loved most was the journey. We took the train to Nice last October and she enjoyed the travelling more than actually being there. She liked being on the move. She was funny like that.'

'It's the symptom of a sheltered home life,' suggested Brook, this time wearing his experience on his sleeve. 'You feel a constant urge to break away.'

'I suppose.' There was a lull in the conversation. 'Where is she, Inspector?'

Brook was sombre. 'We don't know. DS Noble has been working with the PSNI in Belfast.'

'What did they say?'

'That Sergeant Noble's call was the first they'd heard about it,' said Brook. 'You were the only person to report her missing. Mairead didn't contact anyone when Caitlin failed to show up. Not even Caitlin. They checked her phone records. She didn't text or ring to ask Caitlin where she was.'

Laurie was thoughtful. 'I didn't know that. That is weird.'

'And, at first glance, quite suspicious,' said Brook.

'So her family are suspects, then?'

'They were looked at, yes,' said Brook, not wishing to exaggerate the quality of enquiries over which he had no control. 'Especially Mairead.'

Something in Brook's voice alerted Laurie. 'But now she's in the clear.'

'If you can confirm why her sister might not take Caitlin's no-show seriously, yes.'

Laurie looked at Brook and nodded. 'Sometimes Caitlin was . . . unreliable. Is that what Mairead said?'

Brook confirmed it with a blink of the eyes. 'In what way?'

Laurie hesitated. 'She had . . . whims, sudden passions that she had to act on.' Brook prompted her with a raised eyebrow. 'She could go off for days and I wouldn't see her. If she met a man, she'd . . . well, you know.'

'No, I don't.' Brook finished his weak tea with a grimace. 'Tell me.'

'Well . . . she'd drop everything, put her life on hold for as long as the passion burned. It didn't need to be a man. If she found a new band she liked, she'd head off the same day to see a gig, even if they were on tour, not caring if she missed lectures or seminars. They could be playing anywhere in the country but she'd just hop on a train without so much as packing a bag. That was Caitlin.' She closed her eyes to self-admonish. '*Is* Caitlin.'

'And how do you know that isn't the case this time?'

'I don't,' admitted Laurie. 'Not for sure. I should have told the sergeant this, shouldn't I?'

'It might've helped,' said Brook, closing the notebook with a snap.

'I'm sorry. But I know something's happened to her and I didn't want him dismissing her as some flaky student. Her phone is still dead. It's been a month without so much as a text.'

'You said she may have met a man.'

'I don't believe it,' insisted Laurie. 'She wouldn't. Not now.'

The force of Laurie's rebuttal puzzled Brook. 'What does that mean?'

Laurie hesitated. 'Caitlin's off men at the moment.' She

tried to avoid Brook's searching gaze, then took a deep breath, casting around for a form of words before fixing him with a glare. 'This has to stay between us.'

'As far as I'm able to make that promise,' said Brook, beginning to lose patience. 'What happened? Boyfriend trouble?'

Laurie hesitated. 'Caitlin had a . . . termination.'

'She was pregnant?' exclaimed Brook. A few heads turned at the raised voice.

'No, I just said. She had a surgical abortion. A couple of weeks earlier and she could've taken a pill, but she missed it. We were at the Flowerpot celebrating . . .' Laurie pulled up at her choice of words. 'I don't mean it like that. It was more like relief that it was sorted. Kitty was putting on a brave face, but I know she struggled with what she'd done because of her background.'

'And the pregnancy was why she hadn't been drinking,' said Brook.

'Yes.'

'More facts we haven't been given,' said Brook, opening Noble's notebook to write. He was beginning to feel annoyed. Worse, he was being forced to make his own notes.

'It didn't seem relevant at the time.'

'Everything's relevant,' said Brook, squinting at a page. 'She had an ex-boyfriend. Roland Davison. The father?' Laurie nodded. 'As far as you know.'

'Kitty was no skank,' protested Laurie.

'You were the one who mentioned her passions,' said Brook calmly.

'That didn't mean she slept around.'

'So you say.' Brook was stern now, assuming the position – push hard to get the best information. 'According to your previous statement, she broke up with Mr Davison nearly two weeks before she disappeared.'

'Sounds about right.'

'Is that because he was opposed to the termination?'

'The opposite,' said Laurie. 'He was all in favour. She broke up with him because he refused to get involved.'

'Get involved?' asked Brook. 'How? Did she want money?'

'No, nothing like that. Kitty took responsibility. That's what she was like. She didn't want a thing from Rollo except a little help and moral support, like go with her to the clinic and hold her hand, that sort of thing. But Rollo wouldn't man up. He didn't want to know. You know what men are like,' she added with a waspish glare.

'Vaguely,' replied Brook. 'Why didn't you mention the termination to DS Noble? A seismic experience like that in a young girl's life, a Catholic girl, at that. It's what we call a stressor – an event that forces people to deviate from routine behaviour. Like now.'

'It wasn't my place to tell you,' mumbled Laurie. 'She's entitled to privacy. Besides, I thought Rollo would mention it.'

'Well he didn't.' Brook looked at the bracketed note Noble had made next to Davison's name. *Cocky slimeball.*

'I don't see what it has to do with anything.'

Brook stared at her. 'You can't be that naive. A traumatic event like an abortion, the stress of the decision, of the procedure . . .' He sought a delicate path to the inference. 'It could have triggered depression, which can lead—'

'You think she killed herself? No, Kitty would never do that. It's against her religion.'

'So is aborting a foetus,' pointed out Brook.

'But she was upbeat in the pub, having a good time.'

'Perhaps masking the emotional turmoil below,' suggested Brook. 'I'm sorry to put these possibilities to you, but such things do happen. You may not know this, but in a crowded country like England, it's more difficult than you'd think to disappear, and when people do, more often than not it's because they want to escape the life they're living, either geographically or biologically.' He paused to let his words sink in. 'And depression is the most common trigger.'

Laurie stared into her cup. 'So you think Kitty threw herself off the ferry or something.' Brook said nothing; she narrowed her eyes at him. 'Then why aren't the police in Northern Ireland dealing with it?'

'They are,' said Brook. 'But they've drawn a blank. If she'd jumped overboard from a daytime ferry, there'd be witnesses, maybe even CCTV from the boat. And a month later there would have been a body.'

'She could've thrown herself off the train just as easily,' said Laurie.

'You'll be pleased to know she didn't do that either.'

'Well what, then?'

'It's beginning to look like Caitlin never left Derby,' said Brook softly. 'Not on the advance ticket she booked, at least. It wasn't used.'

Laurie's face drained of blood. 'She never left?'

Brook shrugged. 'Unknown. But we do know she wasn't picked up on any CCTV in the town centre or at Derby station on the day of travel. DS Noble checked. None of her friends gave her a lift to the station and no cab company took her.'

'Couldn't she have walked?'

'It's possible,' said Brook. 'But it's nearly three miles and it was thick with snow that day.'

'She's very fit.'

'You told Sergeant Noble she had luggage.'

'Sure, but she liked to travel light,' said Laurie, suddenly encouraged. 'She'd packed her rucksack the day before and it wasn't in her room when I got home on Saturday morning.' She looked hard at Brook. 'So she must have set off at least.'

Brook nodded thoughtfully. 'That seems to be indicated, but it doesn't change the fact that there's no record of her taking the train. If we assume the CCTV cameras at the station were having an off day, it's *just* possible she lost her pre-paid ticket to Liverpool and was forced to buy a replacement on the day. With cash. It's the only way she could have taken the train without her journey being recorded.'

'That would have cost a fortune,' said Laurie.

'Nearly a hundred pounds,' agreed Brook.

'She wouldn't pay that. She would've used her railcard,' suggested Laurie.

'But that purchase would have been logged,' said Brook.

'She has a credit card . . .' began Laurie, stopping as soon as she realised the implication.

'We're going to need more details on that. Any spending with her plastic, especially after her departure date, would be significant. With that in mind, we'd like permission to do a more thorough search of your home, look through Caitlin's room and speak to neighbours. We've got some of her financial details from the university, but old credit card and mobile phone statements would be useful.' Seeing her hesitate, he added, 'Of course, if we find anything incidental to the inquiry, it will be disregarded – within reason.'

'Incidental?'

'Small quantities of recreational drugs, for instance,' explained Brook wearily.

Laurie seemed confused for a moment. 'Search away, we don't do drugs.' She shook her head. 'This is crazy. People can't just disappear into thin air like this.'

'Thousands of people do exactly that every year,' said Brook. 'They drop everything and walk out of their lives, never to be seen again. Nobody knows why, because there's no sure way of knowing what's going on inside somebody's head. On the positive side, most of these disappearances are voluntary.'

'You're certain she wasn't on the train?' said Laurie. 'When I go to Nottingham, I often don't get my ticket punched.'

'That can happen on shorter journeys, Laurie. But there's no record of her getting on the ferry either, or arriving in Belfast. And Mersey police can find no sightings or film of her in Birkenhead station or at either ferry terminal on the day of travel. That's fairly compelling.'

Laurie hung her head. 'She's dead, isn't she?'

'We don't know that,' said Brook sincerely. 'And there's just as likely to be a reasonable explanation. She likes to travel, you said. Maybe she got a better offer, met the man of her dreams and left with him.'

'If she did, she didn't tell me about it.'

'What about that last night at the pub. Did either of you speak to anyone else?'

'Only the barman.' Laurie raised her eyes to remember. 'Jack.'

'Jake,' corrected Brook, reading Noble's notes.

Four

JAKE TANNER HUNG HIS JACKET in the staff cloakroom and jogged up the back stairs into the half-finished upper lounge of Bar Polski. The stairs came out beside the plush new bar with its floor-to-ceiling mirrors and backlit optics. His fellow barman, Ashley, a wiry young man barely out of his teens, was already at work, unpacking boxes of glasses in the evening gloom.

The fitters had gone for the day and the two men were alone to do their work. Every conceivable glass for every possible drink had been ordered, and all had to be stacked carefully beneath the opulent curve of the bar, ready for the grand opening.

Jake opened a box of shot glasses and began to unload them.

'You're late,' said Ashley. 'Better get a shift on.'

Jake halted, dead-eyed. 'Is the boss around?'

'Mr Ostrowsky? Not yet.'

'Then no harm done,' said Jake.

'You've only been here a week. You don't know what he's like.'

'I can handle him,' said Jake.

'Don't say you wasn't warned,' replied Ashley. 'Hey, where's your brother? Don't he come with you no more?'

'Nick?' Jake's lips tightened. 'No, that's not gonna work. What about Ostrowsky's brother? The electrician.'

'You mean Max?'

'Max,' said Jake, rolling the name around his mouth as though he'd eaten something bitter. 'That's the guy. You seen him?' He looked up for Ashley's reply, but it didn't arrive. He followed Ashley's hungry eyes to the cleaner who was unravelling the flex on a vacuum cleaner at the far end of the darkened room.

'Hello, beautiful,' called Ashley. Jake gave the pretty young Polish girl the once over. She had a fine figure and a lovely face, with big brown eyes. Feeling a pang of desire, he took satisfaction from her ignoring Ashley. 'Hey, beautiful,' persisted Ashley at higher volume.

When the girl looked up, Jake noticed something sad about the eyes, though her mouth was set hard, affecting toughness.

'That's not my name,' she barked in her halting English.

'Cassie, then,' said Ashley, grinning at her, expecting her to be flattered that he knew.

Her mournful eyes belied her flinty expression. 'Kassia,' she corrected dismissively, and ignited the vacuum to end the conversation.

Jake watched Ashley watching Kassia.

A few seconds later, the girl glanced contemptuously back towards the younger man with the goofy look on his face, then towards Jake, brief and hostile, before returning her attention to her work.

As the sound of the vacuum dipped around the corner, Ashley winked at Jake. 'Nice, eh?'

Jake aped the girl's look of contempt. 'In your dreams.'

'Speak of the devil,' mumbled Ashley with a swivel of the eyes.

Jake followed his glance to the staff door as it swung closed.

Max Ostrowsky was a scruffy, well-built man in his late thirties, who habitually wore dusty overalls and a five-day beard. He ignored the two barmen and headed around the alcove towards Kassia as she emerged with the Hoover. He leered at her and mouthed something in her direction, appearing also to grab his crotch for good measure.

'What a charmer,' said Ashley.

Kassia glanced malevolently back at Max. Under the noise of the vacuum cleaner, she mimed a return insult and continued her work. Max turned towards the bar with a big grin on his face. On seeing Jake, the grin disappeared and he slowed, dropping his elbows on to the bar.

'Vodka,' he spat out, unable to meet Jake's glare.

You want vodka? Jake's face hardened and he plucked a sealed bottle from an opened box and advanced on Max holding it upside down by the neck. *I'll give you vodka.*

As he raised the bottle to shoulder height, the door swung open again and a sharp-suited businessman appeared. He was a little older and slimmer than Max, but the facial similarity was unmistakable.

Seeing the raised bottle in Jake's hand, Ashley stepped across him, placing two shot glasses on the bar with one hand and snatching the upturned vodka bottle from Jake with the other. He gave Jake a veiled *WTF* glare and, after screwing off the cap, poured out two full measures.

'Leave the bottle,' snapped the well-scrubbed businessman, downing his drink in one and refilling his glass. He began to talk to his younger brother in Polish above the noise of the vacuum.

Jake backed away resentfully to continue unloading glasses. He looked up to see Kassia staring curiously at him until Max turned to face her, a lascivious grin deforming his face as he blew her a kiss. As she absorbed herself in the hoovering again, Max said something to his elder brother. The suited businessman glanced briefly at Kassia, then distastefully back at his brother. He downed his drink and strode away towards the stairs, beckoning Max to follow.

Brook finished his text to Noble in the darkened corridor as a tall young man with jet-black curly hair extracted a key from his pocket and prepared to unlock a door. 'Mr Davison?'

The dark-eyed student turned to look quizzically at Brook, who held his warrant card towards him for inspection. The young man rested one bare foot on top of the other, ignoring Brook's ID. 'What do you want?'

'Are you Roland Davison? I'm told this is his room.'

'Rollo?' said the young man, now deigning to inspect Brook's warrant card. Scratching himself through his torn T-shirt, he came to a decision. 'He's my roomie. You just missed him.' His voice was polished and measured, with that confidence derived from a life in which promise lay ahead, not behind.

'Do you know where he is?'

'Law lecture. He'll be out in a couple of hours if you want to wait.'

'Very kind of you.' Brook found his way barred.

'No, I mean here,' smirked the young man. 'Obviously I can't let you into the apartment. Not without a warrant.' He looked Brook up and down – the ill-fitting suit, the exhausted gait – his expression barely concealing the contempt he reserved for shoddily dressed public servants. 'Is this about his ex?'

'He's going to be a lawyer, is he?' In turn Brook made no effort to disguise the force's de rigueur disdain for members of that profession.

'A barrister, actually,' sniffed the young man, hitting his stride.

'A barrister?' retorted Brook. 'Tough racket.'

'Racket?' The student's lip curled.

Brook's one-note laugh contained an apology of sorts. 'Figure of speech.'

'Can I give Rollo a message?' said the young man, his boredom reaching critical mass.

'Please. Can you ask him if he knows what effect a conviction for obstruction would have on his ability to practise at the Bar?' Brook smiled with that excessive politeness designed to annoy and unnerve. 'Mr Davison.'

The effect was immediate and the young man's eyes sought the floor. His mouth instantly desiccated, he licked his lips. 'I . . . er, what did you want to speak to him about? I mean . . . Rollo, I mean . . .'

Brook took pity on his unprepared opponent. 'We shouldn't talk out here.'

Brook took a hearty sip of the tea his now attentive host had been only too pleased to provide. He looked around the apartment, the shelves lined ceiling to floor with books, apart from one eye-level shelf of compact discs with handwritten labels down the spine. He spotted an expensive-looking video camera on a tripod.

'Film-maker, eh?' he mused. He pulled out a case to examine one of the discs. The title on the label read *La Donna e immobile*. Brook stared at it, puzzled by the misspelt song title from *Rigoletto*.

'Don't touch that!' snapped Davison, taking the case from him. He softened his tone to explain, 'They're in order.' He replaced the disc and moved the camera before inviting Brook to sit. 'You wanted to ask about the last time I saw Caitlin.'

'Can you remember when it was?'

'Not the exact date, no,' replied Davison. 'We broke up over a week before she went into the clinic.' His iPhone beeped on his lap and his thumb jerked across the keypad. He grinned at a message.

'Why did you break up?'

'It was bound to happen sooner or later,' he said as he texted. 'When the silly cow told me she had one in the oven, that was it.'

Brook nodded as though he sympathised. He contemplated the young man studying his phone, wondering how much mental torture to inflict, before realising he was unable to dredge up the moral anger required. Roland Davison had all the hallmarks of a self-centred narcissist with an acute sense of entitlement, and as such was indistinguishable from thousands of other young people. Brook found it hard to summon the energy to rattle his cage.

Davison looked up, misreading Brook's expression. 'Don't judge me. I never pretended I loved her.'

'That's all right, then,' said Brook.

'Sarcasm is the lowest form of humour,' retorted Davison.

'And the most fun.'

'Look, Inspector, the pregnancy was Caitlin's fault. These days a guy has a right to expect precautions to be taken. And if the bitch ain't doing it, she needs to say so or take the consequences.'

'Bitch?'

'Figure of speech,' leered Davison, pleased to have extracted retribution so quickly.

'Not when I was at school it wasn't,' retorted Brook, suddenly convinced that Davison hadn't abducted or killed Caitlin Kinnear. He clearly didn't care enough about her to summon up the necessary passion for such an enterprise. 'Was she depressed about her condition?'

'More pissed off than depressed.'

'There's a difference?'

'Sure. She'd got herself in a jam and she had a problem to solve. It pissed her off. But she didn't mope about it.'

'And you approved of her solution?'

'Hell, yeah,' scoffed Davison.

'So the termination was her decision.'

'Once she'd factored in her options,' said Davison, grinning.

'Her options being to terminate or to raise the child on her own.'

'Bang on. I wasn't about to play happy families with a dumb Irish bitch and her bastard, no matter how good she was in the sack.'

Brook held on to a neutral expression – Davison and his ilk took delight in causing offence to older generations. 'And did she seem at all conflicted about her decision?' Davison prepared to object, so Brook qualified. 'In the small amount of time you had to assess her mood.'

'You're asking me if she was capable of killing herself, aren't you?'

'Was she?'

'God, no,' said Davison, at least taking the trouble to think about it. 'Kitty wasn't the type. Always the optimist.'

'So she never discussed suicide on an intellectual level, or revealed any unnatural fascination with famous people who had taken their own lives, say?'

Davison shook his head as though he'd been asked about a bus timetable.

'Did she know anyone who'd committed suicide?' continued Brook. 'Here at the university, I mean.'

'I don't think so. Look, there are always suicides on campus around Easter, though they like to keep that quiet for obvious reasons. It's the start of the exam season. Some people can't handle the pressure.'

'The majority of FE suicides are overseas students,' said Brook. 'Like Caitlin.'

'Yeah, I heard that,' said Davison. 'They're paying more so their fear of failure is greater. And they're a long way from home. I get that. But Jesus, Belfast hardly counts as foreign. And Caitlin's a pretty tough cookie.'

'Do you know if she'd ever self-harmed?'

Davison's iPhone buzzed and he looked down at the screen and smiled again.

Brook sighed before jerking out a hand and plucking away the black tablet.

'Hey,' protested the student, glaring at Brook and plotting a lunge towards his beloved phone. 'You can't do that.'

'I just did.'

'I know my rights.'

'Glad to hear it.'

'I'm ringing my father,' snorted Davison. 'Do you have any idea who he is?'

'I know you'll be fishing your phone out of the toilet to ring him if you don't listen to my questions,' said Brook calmly. 'Your ex-girlfriend is missing and your indifference is making me suspicious.'

Davison fell into brooding silence, lips pursed, glaring at his phone in Brook's hand. A moment later, a dip of the eyes agreed to terms and conditions. 'What was the question again?'

'Did Caitlin ever . . .'

'Self-harm, right,' said Davison. 'I wouldn't know about that.'

'You didn't notice any cutting scars on her arms?'

'No.' With a lascivious grin he added, 'But when we got down and dirty, I guess that's the sort of thing that would be hard to miss, so I guess not.'

'What about enemies?'

'Enemies?' laughed Davison. 'No chance. Caitlin was an open-hearted country girl. She liked a drink and a good time. She got along with everyone.'

'No students who took a dislike to her?'

'Asked and answered.'

'Nobody come to mind who behaved inappropriately towards her?'

'Define inappropriate.'

'Any male students being excessively attentive, perhaps using over-sexualised language in front of her, that sort of thing.'

'Only me.'

'What about other ex-boyfriends on campus?'

'Nope.' Davison pondered for a second. 'She had a serious boyfriend back in Belfast, but she gave him the heave-ho before she left the bogs.'

'Do you have a name?'

'Paddy Something?' He caught the current of Brook's scepticism. 'Seriously. But she only mentioned him the one time, and only because I asked. She was living a different life in Derby so she cut him loose.'

'What about her tutors and lecturers? Any hint of sexual harassment?'

'She never mentioned it to me if there was.'

'What about her grades?'

'What about them?'

'They're not spectacular. Did she ever complain that someone was marking her down?'

'No. And Kitty's grades are fine. She was happy enough. She wasn't that bright and she certainly didn't work too hard. She was overachieving, you ask me.'

'Was?'

The young man shrugged. 'She's in the past. My past, at least. Are we done?'

Are we done? Brook ignored the temptation to make his next question *Are you American?* 'What do *you* think happened to her?'

Davison shrugged. 'She may have been nabbed by some random sex-starved pervert. Ever thought it might be that simple?'

'Then he's the most careful sex-starved pervert in criminal history,' answered Brook. Davison actually laughed at this. 'What about travel? Could she have simply upped sticks and left?'

'That would be more likely. She loved travel and new places. You should check the airports and ferry ports.'

'Good idea,' said Brook. He held up a hand to forestall another protest. 'Lowest form of humour – I heard you the first time. Anywhere she might go in Britain if she wanted to get away?'

Davison narrowed his eyes. 'Are you saying she hasn't left the country?'

'I'm not saying anything. I'm asking you a question.'

'I guess her top destination would be London.' Brook prompted him with a raised eyebrow. 'Bright lights, big city. Streets paved with gold and all that.'

'Alone?'

'Kitty's self-reliant, and if she wanted to go somewhere badly enough, she'd drop everything and go. I assume that could apply to some man she met, but I have no idea who that might be.'

'She sounds very trusting,' said Brook.

'There's no side to her,' said Davison. 'She takes people as she finds them, but she can handle herself. Depend on it.'

'How did she handle herself with you?' Davison emitted a short laugh. 'Something you want to share?'

The young man sighed. 'We broke up. Was Caitlin happy I dumped her? No. But she was too level-headed to let it worry her for more than a second. She was never clingy or jealous, because she knew how uncool that was. She took the rough with the smooth and didn't hold grudges. And there were no regrets on either side when we split.'

'Final question – can you confirm where you were on the night of March twentieth?'

Five

BROOK SIPPED TEA FROM HIS flask as he looked out across the lights of Derby's dark horizon. Light rain dotted the windows.

Noble closed the door of the office and flopped down on his chair, hands stretched behind his head. 'That's one day I'll never get back. I don't know why we bother nicking burglars. They never get locked up.' He sighed, opting to jettison the rest of the well-worn conversation, flicked on the kettle and stole a quick glance at Caitlin's photograph. 'What about you?'

'I spoke to Laurie,' answered Brook. 'The boyfriend too.'

'And did Davison push your buttons?' Brook gave him a fleeting glance but didn't answer. 'I knew it,' grinned Noble. 'Did you like him for it?'

'There is no *it*, John. And no, I didn't *like* him for it. Roland Davison doesn't care about anyone but himself. Not enough to commit murder.'

'But someone that arrogant . . .'

'Luckily for him, arrogance isn't a crime.' A second later, Brook added, 'Lucky for me too, I guess.'

'Ooh, self-analysis,' teased Noble. 'I'm trembling. Course you know where he gets his arrogance from.'

'Should I?'

'His father is *Councillor* Davison – upstanding member of the Police Liaison Committee.'

'So that's who Roland was threatening to unleash on me,' said Brook.

'I assumed you knew him.'

'I've met him . . .' Brook smiled suddenly, taking Noble's meaning, 'but he's never sat on any of my disciplinary panels. He owned that derelict building on Whitaker Road where young Joshua Stapleton was murdered. Remember?'

Noble lapsed into silence, his mind's eye staring at the pathetic corpse of a boy, barely a teenager, humiliated and killed before life had begun, enduring pain he'd never known and suffering he didn't deserve. 'I remember,' he mumbled, the memory lowering his voice. He roused himself to change the subject. 'Well, sad to say, you're right. Davison's alibi checked out. March twentieth he was drinking with half a dozen friends and went back to student halls on Agard Street with a Miss Polly Cooke. Together all night. She confirmed it.'

'You sound disappointed,' said Brook.

'I am. He treated me like something he'd wiped off his shoe.'

'That I'm used to,' said Brook. 'What depressed me more was his total indifference towards someone with whom he'd recently had a relationship – someone who may be in trouble, even dead.'

'So he got to you too.'

Brook turned back to stare at the night. 'People get to me, John. Especially the young. They seem to think it weakens them if they care for anyone but themselves. What about Laurie Teague's alibi?'

'Cast in bronze,' said Noble, surprised. 'She stayed at the pub until her boyfriend arrived, then took a cab to his place. Barman, boyfriend and cabbie confirm. You didn't really . . .'

'No,' said Brook. 'But now we don't need to take it on trust, do we?'

There was silence for a moment, natural on Brook's part but not so comfortable for Noble.

'So what's next?' said Noble. 'We can scale up and put a team together, canvass the entire campus . . .'

'It's been a month,' said Brook. 'You know what comes next.'

Noble was solemn. 'We pass it along because there's no mileage in it.'

'Afraid so.'

'There'd be mileage in it if she was from Derby and her family were sobbing on *East Midlands Today* every night.'

'That's unfair, John.'

'Is it?' Noble lowered his eyes. 'Have you spoken to the Chief Super?'

'I don't need to. I know what he'd say.'

'Since when did Charlton's opinions carry any weight with you?'

'When they agree with mine,' replied Brook. He sighed and shook his flask. Empty. 'John, Caitlin's not local and the trail's cold. All we can do is hope she's gone walkabout and move on.'

'And you a detective who closes fifty-year-old homicides.'

'If she'd been murdered, I'd be all over it,' argued Brook. 'But Caitlin's young, unattached and likes to travel – she could be anywhere.'

'People who travel leave a trail,' argued Noble. 'You taught me that. And your text said she'd had an abortion. She could have been depressed, suicidal even.'

'Then at least she's making her own choices,' said Brook.

'Now who's being unfair?'

Brook nodded in acceptance of Noble's rebuke. 'You're right.'

Noble was suddenly quiet, and Brook knew what was coming. 'What about the Deity killer?'

'What about him?'

Noble sought the words. 'Do you think he's come back? That he's started again with Caitlin.'

'That case is closed,' said Brook. 'Officially. Deity is dead.'

'You didn't think he was dead at the time,' said Noble.

'Everyone else did.'

'Even so, we should check . . .'

'I did check,' said Brook. 'Before you got back. The Deity website is gone for good. There's no connection, John.'

'But Caitlin's a student who disappeared without trace,' insisted Noble. 'Same as the others.'

'It's not the same,' said Brook. 'Caitlin left no message, no clue. The Deity students left artefacts to show they were leaving of their own volition.' He raised a digit. 'And they left as a group.'

Noble was encouraged, and seized his opportunity. 'Aha, well, Caitlin's not alone. I've been on to Interpol.'

'Interpol?' A smile pulled at the corner of Brook's mouth. 'Being a bit melodramatic, aren't we?'

'Maybe, but I remembered something – a case three years ago. Another Irish girl who went missing. So I checked with Interpol and found the names of *five* young women reported missing over the last three years by parents in Poland, Italy and Ireland.'

'Students?'

'A couple of them,' retorted Noble defensively.

'At Derby University?'

'One was.' Noble cast around his desk for the paper-work. 'Daniela Cassetti from Perugia. She flew to East Midlands in August two years ago to enrol at the university but disappeared after two terms. Easter, this time last year! She was supposed to fly home for the holiday but never arrived and didn't show up for the summer term. Exactly the same as Caitlin!' He reached for a second sheet of paper. 'And there was another Irish girl, a student teacher from Dublin visiting family in Derby. Bernadette Murphy. Also three young Polish girls vanished, all thought to have been in the area . . .'

'*Thought* to have been,' repeated Brook. Noble was quiet. 'The Derby area?'

'East Midlands,' answered Noble, not looking up to catch Brook's sceptical eye. He rustled for another piece of paper on his desk. 'Adrianna Bakula—'

'John, slow down,' said Brook 'Not only are those women not local, they're foreign nationals. They could be travelling anywhere in the UK, even assuming they're still here.'

'But the similarities . . .'

'Such as?'

'They're all young, single women from overseas. Like Caitlin.'

Brook finally trapped Noble's wandering eye. 'You do know there must be hundreds of thousands of young people wandering the globe at any one time, experiencing life. And they're all effectively missing until they walk through their parents' front doors again.'

'Maybe,' said Noble softly.

'Definitely,' said Brook. 'It's part of growing up and leaving the nest. Young people go out into the world, get a taste of freedom and forget they even have parents, never mind communicate with them. It's called freedom. I was the same. I saw my parents as jailers, and when I finally left, getting in touch with them was as alien as . . .'

'As paying attention to Interpol bulletins?' suggested Noble.

'Exactly,' retorted Brook, unwilling to be embarrassed. 'I've had all this with my own daughter. Throw a divorce into the mix, and unless you make a supreme effort to contact your kid, you might easily not speak to them for years. It's a wonder more parents don't report their children missing.'

'How is Terri?' asked Noble.

'She's fine,' said Brook, holding out his hands to make the point. 'I assume.'

'So that's it, then?'

'I'm sorry, John. With no evidence of a crime, we pass Caitlin's file over to the Missing Persons Bureau. They can work this nationally . . .'

'While they look for thousands of other runaways and mispers.'

'We've nothing to work with,' insisted Brook. 'No suspicious spending on her cards. No phone calls, no sightings. I'd suggest she spontaneously combusted, but that's supposed to leave a residue.'

'Then why do I get the impression you know there's something wrong here?'

Now it was Brook's turn to avoid eye contact. 'I don't know what you mean.'

'Yes, you do. What is it? Gut instinct?'

Brook looked up, an expression of derision on his face. 'We're not astrologers, John. We don't read tea leaves. We work on evidence.'

'Agreed,' said Noble. 'And we don't have any, so what is it?'

Brook hesitated. 'You said you searched her room.'

'Apart from her rucksack being gone, everything was in order,' replied Noble.

'That there. That's what worries me,' said Brook. 'It's too tidy. Students are messy – messy in their relationships, messy in their personal lives. The unplanned pregnancy tells me Caitlin was no different. If she left of her own volition, she couldn't have removed herself from the face of the earth more thoroughly. That's either a fluke or takes careful planning.'

'And Caitlin's not that careful.'

Brook rubbed his tired eyes. 'It was just an impression. On the other hand, she did carefully compartmentalise her lives in Derby and Belfast, so maybe that tells us something.'

'So are we passing this on or not?' said Noble.

Brook sighed. 'We don't have a choice. Without leads, sightings or any sign of foul play, the only thing left to do is put her picture on the drinks cartons and wait.'

'You forgot to mention crossing our fingers,' said Noble, trudging to the door, a hand reaching for his cigarettes. No answer from Brook. 'We keep a copy of the file in case we get a chance to revisit, okay?'

'Absolutely.'

* * *

Brook drove home after midnight along the dark, empty roads, uncoupling his mind from the challenges of the day. He loved the night drive out of Derby along the A52 to Ashbourne and then on to his cottage in Hartington. It was a half-hour when he was forced to concentrate on the undemanding task of manoeuvring his aged car through the dark countryside of the Peak District.

Spring had arrived and the promise of a few months walking around the hills after and sometimes before work was a great comfort to Brook. The prospect soothed his overworked brain, and made sleep possible at the end of the journey, if only for a couple of hours before insomnia took over and he rose in the small hours for his first tea of the day.

Thirty minutes later, he dropped his laptop case on the kitchen table and opened the fridge almost as a reflex. For a detective who prided himself on evidence and logic, it was an odd thing to do, as the shelves were just as bare as they had been that same morning when he had reached in for the last pint of milk.

He made a mug of tea and sat at the table, fumbling for his antiquated mobile phone. He hovered over his daughter's number – one of only two on speed-dial – before thinking better of it. A phone call from a parent was bad news at any time, but after midnight it might induce panic. Instead he thumbed out a text – *Not heard from you. How are you?* – being scrupulous to punctuate and avoid text shorthand.

A minute later, the briefest reply. *I'm good.* Brook frowned. A moment later, another message. *Got U. No, I'm not a Yank. LOL. Wassup? Another victim remind you of me? Don't deny it.*

Brook smiled as he tapped the keys. *Am I so predictable? Actually victim not dead, just missing, and reminds me of me as a student.*

Who is he?

He's a she.

V metrosexual ;)

Brook was unsure of her meaning. *Any chance of a visit?*

Rain check on the visit. I'm in Italy.

'Italy?' said Brook frowning. 'I rest my case, John.' He tapped out, *Well thanks for letting me know*. Not enamoured of the nagging tone, he deleted it, instead texted *Ciao x*, drank his tea and trudged upstairs to bed.

Six

21 April

BROOK ARRIVED AT ST MARY'S Wharf later than usual, having slept until nearly five that morning. Even so, he felt tired when he set off, and, assuming lack of food to be the culprit, stopped at the corner shop in Hartington just opening its doors. He bought packs of uncooked bacon as well as other staples like bread, butter and milk, returning briefly to the cottage to dump his supplies in the kitchen.

Once at St Mary's, he walked briskly through the smoked glass doors, carrying his flask and a bacon sandwich from a local chuck wagon. His old sparring partner, Sergeant Harry Hendrickson, was on reception. Brook looked away, though without the trepidation of old. Their animosity had cooled recently and Brook no longer had to run the gauntlet of Hendrickson's jibes about the nervous breakdown he'd suffered while serving in the Met. Now neither of them even acknowledged the other's existence, and that was exactly how Brook liked it.

Trudging towards the stairs, he was surprised to see Chief

47

Superintendent Charlton walking smartly in his direction in his crisp uniform.

'There you are, Brook.'

'No denying it, sir,' answered Brook.

'How was your holiday? Go anywhere nice?' said Charlton with scant interest.

'I live somewhere nice,' replied Brook. 'Why would I go anywhere?' He sifted through the reasons for Charlton's presence at such an early hour. It couldn't be a gathering of the station's prayer group, dubbed the SPG after the now-disbanded Met unit of trained thugs who'd attracted so many negative headlines in the 1980s. No, the SPG gathered every other Friday, and when a meeting loomed, Brook had a rolling list of excuses to avoid Charlton's persistent invitations to bend the knee before 'the Great Chief Constable in the sky'.

'I've just been to your office, Brook. Guess what I found.'

Brook considered the short figure of Mark Charlton glaring at him with all the authority he could summon from his minimum regulation height. 'Desks and chairs, sir?'

'Don't get cute, Brook,' said Charlton. 'I'm referring to the file on Caitlin Kinnear. It was on your desk. You're not actively pursuing that, are you? It's a month old and she's out-of-area. Pass it on to the MPB.'

'Done that, sir,' replied Brook. 'But we retain a copy for when we get an opportunity to revisit.' He paused. 'Cold-case work being a speciality of mine.'

'So then you're free to head up a new initiative I'm putting together on scrap metal theft. After the success of Operation Calanthia—'

'I'm afraid not, sir,' replied Brook without missing a beat. 'DS Noble and I have had an urgent request from Interpol.'

'Interpol? Why haven't I heard about it?'

'We've only just picked it up,' replied Brook.

Charlton raised a sceptical eyebrow. 'What do they want?'

'They have an enquiry about a series of missing women who visited the area recently and they'd like us to check it out. That's why I was brushing up on the Caitlin Kinnear file, in case there were similarities . . .'

'What missing women?' demanded Charlton. 'Recent?'

'I don't have the dates to hand, but the missing girls were from as far afield as Italy, Ireland and Poland.'

'Tourists? Economic migrants?'

'A mixture,' bluffed Brook, not wanting to lie.

'You're not serious,' said Charlton. 'EU citizens come and go as they please these days, Brook. And Interpol have always got some vague fishing line dangled in our waters about this and that missing person. Nothing ever comes of it.'

'Agreed,' said Brook, beaming his admiration for Charlton's grasp of the essentials. 'But one of the girls was also a student at Derby University.'

'And you think she might tie in with the Kinnear girl?'

'Unknown, sir,' said Brook gravely. 'But I told Interpol we'd look into it for them, and they were very glad of our help.'

'Were they indeed?' Charlton's tone was wary. 'And I suppose you're going to need DS Noble to keep you company.'

'If it's not a problem.'

'You must think I'm a complete idiot, Brook.'

Brook paused to control the lure of an honest answer. 'Sir?'

'I see what you're doing.' Charlton eyed him, a sly smile breaking out. 'I should be annoyed. But then you did build up a large reservoir of goodwill with me on the Wheeler case.'

'Nice to know, sir,' smiled Brook. 'Shame about the new

initiative – sounds interesting. And if I had DI Ford's local connections, I'd jump at it.'

'Ford?'

'But if you think I can help . . .'

'All right, don't overdo the smarm,' said Charlton. 'Follow up with Interpol if you think it has merit, but I want to be kept in the loop.'

'Of course.'

'And be aware you're cashing in that goodwill chip now. If a proper case rears its head, you're on it. Understood?'

Brook smiled his acceptance.

Charlton made to turn away before swivelling on his highly polished Doctor Martens. 'By the way, I had Donald Davison on the phone yesterday evening, chewing my ear off about how you treated his boy, young Roland, ex-boyfriend of the Kinnear girl. You do know Councillor Davison's the boy's father?'

'That's the only reason I didn't waterboard him, sir.'

'Be serious, Brook. Davison is on the PLC and we do not want him rubbed up the wrong way. He says you threatened his boy.'

'He's right,' agreed Brook. 'The odious little runt obstructed my enquiries and I threatened to charge him accordingly. Worked wonders.'

'I dare say,' said Charlton. 'And I know from my time as a school governor that the parents of the worst-behaved brats always squeal the loudest, but . . .' he paused to emphasise his point, 'go easy.'

'My new motto, sir,' smiled Brook, continuing on his way. Through the double doors and up the stairs, he turned a corner and walked into DI Ford coming the other way, unlit cigarette in hand.

The grey-haired Ford shot Brook a baleful glance before fixing his gaze beyond the younger man, with whom he'd nearly come to blows a few months before.

'Morning, Frank,' chirped Brook. Ford ignored him, skipping quickly down the stairs. 'The Chief Super was looking for you,' Brook shouted after him.

Almost out of sight, Ford came to a halt, declining to face Brook. 'Why?'

'Something about your pension. Not bad news, I hope.'

Ford scuttled away to find Charlton, not deigning to express gratitude, and Brook smiled at a bullet dodged.

Brook took a bite of his first hot food in forty-eight hours, then opened the file on Caitlin Kinnear. He flicked through the material for the umpteenth time, beginning with the records for Caitlin's mobile phone. Not uncommonly, Caitlin and Laurie, who shared a tiny bungalow on Amber Road near the university, had not bothered to install a landline, relying exclusively on their expensive mobiles for all communications. No calls had been made, no texts or emails sent since Caitlin's final message to Laurie Teague on the night she vanished. *Never better*.

Brook devoured the bacon sandwich, wiped his hands, then skimmed back through the previous month. All calls and texts to Caitlin's mobile had been identified, with the majority of communications coming from best friend and housemate Laurie. Of the others, a large rump had been from Roland Davison's mobile phone and a few from a landline in Normanton, which Noble had identified as the home of Councillor Davison. Those calls had presumably been made at times when Roland was at his father's house.

The calls and texts from her ex-boyfriend ceased twelve days before Caitlin's disappearance, at around the time both Laurie and Roland had identified as the break-up of his and Caitlin's . . . what? Relationship seemed too strong a word for the casual way young men and women interacted these days.

Brook set aside his ignorance of modern mating rituals and circled a call from the councillor's home two days before Caitlin's termination and four days before her disappearance. Roland had denied contacting Caitlin after the break-up, so it seemed noteworthy.

Next he ploughed methodically through her outgoing calls, several of which had been placed to a number identified as the Rutherford Clinic, where she had undergone her termination. There was a sprinkling of other numbers, including a pizza delivery service, a nail bar and a hairdresser.

He tossed the phone records aside and picked up the report detailing the abrupt interruption of GPS tracking on Caitlin's phone on the night of her disappearance. Again he put it aside, as it told him nothing he didn't already know. On Friday 20 March, Caitlin had walked up Kedleston Road through heavy snow, past the university buildings, to her shared bungalow, where she picked up her rucksack. After that, her phone's GPS had been disabled and subsequent movements were a mystery, though it was reasonable to assume that she had disappeared that same night.

He turned to the bank statements. Caitlin's account had been in overdraft after paying her university fees and a security deposit on the bungalow in September of last year. Her student loan had put her back in the black, and for the next six months there had been a steady stream of cash withdrawals as well as regular payments for rent, utilities and her one credit card. The payment for her return train ticket to Liverpool had come out of her account six weeks before the Easter break. There had been no activity on her current account or credit card since her disappearance.

Brook pored over the limited entries on her credit card statement. Caitlin was remarkably prudent in her spending for one so young. Even with a full student grant, he himself could remember the pinch of tight finances at the end of every month, and his old Access credit card had often taken a hammering.

'Her consumption is positively frugal – thirty pounds at the campus Waterstone's and twenty pounds for takeaway pizza,' he said, mulling aloud over the only purchases in the final month of her statement. Granted, the month had been cut short by her disappearance, and as Laurie Teague had attested, the pregnancy had persuaded Caitlin to eschew an active social life for a few weeks. He sat back to ponder. 'Even so, there's a dog not barking here.'

'Who's barking?' Brook was startled out of his reverie. Noble spotted the file and raised an eyebrow. 'Revisiting already?'

'Well, I thought about what you said. About Caitlin and those missing girls.'

'The Interpol girls?' enquired Noble breezily.

'Yes,' replied Brook solemnly. 'And although it's a thankless task, I think you're right – they deserve more than a passing glance.' Noble said nothing. 'And there is something odd about Caitlin vanishing *so* completely. No warning, no trace.' Still Noble was mute and Brook began to falter. 'The emotional trigger of the termination may have tipped over into depression.' Noble raised an eyebrow and a mocking smile began to turn the corners of his mouth. 'You know about the new initiative, don't you?'

Noble's grin erupted and he clapped his hands together. 'Hot off the press. Pity we're so snowed under that we can't give it the attention it deserves.'

'Isn't it?' replied Brook, a guilty smile deforming his face.

'It gets better. Sergeant Hendrickson tells me DI Ford won first prize in the pointless inquiry raffle.'

'A very able choice,' responded Brook soberly.

'Well he's not taking it very well. He reckons you had something to do with it,' said Noble. 'Did you?'

'I don't have that kind of influence with Charlton, John.'

Noble eyed him with suspicion. 'If you say so.' He nodded at the papers in Brook's hand. 'Dog not barking?'

Brook threw Caitlin's financials across. 'I've not been at university for thirty years, so it didn't really strike me at first.'

Noble began to thumb through the papers. 'I've not been to university at all.'

'Well don't feel hard done by,' said Brook. 'I've got a long list of things I'd like to unlearn.'

'So you could be thick like me, you mean?'

'Exactly,' said Brook, ignoring Noble's jibe. 'I was struck by Caitlin's parsimony.'

'And in English for dummies?'

'She didn't spend very much for an inexperienced girl, far from home, unused to managing a budget.'

Noble turned a page. 'Actually, I did notice that. She's got all the big stuff coming out of her current account – rent and bills – but apart from small cash withdrawals, there aren't many . . .' He clicked a finger for the right word, darting a glance at Brook for help.

'Incidentals.'

Noble pointed an approving digit at Brook. 'Not many of those for someone her age let loose on the world. Her credit card is clean, and after her loan went in, she was never close to an overdraft again.'

'No,' said Brook. 'Could she have had another account we don't know about?'

'Possible. But why wouldn't she keep the statements with her other financials?'

'I don't know.'

'Maybe she had a part-time job,' said Noble. 'Cash in hand. Though Laurie said not.' Brook grunted. 'Problem?'

'It worries me how much we rely on Laurie for what we know about Caitlin.'

'You think there's something she's not telling us?'

'She didn't mention the pregnancy at first.'

'An innocent mistake, surely.'

'I'm not saying she's a liar; just that there may be things about Caitlin that Laurie *doesn't* know.'

'They're best friends.'

'According to Laurie,' said Brook. 'But reading between the lines, I got the impression Caitlin kept her at arm's length on some things.'

'What things?'

'I don't know. What are young women usually secretive about?'

'Boyfriends,' suggested Noble.

Brook thought of Terri and her abusive stepfather. 'Boyfriends,' he repeated. 'And what passes between them.'

'That's why we should descend on campus, talk to everyone Caitlin knew or had contact with,' said Noble. 'See if we can get a different spin on things.'

'If we do, we'll be working it without back-up.'

'Would you rather be examining manhole covers at the scrapyard?' argued Noble.

Brook looked at his watch. 'You've got a list of Caitlin's courses?'

'Lecturers, tutors, campus doctor, the works.'

'It'll be a slog,' said Brook.

'You mean you might have to take your own notes,' teased Noble.

'I mean we don't want to repeat it. So let's kill two birds with one stone. Tell me about the Italian girl Interpol mislaid – the one who was also at the university.'

Seven

'PLEASE,' SAID THE GIRL, SEARCHING for the English inflection as she shook the rain from her flimsy coat. The receptionist ignored her. The girl waited, holding her emotions in check, knowing a repetition would harm her cause. This was a familiar routine for Kassia Proch – interacting with resentful locals minded to communicate their disdain of the immigrant in their midst by making her wait. And those were the well-mannered ones.

The receptionist looked up from her computer screen a second later than was polite in case the pale girl standing before her had miscalculated the balance of power in their relationship. She blinked myopically at Kassia, raising spectacles to her face for a proper examination.

'Can I help you?'

'I come see Dr Fleming.'

'Are you a private patient?'

'Please?'

The receptionist's expression hardened, her conclusion already drawn. 'Are you pri-vate or N-H-S?' she said, sounding out the words.

'No, not private.'

'NHS then,' she said, tapping at her keyboard. 'Name, please.'

'I come before.' The sensored main door swept open and Kassia looked nervously towards the noise of the picket line, singing their hymns and chanting their slogans. The door closed and the clamour was muffled until the next unfortunate tried to enter or leave the building.

'Did they give you a hard time outside?'

Kassia looked back at the receptionist. 'Please?'

The woman shook her head, reverting to her previous demeanour. 'I need your name.'

Kassia gave it in a whisper, as though to broadcast her identity would be to invite further shame. But then the severe tone of her interrogator spoke to something deep within her – something hard, something resilient, something that all migrants needed. Suddenly she held the older woman's judgemental gaze and glared back defiantly.

How dare this dried-up old cipa *look down on me?*

Then she thought of the name her mother had given her when she saw those big brown eyes blinking back from the swaddling, and her gaze found the floor again. Kassia. It meant purity.

'Nationality?'

'*Polska*,' replied Kassia. When the *cipa* feigned ignorance, she added, 'Poland.'

'Date of birth?'

'December twenty-five, nineteen hundred ninety-four.'

'Christmas Day?' The receptionist looked up briefly from her keyboard. 'Married or single?' Kassia didn't answer. 'Single,' concluded the woman, checking the appropriate box. 'Have you brought a doctor's referral?'

'I give letter before,' answered Kassia. 'Remember?'

The receptionist sighed. 'Take a seat. Your nurse will be with you shortly.'

'Kassia, isn't it?' said the nurse, pointing to her badge. 'I'm Mary.'

Kassia stood, looked into the smiling face, and nodded in recognition. 'Nurse Moran.' She tried to smile back, but as so often when sympathy accrued, the tears followed and Kassia's sangfroid evaporated. 'No. I can't do it. I can't hurt my child.'

'There, there,' said the nurse, moving in to her, pulling her head on to a chubby shoulder and rubbing her back. 'It's all going to be fine, you'll see. No need for all this upset. We'll get you a cup of tea and Dr Fleming can have a word.'

'No!' said Kassia. 'No talk. I don't want.'

Moran guided Kassia towards a chair, eased her down and clasped her hands. 'Child, your hands are like ice. I'm getting you a hot drink . . .'

'No,' said Kassia, standing. 'Sorry. I go.'

Moran studied her. 'Listen, Kassia. We know this is the most difficult choice you'll ever have to make. But you must think about the child as well. It's not just a question of love. Think about the kind of life you can give it.'

'It?'

'I know we're talking about a human life, but ask yourself if you're ready. You've got your whole life ahead of you.' She shot a glance towards the reception desk, but the hard-faced woman's attention moved back to her screen at once. 'If you decide to go ahead, nobody here will judge you.'

'My mother judge me.' Kassia looked up, her eyes filling

with tears. 'I judge.' She sobbed harder and cupped her freezing hands to her mouth.

'Come on,' Nurse Moran said. 'Let's get you that hot drink . . .'

Kassia pulled away, her decision made, drying the tears on her cheeks with a sleeve. 'No,' she said firmly. 'I can't kill my child,' she added with an involuntary grab of her stomach.

'That's your decision, my love,' said Moran. 'What about the father?'

'The father can go to hell.' She moved hesitantly towards the double doors, shrinking from the ordeal outside.

Moran marched to the reception desk and returned with a card. 'Here.' She pressed it into Kassia's hand. 'If you need to talk, you know where we are.'

Kassia turned back to the nurse, unable to meet her eyes, as though any further communication might dissuade her from her course. The automatic doors opened at her approach and she hesitated, the increased volume of a badly sung psalm giving her pause.

'Come on,' said Nurse Moran, appearing at her shoulder. 'I'll see you out.'

The nurse threw an arm behind the elfin figure and guided her out into the cold. The ground was damp underfoot and a stiffening wind persuaded Kassia to pull her too-thin coat tighter. Moran held her around the shoulder and Kassia braced herself as they approached the small gathering at the end of the path.

The assembled crowd were mostly elderly, huddled under umbrellas and clutching placards bearing an assortment of pro-life slogans.

HALF THE PATIENTS ENTERING AN
ABORTION CLINIC NEVER COME OUT ALIVE!
EQUAL RIGHTS FOR UNBORN WOMEN!

Kassia looked away, hoping not to be noticed. However, the psalm died on the lips of the protesters as all eyes in the group flashed towards her, and she found herself looking round for an alternative route. There wasn't one.

Feeling her slow, Nurse Moran gripped her harder and walked her on. 'To bring a child into this world takes so much love, my girl. You've already shown that love. Now your baby needs you to be brave for just a little longer and then you can get on with your life.'

The silence was broken by an elderly woman wearing an expensive fur hat and matching coat. 'Baby killer!' she screamed at Kassia in an American accent, a gloved finger raised to point. She moved towards the shivering girl but was restrained by the priest next to her.

'We're not allowed to intimidate, Mrs Trastevere,' said the priest. 'The police made that clear.'

'Murderer!' screamed Mrs Trastevere, ignoring him and wrestling for her freedom.

'No,' replied a sobbing Kassia, shaking her head to emphasise her innocence. 'I not kill my child.'

'The Lord is Life,' continued the woman, not listening. She pushed against the priest again. Then, from the back of the knot of protesters, a camera flash briefly illuminated Kassia's distraught face.

Moran's head snapped round to scowl at the figure in the fading light. A man, his face hidden by a hoodie, lowered his hands to pocket his phone and turned away as Moran edged in his direction. 'You, what do you think you're doing?' she shouted at his retreating frame. But Mrs Trastevere pushed towards Kassia once more, forcing the nurse to interpose herself, and in the fracas, he slipped away.

'Murdering bitches!' screamed Mrs Trastevere, looking from Kassia to the nurse.

The priest pulled her wiry frame back. 'Constance, we can't intimidate, or the police will move us on.'

'Burn in hell, the pair of you,' screamed the elderly woman, undeterred.

'Like you'd know about hell, you pampered old bag,' shouted Nurse Moran above the patter of light rain on umbrellas and coats. There was a shocked silence and everyone turned to listen to the fierce Irishwoman. 'Hell is where these poor girls are. I bet you've never had to lift a finger in your life, and if you had someone at home that loved you, you wouldn't be here now, causing grief to the troubled souls who pass through our doors.'

Hushed, the protesters watched the pair pass. Kassia looked furtively into the priest's eyes and instinctively crossed herself. She eschewed a further denial and quickened her step, the tears turning to howls of pain.

'Be safe, my child,' whispered Moran into her ear when they'd cleared the picket. Then she let go of Kassia's arms as though she was an injured bird being released back into the wild.

Once the slight girl had hurried off into the dark, Moran turned a blazing eye on the priest. 'We're throwing that one back, Father O'Toole, so spare me the homily.'

'Praise the Lord . . .'

'Don't you dare mention the Lord!' snapped the nurse, jabbing a finger towards his face. 'And don't think for a second that you and these other gobshites had anything to do with it. You ought to be ashamed of yourselves,' she added, stomping back towards the welcoming glow of the clinic.

Her expression didn't soften as she marched towards reception, her eyes glued to the prim bespectacled woman behind her screen. 'You'd better let Dr Fleming know his eight o'clock has changed her mind, Sally.'

The receptionist picked up the phone and Moran was about to move away but, settled on her choice of words, turned back. 'You know, apart from our job being to help these poor girls, I know for a fact the Rutherford Group makes more money from NHS referrals than it does private. You'd do well to remember that.'

'What do you mean?' retorted Sally.

'I mean best not let management see you putting off potential clients like that.'

'I didn't say anything.'

'You don't have to,' said Moran. 'Your face would sour milk.' She smiled to soften the blow. 'Why upset the poor girls when there's plenty of other folk to do that? Show a little compassion.'

Sally depressed a button on the phone, her face like thunder.

Moran looked towards the double doors and managed a smile. 'And thank goodness for one poor lass able to find her own path.'

Eight

'PRETTY GIRL,' SAID THE ELDERLY round-faced man with the thick spectacles. 'I read in the paper she was missing.'

Brook waited for more. It was the end of a long and frustrating day tramping around campus talking to wary students, bored lecturers and harassed tutors, all unable to offer any insights into Caitlin's disappearance or state of mind. A picture of the Pope behind the doctor's head caught Brook's eye. Stiles followed his gaze.

'We'd appreciate anything you can tell us, Doctor,' said Brook. 'In confidence, of course.'

'Well, it's a bit irregular,' said Stiles, his voice suggesting that a little more persuasion would do the trick.

'It's important,' said Noble, applying the final push. Both detectives knew that members of the doctor's generation were more likely to bend protocols to accommodate the police.

Stiles weighed the gravity of their expressions before peering over his glasses at the computer screen. 'Very well,' he said, clicking the mouse. 'Caitlin came to me last year with an infection. I won't say where,' he added with a suggestion of a smile. 'I prescribed an anti-fungal cream. Job done.' He beamed back at Brook and Noble.

'We'd be more interested in her recent consultations, say the last two months, detailing her condition and how it affected her,' said Brook.

Stiles returned his gaze to the screen. 'The infection was her last appointment with me. That would be last October.' He fixed Brook with a curious gaze. 'What condition?'

'Would she have seen another doctor?' said Brook, ignoring the question.

'Not without my knowledge, not on campus at least,' said Stiles. 'Of course, students are free to choose their campus doctor from the attending list, but she was assigned to me and if she wanted to transfer I'd have been notified. That's the protocol. Now, as her doctor—'

'Caitlin had an abortion,' announced Noble, aware of Brook's instant glare. 'Just before she disappeared.'

The doctor's surprise seemed genuine. 'Indeed. I wasn't aware she was pregnant.'

'Any reason why she might not consult you about it?' asked Brook, deciding he had little choice but to play the hand dealt him by Noble.

'Many reasons,' said Stiles. 'Discretion, embarrassment . . .'

'Fear of religious disapproval,' suggested Brook.

Stiles smiled. 'Yes, I am a Catholic, Inspector. Well spotted. Caitlin too. But do you really think I'd be in a position of trust at a university if I allowed my personal beliefs to influence my work?' He glanced back at the screen. 'I notice Ms Kinnear lived off campus. Perhaps she registered with a local practice.'

Brook shot a fleeting look at Noble, who answered with a shake of the head. 'And if not?'

Stiles shrugged. 'Then I'd suggest she wanted as few people to know as possible. It doesn't take a gynaecologist to flag up your condition if you're missing periods. And any chemist will sell you a pregnancy kit, so self-diagnosis is a simple matter. As for the rest, you'll have to ask her.'

Noble was preparing an acerbic response, so Brook jumped in. 'If you were her only doctor, could she get an abortion without your referral?'

'Oh yes,' said Stiles. 'It's not supposed to happen without one, but things have become very lax these days. A referral clears away the major obstacles – at least within the NHS – but in my experience, it's not unknown for women with a Catholic background to remove that layer of bureaucracy and meet the higher price of secrecy.'

'You think she may have gone private?'

'It can be an affordable option,' said Stiles.

'How much?' asked Noble.

'It depends. Surgical procedure or pill?'

'Surgical,' said Brook.

'Well, again depending on her circumstances and how far along she was, you can get the basic procedure for between five and seven hundred pounds,' said Stiles. 'The earlier the procedure, the cheaper it is, and if you're prepared to dispense with unnecessary sedation and other incidentals . . .' He shrugged. 'Not cheap . . .'

'But not out of reach,' concluded Brook.

'Exactly,' said Stiles. 'Do you know where?'

'The Rutherford Clinic,' said Noble.

Stiles nodded. 'It's local, very reputable. Like most clinics, they'll perform a mixture of procedures depending on the stage of a patient's pregnancy – private and NHS. Rafe Fleming is the top man there – very good in his field. He does a lot of consultancy work at the Royal Derby.' He splayed his hands to suggest closure.

'Could you check your records to see if a Daniela Cassetti was one of your patients?' said Noble, holding a photograph in front of the doctor's face.

'Pretty girl,' said Stiles again, tapping at the keyboard. Brook and Noble exchanged a fleeting glance. 'When was she a student?'

'The first two terms of the last academic year,' said Noble.

'Cassetti,' Stiles sounded out as he typed. 'No, not one of mine, I'm afraid.'

'But you have access to her records,' suggested Brook.

'I'm sorry,' said Stiles. 'It's one thing to bend the rules for my patients; quite another to do it for somebody else's.'

'But you can tell us who her campus doctor was, at least,' said Noble.

'Dr Helen Cowell,' said Miles. 'But don't waste your time looking for her office; she no longer works on campus. University practice was far too dull for her. She consults at the Royal as well.'

'One more question, Doctor,' said Brook. 'It's just procedure. Where were you on the night of March twentieth?'

Stiles stared at Brook, then reached for his diary. 'I left Derby on the eighteenth to attend a medical conference in Northampton for four nights to learn about new drugs coming on to the market.'

* * *

'John . . .' began Brook when they were walking to the car park through the rain.

'I know,' said Noble, pulling out his cigarettes. 'We shouldn't dish out confidential information unless absolutely necessary.'

'Especially when it might colour the information we get back,' added Brook.

'Sorry,' said Noble. 'But with no leads, I think we need to lob in the odd hand grenade.'

'That's not your call,' continued Brook, softening a little.

'Maybe not,' admitted Noble. 'But it's given us an angle.'

'I won't deny it,' said Brook. 'We should have looked into the termination earlier. I assumed that being a student, she'd had the procedure on the NHS.'

'Seven hundred pounds is big money for someone with no income,' said Noble.

'And unless my eyes are gone, not a sign of it in her financials.'

The black skies had opened when Kassia turned on to Vernon Street, and she reached her building out of breath. The whole property was in darkness and she shook the rain from her coat, fumbling sightlessly for her key.

A few minutes later, she'd climbed the three flights of stairs to the bedsit at the top of her building and hung her coat on the back of the door. She ate the remaining *faworki* from her paper bag and licked the sugar from her fingers, then lay back on the single bed, propping herself upright with a pillow. She reached for the bottle of vodka on the floor and, after spinning off the cap, raised it to her lips, then paused in contemplation. A moment later she smiled and replaced the cap on the bottle without taking a drink.

The entryphone buzzed and Kassia slid off the bed, dropping the vodka bottle to the floor.

'Hello.'

Noble finished pinning the pictures of Daniela Cassetti – one from Interpol, one from the university – on to a display board in the smallest incident room in the station and stepped back to look at her. Long dark hair, dark brooding eyes set wide in her face, white teeth beaming out. He hoped it wasn't the doomed image of another victim, another face to carry in his head.

The more cases Noble worked, the more he filed the last head shot, the front-page heart tug, in his memory. It was his personal charnel house, his book of the dead, and though not the healthiest compilation, it was at least preferable to the pictures loved ones never got to see, the snapshots of death, best left to the imagination of seasoned professionals.

He stood back to check his handiwork, drained his Styrofoam cup and stole a glance at Brook, who was poring over Caitlin's file again. He was beginning to understand what robbed his DI of so much sleep, and felt sure Brook's own compendium of death wasn't as sanitised as his own. He'd taken it home far longer, seen much worse.

'Nothing close on the bank statements,' said Brook, picking up the phone. 'And she didn't withdraw enough cash to build up a reserve to pay the clinic. We should get young Davison in and ask him the question.'

'You think he bankrolled the abortion? That's not the impression he gave me.'

Brook squinted at a number on Caitlin's phone records and dialled. 'Nor me, but if he *was* the father and Caitlin didn't pay for the procedure . . .'

'Can he afford it?'

'With a self-made man like Councillor Davison for a father . . . Rutherford Clinic?' said Brook into the receiver. He asked to speak to someone in administration but had to be satisfied with a name to scribble down for the morning. He replaced the receiver, then looked at the display board. Noble had tacked an arrow between Caitlin and Daniela. 'What's the connection?'

'They both went to Derby University,' answered Noble. 'And both are missing.'

'Daniela was there the year before Caitlin arrived. They never met.'

'Dr Stiles was there both years,' said Noble.

'And Daniela is a *pretty girl*,' conceded Brook, mimicking the doctor's leering tone. 'Any word on his alibi?'

'Still waiting on calls,' said Noble.

'Unless he's told us a stupid lie, he's in the clear,' said Brook. 'There must be dozens of fellow delegates to put him in Northampton for four days and nights.'

'Schmoozing in five-star luxury – nice work if you can get it,' said Noble.

Brook glanced at the clock. 'We should wrap it up.'

'I haven't finished putting up all the girls,' said Noble.

Brook's smile was melancholic. 'Take it from a cold-case veteran, there's no hurry. The dead aren't going anywhere.'

'Caitlin's not dead,' replied Noble, as though offended. He looked away, stealing a glance at the enlarged photograph obtained from her student ID.

Brook stared at him. 'You're really feeling this one, John. Any particular reason?'

Noble paused for thought. 'I'll get back to you on that.'

'No need,' said Brook. 'We never know when we're vulnerable. Any case at any time can reach out and bite us, sometimes when we least expect it.'

'Is that how it was with Laura Maples?' asked Noble. He watched Brook stare off into space. Noble had no doubt he was picturing her corpse. Laura Maples – raped, killed with a beer bottle and left to rot in a rat-infested slum, her killer forever unidentified.

'That's how it was,' mumbled Brook, rousing himself 'You've never asked me about my time in the Met before.'

'And don't start now, right?'

'No, you can ask.' Brook smiled. 'Just don't expect a reply.'

Noble reached for his jacket, realising he'd probably never learn the cause of Brook's nervous breakdown in London all those years ago, investigating the serial killer known as the Reaper. His move to Derby CID had been the result, and his mental illness the reason Brook had once been universally unpopular with his colleagues.

'Fancy a late drink?' suggested Noble. Brook raised a disbelieving eyebrow. 'There's a first time for everything.'

'See you in the morning, John.'

Nine

22 April

JAKE TANNER PAUSED AT THE door, hearing the noise of the TV from inside the flat. As he put the key in the lock, he heard Nick scrambling for the remote to turn off the set. Jake pushed open the door and glared at him suspiciously.

'What you got, Jake?' said Nick. Without enthusiasm, Jake brandished two tins of economy baked beans. 'That it?'

Jake slapped down coins on the warped kitchen worktop. 'Eighty-seven pence left,' he said by way of explanation. He rummaged for the tin opener, then poured the contents of one can into a small pan and put it on the hob to warm. He took out the last three slices of bread from the packet, examined the crusts for mould and picked off a few spots. 'Thought I heard the TV.'

Nick looked back at him, confusion written across his face. 'No, Jake. Not allowed,' he said, reciting Jake's mantra.

'Not if we want the light on tonight,' said Jake wearily. 'If the meter runs out . . .'

'If the meter runs out, we sit in the dark,' quoted Nick, pleased with his memory skills.

72

Jake depressed the toaster handle. 'So why is the TV on standby?'

Nick's eyes darted around briefly before he lowered them in shame. 'I just turned it on for a minute, Jake.' He looked up, a smile lighting his face. '*Shaun the Sheep* was on.'

'How old are you, Nick?' His younger brother concentrated hard on the question. Before he could attempt an answer, Jake relented. 'You're nearly twenty.'

Nick's face lit up. 'Is it my birthday soon?'

Jake closed his exhausted eyes. 'Not for three months, Nick.'

'Three months isn't nearly.'

'It's nearer twenty than nineteen.'

'Good, because I know what I want for my birthday,' said Nick. 'An iPad.'

'You'll be lucky.'

'What?'

'I said, the best-laid plans of mice and men . . .'

'The what?'

Jake trudged over to the TV and switched it off at the plug to save power. '*Of Mice and Men*. It's a book I studied at school.'

'What about it?'

Jake met Nick's eyes but decided against further explanation. It would only lead to more questions. 'Nothing.' He spooned hot beans over the dry toast and placed a plate on Nick's lap. 'Brunch is served.'

Nick took up his knife and fork to tuck in, then hesitated. 'I've got more than you.'

'I can nick some peanuts at work.' Jake cut a corner off his unbuttered toast, then laid it on the plate uneaten to watch Nick shovelling his food down like it was a race.

73

'I like your new job,' grinned Nick, bean skins on his teeth. Jake's smile disappeared. 'People were nice to me.'

'It was a bad idea.'

'I liked Max. He was nice.'

'Was he?' said Jake, glaring at his brother.

'Yeah, he . . .' Nick stopped and pursed his lips.

'He what?' said Jake.

'He was nice,' said Nick, clearly pleased with his clever answer. He paused, composing his next utterance, but Jake was way ahead of him.

'The answer's no, Nick.'

'No what?'

'You're not going with me to the bar again.'

'Why not?'

'You're just not. You stay here.'

Nick returned to his eating, sulky. He finished his plateful before eyeing Jake's untouched meal. Jake saw him looking and pushed his plate across the table. Nick gathered it in and began devouring the untouched food with gusto.

'You gonna lock me in again?' Jake didn't reply, an answer in itself. 'What if there's a fire?'

'There won't be.'

'But what if there is?'

Jake blew out his cheeks, coming to a decision. 'Okay, I won't lock you in if you promise not to go out.'

'Why would I go out?' said Nick. 'I got no money.'

Jake considered. He walked to the kitchenette and picked out the 50p coin from the scraps of change. 'For the meter. Watch some cartoons. Don't light any matches. I won't be too late.'

'Can we have beans again for tea?' grinned Nick.

'Did you hear me, Nick?' Jake's eyes burned into his brother's cherubic face. 'Do *not* go out. Promise?'

'I promise.'

Jake trotted down the eleven flights of crumbling concrete steps and out on to the busy road. The morning sky had darkened since his shopping trip to Lidl.

As usual, he glanced over at the ramshackle building that dominated the roundabout at the junction with Lara Croft Way. Every day since the Cream Bar had closed, Jake had looked across at it, and every day the weeds had got a little higher, the iron gate a little rustier and the paint on the brickwork a little dirtier. The place had been closed for several years and was one of many Derby hostelries in which Jake had pulled pints. In fact, he'd been working that last night, the night the police had shut the place down after a gangland fracas had turned ugly. Jake had been a keyholder, and the bar's closure had been so sudden that no one had thought to ask for them back.

Once things had died down, he'd let himself in to see if there was anything worth taking. He was no tea leaf, but he had pay owing and saw no reason not to help himself to anything of value, not that there was anything left after the owners had stripped it. Coppers too, probably.

Shame. It had been good to hold down a full-time job knowing that Nick was only a hundred yards away, safely watching TV in the flat after he got home from school. But when the Cream Bar had closed and Nick left school with no qualifications and no skills, Jake had had little choice but to work part-time and leave his brother outside various bars until he'd finished his shift – it was either that or not work at all.

And with Nick so helpless, not working was often the norm.

But now he'd landed a plum full-time job with good pay, and for the first few days he had been happy to leave his kid brother in Bar Polski's staff cloakroom with a fun pack of sweets and a comic. Not any more. If he wanted to keep hold of his new job, he had no option but to leave Nick alone in the flat. And that was asking for trouble.

The best-laid plans . . .

Jake dragged his thoughts back to the day ahead and how he was going to handle Max if he saw him. He didn't want to lose his job, but something had to be done. He sprinted in front of traffic to beat the lights, then ambled along Osmaston Road towards the centre of town.

From the comfort of his van, Max watched Jake pass, sinking down into the driver's seat at his nearest tangent. When Jake had disappeared from view, he took a hearty pull on a bottle of vodka before spinning the top back on and tossing it on the passenger seat. Grabbing a large bunch of keys from under the seat, he got out and locked the vehicle before spitting contemptuously in Jake's direction.

He looked up at the tower block. He could make out Nick pressed up against the window, scanning the people below. Max ambled across the road, keeping his eyes on the eleventh floor. He plucked out a large packet of Haribos from his overalls and opened it, popping a handful in his mouth and eating with exaggerated pleasure. When he looked back up to the window, Nick was gone.

That afternoon Brook sat in the incident room and gazed absently at the display boards. Six missing young women now stared, smiled or laughed happily back at him. In addition to Caitlin Kinnear and Daniela Cassetti, Noble had posted brief biographies and last known movements of four other girls, three from Poland and one from the Republic of Ireland, who had travelled to England as tourists or economic migrants.

Taking a pair each, Brook and Noble had spent the morning looking separately into the four young women's last known movements, and now Brook read through his meagre notes.

Adrianna Bakula had flown to East Midlands Airport from Gdansk in February 2014. She had taken a cleaning job at the new Riverlights Hotel and had worked there for the best part of six months, living frugally in a nearby Catholic women's hostel. She had quit the job, packed all her belongings and left the hostel in the middle of the night of 25 July, and hadn't been seen since.

Unfortunately, it had been a further four months before relatives in Gdansk had begun to worry, and her mother duly reported her missing in early December, but by then it was too late for meaningful enquiries. Derby CID had been able to do little more than a cursory check, discovering that Adrianna had had a return Ryanair ticket for a flight in May. It hadn't been used, but then it was scheduled for a time when Adrianna was known to be working at the Riverlights, so it was clear she had herself declined to use it *before* she disappeared in late July.

At the time, nobody in Derby had thought her sudden departure suspicious, because it was in the nature of economic migrants to leave jobs at a moment's notice. Indeed, all of Adrianna's friends and work colleagues at the time – most of them migrants – had also moved on, a function of the temporary nature of hotel work, so getting witness statements – then and now – was impossible.

One solid fact was that since her disappearance, Adrianna's passport had not been logged at any border control exiting the UK, either by air or sea. As a result, Interpol believed she was still in Britain.

With no evidence other than a name, passport details and a photograph, her particulars had been passed along to the Missing Persons Bureau, who worked in partnership with the British Transport Police and other agencies on thousands of disappearances every year.

Neither agency had turned up anything. And unless a body was found, dead or alive, Adrianna Bakula's final resting place would be a database entry in their files, the only thing to show that she'd ever visited the UK. No coffin, no grave, in fact nothing to mark that she had ever lived, apart from a few fading photographs clutched to the bosom of a bewildered family in Gdansk.

'How easy it is to fall through the cracks,' mumbled Brook, flipping a page. The second girl was Nicola Serota from Poznan, and again Brook had discovered nothing new to add to her skimpy file. Nicola had also flown into East Midlands on Ryanair, just after Christmas 2013, to stay with her sister Veronika, a waitress in a Derby restaurant. A week later, on 3 January, she had vanished while Veronika was at work. Apparently she had packed her belongings, left her sister's flat and walked out into the night, never to be seen again. To make matters worse, her sister hadn't initially reported her missing because the flat's spare key, which she'd given to Nicola, had been pushed back through the letter box.

A few weeks later, when Nicola hadn't phoned or texted, Veronika began to worry and took the next step of reporting her sister missing, but because of the delay, little or no time was spent on such a futile enquiry. Nicola Serota could be anywhere. A foreign tourist with few ties to the community moving on. What's to investigate?

Brook could sympathise: he'd tried to make contact with Nicola's sister Veronika that very day, but Veronika herself had left Britain nearly a year ago.

He booted up his laptop and logged on to the PNC database to find the name of the case's supervising officer – he could hardly use the word *investigating* – who turned out to be DC Read, a member of his own squad. He scrolled through Read's notes on Nicola Serota, cheered to find an element of thoroughness. The detective constable had at least made the effort to follow up and check whether Nicola's return ticket to Poland, dated a month after her arrival, had been redeemed. It hadn't. With no further indications, Read had filled in the paperwork and sent it on to the MPB.

Brook's mobile vibrated. It was a message from Noble.

Brook sat in Starbucks in the Intu Centre, his back to the tide of pedestrians shuffling aimlessly along the concourse. Noble arrived, ordered a coffee and spotted Brook in the corner hunched against humankind. He nodded at his empty cup.

'Want another?'

'I'll pass,' replied Brook. 'I asked for a cup of coffee with milk and nearly started a riot.'

'If only it were that simple,' laughed Noble, darting back to the counter and returning with a frothy concoction in a cup the size of a soup tureen. 'Any joy at the Rutherford?'

'They were pretty cagey over the phone,' said Brook. 'They need a warrant for a patient's medical details, but I impressed upon them that we're looking for a missing person, and that tracing all Caitlin's financial transactions was vital.'

'And?'

'She paid the lot in cash, up front – six hundred and sixty-two pounds.'

'A clinic takes cash?' puzzled Noble.

'It makes sense when you think about it.'

'I suppose,' said Noble. 'Doesn't help us trace the money, though, and Caitlin definitely didn't take that from any account we've seen.'

'So we're still looking for an extra source of income.'

'Davison?'

Brook looked at his watch. 'You can ask him this evening. I invited him to the station.'

'Invited?' exclaimed Noble. 'That arrogant . . . He won't come.'

'And miss the chance to look down his nose at us?' said Brook. 'He'll come.'

'And your Polish girls?'

'Not a thing that's not in the files. You?'

Noble handed Brook a smaller version of one of the new photographs on the display boards – bright smile, natural blond hair and cornflower-blue eyes.

'Valerie Gli . . .' he stumbled over the pronunciation, 'Gli . . . szc . . .'

'Gliszczynska,' said Brook, leaning over Noble's notebook.

'That's easy for you to say.'

'University education,' said Brook, teasing Noble with his own ammunition.

Noble grunted over his coffee. 'Valerie arrived in England in April 2012 and worked as a barista in London for a year.'

'She's a barrister?'

'A barista,' repeated Noble, rolling his eyes at their surroundings. 'It's someone who serves coffee – in a coffee shop.'

'Whatever happened to waitressing?'

'It's because they work behind a bar ...' began Noble, giving up immediately. 'Take my word for it. Anyway, she packed that in and went to Liverpool for a couple of weeks, and we know she went to the Download Festival in Castle Donington in June of 2013 because she met a man there ...'

'Is this going somewhere?'

'Just background to show she's more at home here, speaks good English.'

'Tell me she ends up in Derby.'

'She ends up in Derby ...'

'And gets a job in this branch of Starbucks,' concluded Brook. 'And that's why we're here.'

'Correct,' said Noble. 'That same summer, she moves in with the manager, Leon LaMotta, the guy she met at Download. His shift starts in ten minutes.'

LaMotta stared at the photograph for several minutes, his mouth tightened by melancholy. Then he placed it on the coffee table. 'I lived with Val for a few months ...'

'This is at your house in Allenton,' said Noble.

LaMotta nodded. 'Everything seemed to be going well, then one day I went to work and when I got home she'd gone. Cleared out her bags and everything. I don't know what else I can tell you.'

'And the relationship was good?'

'I thought so.'

'Did you argue before she left?' asked Brook.

LaMotta took a deep breath, then picked up the photograph and brandished it. 'Look at her. Isn't she the most beautiful creature you ever saw? I wanted to marry her and start a family and she kept turning me down. I argued with her all the time about it.'

'And that caused friction?'

'Listen, I was with her so I was happy. The relationship was great. Or so I thought. She didn't want kids but that didn't matter. There was time for that. What's this about?'

'You know she was reported missing by her family.'

'In Katowice, yes.' LaMotta shrugged. 'Last year a female detective told me she was looking into it.'

'DC Liz Rawson.'

'That's her.' His expression implied a question.

'She transferred to Nottingham,' said Noble.

LaMotta nodded. 'Good. She was a bit keen. She didn't believe me when I told her Val was probably travelling and it's not always easy to keep in touch with family.'

'For two years?' said Noble.

LaMotta's head dipped. 'I thought she'd be back in Poland by now. Or at least in touch with her old man.'

'I'm afraid she's still missing,' said Noble.

'Oh, Jesus.'

'Tell us what happened the day she disappeared.'

LaMotta gathered himself. 'I went to work as usual, leaving Valerie at home – she was on a later shift. She never showed up. I tried ringing and texting, but her mobile was dead.'

'What did you do then?'

'Nothing. I assumed she was ill or something. I went home at the end of the day – still no Valerie and no note saying where she might be. A bit odd, but I've got a night out arranged with the lads, so I go and have a few beers, thinking she'll be home when I get in.'

'But when you got back, still no Valerie.'

'No,' said LaMotta. 'And that's when I realised all her stuff was packed and gone.' He exhaled heavily. 'I've not seen her since. I told all this to DC Rawson.'

'And that was the tenth of September that year.'

'If you say so.'

'You didn't report her disappearance.'

'Disappearance?' laughed LaMotta. 'Her stuff was packed and cleared out. I thought . . .'

'Boy wins girl. Boy loses girl,' offered Brook.

'Something like that,' said LaMotta. 'Val's Polish. No local roots. I was pretty broken up about it, but I had to take it on the chin.'

'In her report, DC Rawson mentioned something about a van.'

'Yeah, well I was talking to a neighbour about a month after Valerie left, telling him what had happened. And he said he'd seen a white van parked across the street for three consecutive nights. He didn't know the dates but reckoned it had been the week Valerie disappeared. He also said that on the third night, he saw two people get out of the van and walk down my drive.'

'What happened?'

'It was dark. He couldn't see much, but he assumed they were making a delivery or doing some work. The next time he looked, the van was gone.'

'Same old problem, John,' said Brook, back in the incident room. 'A young girl with no ties who could be anywhere.'

'But lump all six disappearances together and it starts to take on a pattern. Foreign nationals enter the country for travel, work or study, come to Derby and disappear without a trace. And when they're eventually reported missing, there's no record of them leaving the country . . .'

'Our border controls are not the best—'

'Or entering another country,' interrupted Noble.

Brook was silent, seeking an objection. 'Caitlin Kinnear's not a foreign national.'

'She's overseas,' said Noble. 'And even though you can sometimes get away without showing photo ID on a Belfast ferry, it doesn't change the fact that over a three-year period, six young women have vanished in Derby with no record that *any* of them left the country.'

'That's not proof of a crime,' said Brook.

'It's proof of a pattern and evidence that the girls are still here.'

Brook sighed. 'What about LaMotta? He mentioned a lads' night out. Was he alibied for that night?'

'To the hilt,' said Noble.

'But there's only his word that Valerie disappeared while he was at work or on a night out with friends.'

'True,' agreed Noble. 'But when I spoke to Rawson, she said she went at him pretty hard and couldn't find fault. No criminal record. Steady job. And in all his statements he came across as genuinely puzzled and upset. Especially when, a year after the love of his life leaves him, DC Rawson goes round to tell him Valerie's officially missing. You saw him. He still feels it.'

Brook conceded with a shrug. 'How did she leave it?'

'The way they're all left. No leads, no body and no case – her file went to the MPB.'

'Anything on the pair in the van? Description? Number plate?'

'Nothing. But the van suggests an MO at least.'

'Or a takeaway.'

'Look, just suppose we've got two men targeting young foreign females travelling alone, young women who won't be missed for months, maybe even years, if they're taken. They have a van and know where the girls live. They watch them and wait for their chance and once the girls are alone they make their move. They knock on the door, grab the girl, then pack all her gear and take it with them. As far as anyone can tell, she's walked out never to return.'

'A home invasion?' Brook shook his head. 'Too risky. It requires a level of violence that sooner or later draws attention. Much easier just to grab the girl somewhere secluded, get hold of her keys, then slip in and clear out her gear.'

Noble nodded slowly. 'That makes more sense. But then they were seen watching LaMotta's house.'

'Maybe making sure he was out,' said Brook. 'They may have already snatched Valerie and were coming back for her luggage.'

'Sounds plausible.'

'Except they were seen, John.'

'But that was the only time,' said Noble. 'So maybe, being one of the first to vanish, Valerie was part of an emerging MO, which they've refined with Caitlin and the others. And working as a pair offers them scope to alter their method.'

Brook steepled his hands over his nose. 'We're just talking here, but assuming all this is true, why are they doing it?'

'Why abduct attractive young women?' asked Noble. 'Is simple rape so unlikely?'

'Rape is rarely simple,' said Brook. 'And rapists are never this organised, even the ones that plan. It's the nature of the beast, John. They always leave trace evidence, especially with a series. And the more they get away with it, the more careless they become. Doubling the number of offenders just doubles the exposure.'

'Then that's why they're snatching them first,' argued Noble. 'So they can clean up after themselves.'

'Cleaning up, fine,' said Brook. 'And murder to prevent them being identified. It happens. But that's usually only child-abusers and high-status rapists. Invariably rapists don't kill. Removing their victims from the face of the earth is not part of their profile. Rapists *prefer* their victims alive because their ongoing fear feeds the rapist's sense of his own power. It's part of the ego trip. Believe me, if the motive was rape, we'd have evidence.'

'We should check the SO database—'

'I did,' interrupted Brook. 'Nothing about pairs of rapists operating at this level anywhere in the country.'

'What then?'

Brook sighed. 'If these guys exist and are going to *this* much trouble to stay off the radar, it has to be something much worse.'

'And abducting the girls means they can take their time doing it,' added Noble, his expression grim.

'Right. They can savour it; maybe record what they're doing. They might even be filming.'

'Christ.'

'I'm not sure Christ plays any part, John.'

'They'd need privacy if they were filming torture and abuse.'

'Agreed,' said Brook. 'Which means . . .'

'What?' said Noble.

'Film,' said Brook softly.

'What about it?'

'Who's on reception?'

'Sergeant Grey.'

'Then you talk to him,' said Brook, jumping out of his chair. 'When Davison turns up, I want him brought in here.'

'To the incident room?' Noble gazed round at the artefacts. 'With all this confidential—'

'You were the one who suggested lobbing in a hand grenade,' said Brook. 'Give me a hand with this display board. I want the pictures visible from the door.'

Ten

ASHLEY UNBUTTONED HIS WAISTCOAT AND hung it on a hook while Jake unpacked another box of bottles. 'Ten o'clock. Get a shift on, I got plans.'

'Get a shift on, get a shift on,' mimicked Jake.

'Put the box down,' insisted Ashley. 'We're not open for another month. We'll be standing spare for two weeks, you keep that up.'

Reluctantly Jake lowered the box and in unison the pair of them pulled the huge tarpaulin over the bar as a dust cover, making sure it reached the floor on both sides.

'Seen Max today?' said Jake, trying to be matter-of-fact.

Ashley eyed him suspiciously. 'What is it with you and him? He don't even work here.'

'Have you seen him?'

'Tell me why, first.' A raised eyebrow was Ashley's only answer. *Mind yer own business.* 'I hope you're not gonna queer this job for us, Jake. We're on a good screw here.' No answer from Jake, so Ashley headed for the stairs. 'Sort your attitude out and do yourself some good. If Mr O likes you, he treats you real well, even gives you little jobs for cash. And I mean decent cash.'

'Like what?'

'I've got one tonight – fifty notes for a few minutes' work.' Ashley glanced at his watch. 'Be finished by half eleven.'

'I don't believe you,' said Jake. Ashley pulled out a fifty-pound note and snapped it in front of Jake's eyes. Jake looked at it greedily. 'Doing what?'

Ashley touched a finger to his nose. 'Never you mind, but I don't want him thinking he can't trust neither of us, so be careful. He's about and he's already pissed off.'

'Why?'

'Ain't you noticed? That sexy little cleaner didn't turn up and there's sawdust all over the floor. So whatever you got planned, forget it.'

'What's that supposed to mean?' said Jake.

'I mean teafin',' said Ashley. 'Mr O's all over the stock and he don't look the forgiving type. And then there's that big Polish goon he's got in to keep an eye on things. A bag of nuts, fine, but a case of vodka . . .'

'Night, Ash,' snarled Jake.

His piece said, Ashley headed for the stairs. 'Don't say you wasn't warned.'

Moments later, Jake threw his waistcoat on the same hook and trudged downstairs, hesitating at the staff entrance. When he was sure Ashley had gone, he knocked on the door of the manager's office. No reply. He opened the door quickly and bolted inside, closing the door behind him softly. His eyes flicked around for what he needed, spying a batch of unsealed envelopes on a desk, stacked like a concertina, each with a printed label. He plucked out the envelope marked 'M. Ostrowsky' and read the address before putting it back in the stack. Arboretum Street! That was just round the corner from the flat.

As he hurried from the office, he ran straight into the

owner. A large bald-headed man Jake hadn't seen before stood behind him.

'Mr Ostrowsky,' said Jake, trying to sound calm. He looked to the other man. Ashley was right. The guy was massive; bald, with a thick neck, well over six feet and almost as wide. Jake was reminded of Oddjob in one of the Bond films.

Ostrowsky – slim, handsome, expensively dressed and supremely self-assured – trained his steel-blue eyes on Jake. Oddjob bristled behind him. 'What were you doing in the office?'

'Looking for you, sir,' said Jake quickly. 'I was hoping I could ask for a sub.'

'You want I should make you a sandwich?'

Jake's smile was involuntary. 'Not that kind of sub.' He cast around for a better word. 'Er . . . an advance. On my wages. Things are a bit tight.'

Ostrowsky shrugged. 'We're not open yet, so no cash.'

Jake nodded philosophically. 'Understood.' He made to leave.

'Wait.' Ostrowsky put a hand in his back pocket and pulled out a thick wad of notes, peeling off a twenty. He held it out to Jake. 'Enough?'

Jake took the note gratefully. 'Thank you. I'll make it up on payday.'

Ostrowsky smiled back, his eyes failing to join in. 'I know you will.'

Jake pushed open the exit door and turned. 'Did I see your brother's van outside?'

'Max? No. He's wiring a house again.'

'Rewiring,' offered Jake.

Trying out the word for size, Ostrowsky disappeared into the office. As Jake stepped into the dark, clutching the note like a lifebelt, he saw his boss return with a set of car keys and throw them to Oddjob.

Brook stared at the display of photographs, now strategically positioned to face the door. 'You didn't tell me about girl six.'

'Bernadette Murphy from Dublin.' Noble stared at the final photograph, of a young redhead with grey eyes and freckles. 'We can't be sure of dates, but she seems to have been the first to disappear. By more than a year.'

'So she's actually girl one.'

'We're working on incomplete information, but yes,' said Noble. 'And there could be more girls as yet unreported.'

'Let's not get ahead of ourselves,' said Brook. 'Work with what we have in front of us. When was she in Derby?'

'A couple of weeks in June 2012, at the end of her gap year. She was staying with her aunt, a nurse called Mary Finnegan who works at the Royal Derby. She left on the fourth of July. Not officially missed until the start of September, when she failed to turn up for her first teaching post in Dublin.'

'And the aunt was the last to see her. In Derby, I mean.'

'Apparently. Finnegan left for her nursing shift at eleven that morning. Bernadette was gone when she got home twelve hours later.'

'Was there an uncle?'

'Barry Finnegan was working away from home. Oil rig.'

'Luggage?'

'All her belongings were gone and she didn't leave a note. Like the others.'

'And the aunt thought nothing of it until relatives in Ireland started to worry.'

'Exactly,' said Noble. 'Jane picked it up two months later.

She thought there'd been tension between the aunt and her niece but nothing to suspect she'd done her any harm. And there was no evidence of anything untoward, no unidentified YWFs in the mortuary. Bernadette was just gone.'

'And no reason to dig deeper,' said Brook.

'None. I've got a new address for Finnegan but haven't had a chance to call round.'

'Is there much point?' said Brook with a sigh.

'It's not too late to head up the scrap metal team,' said Noble.

'Might not be a bad idea at that. This is a haystack that might not even have a needle in it.'

There was silence while Brook stared at the photographs in turn. Six young faces gazed happily back. 'You couldn't handpick six better candidates to abduct. Transient, no roots in Derby and all the girls clear out their belongings.'

'That's the clever bit,' agreed Noble. 'Makes their disappearance seem voluntary.'

'Or it is what it looks like,' said Brook. 'A handful of independent young women continuing their travels – no division worth its salt is going to waste time on a crime they don't know has been committed.'

'Until now,' said Noble. Brook threw him a glance. 'So assuming we're leaving Derby's manhole covers to fend for themselves, what next?'

'Concentrate on Caitlin,' said Brook. 'She's got the freshest trail.'

'And with no common link between the girls and no clear motive, we concentrate on method, I suppose,' concluded Noble.

'You suppose right.'

'Do we accept LaMotta's story?'

'We've got to start somewhere, John.'

'Then we have two perpetrators with a white van big enough to hold a body and luggage.'

'And without windows, so the cargo can't be seen.'

'A panel van, then. Do our suspects already know where the girls live ahead of the abduction?'

'Definitely,' said Brook.

'So maybe they followed them home then stalked them over a period of time.'

'They'd stalk them once they had an address, John. Following six girls to find out where they lived is too risky. It would increase their visibility.'

'Agreed. So, taking Caitlin as a template, I'd want to know her movements and habits, work out the best time to strike. That way I eliminate variables like a boyfriend or housemate getting in the way.'

'So?'

'So I might need basic surveillance equipment, like a camera or binoculars.'

'Which suggests some kind of income and a job,' added Brook.

'Another reason for snatching Caitlin at night,' said Noble. 'I work during the day.'

'Okay, it's March twentieth. Caitlin's been chosen. You know where she lives. You're in the van watching her house. What next?'

'It's thick with snow so I don't park too near the bungalow,' said Noble. 'I don't want to leave tyre tracks or park in a resident's space and draw attention to the van. Laurie and Caitlin take a cab because of the weather and I . . . we follow them to the Flowerpot.'

'Do you park near the pub and wait?'

'If we're confident she's going home after the pub, we could park the van at any point on her route and wait . . .'

'But you can't be certain,' said Brook. 'It could be several hours before she leaves the pub. She might be going on somewhere, so you have to monitor her departure.'

Noble nodded. 'Besides, she left early.'

'You checked the Flowerpot's cameras?'

'If somebody followed Caitlin from the pub, it's not on their film.'

'Then they don't follow her from the pub. They follow her *to* it, then park along the route back to the bungalow but close enough to *see* the pub.' Brook jabbed a finger at the large map of Derby taking up most of one wall. 'King Street or Garden Street, maybe.'

'And sit in the warm van to watch and wait,' said Noble. He looked up at Brook. 'Caitlin must have walked right past them.'

'At which point they turn and drive past her to the abduction site.' Brook gazed at the map, traced a finger along the route and jabbed at a large green space. 'Markeaton Park.'

'Perfect,' said Noble. 'Nobody will be in the park on a night like that. In fact nobody's out on foot at all. We drive past her, park the van and wait, knowing it will only be a few minutes. And when she reaches Markeaton Park, we knock her out, take her house keys and throw her body in the back of the van for the short drive back to her place. We know Laurie is still in the pub so the place is empty and one of us goes in to fetch Caitlin's rucksack, all packed and ready to go.'

'While the other dismantles her phone to disconnect the GPS,' said Brook.

'Caitlin's going away the next day, so as far as anyone can

tell, she's left for Belfast and won't be missed for weeks. You think they knew she was going away?'

'Possible.'

'How?'

'A product of the planning and surveillance,' said Brook.

'Or maybe my access to her details means I know it's a reading week and she's going to Belfast the next day. Someone at the university, like Stiles.'

'Not everybody heads home during a reading week,' said Brook. 'And Stiles was at the conference in Northampton that night. The hotel confirmed it.'

'I don't care,' said Noble. 'Until I get confirmation from someone who actually saw him there, I'm keeping him in the frame. What's to say he didn't drive up for the night to snatch Caitlin and still be back at the hotel for breakfast?'

'John, he's got no history and he's not strong enough to overcome someone as young and healthy as Caitlin.'

'He wouldn't have been alone,' said Noble. 'And even if he was in Northampton, he could still be involved, maybe in the background, a sleeping partner. He has access to Caitlin and Daniela's details, as well as drugs in case they need to be controlled.'

'So now there are three of them.'

'Why not?'

'Well if we're ignoring alibis, Davison is more likely to know her travel plans. Caitlin booked her train while they were still going out together.'

'That's right,' said Noble, his face lighting up.

'But only one person would be one hundred per cent sure of her plans, and that's Laurie. No, I don't like it either, John. Or the notion of a sleeping partner. You can explain Daniela and

Caitlin with it, but how do you link in the other girls?'

'Maybe Daniela and Caitlin are a separate case.'

'No, there has to be a common connection – beyond all six being single white females from overseas.'

'You forgot young and sexually attractive.'

'And if we're using Caitlin as a template, sexually active too,' added Brook.

'So we're back to rape again.'

'I didn't say that,' said Brook. 'But temptation *is* the oldest sin. You covet what you can't have.'

'Which would tend to rule out Davison,' said Noble. He tapped his watch.

'His alibi already did that,' said Brook. 'And you're right. Davison's not coming.'

'Good.' Noble rubbed his temple. 'My brain hurts. Is it always this thankless?'

'Cold-case work? Try doing it alone in a room without windows. This isn't the best incident room, but at least it has natural light.'

'It's tiny,' said Noble, looking around. 'I booked it because no one else wanted it and we can shut it down quickly if . . .' He declined to finish the sentence.

'If a *proper* case crops up,' finished Brook.

Before Noble could prepare an objection, Duty Sergeant Gordon Grey, his uniform straining at the waist, knocked and entered, looking past Brook as though he didn't exist. 'Sergeant Noble. Got a Mr Davison here to see you.'

'Show him in,' said Brook, glancing at Noble.

Grey was taken aback. 'I've got interview rooms free.'

'You heard the man, Sergeant,' shouted a voice from the corridor. A burly figure pushed past Grey.

'Councillor Davison,' said Noble, as a large, red-faced man strode in, his son slipstreaming behind him. He stood in a limp attempt to conceal the display boards.

'Inspector Brook,' boomed Davison Senior. 'What're you playing at? My lad's not going to be treated like a bloody criminal.'

'Councillor,' said Brook, standing.

'Oh, you remember me, do you?' blustered Davison, Roland smirking behind his back. '*Councillor* Davison – member of the Police Liaison Committee and generous supporter of police charities.'

'And your son – the future barista,' said Brook. Roland's expression darkened and he opened his mouth to complain.

'And don't you forget it,' boomed Councillor Davison, jabbing a finger. 'So what do you want to talk to him about now?'

Brook gestured feebly towards the corridor. 'Sir, you can't be in here. This is an incident room.'

'I'm not going anywhere until you tell me what this is about. My boy's answered all your questions and he knows nowt about that girl's whereabouts.'

As Brook had hoped, Roland's eyes had alighted on the portraits of the missing girls and his Adam's apple took a dive.

'You can't be in here, sir,' repeated Noble. 'We have confidential information on show.'

Davison Senior followed his son's eyes to the display, and he too paused to stare for a few seconds. 'Aye, well. Maybe you're right. Being on the PLC, I don't want to ride roughshod over procedure.' He touched his son on the arm and, prompted by a flick of his father's head, Roland headed for the corridor.

Eleven

CAITLIN WOKE IN DARKNESS, HER head aching and her neck sore. She blinked her eyes open but in the blackness it felt like she hadn't opened them at all. Lifting her head, she realised it was held, her neck almost immovable in some kind of restraint. She couldn't sit up, and when she attempted to lift her feet, she found her legs were also bound. Worst of all, a piece of cloth filled her mouth and, try as she might, she was incapable of spitting it out. Powerless to touch or even see her face in the dark, she was aware of the sticking plaster covering her mouth keeping the gag in place.

Panic began to rise in her and she could feel herself starting to choke. She tried to thrash and kick but her hands and feet wouldn't budge, and no matter how urgently she struggled, she couldn't free herself. Trussed like a chicken, she slumped back on to cold, hard concrete.

It took several large pulls of oxygen before her nerves steadied and her heart rate began to slow. She tried to think and get her bearings. Making a supreme effort, she was able to prop herself on to her right elbow and lift her head. With more deliberate movements, she found she had limited play side to side in her hands, though not nearly enough to reach any of her bonds or the large plaster over her mouth.

She could hear at least. There was a definite hum of working machinery, and above that what sounded like animal noises. *A pig squealing? Am I on a farm?* Come to think of it, when she sniffed at the cold air, she realised there was a definite odour of excrement reaching her nostrils. Not the pungent, repulsive ordure of human waste but the manure-rich aroma of a well-grazed field.

I'm on a farm or smallholding. She listened again. The squealing was high-pitched and didn't sound like the contented grunting of a feeding animal, so perhaps the poor beast was being slaughtered. To add weight to this, the machinery stopped humming shortly after the pig ceased squealing.

Her elbow began to hurt so she sank back down to the rough concrete to think. *Who is doing this to me, and why?* She closed her eyes to piece together what she could remember. The Flowerpot, the walk home through the snow and the angry mocking voice calling her name she could recall with crystal clarity. She even had a sense of being thrown on to the floor of a van, where she'd lost consciousness. She'd come round once or twice while the van was still moving. It must have been a long journey, because whenever she woke, her arm and leg under her body were completely numb on the metal floor.

She heard a door open and close somewhere behind her. Then footsteps, and a few seconds later daylight illuminated her space. Caitlin struggled to lift her head and darted her eyes hungrily around for information. She immediately saw that she was in a large hangar or barn with a high ceiling. Off to the side there were small pens, some empty, some containing bales of straw, but all devoid of livestock. On one wall was a large stainless-steel door from where the footsteps had emanated before crossing the barn to open the outer door.

In the light she could run an eye over her bonds to register the criss-crossing network of leather straps, not unlike the bondage gear Rollo had had her wear a couple of times, only thicker and less pliable.

A figure approached through the outer door, walking purposefully towards her. It was a man, large and bear-like. The glare of sunlight hitting snow obscured her search for detail on his face.

Many things to say sluiced through her mind, some aggressive, some submissive. *Please let me go. I won't say anything. Who the hell do you think you are? You've no right. People will be looking for me.* Frustration followed immediately, as the gag in her mouth meant she was unable to say any of them even supposing she could settle on a script.

She manoeuvred herself with difficulty, keeping her eyes trained on her captor. The man ambled cockily towards her as though he hadn't a care in the world.

'Hello, Kitty.' The voice was gravelly and deep, the accent local to Derbyshire as far as her untrained ear could tell. His greeting was accompanied by an expulsion of air, condensing in the cold. He was laughing at her, mocking her helplessness. 'Not so mouthy this time, are you?'

This time? Have we met?

'Don't remember me, do you?' said the man. 'Something for you to think on.'

His confidence was unsettling and Caitlin forced herself to look for information that might help her. She didn't know the voice, of that she was certain, but this only made her unease climb a notch, extinguishing the forlorn hope that her abduction might have been some elaborate prank. She stared hard, trying to get a glimpse of his face, but the glare defeated her. She mumbled an acknowledgement to let him know she wasn't paralysed by fear.

The man stood astride her prostrate frame and reached down with a gloved hand.

'*Please* ...' she tried to say, sounding like Frankenstein's monster bemoaning its reflection.

The sticking plaster was pulled roughly away, accompanied by a yelp of shock from Caitlin.

'Please ...' she repeated, coughing out the gag. But her appeal was cut short when he jammed a piece of dowelling, like a brush handle only thinner, into her mouth and forced it up against her back teeth. It made her choke on accumulated saliva and she began to splutter, but she was powerless to voice a protest as the figure hooked his hand through one of the straps and dragged her across the floor towards the entrance. She winced as the rough concrete scraped her bare midriff. Fortunately her jeans protected her legs from the worst of the friction.

She trained her eyes on the entrance as it loomed larger. This door too was metal, and slid open sideways on well-oiled runners. About five yards from the warmth of sunlight, her captor let go her bonds and she dropped like a sack of potatoes on to the concrete. She tried to right herself and wriggle towards the life-affirming sun, but was flipped roughly over on to her stomach. She felt the weight of him sit astride her, pinning her down, before he lay on top of her, his chest pushing her face into the concrete. Strong hands grabbed her right arm and held it fast to the ground, and Caitlin could see what looked like a tattoo of a cross on his hand, another on his forearm. She struggled against his grip but was completely immobile, though she managed to spit out the wooden peg.

'You'll be sorry you did that,' said the man.

'Fuck you,' she screamed, writhing in vain to get away, her ordeal finally bringing tears.

'Keep still, whore,' the man breathed in her ear. 'Accept the Lord into your heart.'

Another figure, of slighter build, appeared at the barn entrance, framed in dazzling winter sunshine. Caitlin saw small feet moving to stand over her.

'Who the fuck are you?' she panted, unfurling her broadest Irish snarl for the occasion. 'Get this fucking ape off me . . .'

'The language on her,' said the man, chuckling softly in her ear. He grabbed her hair to pull her head back and make her watch while his partner moved closer, holding a thin metal rod, solid like a golf club, brandishing it lovingly before Caitlin's eyes. The tip was bright orange and shaped like a crucifix. With a gulp of horror, Caitlin saw the air shimmer around it as it moved, and she felt the heat warm her face.

'And the Lord said they shall be cleansed by the purifying fire,' said the man in her ear.

'No . . . please.' Caitlin struggled again.

'Hold her.' Caitlin was shocked to hear someone else's voice.

The man's hands redoubled their grip on her arm. 'Do it!'

Caitlin sobbed and closed her eyes to imagine herself elsewhere. A second later she felt searing heat on her right forearm and screamed as she heard the sizzle of the red-hot iron on her skin. A millisecond later, pain a thousand times more intense than anything she'd ever felt before tore through her nervous system and her teeth jammed together on to the tip of her tongue as she lost consciousness.

* * *

Caitlin woke several times but drifted back into the netherworld on each occasion, until consciousness took a more permanent hold and the pain of her burn kicked in. She began to sob, quietly at first but then full-on, her shoulders shaking in accompaniment. She'd bitten down hard on her tongue and could taste the coppery bitterness of blood mingling with what little saliva she was able to produce.

Eventually the tears subsided and she lifted her head to look around her, eyes better accustomed to the shadows. Nothing had changed. She was still in the large concrete-floored barn and she sagged back to the ground, helplessness and rage washing through her. A second later, she stirred again, muscle memory sending its message.

'I can move,' she croaked, and was shocked at the tremor in her voice. She pushed herself to her bare feet with her bound hands and managed to stand, biting her lip at the pain. All restraints except those binding her wrists in front of her had been removed. She examined her arm. It was raw, the weal on her skin in the shape of a cross.

She tore with her teeth at the heavy straps and stiff metal buckle binding her wrists, but the leather wouldn't budge. When she eventually withdrew her mouth, there was blood on the leather. She spat out more in despair and gave up, looking instead to her surroundings.

The barn was dark, but her eyes alighted on a plastic bag by the door. She ran to examine it, removing a leather-bound bible. There was an inscription on the inside cover: *Something else for you to think on, Kitty.* She returned the book to the bag and took out three litre bottles of water, greedily spinning the cap from one and downing half of it in one go. She felt better having done so but then realised she might have to ration the water, so she resealed the bottle and laid all three carefully on the ground.

Also in the bag was a Tupperware carton. She flicked off the lid, sniffed at the meaty aroma of cooked chicken and picked at a shard to nibble at. It was tasty, and though she couldn't describe herself as hungry, she finished the entire carton in one go, not sure when she might eat again.

After her meal, she replaced the sealed carton in the plastic bag, discovering something she'd missed in her eagerness to eat and drink. It was shaped like a tube of toothpaste. She couldn't make out the label in the gloom so unscrewed the small cap and sniffed at the tiny spout. It was Savlon.

She scoured the floor until she spotted the plaster the man had torn from her mouth. She knelt down and laid the plaster upside down before squeezing out a generous blob of the ointment on to the cotton pad. Very delicately, she manoeuvred her stinging burn over it, and when she felt the cream smearing against the wound, she gritted her teeth and pressed the plaster firmly into place. She used her chin to smooth it on, and could feel the ointment beginning to do its work, at first bringing more pain before the medication began to soothe a little.

With her field dressing in place, she explored her prison, examining the outer door and the large steel door on another wall, both locked. The internal door was modern and sturdy, like a walk-in freezer in a butcher's shop.

After inspecting each of the animal pens in turn, Caitlin located the small wooden stake that had been shoved into her mouth – to prevent her biting her tongue, she now realised. One end was sharper than the other, and she sank gingerly to her knees to begin the long, slow process of sharpening it further against the smooth floor.

A couple of hours later, she felt the tip of her new weapon and nodded with satisfaction before positioning herself behind the cold metal door to wait.

Caitlin waited, coiled behind the door, for hours before exhaustion overtook her. Resigned, she left her vigil and went to lie on the straw in one of the pens. She was beginning to lose a sense of time passing.

Sleep came easily but it was never restful, and she woke several times. Once she stretched, expecting to find herself in the room next to Laurie, hearing her best friend flushing the toilet in the small hours. But Laurie wasn't there.

Hours later, she woke again and returned to crouch at the metal door, sharpened stake between her cupped hands. But as the hours passed, her state of vigilance waned, sapping energy and will from her. After what felt like half a day but was probably only two or three hours, she returned to the relative comfort of the pen, with its itchy but comfortable straw, still clutching her wooden weapon in white knuckles, to watch and wait between fitful naps.

This pattern repeated itself for what must have been days. In between periods of readiness, Caitlin slept. Every so often, when she was asleep in the straw, a new bag of provisions would be slipped into the barn. But it never happened when she was waiting by the door.

From time to time she would carefully remove her dressing to prod at her burns, reapplying ointment when necessary. Fortunately the outbuilding was cool and airy, which, with decent luck, made infection less likely.

However, there was no toilet, and Caitlin had been forced into the indignity of relieving herself into a trough at the far end of the barn. After wiping herself on a clump of straw, she covered the offending matter with more straw and resumed her desperate vigil, fighting back the tears. Eventually she stood and flexed her aching leg muscles. Suddenly, as though a white-hot needle had been pushed into her brain, she could stand it no longer and launched herself at the door, pounding against it with bound hands, and when they tired, kicking out with bare feet.

'Open this door, you bastards,' she screamed. 'You hear me? Let me out.' She continued to beat and kick at the door until she fell in a heap against it. 'What's wrong with you, you pervert?' she sobbed, her voice cracking under the strain. 'If you want to fuck me, get in here and get it over with.'

Hoarse with screaming, she dragged herself across to the straw-filled pens and threw herself down in despair and exhaustion, tears filling her eyes. She lay still for several minutes, panting, her eyes closing, hoping oblivion would come. Eventually it did, though it was more a symptom of her weakened condition than any regular sleep pattern.

Twelve

'YOU WERE RIGHT,' SAID NOBLE, picking up a tray of hot drinks. 'Roland was staring at Daniela's picture.'

'He probably has no idea she's missing,' said Brook. 'Must have been quite a shock.'

'How did you know?'

'I didn't. Not for sure. But Daniela started her first year at university the same time as Roland. There was a good chance their paths crossed.'

'I thought you didn't operate on hunches,' said Noble.

'It wasn't just that,' said Brook, checking his watch. 'You're not an opera buff, are you?'

'Do I need to be?'

'Tell you later,' said Brook. 'Cooper?'

'He'll knock on the door in ten minutes and hand you a piece of paper.'

'Good. Better not keep them waiting.' He reached for the door handle.

'There's something else,' said Noble.

'What?'

'The councillor recognised Daniela's picture as well. I saw him looking.'

Brook considered for a moment before opening the door.

'So you don't deny being the father?' asked Brook.

'He doesn't deny he had a sexual relationship with the girl,' said Davison. 'Natural and healthy, but whether or not—'

'Councillor,' interrupted Brook. 'Please be quiet.'

'I beg your pardon.'

'Your son is old enough to answer for himself,' explained Brook. 'We've allowed you to sit in as a courtesy—'

'The boy's allowed legal representation,' barked Davison.

'That's not what you're providing,' said Noble. 'So either let him answer or leave.'

There was silence while Davison's hooded eyes burned into Noble's. A few seconds later his gaze dropped.

'Go on,' prompted Noble.

'We had regular sex,' said Roland. 'But do I know for certain I was the father? No.'

Brook considered him. 'You're suggesting Caitlin had other sexual partners.'

'I wouldn't bet against it,' replied Roland.

'But you can't give us any names,' said Noble.

'No.'

'You stated previously that your relationship ended ten days before Caitlin had the termination,' said Noble. 'That would be on or around the eighth of March.'

'Sounds right.'

'And when you broke up, that ended all contact between you.'

'I saw her on campus from time to time but only from a distance.'

'But you didn't speak to her.'

'I thought a clean break was best,' said Roland, grinning. 'Didn't want her under any illusions.'

'You didn't speak to her on the phone, for instance?' said Brook, slipping in the key question without fanfare.

'Asked and answered.'

Brook looked at him before making a note. 'The witness answered no,' he said as he wrote on his pad. Roland looked at him curiously.

'What about the actual termination?' said Noble. 'Did you give Caitlin money towards the cost?'

'No,' said Roland firmly.

'What about your father?'

'Pardon!' exclaimed Davison Senior. 'Are you suggesting I paid her off?'

Brook addressed Roland. 'Well, did he?'

'No I bloody didn't,' boomed the councillor, his face reddening. 'And I resent any such implication.'

'Why?' asked Brook. 'It makes perfect sense. You give Roland cash to give to Caitlin for a procedure that everyone wants to happen. The chances are it's your son's child, so you go private for the sake of confidentiality and the matter's closed. Why all the bluster?'

'Because it didn't happen,' said Davison.

Brook contemplated him. 'Did she at least ask for money?'

'No, she didn't,' said the councillor, his face reddening.

'You wouldn't object to us checking your financial statements to be certain?' said Noble.

'Yes, I would object,' said Davison. 'The law requires you get a warrant. Isn't that right, son?'

'Right, Dad,' agreed Roland.

'Something to hide?' chipped in Brook.

'Neither of us has anything to hide,' said Roland confidently. 'But my dad's finances are private and irrelevant to Caitlin's disappearance. So if you want to look, get a warrant – if you can.' Brook smiled quietly as if pleased that Roland was putting up a fight. Roland caught the mood and uncertainty invaded his eyes. He glanced at his father, keen now to be away. 'Are we done?'

'No,' said Brook. 'When I asked if you'd spoken to Caitlin after your break-up, you said you hadn't. Yet on March sixteenth, two days before Caitlin's termination, and four days before her disappearance, you phoned her mobile.'

'No I didn't,' said Roland, his expression scornful.

'We have her phone records,' persisted Brook, waiting for Roland to dig himself a bigger hole.

'I don't care. I didn't phone or text the silly bitch after we split.'

Brook glanced at Noble, who pushed a photocopy across the table. 'For the benefit of the tape, DS Noble is showing the witness a copy of Caitlin Kinnear's mobile phone records.' Roland stared at it, then looked at his father. 'The call was placed from your father's house to Caitlin's mobile at ten thirty that night,' said Brook. 'It lasted for five minutes and twenty-one seconds. As you can see.'

Roland seemed confused. 'But I wasn't even—'

'You did call her, son,' interrupted Davison Senior.

'What?' said Roland.

'You did call her,' said Davison, his eyes burning into his

son's face. 'I heard you on the phone in the hall. You dropped in to pick up your laundry. Do you remember?'

Roland stared at his father until he'd processed the information, then stared at the ceiling to recollect. 'That's right. I did swing by for my laundry and I did call her.' He looked sheepishly at Brook. 'Sorry. Forgot.'

'Why did you ring her?'

'You said it was before she was going into the clinic,' said Roland. He looked down at the floor, then up again. 'I wanted to wish her well.'

'I see.' Brook smiled, leaving a pause to relish the shock and awe to come. 'Let's move on to your relationship with Daniela Cassetti.'

'My . . . what? Who?' Roland exchanged a glance with his father.

'Daniela Cassetti,' said Noble, offering Roland a smaller version of the display photograph for the pair to examine and introducing it verbally for the tape. 'She was a first-year student for two terms, same year you started. She disappeared at Easter and didn't return for the summer term, same as Caitlin. You had an intimate relationship with her – same as Caitlin. And eventually she was reported missing.' Noble paused for effect. 'Same as Caitlin.'

The two detectives waited, allowing the silence to work its magic on Roland and his father. The young man kept his rebuttal simple. 'I don't know her,' he said softly.

'We have information that not only did you know her, but you had a sexual relationship with her,' said Brook.

'If my boy says he doesn't know her—'

'What information?' demanded Roland.

There was a knock at the door and Noble halted the tape

after documenting the interruption. DC Cooper handed Brook an A4 copy of the staff canteen menu from two days ago. 'Your warrant, Inspector.'

Brook folded the paper and meshed his fingers over it, staring between Roland and the councillor. Noble restarted the tape.

'Do you like Italian opera, Roland? Verdi, for instance.' The young man stared back at Brook, the detective's confidence eating away at his sangfroid. '"La donna e mobile", in particular.'

'You what?' scoffed Davison Senior. 'Are you off your trolley, Brook? Actually, don't answer that. I already know about your problems, fella.'

'It's Italian for *the lady is fickle*,' said Brook, ignoring the councillor. 'It's a song from *Rigoletto*. You had a disc in your apartment. The one I picked up, in fact. But you changed the title to *immobile*. I assume that's some kind of sniggering undergraduate humour. The Italian lady is immobile. Did you tie Daniela up and film yourself having sex with her?'

'This has gone far enough,' said Davison, standing.

Brook turned a cold eye on him. 'Feel free to leave, Councillor. Your name isn't on the warrant. Yet.'

'You cheeky bugger . . .'

Brook tapped the out-of-date menu with a finger. 'I'll be searching your son's apartment . . .'

'You've got no right,' said Davison.

'Dad . . .'

'I have every right,' said Brook. 'I have reasonable suspicion that two of the missing girls in our inquiry were filmed by your son in a series of compromising sexual encounters. I suspect money changed hands for their participation in those recordings, though I can't prove it. Furthermore, I suspect you're aware of your son's activities, Councillor, although the extent of your involvement remains as yet unclear . . .'

'How dare you?'

'*You* rang Caitlin that evening, Councillor, because she'd asked for money to pay for terminating her pregnancy. Either you knew about the films already, or she told you and gave you a subtle hint that paying for the procedure would prevent damaging and embarrassing revelations.'

'I'll have your job—'

'Dad,' said Roland. 'Leave it to me.' He turned to Brook. 'You didn't have a warrant when you picked up that disc in my flat. So your search was illegal.'

'That's true if it's the only film,' said Brook. 'But it isn't, is it?'

'But you developed your suspicions based on an illegal search,' said Roland.

'You invited me into your flat . . .'

'That doesn't mean I waived my right to privacy. I didn't invite you to tamper with my possessions; in fact I expressly forbade it.'

Brook smiled, exuding more confidence than he felt. 'How sure are you of your legal ground, Roland? By the time we're arguing the case in front of a judge, it may be too late for your father's reputation.' He turned to Davison; the councillor's expression was uneasy. 'You know about or have seen these films, haven't you, Councillor? That's why you agreed to pay cash to Caitlin Kinnear before her termination.'

'I don't—'

'Look,' said Brook, banging a fist on the table, making everyone jump, Noble included. 'We've spent enough time on you and your son. If those films involved Roland and his girlfriends having consensual sex, I want to know now. If they have no bearing on the disappearances of Daniela and Caitlin, I'm not interested in wasting any more of my time. The fact that you may have compensated the girls for their efforts is not a matter of record or something that I'm able to prove easily. So if I get full disclosure *right now*, we can all get on with our lives. Roland will lose his collection either way. The camera too, for the time being. But that's all you'll lose, because I've got better things to do than police consenting adults at play.'

He waited to let his speech sink in, then continued quietly. 'But if I don't get full disclosure, I'm going to start thinking those tapes may be significant in the *serious* crimes I'm investigating. And if I find other abductees on those tapes, or you, Councillor, participating, or young women who appear lethargic as the result of being drugged, then charges are going to be laid and people are going to go to prison. So decide now.'

Brook sat back and contemplated father and son, his face set in stone. The pair seemed to have shrunk since the start of the interview, and searched each other's eyes in silence for the way forward. Eventually they both nodded.

'What do you want to know?' said Councillor Davison, barely able to raise a croak.

When Davison and his son had left with DC Cooper and DS Morton to retrieve the tapes, Noble could contain himself no longer. After allowing a few seconds for father and son to disappear out of earshot, he sighed heavily and closed his eyes with satisfaction. 'Oh my God,' he panted. 'That was better than sex.'

Brook was unable to hold back a smile. 'I'll take your word for it.'

'Roland's face . . .' began Noble, clenching his fists in ecstasy.

'I thought he was going to call my bluff,' confessed Brook.

'When you asked for permission to remove his discs and camera . . .' continued Noble. '*Why do you need my permission if you've got a warrant?*' Noble shook his head. 'And you showed him the menu.'

'I don't think he was overly impressed by the canteen's selection.'

'So what do you think?' said Noble, laughing. 'Do we believe them?'

'I think so,' said Brook. 'Obviously we can't corroborate consent with Caitlin and Daniela, but if the tapes show what Roland says they show, then their only crimes are stupidity and arrogance.'

'We are looking for a pair of kidnappers, and that's now two missing girls they know.'

'We're not even certain they're missing, John.'

'*I'm* certain.'

'Well, Roland has an alibi and the councillor says he was in the chamber the night Caitlin disappeared,' said Brook.

'Easy enough to check.'

'And assuming he's telling the truth, that puts them both in the clear,' said Brook.

'Think the dirty old sod is in the films?'

'He's not stupid enough to lie about something so easy to verify.'

'He could have had sex with Caitlin or Daniela off camera,' suggested Noble.

'We don't know that,' said Brook. 'And if he had, I suspect Caitlin would've asked for a lot more than a thousand pounds.'

'Then why else would he ring her?'

'To protect his son's good name,' suggested Brook. 'Reputation is everything to people like him.'

'But what was there to stop her coming back for more?'

'Once the pregnancy was terminated and the films were destroyed, she would have no way of backing up her claims,' said Brook. 'Crisis over.'

'And cheap at twice the price,' nodded Noble. 'So why didn't Roland destroy the films after you saw the discs?'

'Arrogance, John. People like that think they're untouchable.'

'So we're back where we started.'

'Not quite,' said Brook. 'Eliminating suspects is always progress.'

Jake opened the door of the flat and hurried inside.

'Where've you been?' demanded a sulky voice.

'Shopping.' Jake snapped on the light. It didn't work.

'The lecky ran out in the middle of *Pointless*,' said Nick.

'Here.' Jake tossed a couple of coins on to the kitchen counter. Nick moved out of the darkness and picked them up. He knelt before a small cupboard and slotted them home before turning a switch on the meter. The light and the TV came on.

'Where've you been?' he repeated, staring hard at his cheap plastic watch to be certain of his facts. 'It's gone eleven and I'm hungry.'

Jake slung a groaning carrier bag on to the kitchen counter. 'Glad to hear it.' He tipped out a dozen cans of economy beans, a pack of sausages and a loaf of bread. 'Get a couple of tins open and put the rest away.'

'Sausages,' breathed Nick in wonder. 'You bought meat.'

'No guarantees,' grinned Jake, pulling out the tin opener and tossing it to Nick. His smile dissipated. 'I've got to go out again after we eat.'

'But it's past bedtime.'

'It can't be helped.'

'Where?'

'Just out,' said Jake. 'Don't worry, I'll lock you in.'

'No, I'm coming with you.'

'You can't. Get the frying pan out . . .'

'I'm coming with you,' repeated Nick. 'I've been cooped up here all day.'

'It's not safe,' insisted Jake. 'You can watch telly.'

'I'll scream the place down and then the social will come round and cart me off,' insisted Nick, panting with determination.

'You'd like that, would you?' snarled Jake. 'End up in some poky residential again. No computer games – fighting over the TV remote with some skell who'd beat you to a pulp just for looking at him funny.'

'At least I'd get to go outside,' growled Nick.

Jake bent down to stack tins on top of the yellowing newspaper in the cupboard, avoiding Nick's gaze. A moment later, he relented. 'Maybe you should be there. See what happens when you fuck with a Tanner.'

Nick grinned. 'Fuck with a Tanner.'

'Listen,' said Jake, grabbing him roughly by his T-shirt.

'Gerroff,' complained Nick, finding his sulk again.

'I said listen!' repeated Jake, forcing Nick to meet his eyes.

'No matter what you see tonight, you don't speak and you never mention it after. And you don't get in the way. Got it?'

A little after midnight, Jake and Nick made the short journey to Arboretum Street, where they spotted Max's white van parked up. Jake scoured the ground, eventually bending to pick up a half-brick from the road.

'What you doing, Jake?'

'Shut up!' hissed Jake as he approached the driver's door. He raised the brick above his head, preparing to launch it through the driver's window, but something gave him pause and, puzzled, he lowered his arm and allowed the brick to drop at his feet. He peered into the cab and tried the handle.

'It's not locked,' he hissed in Nick's direction. He bent into the cab and emerged holding a set of car keys, grinning at his brother. 'What a dick.'

'What a dick,' repeated Nick, giggling.

'Get in,' said Jake, climbing into the driver's seat and starting the engine. 'We're gonna have some fun.'

Thirteen

TIME PASSED, NOT THAT CAITLIN had any way of marking its passage. Hours felt like days and days felt like weeks and her routine never varied. Every two or three days, a new plastic bag with water bottles and cooked chicken or sometimes fish would appear by the locked door. At less frequent intervals, a bucket of cold water would also materialise. As Caitlin was well supplied with bottled water, she assumed this was for washing, and the block of chemical-smelling carbolic nestled at the bottom of the bucket confirmed it.

By now she had begun to believe her captors were watching her, at least part of the time. It was too much of a coincidence that the door to the barn would only ever be opened when she was collapsed in fitful slumber in the straw, exhausted from fruitless hours spent crouching in readiness, sharpened stake in her hand.

So she abandoned waiting by the door and kept the stake concealed in her pocket during waking hours but in her hands while she slept. Instead she concentrated her efforts on her body language, hoping to appear as servile and beaten as possible. She even took to reading the bible when the ambient light was bright enough.

'Getting my head right, boss,' she would shout occasionally, aping a Paul Newman film she'd once watched with her parents. Regret pulled on her stomach. How she'd reviled her home life in Belfast, but now she yearned to be there, safe and warm, getting ready to go to church after a hearty fried breakfast.

One morning – she assumed it was morning – she woke to find her bag of supplies and a bucket of water as before. But this time something was different. Steam was rising from the bucket. The water was hot. She hurried over and plunged her bare feet in one at a time, closing her eyes to the pleasure of the warmth caressing her toes.

'Thank you,' she shouted, remembering her strategy, then stepped out of the bucket and proceeded to wash her face while the water was still fairly clean before returning her cooling feet to the bucket and washing them thoroughly.

She made her way back to her bed in the straw, taking the food and drink with her, and devoured a chicken leg, barely stopping to chew, then washed down her meal with water. As she lowered the bottle, she noticed something. Her hands were much freer. The hot water had softened the binding on her wrists, making the leather pliable. Glancing around, she sank into the straw as though going to sleep, but instead held her hands to her mouth and worked at the strap with her teeth.

The strap gave slightly and she stifled a yelp of excitement. She repositioned her mouth and sank her teeth into the leather, gripping as tight as she could before slowly yanking her head back. Her heart gave a leap of joy as the strap moved out of the buckle, the prong was dislodged from the hole and the binding unfastened.

She removed the strap with a heartfelt sigh of pleasure but resisted the urge to stretch out her arms. Instead she squeezed out the last of the Savlon on to her chafed wrists and settled down to wait, the wooden stake gripped in her palm.

A noise woke her, and Caitlin opened her eyes without moving, still clutching the stake in her fist. She could hear the metal door being pulled slowly open. Enough for one person to slip into the barn. There was no sound of the door closing again.

She closed her eyes to feign sleep. Her hands were hidden underneath her prostrate body and she manoeuvred the wooden stake into a stabbing hold, waiting, all her senses supercharged.

When she could feel the warm breath of someone peering down at her, she lashed out in the darkness with all the force she could muster, thrusting the wooden stake as hard and accurately as she could in the presumed direction of her captor.

A high-pitched squeal rent the air and Caitlin felt the thin blade snap in her hands as it met the resistance of bone. Dropping the remaining shard, she leapt to her feet and, loosing off her own shriek, grabbed hair to fling the shadowy form between her and freedom to the ground. Running at full pelt, she aimed a sharp kick into her captor's midriff, registering a satisfying yelp of pain before dashing towards the starry canopy of a clear night.

At speed, the concrete floor was treacherous, and she slipped and stumbled her way towards the partially open door as best she could on bare feet. Once there, she stepped through into the sweet cold air and pulled the door closed, the handle clicking on to a latch. There was an open padlock on the ground with a key protruding, so for good measure she fumbled it into both rings, snapped it shut and flung the key off into the darkness.

'Enjoy your stay, fucker,' she hissed at the metal door.

She flicked her head left and right, but despite the full moon, an escape route wasn't easy to pick out. On a whim, inspired by her religious upbringing, she turned right instead of left and hurried along the side of the barn towards a five-bar gate, and beyond that a small track that stretched out into the gloom.

The briefest glimpse over her shoulder reassured her that she wasn't being pursued, so she vaulted the gate and sped off down the slippery downhill track, slick with mud, until she came to a cattle grid lying between her and the road. She didn't hesitate, stepping determinedly across the cold bars in her bare feet, leaping from the last rung on to slippery tarmac.

She was at a T-junction. The road wound uphill to her left and downhill to her right. Again she shunned the Devil's hand and turned right, hurtling along, making light of the occasional pothole trying to snap her ankles as she struck out into the night.

After nearly a mile of good progress, she paused for breath, and in so doing realised that her feet were raw. She'd reached the bottom of a dip and saw moonlight bouncing off a babbling river through some trees. She was debating whether to head for the river and open country, where she could at least walk on grass, when she saw headlights moving towards her from the opposite direction to which she'd come.

She let out a yelp of delight and ran towards the vehicle, waving her hands wildly in the air.

'Stop. Please stop. Help me.'

As the headlights approached, the vehicle slowed until it was about twenty yards away. Caitlin stepped into the middle of the road, wondering what she was going to say to the driver. But as her sore feet left the muddy bank, she gasped at the sound of wheels spinning and looked up in horror to see the vehicle hurtling towards her.

She braced to leap for the bushes at the side of the road but was a split second too late, and as she left the ground, the wing of the vehicle clipped her left leg, sending her spinning through the air. She landed with a sickening crunch on the bank and lay spread-eagled, her limbs splayed lifelessly about her.

Slowly, deliberately, the driver's door opened and a man stepped casually around the vehicle to gaze at Caitlin's stricken body.

'Bitch been getting some exercise.' He stooped to press his mouth into Caitlin's inner ear. 'Good girl. Don't want you letting yourself go just because you're spoken for.'

He put a hand on her brand mark and squeezed. No reaction. She wasn't faking. He strode to the van and opened the back doors, then returned to pick up Caitlin's inanimate form from the roadside, tossing her unceremoniously inside before chuckling his way back to the driver's seat.

Fourteen

23 April

THE WHITE VAN TURNED ON to Meadow Lane at the edge of the River Derwent in Derby's city centre, the roar of the adjacent weir instantly audible. Jake Tanner closed the driver's window but, unable to abide the smell from the rear, opened it again at once. He looked across at his brother fiddling with the radio.

'Turn it off, Nick.'

Nick grinned when he found a station he liked, started writhing to the beat. 'I love this song.'

'Turn it off!' shouted Jake. Nick's sulk was immediate, bottom lip pouting, eyes cast down. 'Someone might hear,' reasoned Jake, not taking his eyes from the road. Not mollified by the explanation, Nick jerked an arm to turn off the radio, making his displeasure apparent.

Jake scanned the horizon. It was even darker here, in the shadow of the underpass, with not a soul stirring in the small hours. He was glad he'd thought of it. If he'd remembered the layout right, it would save them a lot of hard foot-slogging cross-country.

'Camera up there, Jake,' muttered Nick, scanning the dark building on the left, with its squat sixties ugliness and gated barbed-wired car park. He waved up at it.

'The hell you doing?' spat Jake. 'Stop that.'

'Can't have no fun,' said Nick, scowling.

Jake didn't bother to explain. That was what exhausted him the most – explaining. He extinguished the van's headlights as it rolled gently past the *Derby Telegraph* complex on the north bank of the river towards its destination.

'You've turned the lights off,' pointed out Nick.

Jake tried to tune his brother out, stifling the urge to drive the van off the road and into the river and let the sweet black water close over his head. 'Keep your hood up,' he muttered, looking for the dirt track he knew was at the end of the cul-de-sac. 'And don't stare at the cameras.'

'Why'd you come down here, Jake? I don't like it. It's dark.'

'Did you wanna dump the van in the countryside in the middle of the night and walk miles back to town?'

'Why not? There were horses.'

'Horses?' Jake repeated in disbelief. 'It'd take all night walking across the fields.'

'We could have walked along main roads.'

'Yeah?' replied Jake, the sarcasm rising. 'And get seen legging it by any passing traffic, maybe even a cop car. Then we'd be proper screwed.' The younger man started to smile but remembered his annoyance about the radio and shrugged. 'If we stay in town, Nick, we've got a chance of getting away clean,' persisted Jake. 'We leg it over the footbridge into the park and then we're just two more punters walking the streets.'

Nick's grin finally emerged. 'Screwed,' he sniggered.

Jake didn't answer; concentrated on guiding the van off the tarmac and on to the grassy scrub of a short, purposeless trail penetrating no more than two hundred metres into the overgrown wasteland that encroached along the north bank of the Derwent. Beyond was Pride Park – the only industrial estate in Britain named after one of the seven deadly sins – a soulless mix of ultra-modern office blocks and half-empty new-builds dotted around Derby County's football stadium, crawling to completion after the recession had sunk its teeth into the local economy.

Once they were hemmed in on both sides by undergrowth, Jake flicked the headlights back on and followed the track to the arch of an ancient brick-built bridge, applying the brakes a few seconds later as the track petered out on this appendix of a road. The van was now out of sight of the main drag, halted in front by robust thorn bushes and flanked by the damp bricks of the bridge.

He turned off lights and engine, and darkness and silence enveloped them. He opened the driver's door to illuminate the cab. 'Let me see your hands.'

The younger man waggled his gloved fingers.

Jake stared at the stains on his own bare hands. The dried blood was black on his fingertips. 'Get a rag from the back and stuff it in the petrol cap. Quick as you can.'

'Why do I have to go in the back?' wailed Nick. 'It's smelly.'

''Cos I'm wiping . . . Forget it,' replied Jake, pulling out a handkerchief and smearing it around the gearstick and steering wheel, knowing it was probably hopeless. His dabs would be all over the back of the van too. Only the purifying caress of fire would do the trick. Nick didn't move.

'Get out then,' seethed Jake, jumping out and rubbing his

handkerchief over the door handle. 'I'll do everything for a change, shall I?'

No answer from Nick, so Jake quietly closed his door, threw the ignition keys towards the river and hurried to the rear of the van. Nick slammed the passenger door.

'What the fuck!' hissed Jake.

'Soz,' whispered Nick. 'Hand slipped.'

'Get the petrol cap,' ordered Jake. He pulled open the back door. The smell of death hit him as he leaned in, and he swayed back out for a breath of air. Without looking at the corpse, he reached into the van and rummaged around the dark interior, careful to avoid the cold, clammy flesh wrapped in polythene.

Long-forgotten smells from his first summer holiday job made him gag. The putrid aromas he remembered from his days sorting surgical gowns and theatre sheets at the old hospital laundry were unmistakable. Blood-soaked garments arrived at the laundry in hazard bags and were washed separately from regulation laundry such as sheets and hospital-issue nightwear.

The odour of ageing blood mingled with the putrid stench of faeces and urine, the inevitable consequence of dying patients no longer able to control their bodily functions. Foul Money, they'd called it on his payslip – £3.27 a day extra for handling the essence of the dead. *More than I'm making tonight*.

'Found any tools?'

'Forget the fucking tools,' spat Jake under his breath, the last of his patience spent. 'Go wait by the footbridge and give me a shout if you see anyone.'

Nick blew out a relieved breath, glad to be away from the smell. 'You can rely on me, Jake.'

'Yeah, right.'

While Nick scampered off into the darkness, Jake held his breath and leaned further over the body to feel around for the small billycan he'd seen in there. He also located what felt like an old towel.

Standing upright, he shook the can, glad to hear the deep slosh of liquid inside. He opened the cap, poured the fuel generously over the towel, then emptied the rest of the liquid into and over the van, glad to swap the odour of putrefying flesh for the pungent fumes of petrol. He closed the back doors softly and stepped around the van to wedge the towel in the fuel tank's spout, fumbling for his lighter and igniting the soaked material. He waited a moment for the blaze to catch, then turned to run back along the track.

Before he reached the safety of the road, he heard a distant shout above the crackling and spitting of the flames.

'Look out, Jake!'

An overweight man in a snug brown uniform stood across his escape route. 'All right, fella,' said the security guard, shining a torch into Jake's hooded face. 'Stop right there.'

After a split second to consider, Jake put his head down and raced towards the guard's ample midriff, bulldozing through him and knocking him to the floor. The guard grunted in pain as he fell. Jake stumbled on but fell over a flailing arm and ended up on the ground as well. A hand grabbed his ankle but he kicked it off. At that moment a muffled explosion rent the air, and as soon as he was able, Jake scrambled to his feet and sprinted away, leaving the guard spluttering and swearing after him.

A few seconds later he joined Nick, who was mesmerised by the flames.

'Wow! Look, Jake. It's like New Year.'

'Come on,' shouted Jake, spinning him round. Together they sprinted across the footbridge to be swallowed up by the darkness of the deserted riverside park on the opposite bank.

Fifteen minutes later, a grim-faced Jake slowed from a jog to a walk.

'Did I do good?' asked an expectant Nick, barely out of breath. Jake kept his eyes glued to the pavement, panting. 'Jake. Did I do good?'

Jake wheeled round on him and grabbed his collar, pulling Nick's shocked face to within an inch of his own. '*Look out, Jake!* Shout my fucking name, why don't you? Jesus, the fuck are you using for brains?'

'I-I'm sorry, Jake.' Nick was ashen. He hadn't done good. 'I di'n't think.'

Eventually Jake's grip slackened and guilt rushed in. His brother wasn't to blame. He'd been starved of oxygen at birth and his brain had been affected. Their late mother had taunted him with it during those small windows between her drug and alcohol binges when she was alert enough to string two words together.

Got a mental case for a son. Can't believe the dopey fucker's mine.

Nick had finished school three years ago with no qualifications and no prospects. *No prospects.* The phrase his teachers had used. Nick should be in a special school, they said, but his mother – an alcoholic prostitute and drug addict – couldn't face the social stigma. Jake hadn't needed extra English lessons to see the irony.

He thought about his own days at school, followed by the parents' evenings he'd attended in place of that drunken, whoring bitch. Evenings spent watching Nick's teachers shake their heads in frustration before washing their hands of him. Worse, they'd remind Jake what a promising student *he'd* been and ask after his career. Career? What was the phrase he'd heard about that washed-up footballer? A great future behind him.

Well, that's where my future is, if I even have one after tonight.

Jake smiled at Nick to reassure him and slung an arm playfully around his brother's head. 'Sorry for shouting. You did good, Nicky. Just got to be more careful in future. One slip and we get fucked over by the system for the rest of our lives.'

'Fucked over,' laughed Nick, relishing the obscenity's harshness in his throat.

'Careful,' repeated Jake. 'Try remembering *that* word, Nick.'

'Fucked over,' repeated Nick, still chuckling.

Jake sighed and continued briskly past the window of Marks & Spencer and on up the hill towards home, Nick keeping step beside him. He felt around for the cigarettes, his first pack in weeks courtesy of Mr Ostrowsky's advance. He threw one into his mouth, able now to confront the kernel of self-reproach flourishing inside his gut. He looked hopefully across at his brother.

'Got a light, Nick?'

'I'm not allowed matches,' said Nick gravely. 'You said.'

'That's right, I did.'

'And you said you'd stopped. Can't afford smoking, you said.'

'That's right, I did.' Jake returned the cigarette to the packet and threw it at a pile of blankets in a doorway, the image of the explosion and his collision with the security guard playing over in his mind.

'Where's *your* lighter, Jake?' asked Nick.

Jake exhaled deeply, remembered the sickening force with which he'd hurtled into the fat jobsworth standing in his path, remembered being on the ground, remembered the hand that had held the lighter as it opened.

'I don't know.'

Fifteen

BROOK WOKE WITH A SHUDDER on the hard chair of his box-sized office at home. It was dark and deathly quiet outside – that massive, almost oppressive silence only to be found in the countryside once the night predators had gorged and fallen silent in their nests and burrows and before the dawn chorus had taken up the day.

He sat up to massage his aching back, feeling clammy in his day-old clothes and stubble. The clock showed nearly four. His eye alighted on the chessboard, pieces black and white scattered in mid-struggle. The game had not progressed in a month though Brook had received his opponent's move two weeks previously. He glanced at the unopened envelope that contained the gambit, its child-like scrawl inducing a shudder, then pulled it towards him and eased a thumb under one end of the seal. He'd made a promise to a beaten opponent now languishing in prison for the rest of his days, and it was time to deliver his end of the bargain, absorb his next move while trying to ignore the stab at his peace of mind.

Pawn to King's Rook 4, Inspector. Our game seems to be slowing. Are my moves that good? Or do I remind you of what you've done? The dead are always with us. Do you see them yet?

Brook screwed up the handwritten note and launched it towards the blackened woodburner. He hesitated before advancing the black pawn, then marched through to the kitchen to flick on the kettle.

'Leave that,' commanded Jake, tearing around the flat throwing clothes into a case.

Nick looked down at the tatty stuffed bear in his hand. 'I can't leave Mr Ted.'

'You have to.' Jake avoided eye contact or the edict wouldn't take.

'*Why* do I have to?'

Jake closed the case and put it by the door, then began tipping all the tins bought the previous evening into a cardboard box. 'He'll be safer here.' Having emptied the shelf, he pulled out a drawer and flung a few items of cutlery and a can opener into the box with a clatter. He tossed the chipboard drawer on the floor and looked around, irritated. 'Where the hell are those damn keys?'

'Safer?' continued Nick, preparing to wail. 'Why won't he be safe with me?'

'Because . . .' Jake folded the box lid closed and contemplated his brother, his anger at their situation beginning to bubble over. He snatched Mr Ted from Nick and prepared to tear him limb from padded limb.

'Nooooooo,' screamed Nick, suddenly at Jake's throat, grabbing at the air to reach his friend.

'Shut up!' shouted Jake, holding the toy out of reach.

'Give him back,' screamed Nick, still clawing. 'Give him back.'

'Stop screaming!'

'Give me Mr Ted then.'

Exasperated, Jake heaved Nick backwards over the coffee table and down on to the floor. The wailing increased and Jake hung his head, closing his eyes to wish himself elsewhere. Finally the noise quietened a little, but only because Nick had graduated to that soundless, breathless grieving born of the truest despair.

'Oh, Jesus.' Jake dropped Mr Ted into Nick's greedy hands, his brother enveloping the soiled bear in a tight embrace to shield him from his wicked sibling's malice.

Jake slumped on to the table. 'Okay. We take Mr Ted. But Nick, look at me.' He stared at Nick's tear-streaked face, choosing his words with care. 'Bad people are going to come for us. We have to be quick and we have to be quiet. We're not going far but no one can know we've gone there. Are you listening?' Nick gulped and nodded at the seriousness in Jake's voice. 'When we get there, we won't have telly or radio because we can't make any noise, and we have to stay there for a long time or we're going to get . . .' He tried to find the right words.

'Fucked over?' suggested Nick, remembering the phrase from earlier.

Jake smiled and Nick giggled gleefully into the break of tension. 'Fucked over,' agreed Jake. He pulled Nick's head towards him and hugged it, fondling his greasy hair.

'Have you seen those keys, Nick? The big bunch. They were in the drawer a couple of weeks ago.'

'What keys, Jake?' Nick mumbled into his brother's chest.

Jake stared at the top of Nick's head. *Something in his voice.* 'Never mind.' He jumped up to finish packing, then pulled on his coat and lifted the box of cans. Finally he picked up a screwdriver from the tangle of metal on the floor. 'Come on. We don't have much time.'

Unable to sleep, Brook padded out into the darkness of his cottage garden with a fresh mug of tea, regular practice when the weather allowed. It eased the constant burden of his thoughts, whirring around his head like a hamster on a wheel, robbing him of all but the briefest slumber. The dreams had started again, as they always did when he was immersed in a case – dreams of rotting corpses and feeding rats.

He warmed his hands around the mug and shifted his weight on the harsh garden bench. He heard a noise from the tree and turned to see a pair of cat's eyes blinking at him, that other-worldly light shining back at him. Tigerbob, his neighbour's tabby cat, lay still on the branch until Brook made a noise with his lips and the cat poured himself to the ground and came to nuzzle at his hand.

'What a life you lead,' said Brook, scratching at the white fur on the cat's chin. He took a mouthful of tea and turned his face to the sky. The stars were starting to disappear behind a fast-moving grey canvas of cloud, now shedding a fitful spray of light rain and eating its way into the buttery moon until it was covered.

His old boss in the Met, DCI Charlie Rowlands, had once warned him against looking to the night skies when the darkness enveloped the light. 'It's called a killing moon, Brooky. Nothing good comes of it, so best to look away.' Brook splayed his hand, searching for the cat in the dark, but it had skittered away.

An unwelcome sound invaded the brutal quiet and Brook trotted into the kitchen to answer the phone. Only his daughter and Noble ever rang him at home, and he knew Terri wouldn't be awake at this hour.

'John?'

'You're up,' declared Noble at the other end of the line.

Brook glanced at his watch – not yet five o'clock. Dawn was starting to rehearse over the eastern horizon. 'I'm stirring,' he answered, unwilling to explain his nocturnal vigil.

'We've got a murder.'

'Where?' Brook knew the location that Noble reeled off, and began to plot the route in his head. 'Do we have an ID?'

'No,' said Noble softly. 'And it won't be easy.'

Brook's heart rate headed up a notch. 'Okay.' He didn't enquire further; he didn't like to prejudge a crime scene before he'd seen it. 'So much for our cold case.'

'I wouldn't be too sure,' said Noble. 'The victim is a young woman – late teens to early twenties by the look.'

Brook drew the phone closer. 'Caitlin?'

'Hard to tell.'

'I'll be there as soon as I can.'

'No hurry. As you said, the dead aren't going anywhere.'

Jake opened the door and peered out into the dark passage. Everything was quiet, even the neighbouring flat that was often rocking and rolling into the small hours, when the young mum that lived there wasn't screaming at her kids or their latest uncle.

Stepping towards the stairwell carrying the box of tinned

food under his arm and a holdall in each hand, he looked back and beckoned Nick out of the flat. 'Close the door quietly,' he hissed. 'No need to lock it.'

This time the door closed without noise and Nick looked eagerly for feedback. Jake nodded his approval and Nick swelled with pride. The pair walked swiftly and quietly to the stairwell and scampered down, Jake in the lead.

A few minutes later, the brothers stood on the ground floor, panting under the burden of their luggage.

'I'm tired, Jake,' said Nick. 'I want to go to bed.'

'Quiet,' hissed Jake, moving to the communal exit, which was thankfully cloaked in darkness. The sensored light on the ceiling had been vandalised so many times that it was no longer replaced, and more vulnerable residents knew to get behind their doors before the sun dipped.

He followed a passage that led towards the back of the flats and out into the car park, with its shabby population of rusting, scuffed vehicles. There wasn't a car less than ten years old, and each represented if not the limit of the residents' income then at least their tolerance for having their property coveted and vandalised. New cars were a magnet for crime at Milton Flats, so nobody owned one.

'Are we boosting a car?' asked Nick.

Jake put down his bags and box of tins and pulled out the large screwdriver from his back pocket, brandishing it at his brother.

Sixteen

BROOK GUIDED HIS BATTERED BMW around the tricky one-way system, trying to get his bearings in the faint morning light. He knew the area around Exeter Bridge and the weir well enough – it had been a crime scene in the Deity case a year or so before, when a missing student had been recovered from the Derwent – but Terri had driven him to the scene that day because Brook had been suffering from concussion.

He located the Exeter Street underpass and drove past a line of cars parked along the length of its double yellow lines, then turned right at a small roundabout, gliding past the Meadow Lane bus depot on his left, its forecourt also jammed with cars. On his right, he passed a brightly painted pub called the Smithfield, before coming to a halt at the police tape. A uniformed female officer was directing cars and pedestrians away from the crime scene. She squinted at Brook in recognition, then lifted the tape for him to drive under and park.

'Morning, Constable,' said Brook, locking the car, not even making the attempt to remember her name, if he'd ever known it. As usual, without Noble there to quietly slip him the information, he was adrift in a sea of anonymous faces.

'Inspector,' replied the female officer, returning the compliment.

'Everything under control?' ventured Brook, risking a line of small talk.

'The bus drivers have started their routes, so most of the crowd control is outside the *Telegraph* building.'

Brook realised that in all his years in Derby division, he'd never assigned a location to the home of the *Derby Telegraph* and his tormentor-in-chief, crime correspondent Brian Burton. He surveyed the crowd, looking for his familiar pinched face. Maybe the chilly morning and poor view was forcing Burton to rubberneck from behind the tinted windows.

'And the cars?'

'*Telegraph* employees who can't get to their car park.'

Brook nodded, unsure how to proceed. His bag of conversational tools was light at the best of times. 'Carry on,' he said over his shoulder, feeling foolish.

He strode past the squat building looking out across the swollen river towards the huddle of police and CID standing by a footbridge a hundred yards away. Like driving past a cricket match, it was possible to believe that absolutely nothing ever happened at a crime scene. And if it weren't for scene-of-crime officers and the duty police surgeon, nothing much did.

Brook snaked a glance across at the few onlookers, struck by how mobile phone technology had changed bystanders' behaviour down the years. Once they would have directed their gaze towards unfolding events; now faces were hidden behind camera phones, pausing only to send images to excited friends or disinterested social media.

Noble broke away from the throng and marched towards

him. 'He's on holiday,' he said, seeing Brook scanning the area.

'Result.' Brook's smile was heartfelt. 'Be nice to do our work without his toxic presence. What have we got, John?'

'IC1 female, late teens to early twenties, found in the back of a burned-out van – no ID.'

'Cause of death?'

'Unknown – though probably not the fire.'

'Do we know how long dead?' said Brook.

'Higginbottom thinks around forty-eight hours.'

'Two days,' mumbled Brook, absorbing the implication. 'So if it is Caitlin . . .'

'She's been held somewhere for more than a month until the killer had no more use for her.'

'Killers,' corrected Noble. 'Two men in a van. Just like Valerie G.'

Brook raised an eyebrow. 'We've got witnesses?'

'A security guard disturbed the body dump. We've got film too.' Noble indicated the cameras above the empty car park.

'Any good?' said Brook.

'Good enough to tell us we're dealing with two suspects. It's being sent over.'

'Outstanding,' said Brook with no evident enthusiasm. He looked around. 'Odd spot for a body dump – so close to the *Telegraph* building.'

'It's better than it looks, especially at night,' said Noble, nodding towards the footbridge as they passed. 'It's usually deserted and there's an instant getaway into an empty park. From there you're straight into the city centre.'

'Check all CCTV,' said Brook, not looking at his DS for a response. Noble knew the drill. He turned his gaze to the burned-out shell of the van as they approached. 'Could it be her?'

'Possible,' said Noble. 'I took a rough measure before you got here. It's hard to tell with heat-stiffening, but she's a reasonable match on height. No other indicators. She's also naked, so no ID from clothing or contents, and the fire makes prints unlikely.'

'Did we ever rustle up any DNA on Caitlin?'

'We took a toothbrush and a hairbrush.'

'Good,' said Brook. 'Whose van?'

'We're running the plates as we speak.'

With a grown-up daughter, Brook was the more sombre as they stepped up to the charred van. The back doors were hanging off at an angle. Whether prised away by officers or blown apart by the exploding fuel tank, Brook didn't have time to ask as the police surgeon stood upright at that moment and contemplated the two detectives before him. As he straightened, the smell reached Brook's nostrils. Burned flesh. Not an odour with which he'd ever become comfortable.

'Brook,' said Dr Higginbottom. 'You finally got here.'

Brook sighed. 'What have you got for us, Doc?'

'Nice to see you too,' retorted Higginbottom, arching an eyebrow across at Noble. He stepped away from the van and fumbled in a pocket to produce a small jar, which he threw at Brook. 'Here. Better apply some of this. Cooked people's not everyone's cup of tea. Not without a dab of HP sauce at least.'

If possible, Brook's expression became even wearier. 'Leave that observation out of your report,' he said, unscrewing the jar and dabbing camphorated chest rub under each nostril before taking the PVC gloves offered by Noble. 'I'm listening.'

'Not much I can tell you here, Inspector,' continued Higginbottom. 'Young white female – between eighteen and twenty-five years. She's been wrapped in sturdy plastic sheeting, presumably for ease of carriage; naked underneath, so the fire has melted the plastic on to her skin, which means I can only comfortably get at the head and neck for now. There's a little wisp of hair left at the root that suggests she was a brunette. See there.'

'What was Caitlin?' said Brook, squinting at the indicated section of charred skull.

'Bottle blond,' said Noble. 'But a natural brunette.'

Brook stepped nearer for a better view of the body, an odour of barbecued meat fighting its way past the camphor. The girl was laid on her back, arms and legs tight together inside the still faintly steaming plastic shroud, which had moulded to what was left of her contours like a second skin. Her mouth was closed, teeth jammed together, partially exposed by the shrinkage that occurred when fat and tissue were rendered by heat. A couple of teeth at the front were broken.

'John tells me she didn't burn to death,' said Brook.

'Trying to put me out of a job, Sergeant?' quipped Higginbottom. 'A blood test for carbon monoxide will be definitive, but I can't see any telltale scarring in the airways. Also the blistering of the skin appears to be post mortem.'

'How can you tell?'

'If she was burned alive, the body's defence mechanisms would have bombarded the injury site with white blood cells to begin the healing process. That results in inflammation and blisters full of fluid . . .'

'And what blistering you can see contains little or no fluid because her body's defences were dead,' concluded Brook, staring at the blackened head. The eyes were closed and sunken and the nose tissue had partially burned away to expose cartilage.

'Precisely. Also her teeth are clamped shut, which suggests her mouth was closed when she died. You see enough fire deaths, you never forget the contortions of the body. The hands clench and the mouth opens to fight for breath.'

'Or scream in mortal agony.' Brook was lost for a moment, a memory returning to unsettle. 'So the fire's a cover.'

'That would be my assessment,' said Higginbottom.

'And she died elsewhere.'

'Almost certainly.'

'Of what?'

'She's been bashed about. There are blunt-force trauma wounds on the top and side of the skull. Also the chipped teeth are recent, as is the dislocated jaw. Could be a heavy object, or she could have been slammed against something with great force. Maybe even hit by a car or thrown out of a window. Hard to tell in these conditions.'

'But the blunt-force trauma didn't kill her?'

Higginbottom raised an eyebrow. 'You're wasted in CID, Inspector.'

'So everyone says.'

'As a general rule, it's hard to beat someone to death, and such attacks often end with stabbing or strangulation,' said Higginbottom. 'No knife involved, so I'd wager on strangulation. You'll have to wait for the PM to be definitive, though.'

'Dead for about forty-eight hours?' said Brook.

Higginbottom hesitated. 'Look, it's too early . . .'

'I just need a working number,' insisted Brook. 'Until the post-mortem.'

'Very well. Through the plastic I can see some discoloration of the abdomen, which is evidence that putrefaction has begun. So, ballpark, I'd say no more than forty-eight hours. But don't quote me.'

'I also won't ask if you're American.'

Higginbottom's smile was tight, remembering Brook's aversion to transatlantic grammar. 'That's me done. You'll have my report soonest.' He bade them farewell and ambled back towards his car as Noble beckoned to an overweight man in a hoodie and tracksuit, waiting eagerly on the other side of the tape. He made his way over, clutching a white plastic bag in his flabby hands.

'Norman Stansfield,' said the man, before Noble could speak. 'It's an honour to meet you, Inspector.'

'Norman's a security guard—' began Noble.

'Night security concierge,' interrupted Stansfield. 'It's just to pay the bills, mind, before I can join the force. I know what you're thinking . . .' Grinning, he gripped a small portion of his flabby stomach between fingers and thumb. 'My glands. But I'm getting help with that, and when I lose—'

'You saw who dumped the van, Mr Stansfield?' said Brook.

'Better than that,' beamed Stansfield, 'I tackled the slippery fucker.' Brook frowned and Stansfield looked guiltily at Noble. 'Right. You said not to swear.'

'It's not the swearing,' said Brook. 'Your job is to protect property, not tackle criminals, Mr—'

'Norman,' insisted Stansfield. 'And I'm sorry, but you can't stand by and let these scumbags get away with it. Someone's got to have a go, so I brought the bastard down . . . Sorry,' he said with another apologetic glance at Noble. 'The suspect, I mean.' He thrust the white bag at Brook. 'Here. He was on top of me for a minute as we wrestled.'

'What's that?' asked Brook.

'My uniform. You'll need it for DNA. Dibs and dabs, as coppers say. I couldn't get my nails under his skin 'cos I had gloves on, but I'll bet there's DNA and fibres from his clothes . . .'

Brook handed the bag off to Noble. 'Can you give us a description?'

'There were two of them,' said Stansfield, staring into space to remember. 'One tall, one medium height, both slim build, both wearing hoodies. Both Caucasian – IC1 males,' he added, grinning at Brook then Noble. 'That's the proper phrase for it. They were white, in other words.'

'So that's what it means,' nodded Noble.

'Age?'

'One was young,' said Stansfield. 'Late teens maybe. The other was older, the one I tackled. Still young, mind. Mid twenties, no more than thirty.'

'Anything we can't get from the film?' asked Brook. 'Distinguishing features?'

'You mean like . . .'

'Tattoos, scars, limbs missing, extra heads.'

'It was dark, Inspector,' said Stansfield, for the first time crestfallen. 'I had my torch but the older scumbag gave me the bum's rush. Knocked me clean off my feet. I brought him to ground and I might have had him but for the explosion.'

'Where was the young one while all this was going on?' asked Brook.

'He was already at the footbridge when I come out, but I

nearly had the other one trapped.' Stansfield beamed at the two detectives.

'Norman,' said Noble patiently.

'Oh right, yeah,' spluttered Stansfield apologetically. 'The one at the bridge tried to warn the one setting the fire. He called out a name. "Look out, Jake," he shouted.'

'You're sure it was Jake?' asked Brook.

'Definite.' Stansfield grinned. 'I mean, how dumb are these scumbags?'

'Did you pick up an accent?'

'Local, I'd say,' said Stansfield. 'Yeah, definite.'

'Thank you, Norman.'

Noble beckoned over DC Cooper, who approached keeping his eyes on the van.

'Dave, take . . . Are you all right?'

Cooper nodded. 'It's that smell. Don't think I'll ever have a barbie again.'

'Shame,' said Noble. 'Take Mr Stansfield to the station and tell DC Smee to get a full statement and see if he can't rustle up an artist. And then get to work on the film they're sending over.'

'It's Norman,' said Stansfield to DC Cooper as they walked away. He turned back suddenly, waddling towards Brook. 'Inspector, when I put in the application, can I put you down as a reference?'

Noble pretended to look at his notes as Brook hesitated. Eventually Brook cracked. 'Why not?'

Stansfield left with DC Cooper, smiling from ear to ear. 'Dave, is it?'

Brook turned back to the van, avoiding Noble's mocking smile. 'Don't bother, John.'

'I didn't say anything.'

'You didn't need to. Let's face it, if Ford can make it to DI, why the hell can't Norman?'

'He's certainly keen.'

'That he is,' agreed Brook.

A suited and masked SOCO approached, plastic evidence bag in hand. 'Found this, Inspector. Looks like we've got smudges and maybe even blood.'

The detectives peered at the cheap plastic lighter nestling in the bag. 'The miracle of fire. Get it processed . . .' Brook hesitated.

'Good work, Col,' said Noble, quick to provide a name for Brook. 'Any prints soonest, please.'

'Thanks, Col,' Brook called after the SOCO with a weak smile, then returned his gaze to the van with the girl's body still inside. The SOCOs had swarmed back round it on Higginbottom's departure, so Brook walked past the burned-out wreck looking off into the scrub. 'Bit of a dead end.'

'We've got the film and possible prints,' replied Noble, deadpan.

'I meant this track . . .' Brook looked round at him.

'Sorry. I shouldn't crack wise with a dead girl lying there.'

'She won't be complaining, John, so deal with it however you can, unless you want to end up like me. Did you know about this track?'

'Never been down here,' said Noble. 'But it's not on the way to anywhere. So whoever dumped the body must know it.'

'That's my thinking,' said Brook, his eyes sweeping back over the *Telegraph* building. 'And whoever knew it existed must once have had a reason for being here.'

'Think our killers are journalists?'

'I wouldn't have said so, but not everyone who works in the building will be a professional,' said Brook. 'Get on to their personnel department and get details of any Jakes between twenty and thirty-five working at the building in any capacity. Ex-employees too. Go back at least five years . . .'

'What about the bus depot? Maybe Jake was a driver.'

'Good idea.' Brook looked around. 'And check the pub, too.'

They walked either side of the van. Both passenger doors were closed, but the glass from windows and windscreen had blown out. Brook and Noble crunched across the blackened shards to look into the cabin. There wasn't much to see.

'Not hot-wired,' said Noble, gazing at the steering column.

'And no keys in the ignition.'

'Can we get in, Col?' shouted Noble from the passenger side.

'Not yet,' replied Col through his face mask.

'What about in the back? Anything?'

'Besides the body, what looks like a canvas bag of tools for a tradesman of some kind. Oh, and a big bunch of keys,' said Col.

'For the van?'

'Negative,' said Col. 'We also found an empty billycan in the bushes. Petrol,' he added before being asked.

'Anything capable of BFT in the toolbag?'

'There's a claw hammer that was next to the body instead of the canvas bag.'

Brook nodded. 'Off to the lab as a priority.'

Seventeen

LATER THAT MORNING, BROOK HUNCHED over a mug of tea as he watched a second showing of the CCTV footage of the van being dumped. Brook and Noble had opened a larger incident room appropriate to a murder inquiry, although without victim ID, they hadn't moved in any of the materials from their smaller incident room.

Brook sat on a padded chair amongst the desks, terminals and phones staring at the whiteboard screen. Noble, DS Rob Morton and DCs Cooper, Read and Smee watched with him, sitting in silence, noting the odd question to ask the technician. Norman Stansfield had already watched the film and had left after one viewing, having talked all the way through. He'd been taken away to provide facial composites of the two suspects.

'Can we get that any clearer, Gavin?' Noble asked the technician.

'I doubt it,' replied Gavin.

'What about other cameras?' said Brook.

'Other cameras?'

'They ran across the footbridge,' explained Noble. 'We've got their timeline so we might be able to pick them up and track them through the city centre.'

'If that's where they went,' said Morton.

'I'll get on it,' said Gavin, standing. 'All the business and public area cameras are in the centre, so *if* they walked through, we'll find them. It's unlikely to get you more than a general direction out of town, though – most people don't live in the centre.'

'Some people do,' said Brook, having lived in a run-down city-centre flat before his move out to Hartington.

'Maybe they were heading for a second vehicle stashed in a city car park,' suggested Gavin.

'Thanks, Gavin,' said Brook, giving the technician his politest smile. 'We'll do the thinking on this one. DC Cooper will liaise with you.'

After the crestfallen technician had left, Morton said, 'They're not going to have another vehicle in a monitored car park if they've got a brain cell between them.'

'Remind me when criminals had brain cells,' said Cooper.

'With or without brain cells, it's unlikely with *two* suspects,' said Brook. 'Dumping a body in the city was a risk. If they had a second car, they'd drive both vehicles somewhere remote, dump the van and drive off into the sunset.'

'Sunrise in this case,' offered Noble.

'Assuming the kid can drive,' put in Morton.

Brook conceded with a lift of his tired eyes. 'We'll see when we have IDs.'

'Shouldn't take long,' said Noble. 'We've got clear prints from the lighter and I'm betting these two are in the system.'

'I know that footbridge,' said Morton. 'It could have taken them away from the centre just as easily – on to the Pride Park cycle path or even to the railway station.'

'There wouldn't be any trains at half two in the morning,' said Noble. 'Not for passengers, at least.'

'Make certain,' said Brook. 'But a train suggests out-of-towners while the dump site points to local killers. Nobody would know that track or how to get to it on the one-way system if they weren't from Derby. I struggled to find it.'

There was a brief silence in which someone might once have pointed out that Brook wasn't a local man either.

'How long on the lighter?'

'I put a rush on it with EMSOU,' said Noble. 'Should only be a few hours unless they've had another shoot-'em-up in Nottingham.'

'And the van?'

'It's a Ford Transit 350 Jumbo – 2012 model. According to the database there have only been three possible thefts in the county this last month. But I've just picked one off the dailies – a van matching those plates and description was reported stolen in Arboretum Street this morning.'

'Time?' said Brook.

'The owner noticed it gone around six thirty a.m. and phoned it in half an hour later,' said Noble.

'Half an hour?' said Smee.

'People often forget where they've parked their cars the night before and walk round the neighbourhood,' said Brook. 'Especially if they'd had a few drinks. Do we have a window?'

'Better than that.' Noble squinted at a piece of paper. 'There was an anonymous call at eleven twenty-one last night. An upstanding citizen saw someone trying the van doors and called it in. Unfortunately it was chucking-out time, so by the time the response car got there an hour later, the van was gone.'

'What did they do?'

'Nothing they could do,' said Noble. 'There was no broken glass or any sign of a break-in. The van was registered to an address in Pride Park, so they assumed the owner had driven it away. Want me and Rob to follow up?'

Brook looked at his watch. 'No, we'll take it while we wait for the print and the forensics to unravel. Do we have a PM slot?'

'Tomorrow morning at the earliest.'

Brook nodded, then wished he hadn't. His head felt like it weighed a ton after a disturbed night. 'Get the room set up, Rob,' he said to Morton. 'And when they're done, get the composites on to the regional news for the lunchtime bulletin if you can, then off to the press. The *Derby Telegraph* is going to have plenty of pictures from their building so they'll jump at some hard facts to run.'

'What about transferring the Interpol display from the other incident room?' ventured Noble. When heads turned in confusion, he explained. 'A possible link to another inquiry.'

'We don't move on that without victim ID,' said Brook. 'Right now it's a straightforward manhunt. The missing can wait.'

'Tired?' asked Noble, catching Brook stifling a yawn.

'Tired of stupid crimes committed by stupid criminals, John.'

'About that. I'm wondering if these two are our guys,' said Noble, dropping his speed to scan buildings along Friargate. 'A dump and run is a bit panicky for people who've lifted Caitlin without a trace and kept her for weeks.'

'People don't always behave logically under pressure.' Brook snaked a glance at Noble. He was taking this personally. 'And this may not be Caitlin.'

'She's the right age,' said Noble.

Brook raised an eyebrow. '*She?* It's a corpse now, John. Whoever it *was* is gone.'

Noble turned to reply but thought better of it.

'There.' Brook indicated an empty double-fronted unit with whitewashed ground-floor windows obscuring the interior. 'Who's the owner?'

Noble pulled up outside and reached for the freshly printed pack on the back seat. He flicked through the papers, extracting a log book photocopy, part of the stolen vehicle report.

'A Mr Grzegorz Ostrowsky,' he said with care. 'He's a Polish businessman in his early forties.'

'No chance he'd have Jake for a nickname then,' quipped Brook.

'And a good job I don't have a sore throat. The van is registered to a unit in Pride Park but Ostrowsky lives in Quarndon. Nice.'

'Why was his van in Arboretum Street?' When Noble shook his head, Brook considered for a moment. 'We don't mention the body or that we have a definite match to his van. Let's see how he plays it.'

Brook and Noble stood outside the empty unit. Building work was in progress somewhere behind the glass facade, but it was hard to see where through the whitewash. Noble pushed at a glass door.

'Locked.'

Brook stepped back to read the large banner hanging above the windows.

BAR POLSKI. GRAND OPENING 5 JUNE

He saw an open window on the second storey. 'Hello!' he shouted. After a louder hail, the window opened further and the sound of hammering and sawing increased. A handsome man with piercing blue eyes popped his head out.

'Building inspector, yes?' he shouted down.

'Half right,' mumbled Brook, nodding vigorously. The head disappeared and thirty seconds later a shadow appeared on the other side of the glass door.

'Welcome to Bar Polski.' The man was tall and lean with a tanned face and cropped blond hair with a tinge of grey at the short sideburns. He wore a sober, expensive-looking grey suit and carried a smartphone.

'Mr Grzegorz Ostrowsky?' said Brook.

'You pronounce it perfectly.' He beamed solicitously at Brook. 'Please come in. The plans are inside. You'll see—'

'We're police officers,' interrupted Noble, brandishing his warrant card.

'I thought . . .'

'Detective Inspector Brook, Sergeant Noble,' announced Brook. 'Sorry about that little confusion.'

Ostrowsky stared at Brook, conspicuously failing to step aside. 'What do you want?'

'We have a report of a stolen van belonging to you.'

'What van?'

'A Mr Ostrowsky reported it stolen several hours ago,' said Noble. 'Not you?'

'My brother Max uses one of my vans for his work. Stolen, you say?'

'You didn't know?'

'I did not,' he said slowly. 'Max doesn't care to tell *me*. But you've found it?'

'We've found a van matching the make and model,' said Brook. 'But we're having difficulty reading the plates.'

'Difficulty?'

'The van was . . .'

'Set alight,' nodded Ostrowsky. 'It's okay. I have insurance . . .'

'How do you know it was burned?' asked Brook.

'Inspector, I'm from Eastern Europe but I'm sure it's the same here. You steal a car and when you don't need, you burn to get rid of fingerprints, no?'

'I suppose.'

He shrugged. 'So where do I sign?'

'It's not that simple,' replied Brook. 'We're going to need more details about the theft – whose possession it was in, when it was last seen, that sort of thing. Just routine.'

'Just routine,' echoed Ostrowsky, gazing at Brook. 'In my country, inspectors don't dirty their hands with stolen vehicles.'

'No?' Brook smiled into the gap the businessman left for elaboration.

'You'd better come upstairs,' said Ostrowsky.

Brook and Noble followed Ostrowsky past the gutted ground floor and up the wide staircase to a similar space that was much nearer completion. Even so, it was a hive of activity. Half a dozen men in dusty, stained overalls were hammering, sawing and drilling for all they were worth. One of them barked an instruction to a colleague in Polish.

A younger man in smart apparel stood behind a tarpaulin-covered bar stacking boxes. Unbidden, his eyes flicked solicitously towards Ostrowsky.

'Espresso,' said Ostrowsky, turning to Brook and Noble. 'And whatever these officers want.' Brook and Noble demurred with a swift shake of the head, and the barman headed for a door at the back of the bar. 'Where are you going, Ashley?' barked Ostrowsky.

The barman hesitated. 'To make the espresso.'

'Where is . . . ?' Ostrowsky waved a hand in frustration.

'He hasn't shown up yet, sir,' mumbled Ashley.

'*Sukinsyn!*' exclaimed Ostrowsky. 'Fucking British workers,' he continued without concern for the sensibilities of the nervous barman.

'Do you still want the coffee, Mr O?' Ashley asked timidly.

Ostrowsky nodded and the barman dutifully disappeared. The businessman plucked a burning cigarette from an ashtray and stubbed it out. A bottle of vodka and a half-full shot glass stood next to it. He took a sip and contemplated the two detectives, composure regained.

'I hope you're not planning to drive later, sir,' said Noble.

Ostrowsky looked at the glass. 'I never drive, Sergeant – one of the perks of success. Excuse me. Tymon,' he shouted over the din of the workmen, beckoning to a large, bald-headed man who was clearly not involved in the building work because he wore an ill-fitting suit that looked like it had shrunk in the wash. Not that the suit was cheap, more that the man inside it was so muscle-bound that the material clung to his physique like skin, riding up over his wrists and ankles in search of a smaller man.

Tymon sidled over to them, unable to describe a straight line with his thick legs, which rotated in their sockets. His gimlet eyes flicked briefly up and down Brook and Noble with distaste.

'*Gdzie jest makszi?*' Ostrowsky gestured at Brook. '*Policji.*' Brook raised a discreet eyebrow. *Policji* – police.

Tymon shrugged at Ostrowsky in reply, his neck squeezing over his tight collar like a rubber ring. Ostrowsky made the international signal for a telephone and Tymon took out his mobile and depressed a flabby thumb on to the keypad as he made his way to a quieter part of the room.

'Max is an electrician. We're calling him.'

'But you're the registered owner,' put in Noble.

Ostrowsky held out his hands. 'I'm a businessman. I import goods. I have vehicles.'

'Where did you keep the stolen van?'

'Max kept it with him.'

Tymon returned and barked something in Polish at Ostrowsky. '*Huj w dupe policji.*'

Ostrowsky grimaced at Brook with theatrical regret. 'Max isn't answering his cell, I'm afraid.'

'Do you know where he might be?' asked Noble.

The businessman's beaming smile returned. 'Probably out on a job. I'd ask him to ring but his English isn't very good.'

'Then how did he manage to report the stolen van to the police?' asked Brook.

'He knows his name, also street names he needs,' said Ostrowsky, without missing a beat.

'Arboretum Street,' said Noble. 'Is that where he lives?'

'Or it's one of his jobs,' shrugged Ostrowsky. 'I don't know. He's looking for a place to live. He's not long in your country.'

'You say you have other vehicles,' said Brook. 'Where are they kept?'

'They are delivered to my warehouse in Pride Park and my drivers pick them up from there.'

'We went there first,' said Brook. 'What else do you keep in your warehouse besides vans you don't drive?'

Ostrowsky picked up on the tone. 'I import Polish goods for my bar. In a container. Twice a month. I have three Polish grocery shops also. I can show you invoice and paperwork for vans tomorrow if that helps.' He handed Brook a business card from a hip pocket.

'Thank you,' said Brook, taking it without a glance. 'But in the meantime we need a word with your brother. Where does he work?'

'Who knows? He doesn't tell me. Many different houses.'

'He must be staying somewhere.'

'Let me check,' said Ostrowsky, looking round theatrically.

'We need his mobile number too,' said Noble.

'Of course.' Ostrowsky turned to rummage through a pile of documents on the raised bar and plucked out a card to give to Noble. 'Max was staying in this boarding house while he looked for accommodations. He's a very hard worker if you need . . . rewiring.'

'Phone number?'

'Tymon.' Ostrowsky held out a hand for the big man's phone without looking at the giant and flicked at a button to read out the number. Noble jotted it down. Brook was tempted to demand the phone to verify but he resisted. It would be simple enough to check.

'Is that on a Polish network?' asked Noble. The lead in his pencil snapped.

'Bought in UK.' Ostrowsky smiled. 'Everything's cheaper here. Except electricity. But that's because you closed your mining industry and import Polish coal.' He guffawed long and violently, stopping as suddenly as he'd begun. 'You English.' He reached for a pen. 'A Bar Polski pen,' he said, handing it to Noble. 'With compliments.'

'Normally we prefer pencils,' said Brook. 'It's easier to alter our notes later.'

'Ah, you have served with the PRP, I see,' said Ostrowsky, grinning. 'In Poland, the evidence is never settled until money changes hands.'

'May I take a pen in case I want to book a table?'

'Of course, Inspector.' Ostrowsky was quick to oblige and Brook took the offered pen and slipped it into a breast pocket. 'Naturally your first meal here with your lady friend is free.'

'That's very kind,' said Brook, ignoring Noble's sly glance. 'Tell me, Mr Ostrowsky, how do you say *screw the police* in Polish?'

Ostrowsky's smile faded and he contemplated Brook. He was about to respond when a workman called out and gestured towards a soberly dressed man carrying a battered briefcase, staring intently at the ceiling. The bar owner's smile returned.

'The inspector of buildings. Forgive me, officers, but I have a bigger fish to cook.' He extended an arm to usher them away, eyes cold. 'You know where you can reach me if you need.'

'You didn't push him very hard,' said Noble, mobile phone held to his ear as soon as they were outside. Brook fished out his own antiquated mobile, switched it on with a huge depression of the thumb and called the number on Noble's notepad.

'No answer from the B and B,' said Noble.

'There wouldn't be. Max lives in Arboretum Street.'

'Then we should go back in and get a house number,' said Noble.

'Anything in the pack?'

Noble flicked through the wallet. 'The attending officer took down the Pride Park address. Ostrowsky's brother either didn't understand or didn't want us to know where he lived.'

'The mobile number doesn't exist,' said Brook lowering his phone.

'Honest mistake?'

'Not a chance,' said Brook.

'To be fair, I'm not sure I'd hand over my brother's contact details to a foreign police force.'

'You haven't got a brother.'

'But if I did. Do we go back?'

'On what grounds?'

'On the grounds that we were lied to,' said Noble.

'Everybody lies to us, John.'

'Okay. On the grounds that we've got a young girl lying on a steel trolley who was dumped in one of his vans.'

'Which was stolen,' said Brook. He came to a decision. 'He's not under thirty or called Jake and he didn't appear unduly worried about the theft of his van, so it'll keep.'

'I still don't like being lied to.'

'You should be used to it.'

'I am. Doesn't mean . . .' Noble held up a hand as his phone rang. 'No, go ahead,' he said into the phone. He looked significantly at Brook.

'Fingerprint?' ventured Brook.

Noble nodded. 'Got a current address?' He looked at Brook and gave a thumbs-up. 'Milton Flats. We're ten minutes away.'

* * *

The building inspector shook Ostrowsky's hand. 'Everything seems fine, though I don't know if you'll be opening on time, Mr . . .'

'We will if we don't employ any more British workers,' replied Ostrowsky coldly. He showed the inspector the staircase. 'You can find your way, no?'

When the man had left, Ostrowsky bellowed across at Tymon in Polish. 'Go find Max and get him here. Now!'

Max took another long slug of vodka and wiped his mouth with the back of his hand. He slammed the near-empty bottle down on the cigarette-singed bureau beside the bed. To manage the feat he was required to stop stroking his genitalia under the thin nylon sheet that crackled every time he moved his rough hands across it.

Propping himself up against the flimsy velvet headboard, he gazed at the undernourished girl as she dressed, scratching at his bare stomach as he stared. She was barely out of school and had hardly any meat on her. Her breasts were little more than bumps and her arms and legs were like the thin branches of a sapling. Her flesh was white – apart from the line of dark red blemishes and bruises that marked her from shoulder to wrist.

'What your name?' enquired Max in his broken English.

The girl smiled nervously. 'Are you a copper or summat?'

Max guffawed, nodding with amusement. 'You think if I copper, I pay, *cipa. Idiota.*'

The girl pulled her slip over her head. No bra. Too time-consuming when some of the cheapskates just wanted a quick suck and tit-fuck. 'Whatevs.'

Play ball, her mum had taught her. Keep talking but sort the money and get the fuck out asap.

'Tell me,' insisted Max.

The girl stepped into her denim skirt and pulled it up to her tiny waist, buttoning it before swivelling it round the right way and brushing herself down. She slipped into her shoes. No tights – impossible in cars. 'It's Lola, if you must know.'

'Lola?' Max laughed again. 'You lying *cipa*.'

His eyes pierced her and she reached into her clutch bag for a cigarette. 'Whatever you say, lover.'

'Cut your hair,' said Max softly, still contemplating her.

'You what?' she replied hoarsely, turning her dead eyes to him as she fumbled for her lighter.

'Cut your hair.' He reached drunkenly for the bottle again and took another gulp of fire. 'And then. *Ssij suko.*'

'Come again?'

'Exact,' nodded Max, his eyes flashing, slurring, 'Then you can suck my dick, bitch.'

She smiled nervously, her teeth already rotting under the assault of drugs, booze and smokes. She turned back to the cracked mirror for a last onceover, perhaps hastening her movements imperceptibly. 'My, aren't you the frisky one,' she said, keeping her reply airy, unconcerned.

'You don't want suck my dick?' asked Max plaintively, swinging his legs from under the cheap duvet to the music of ancient springs.

The girl thought of the money already in her clutch, nestling next to the nickel bag of *one-on-one* calling her to deaden the pain. The john had coughed fifty for anal and he didn't look like no roller with his filthy overalls and scuffed boots. But another thirty and she might have enough left over to get chips for the kids . . . 'That's an extra thirty. You got that, lover?'

'I got,' smiled Max, walking naked towards her from the

bed, his semi already preparing for her attentions. Quick as lightning, belying his thickset middleweight's frame, he grabbed her arm.

'You got to wash it first,' said Lola. 'I don't know where it's been.'

Max grinned at her, his eyes cold and black. 'Yes you do,' he whispered. He guided her across the threadbare carpet, noxious substances gripping the soles of his feet, and stopped near the chair. He put a hand down to his satchel, pulled out his wallet and took out a note. 'Here is fifty.'

Lola eyed the money greedily, then grabbed the note and scuttled across to her tiny handbag and thrust it deep inside, as though the further down she drove the bill, the more certain it was that the money was hers.

When she turned back to him, rearranging her limbs into a more coquettish pose, she froze at the sight of the scissors in his hand.

'What are you doing?'

'First, cut hair. Short, like boy.'

'What?'

'So I can hold.' He grinned at her, relishing his power over this weak, drug-addled girl; made a fist in front of his penis to make his meaning clear.

'I'll pass on the haircut, if it's all the same to you.' Lola tried to keep her smile intact but her fear began to bite. She wasn't a stranger to a punch. Sometimes she even took a more sustained beating but no-one had ever used a blade on her. No-one had ever cut her – except herself back in school. She backed slowly away, her phoney desire disappearing like heat haze on a road.

Max's grin disappeared and he stalked after her at the same

speed. 'Not all right,' he growled. 'I give you bonus. You get short hair for free.'

'Well I don't want it cut,' she said defiantly. 'My old man—'

'Fuck your old man,' snarled Max. 'And fuck you. Keep still or I cut you good.'

Lola gulped and her breathing quickened. At the wall she could retreat no further; she opened her mouth to scream, but nothing came out. Not that anyone would have rushed to her aid in this scarcely furnished fleapit, where the noise of violence and discord rent the air at regular intervals.

Max pressed against her, rubbing his penis into her stomach with glee, watching her fear as he held the scissors to her face. Lola closed her eyes to them, the only self-defence mechanism in her pathetic armoury. At least not to see made it quicker. She'd learned as much in previous attacks. Look away so they can't see the hurt. Then maybe they won't linger, won't take the pleasure from it.

'You don't want watch,' he said, banging her head gently against the wall.

She gave out a little whimper and began to slide down to the floor, but Max pulled her up roughly by the hair and pushed her back against the mildewed wallpaper.

'Keep still,' he said, looking intently at her scalp. He grabbed a fistful of her lank brown hair, raised the scissors and cut a huge clump close to her head, discarding it on to the wafer-thin carpet. He grabbed another strand and yanked her head towards him.

In the corner of the room, a tinny rendition of the Ride of the Valkyries erupted – his brother's call sign. Max cursed, let go of Lola's hair and returned to the bedside bureau to inspect his phone.

The commotion of Lola gathering her courage and streaking for the door distracted him, and he threw the phone on the mattress and leapt after her.

'Where you going, *cipa?*' shouted Max.

'Let me go,' screamed Lola. She'd managed to get the door half open when Max arrived to block her path and push her back into the room.

He stood panting in front of her, his face angry, his erection waning. Gesturing with the scissors still in his hand, his grin returned and he moved to close the door, but a strong, pudgy hand prevented him.

'Tymon,' exclaimed Max, releasing the door.

'You're a hard man to find,' said Tymon in Polish, stepping across the threshold. He looked distastefully around the seedy room. 'Get dressed. Your brother wants you.' He saw Lola cowering in a corner. 'Get out, whore,' he said, also in Polish, thumbing at the door to translate.

Slowly, like a cornered animal, Lola accepted her reprieve. After gathering her belongings, she moved warily around the room to the door, keeping her distance from Max. When she was closer to the door than her naked client, she darted up to him and spat in his face, screamed, 'Fucking freak!' and scuttled out.

Max made a move to grab her, but Tymon interposed himself between the naked man and the retreating girl. Tapping his watch, he grinned at Max. 'Get dressed.'

Eighteen

BOOTED AND SUITED, BROOK WATCHED as scene-of-crime officers went about their work, examining, photographing, bagging and tagging the few artefacts in the three-room flat. The real search would be for the small stuff – DNA, hair and skin samples, fibres and blood. If the girl had died before being dumped in the van, every site connected to the suspects was a potential murder scene, and what better place to find evidence of murder than a killer's home. It was what the Crown Prosecution Service called a slam-dunk. The lawyers over there watched far too much American TV.

Brook gazed methodically around at the rudiments of comfort. There was a grubby sofa and a stained chipboard coffee table facing a massive TV on a stand – funny how poverty seemed to affect the size of the television in a home. The more deprived couldn't afford to go out, so a serious investment in home entertainment seemed like money well borrowed. A hideous wrought-iron standard lamp with no shade completed the furnishings.

And that was it for the lounge. The kitchenette, on the other side of a token partition, contained a seriously dilapidated oven that didn't look like it had roasted a chicken in decades.

A dirty saucepan and frying pan on the hob suggested a life of fried meats and beans, though there were no supplies in the cupboard to confirm it, and no fridge either. The stainless-steel sink was only slightly cleaner, though the ancient worktop was rotting around it.

There wasn't much more to see. The space was tidy, but Brook put that down to the absence of furniture rather than a woman's hand. Only the mess on the floor suggested a hasty departure – underwear, a sock, a cutlery drawer pulled out.

'They packed,' said Brook. 'Which means they had a plan.'

'Sorry?' enquired a SOCO.

Brook shook his head.

'Imagine living in a dump like this,' said Noble, returning from the only bedroom.

Brook fancied he saw the sliver of a smile on Noble's lips but didn't react. It had been several years since Brook had lived in a similar hovel, immediately after his move up from London, and Noble occasionally made oblique reference to it.

Having taken the first accommodation offered, Brook didn't care if it was comfortable or stylish, only that it had walls behind which he could retreat after his shift had ended. Walls that he'd stare at blankly as the demands of his new life in a strange city – post-breakdown – made themselves apparent. It had taken him three years to snap his addiction to the solitude offered by such lodgings; Noble's appalled reaction on his first, and only, visit had been the chief catalyst.

'Imagine,' retorted Brook drily.

Noble's smile found its fuel. He gestured to the source of daylight behind him. 'Stunning view, though.'

'Anything in the bedroom?'

'Not even curtains. Two single mattresses. A chair.'

Brook nodded. 'It's easy to forget what life on the margins is like. What background do we have?'

'There's a gas bill in the name of Jake Tanner,' said Noble.

'Tanner?' exclaimed Brook.

'Lives here with his younger brother, Nick. The descriptions match our composites. And his prints are a match to the lighter.'

'How do we know them?'

'Jake's got form, though he's strictly Cat D. Or was until today. Cautions for theft and shoplifting. A couple of years ago he managed to get himself a short stay in Sudbury for an assault, but he's no Moriarty.'

'Open prison to abduction and murder suggests ambition at least,' said Brook. 'That should have shown up before now.'

'You sound like you know him.'

'Not as well as you, John. You met him.'

'I met him?' Noble's eyes closed briefly before enlightenment arrived. 'Jake Tanner was the barman at the Flowerpot the night Caitlin disappeared.'

'He was. Maybe still is.'

'No,' said Noble. 'He was a casual for a day or two, does temp work all over town apparently.'

'So maybe he also did a few shifts at the Smithfield.'

Noble smiled. 'And then he'd know the dump site. I'll get Cooper to check.' He hesitated, feeling a need to explain. 'I didn't dig any deeper on Tanner because he was in the clear on Caitlin. He didn't leave the bar until lights out.'

'Since we're looking for two assailants, he wouldn't have had to.'

'Of course,' nodded Noble. 'He could just have tipped off his partner when Caitlin left – his brother, presumably.'

Morton marched in. 'Neighbours say they saw them both yesterday. No hints about when they scarpered.'

'As soon as they got back from torching the van, I'd say,' said Noble. 'When Jake realised he'd dropped the lighter, he must have known they'd have to run for it.'

'Descriptions fit with our film and the security guard,' said Morton. 'It's them.'

'Neighbours share any insights?' asked Noble.

'No one has a clue about their personals or where they might have gone.'

'Women? Visitors?'

'They were inseparable according to everyone I spoke to,' replied Morton. 'And no one saw them with any guests or girlfriends. Jake was very protective of his brother. He's got special needs.'

'On the eleventh floor, I assume they're educational and not physical,' said Brook.

'Right,' said Morton. 'Next door said the kid's none too bright though nice enough with it.'

'Any grumbles?'

'I couldn't find anyone with a grievance. Everyone says they were quiet, polite and helpful, kept to themselves. I'm not getting any vibe that they might have been killers.' As Brook made to speak, Morton qualified his observation. 'Which people always say about murderers who lived next door, I know.'

'Vehicle?' asked Brook.

'Cooper says Jake passed his driving test five years ago but he's never owned a vehicle,' said Noble.

'Doesn't mean he didn't keep an uninsured banger downstairs, although neighbours weren't aware of one,' said Morton.

'Can Nick drive?' asked Brook.

Noble shook his head. 'Not qualified, at least.'

'Check the car park. And better get on to local taxi firms,' said Brook. 'They left in a hurry, probably with baggage, so they couldn't have got far on foot.'

'Maybe they nicked another resident's car,' suggested Noble.

'Easy enough to ask,' agreed Brook, lifting an eyebrow to Morton. 'Put uniform on it and circulate our suspects' names. There are no photographs here, so make that a priority in Nick's case. Check if he has form as well, then get his likeness released with his brother's. Failing that, find next-of-kin and ask for a picture. John, tell Cooper I want chapter and verse on the pair of them.'

'Already on it,' said Noble. 'We'll know what they had for breakfast in two hours.'

'I doubt they had time,' said Brook, looking at his watch. The light was beginning to go. 'Chief Super?'

'I've made him aware,' said Noble.

'He's going to want to brief local media,' said Brook. 'Better get Cooper to liaise with Corporate and put a statement together. We don't have time.'

'Charlton's not going to like you ducking out of media briefings,' teased Noble.

'I know what Charlton doesn't like, John.'

'We're clear in here if you want a closer look, Inspector,' said a SOCO through a face mask.

Brook and Noble moved quickly around the small room, opening drawers and kitchen cupboards, examining artefacts in gloved hands before putting them back. Brook's eye lingered on the old newspaper lining one cupboard's shelves. It was marked by circles made by cans of food stored on top. He picked up a nearby waste bin, emptying the contents into the sink. With a pencil he moved bits of detritus around for a proper inspection – several empty cans of economy baked beans, a discarded wrapper for sausages, toast crusts. He examined a stained receipt before returning the empty bin to the floor and opened more drawers, poking keenly through the cutlery.

He called out to one of the SOCOs. 'Can we have a look in the bathroom . . . er . . .'

'Ben Shaw,' said the officer, holding out his ID lanyard. Brook's reputation for forgetting people's names didn't go down well with the rank and file.

'Course.' Brook smiled sheepishly. 'Sorry. Early start.'

'You and me both,' he retorted. 'Inspector Brook.'

Brook caught Noble's amused eye. 'I asked about the bathroom.'

'There's nothing in there,' said Shaw.

'Nothing at all?'

'Just a bath, a bar of soap and a towel.'

'No other toiletries?' prompted Brook, unable to trust evidence unseen. 'Things a woman might use,' he continued, trying to recall the glut of products his daughter left behind after a visit to Hartington. 'Tampons, shampoo, cotton buds, gels, hand creams . . .'

'Hand cream?' exclaimed Shaw, excitedly raising a finger.

'Yes?' said Brook.

'No,' continued Shaw, deadpan. 'There's a bath, a bar of soap and a towel,' he repeated, speaking as though to an idiot. 'Now can I get on with it?'

Brook nodded, glancing at the smiling Noble. 'I didn't get much sleep, John.'

'You couldn't delegate if you slept like a baby,' observed

Noble with a grin. Brook didn't contest. 'But there's definitely nothing to suggest a woman was here for a month. No clothing, toiletries . . .'

'Eleven flights of stairs and the lift out of order,' said Brook, nodding. 'They kept her somewhere else.'

'I'd go further,' said Noble. 'Sounds patronising, but looking at this place doesn't suggest they're capable or organised enough to pluck a healthy young woman off the face of the earth and keep her hidden for four weeks.'

'Agreed,' conceded Brook. 'And trusting a kid brother with special needs to abduct a teenager while you serve drinks . . .' He left the rest unsaid. 'But two things are certain, John. Somebody killed the girl, and the Tanners torched the van we found her in, so we shelve our reservations because they're all we've got.'

'Maybe Cooper can connect them to a lock-up or a garage,' suggested Noble. 'Somewhere private where they could take their time with her. And that's where they are now.'

'It would have to be close. They're on foot and they packed – after a fashion. Some clothes, I think, and supplies for a longer stay.'

'Supplies?'

'The larder's empty,' said Brook, showing him the cupboard. 'They cleared out all the canned food. Tin opener too.'

'Maybe they didn't have any cans to start with.'

'They'd just stocked up,' said Brook, showing him the receipt itemising food items bought the previous evening.

'So maybe they're lying low instead of running,' said Noble, yawning as he spoke.

'Maybe,' said Brook on his way to the door. 'Come on. We need tea.'

'You buying?' said Noble, following into the corridor and ducking under the police tape. Brook gave him the arched eyebrow. *Don't I always?*

They trotted down eleven flights of crumbling concrete stairs, breathing shallow to defeat the omnipresent stench of urine. It was nearly dark when they emerged from the block, and a light drizzle insinuated itself on to their faces.

'Jake Tanner,' purred Chief Superintendent Mark Charlton, as though he'd cracked the case himself. Noble and Brook exchanged a lazy glance. Charlton stroked his chin, swivelling his executive chair as he contemplated the documents in hand. 'How old is this picture of Nick Tanner?'

'Fifteen when it was taken,' replied Brook.

'A school photo? How old is he now?'

'Nineteen.'

'A murder suspect and this is the best we can do?'

'Working on it, sir,' said Noble. 'He may be an adult, but he's pretty much a dependent, from what we can gather.'

'No form? No DVLA photo? No passport?' Brook smiled with his lips to confirm. Charlton brandished Nick's picture. 'You'll never catch him with this.'

'We're checking social media for something more recent,' said Brook, looking at the clock behind Charlton's head. 'But as John said, he's dependent. They don't appear to own a computer, which means no email, no Facebook . . .'

'And neither of them has a mobile phone on a contract,' added Noble.

'So we find Nick when we find his brother,' concluded Brook. 'They're a pair.'

'And not the sharpest knives in the box,' said Charlton.

'We'll have them inside twelve hours.'

Another glance from Brook to his DS. A quick result was always *we*, but if things turned sour, collective responsibility quickly mutated to *you*.

Charlton stood and took his own glance at the clock, the media briefing fifteen minutes away. 'Is this everything?'

'Yes, sir.'

'No ID on the body yet?'

'No, sir.'

'It may come down to dental,' added Noble.

'But prime candidate is this Caitlin Kinnear.'

'She's missing and the right age,' allowed Brook.

'And she encountered Jake Tanner on the night of her disappearance, sir,' said Noble.

'Anything at the Tanners' last-known?'

'Cleared out, sir,' said Brook wearily. 'SOCO are on it, but no sign the girl was ever there.'

'And she wasn't killed at the scene?'

'No, sir,' answered Noble. 'Post-mortem results tomorrow.'

Charlton nodded and checked his appearance in the full-length mirror in his office. He pulled down his tunic, half turning left and right to assure sartorial precision. He identified a stray piece of lint on his thigh and brushed it away. 'Better remind me about Caitlin Kinnear in case I'm asked.'

Ostrowsky sat on a stool in the darkened bar, illuminated only by the lights behind the optics, a fresh bottle of vodka and a full shot glass beside him. He lit a cigarette and contemplated his brother. Tymon loomed behind Max, a giant in the shadows.

'Look at yourself,' said Ostrowsky in Polish, running his gaze up and down his dishevelled brother in disgust.

'I need a drink,' said Max, eyeing the bottle.

'You need a shower, little brother.'

'I've been working,' protested Max.

'You've been whoring,' shouted Ostrowsky, standing off the stool. He glanced briefly at Tymon's impassive features for a contradiction. It didn't arrive. He slipped off his jacket, draped it over the bar stool, loosened his silk tie and moved to stand face to face with his brother. Max looked away, so Ostrowsky leaned in close to ensure his undivided attention. 'And while you've been throwing your money away on whores, I've had the police here.'

'Here?'

'A detective inspector, no less . . .'

'Is that my fault?' sneered Max, his face distorting with sudden petulance.

Ostrowsky glanced at Tymon, who gripped Max by the shoulders to position him for the blow, which the business-man landed just above the midriff. Max doubled up in pain, and sank towards the floor to avoid further blows, but Tymon pulled him upright in case additional sanctions were required.

'Your stupidity pains me, little brother,' said Ostrowsky softly, examining then massaging his left hand. One of the knuckles was skinned. 'Now look what you made me do.' From his trouser pocket he drew out a knuckleduster and slid it carefully over his fingers.

'No more, Grzegorz,' pleaded Max. 'I'm your brother.'

'I sometimes wonder.'

'It's not my fault the van was stolen.'

'But it's your fault it was reported,' spat Ostrowsky. 'It's your fault the police have my name.'

'They would have found out, wouldn't they?' pleaded Max. 'What choice did I have?'

Ostrowsky was incredulous. 'What choice? Have you seen the news? Someone used my van to dump a body. *My* van. And what do you do? Come to me so I can fix the problem, or speak to strangers?'

'Would I have reported it missing if I'd known there was a body inside?' retorted Max sourly.

'Perhaps you did it to distance yourself. To point to the thief as the killer.'

'No, brother . . .'

'Perhaps the problems you had with women in Warsaw are coming back?'

'No. That is past.'

'Are you sure, *braciszek*?'

'I wouldn't lie.'

'Yet still you seek out whores.' Max lowered his head in shame. Ostrowsky considered him with an implacable expression before softening. He gestured to the giant and Tymon let him go. The shabbily dressed workman sank to one knee, rubbing his stomach and emitting short moans of pain.

'But you're right,' said Ostrowsky. 'I must take the blame. I have been indulgent. Left you to fend for yourself knowing you would not manage. All this freedom and money in a new country. I should have seen.'

He returned to the bar, took another draught of vodka. 'I hope you understand that I am strict with you now because I love you, Max. You're the only family I have. I should have paid more attention. But now, because of you, I've told a lie to the British police about your whereabouts. And they knew I was lying, I think. But this policeman, this Inspector Brook, said nothing. He kept his ammunition in the chamber, not sure if my lie was relevant, while I . . .' he took an exasperated breath, 'while I exposed myself in that lie. And I do not want to be exposed to the police in a foreign country.'

'I need a drink,' whined Max.

'A drink?' said Ostrowsky. 'Did you not hear me? The police found a dead body in my van.' Max stared at his feet again. 'Who was it?' Max shook his head, unwilling to look his elder brother in the eye. 'You don't know?'

'Why would I, brother?'

Ostrowsky snorted in disgust. 'Because it's your van!'

'Don't the police know who it was?'

'If they do, they're not saying,' said Ostrowsky. 'This Inspector Brook was on the news. He must have known this morning that my van contained a body. But he said nothing. He observed me to see if I gave myself away. He's clever, this one. He watched and waited for me to show guilt. Lucky for me I am ignorant, because my brother prefers speaking to strangers ahead of his own blood. And lucky for me this policeman could see that when he watched, I think. And he has other suspects so he didn't challenge my lie.' He drained his glass and refilled it. 'But he will.'

'That's good then, isn't it?' said Max. 'These bastards who stole the van . . . they must've killed the girl.'

'Girl?' snapped Ostrowsky. 'I didn't mention it was a girl, did I?'

'No, I . . .' blustered Max.

'Tymon?' The big man shook his head.

'I saw it on the news, brother,' nodded Max. 'Like you. They think it was some Irish girl.'

'Yet you feign ignorance when I ask about a body.'

'No, Grzegorz,' said Max hastily. 'I don't understand everything on the news. My English . . . But they showed a picture of a missing girl. Some student.'

Ostrowsky lit another cigarette and considered Max. 'Then you also saw pictures of who the police suspect stole my van.'

Max lowered his head. 'It was Jake, the new barman.'

Ostrowsky became tight-lipped, nodding at his brother. 'That's right, *braciszek*.' He gestured towards one of the large flat screens suspended on the wall. 'They're looking for Jake Tanner. And *his* little brother. And because Jake works for me, they'll be back here with a second reason to interrogate me.'

'I'm sorry.' Max managed to stand. 'It's not my fault.'

'So it's *my* fault, is that what you're saying?'

'No, brother. It's Jake's fault. He stole the van. He must have killed that girl.'

'Yes, he must. But here's my confusion, brother – why steal *my* van to put her body in? Explain that to me. Then I'll have something to tell this Inspector Brook when he comes back to ask me.'

Max shook his head. He looked around for a seat and slumped on to it. 'I need a drink,' he repeated. Ostrowsky sanctioned it with a lift of his eyes and a moment later Tymon handed Max a large shot of vodka. He downed it in one before rummaging for cigarettes. Ostrowsky threw over his own pack, hitting him in the chest, and Max grabbed them up and lit one.

'Well?'

'I don't know.' Max exhaled blue-brown toxins with a sigh of relief. 'All I know is the van was outside my flat last night and this morning it was gone.'

'I'll ask again. Why would Jake steal *my* van?' said Ostrowsky. 'Did I not treat him fairly? Tell me.'

'Why the fuck are you asking me?' demanded Max. 'Why don't you ask *him*?'

Ostrowsky took a sharp breath, then considered for a moment, examining his hand. 'I intend to.' He stood up again and extinguished his untended cigarette. 'You've hurt my knuckle, Max. But for the sake of our father – God rest him – I was glad to endure the discomfort. Normally I would ask Tymon to inflict the damage on those who have angered me, but I thought of our father and our long-departed mother . . .' he crossed himself and kissed his fingers, holding them against a small crucifix beneath his shirt, 'and I took the burden upon myself so that you wouldn't feel the weight of Tymon's greater strength.' There was silence as Ostrowsky considered his younger brother, profound disappointment weighing heavily on him. He threw the knuckleduster to Tymon, who caught it with glee. 'But now . . .'

Tymon slid the duster as far along his podgy knuckles as he could manage and moved towards Max, flexing his neck.

'Wait!' shouted Max.

Tymon froze at the tiniest hand movement from his boss.

Max took another pull on the cigarette and tried to speak calmly but glanced nervously at the eager Tymon. 'There was a problem. With Jake's kid brother.'

Ostrowsky's brow furrowed. 'Jake's brother?' He waved an arm at the TV to recall the name.

'Nick,' said Max.

'Nick,' nodded Ostrowsky. He whirled a forefinger close to his temple. 'The *idiota*?' Max confirmed with a blink of the eyes. 'What problem?'

'The cleaner,' continued Max. 'The one from Warsaw. The one who doesn't turn up for work.'

Ostrowsky glanced at Tymon. 'Kassia. What about her?'

'I don't think she's sick, brother,' said Max. 'She was upset because of Nick.'

'I don't understand.'

'When Jake was stocking the bar, Nick used to sit in the storeroom in the basement. Remember? Jake gave him comics to read. He couldn't leave him home alone.'

'What of it?'

'Well, Nick . . . he used to do things when Kassia was around. Try to, at least.'

'Things?' demanded Ostrowsky.

Max hesitated. 'He touched himself in front of her.'

'He touched himself? What did Kassia do?'

'At first she laughed, but it got worse. He starts taking his dick out and asking her to touch it.'

'And?'

'And she say no to the *struntz*,' said Max, indignant.

'Did you know about this?' Tymon shook his head.

'Got so Kassia was scared to go in there,' said Max, warming to his theme. 'He touches her breasts, tries to kiss her . . .'

'How do you know all this?'

'She told me,' said Max, unable to meet his brother's eyes.

Ostrowsky lit another cigarette and contemplated Max. 'What did you do?'

'I tell him to stop,' said Max. 'Then I tell Jake that Nick can't come to Bar Polski no more.'

'And *that's* why this Kassia hasn't been to work?' Ostrowsky looked doubtfully across at Tymon. 'You're sure, little brother? Maybe she got homesick and went back to Poland.'

'I only know what happened with Nick. I walked into the storeroom last week to pick up that cable for the new house and she was crying.'

'Why didn't the girl come to me? Why didn't you?'

Max spread his arms wide. 'I should. But the kid's a fucking baby and starts crying when you tell him off.'

'And you think Jake stole the van to get back at you,' nodded Ostrowsky.

'Nick must've told him some story about me and Kassia accusing him of bad things.'

'Where was I?'

'You were at the warehouse, I think.' Max shrugged. 'From that moment, Jake's had it in for me. That's why he stole the van. Hey, maybe it's Kassia's body in the van.' He nodded. 'Yes. Maybe he kills her to shut her up. And puts her in the van to . . .' He jiggled his hand for the right word.

'Implicate you,' said Ostrowsky. He drained his glass. 'And I'm just hearing about this when the police are involved.'

Max looked at the floor. 'I should have spoken sooner. But what do we do with snitches in our country, brother?' He picked up his glass and Tymon refilled it at Ostrowsky's behest.

'You should *not* have reported the van missing,' said Ostrowsky sternly. 'Always come to me. I deal with problems. Now you're connected to the van. I could have said it was stolen from the warehouse not your street.'

'But the insurance—'

'Fuck the insurance,' shouted Ostrowsky. 'Are we poor?'

Max downed his vodka. 'You're right, Grzegorz. I'm sorry.'

Ostrowsky eyed his brother. 'Very well.'

'What happens now?'

'Now?' Ostrowsky looked over to Tymon. 'Kassia was not official?'

Tymon shook his head. 'Only the English workers are official.'

'Good. Now she doesn't exist. Did Ashley know her?' Tymon nodded.

'Then get rid of him.'

Tymon seemed unsure for a moment and pulled a stiffened hand across his throat in enquiry.

Ostrowsky smiled for the first time. 'We're not in Hong Kong now, my old friend. No. Get him out of the bar and off the payroll, quietly. Pay him off – cash. Two thousand. Then offer him a job in the warehouse at higher pay but self-employed. Nothing on our records.'

'Yes, boss,' said Tymon.

'One more thing,' said Ostrowsky. 'You have an address for this Kassia?'

'Yes, boss,' said Tymon.

Ostrowsky looked over at Max. 'Go and see what her situation is.'

'Is that a good idea, Grzegorz?' said Max. 'The police might be there.'

'Let me worry about the police.' He looked his dishevelled brother up and down. 'You go home and get cleaned up. Respectable. The police will want to talk to us.'

'What about Nick and Jake?' asked Max.

'Leave them to me,' said Ostrowsky, with a long glance at Tymon. The big man acknowledged it with a dip of his eyes. 'Now go, little brother.' Max turned to leave. 'And Max!' The shambling figure returned a red-rimmed gaze. 'No more whores.'

* * *

'Find Jake and his brother and bring them to me before the police get to them,' Ostrowsky said to Tymon once Max had gone. 'Check the payroll database. Jake's home address is probably compromised, but maybe his work record will tell you something. One more thing. Max is lying. I don't know what he's been up to, but keep your eyes and ears open.'

Tymon nodded, then hurried down the back stairs as fast as his legs could carry him. Ostrowsky poured another glass of vodka and flicked on one of the wall-mounted televisions. He scrolled away from the muted football match looking for a local news station. He stopped abruptly when he saw Brook's face on the screen and turned up the volume. Brook was sitting impassively next to a small man in a uniform. The small man was speaking and seemed very pleased with himself. The inspector looked bored. It was a repeat of the earlier broadcast but Ostrowsky watched it anyway.

'Yes, the fingerprint was sent to EMSOU, which is the East Midlands Special Operations Unit, opened to provide the best-value forensic support for forces in Derbyshire, Nottinghamshire and Lincolnshire, at a saving of millions of pounds, I might add.' Brook coughed diplomatically and Charlton returned to the relevant topic. 'The suspect has a history with us so we had a result back within three hours. The men we're looking for are Jake Tanner . . .'

Ostrowsky glared at the mugshot of his former employee, a smile breaking out across his face. He held the glass up towards the screen. 'See you soon, Jake.'

Nineteen

'I'VE EDITED ALL THE SEQUENCES together, starting at the Cock Pitt, where they left the park,' said DC Cooper out of the darkness of the incident room. 'There.' He stood to point to the two figures frozen on the whiteboard screen. 'This is a few minutes after they ran across the footbridge.'

'That's our timeline,' agreed Morton, glancing at the digital display.

Six detectives watched as the film restarted and the two male figures emerged from the shadows of Bass's Recreation Ground, moving away from the river towards the Intu Centre. Then a different piece of film showed them stepping smartly along Traffic Street in the direction of Marks & Spencer, bordering the shopping precinct.

The younger, shorter man walked as though he hadn't a care in the world, but the older man – Jake Tanner – seemed to be on constant alert, glancing around anxiously, chivvying his brother along when he slowed to look in shop windows. At one point he seemed to grab his brother briefly. They appeared to be having an argument about something before they resumed their journey. Finally, a third camera showed them crossing the London Road roundabout before heading up Bradshaw Way in the direction of their block of flats.

'That's it,' said Cooper, flicking on the overhead lights.

'They went straight home after torching the van,' said Morton.

'What about later?' said Brook.

'Later?' asked Cooper.

'It's likely they flew the nest not long after they got home.'

'And you think they went back through town,' said Cooper.

'No idea,' said Noble. 'But we need to be sure.'

'Be a bit stupid getting themselves on film again,' said DC Smee.

'I doubt it was an issue by then,' said Noble. 'Jake knew he'd dropped his lighter when Inspector Gadget tackled him . . .'

'And that we'd be all over them when we matched his prints,' nodded Smee. 'World's Dumbest Criminals.'

'Who aren't yet in custody,' pointed out Noble.

'Transport?' asked Brook.

'None of the taxi local firms picked them up,' replied Morton. 'And no residents with nicked cars either, far as we can tell from door-to-door.'

'So they left on foot,' said Cooper. 'With luggage?'

'They panicked and grabbed what they could carry,' said Read.

'We don't know that,' said Brook. 'They may have had a plan and a destination in mind, but if they did panic, being on foot makes them desperate and dangerous.' He looked over at Cooper.

'They don't have any family in Derby, or anywhere else for that matter,' replied Cooper. 'Their mother died of a drug overdose eight years ago. Father unknown . . .'

'He may be unknown to us, Dave,' said Brook.

'But not to them,' agreed Cooper, making a note. 'I'm still checking for friends, but they don't seem to have any. They were pretty tight.'

'Then check again,' said Brook. 'Use Jake's work history. And coordinate a more thorough canvass of Milton Flats with uniform, make sure every resident is spoken to. All floors.' He turned to Read and Smee. 'Chances are they're still in Derby, but alert security at the bus and rail stations. You know the drill.'

'What about East Midlands Airport?' asked Smee, gesturing Read to his feet.

'The Tanners don't have passports,' said Morton. 'Not legal ones, anyway.'

'I'm guessing a pair of dodgy passports would be out of their price range,' said Noble.

'Agreed,' said Brook. 'Flag it up for the airport, but stick to bus and rail for now and gather any relevant film.'

'Bus station first,' suggested Noble. 'It's closer to their price bracket and they're more likely to have a skeleton service through the night. Check with National Express and Megabus for bookings out of town.'

'Night buses near the flat?' enquired Read.

'That won't get them out of Derby, but check anyway,' said Noble.

'What about hitching a ride?' suggested Morton. 'I know they've got luggage, but . . .'

'Circulate to Traffic, Rob,' said Brook. 'But they've had the best part of a day's start. If they've got as far as the motorway, they're gone. As for the rest of us, we concentrate on the area around the flats. I want uniform going house-to-house within a mile radius of their block. Dave, if they're still in Derby, we need to know anywhere local they might go or anyone who is prepared to hide them. Check Jake's known associates from Sudbury prison. And bump up patrol cars in the area. I want outbuildings checked, empty properties and derelicts top of the list.'

'Let's hope they haven't got the stones for a home invasion,' said Cooper.

'They're too small-time for that,' said Morton.

'A girl is dead,' said Brook. 'How is that small-time?'

'A fiver says the black rats pick them up thumbing on the M1,' said Smee.

'Then make sure they've got all the details,' said Noble, nodding at the door. Smee and Read departed, grabbing a radio each from the rack.

Brook looked to Cooper. 'Any more background, Dave?'

'I've been on to the Flowerpot,' he said. 'Jake left shortly after Caitlin disappeared. He was a relief barman and gave references from pubs and bars all over town . . .'

'Doesn't seem to hold down a job for very long,' observed Morton. 'Is he trouble?'

'The opposite, apparently,' answered Cooper. 'The Flowerpot manager said it was a case of him not being able to work full time, presumably because of his brother. He said Jake was polite and good at his job and left on amicable terms.'

'Did they know he had a criminal record?'

'He didn't declare it.'

'How sure are we that the Jane Doe is Caitlin Kinnear?' asked Morton.

'Jane Doe?' echoed Brook, turning to him.

'Are you American, Rob?' enquired Noble, before Brook could ask the question.

'We're sure of nothing until we get an ID,' said Brook, looking sideways at him. 'But Caitlin disappeared after a night at the Flowerpot and Tanner served her.'

'There's something else,' said Cooper. 'Jake applied for another job while he was at the Flowerpot; the manager said he got a request for references.'

'Where?'

Cooper rummaged around for a piece of paper. 'Some address in Pride Park.'

'Did he get it?'

'Unknown,' replied Cooper.

'Is it a pub?' asked Noble.

'No, strangely,' said Cooper. 'Some outfit called Warsaw Import and Export. They supply Polish minimarts.'

Brook and Noble looked at each other. 'Know any Polish bar owners, John?'

'The coincidences are starting to stack up. It's a company fronted by a Grzegorz Ostrowsky,' explained Noble. 'He owns Bar Polski, which is opening in Friargate. I'm running him past Interpol and the Polish police because he also owns the burned-out van, though it was his brother Max who used it for work.'

'What kind of work?' asked Morton.

'He's an electrician,' said Noble. 'SOCO found a bag of tools in the van, some workman's boots and gloves – nothing out of the ordinary. I've emailed an inventory.'

'Interesting,' said Cooper, staring at his monitor.

'What?'

'I've just noticed that Jake was working the bar at the

Cream when we closed it down nine years ago. One of his first bar jobs and one of his longest spells of employment.'

'The Cream?' said Brook.

'It's a hundred yards from Tanner's tower block,' explained Noble. 'On the roundabout.'

'Why is that significant?' asked Brook.

'Well, it's been empty since it closed and Jake was working the night it shut down,' said Cooper. 'It's derelict.'

'Might be a good spot to lay low,' said Morton.

'And if he had responsibilities, he may even have a set of keys by default,' said Brook, nodding. 'Divert some bodies from the Milton tower block to check doors and windows and look for any signs of recent occupation or ingress.'

Morton propelled his wheeled chair to a desk to pick up a phone, exchanging a smile with Noble. *Ingress?*

'You haven't mentioned the Smithfield, Dave,' said Brook.

'Just about to,' replied Cooper. 'How did you know?'

'Whoever dumped the van along that track would need local knowledge.'

'You're right, Jake did a four-month stint there five years ago,' said Cooper. 'Quite long by his standards.'

'His brother was probably still in school.'

'He works pretty hard for a criminal,' observed Noble.

'Another myth laid to rest,' remarked Brook.

'Hasn't kept him out of mischief,' added Morton, wheeling his chair back to the throng. 'Uniform are still knocking on doors at the flats. They're taking a peek at the Cream as we speak.'

Brook checked his watch when he saw Morton yawn. Twenty minutes to midnight. The other three detectives yawned in sequence. 'Long day.' Nobody argued. 'What time's the PM tomorrow, John?'

'Nine,' answered Noble.

Brook nodded. 'Go get some rest, everybody. We've done all we can tonight. Let's pick up tomorrow when we may have a name for our victim.'

Morton stood, but Cooper didn't move. 'I've still got film to check,' he said. 'See if the Tanner brothers bolted back through town.'

'I think it'll keep,' said Brook. 'If they went through town, they're likely heading for the bus station, and Read and Smee should pick up their trail from there.'

Cooper logged off and rose to leave. 'Okay, but I'm checking the rest of the film from home.' Feeling the need to explain, he added, 'Those two scumbags killed a girl and God knows what else beforehand.'

'We don't know that,' said Morton.

'We know she's dead, Rob,' said Cooper striding to join him at the door. 'And you didn't see her.'

Brook's voice halted their exit. 'Dave.' He hesitated, not sure what to say, knowing only that he had to speak. 'I don't sleep well most nights. You're a young man. Take my advice and train yourself *not* to imagine what's happened to a victim unless absolutely necessary.' There was silence for a moment and he began to wish he'd said nothing. He dredged up an exit line for them. 'And good work today.'

The pair retreated, sombre. Brook looked across at Noble. 'That went well.'

Noble smiled. 'They're not used to the new you.'

'The new me?'

'More relaxed, more confident now you're out of the

doghouse with Charlton. You even remember Cooper's name.'

Brook grunted his amusement. 'It won't last.'

'I dare say. And as we're discussing the new you, isn't it time you stopped asking people if they're American?'

'I thought that was you.'

'Just wanted to show you how daft it sounds.'

'There are some things I can't let slide,' said Brook, after a moment's thought. He glanced to the door. 'As for Cooper, I had no idea I inspired such a work ethic.'

'That's because you're not career-minded like the rest of us.'

'Meaning?'

'Meaning Jane's promotion has opened a vacancy for DS.'

'That's very cynical.' Brook reached out to flick on the kettle. 'I miss Jane. Whatever happened to positive discrimination?'

'There's plenty of female CID in the division.'

'But they're not on my team,' said Brook. 'And I want them. They've got skills male CID can't offer.'

'You mean to help with the tea,' suggested Noble, looking away.

Brook's face tightened. 'I'm not going to dignify that with an answer.'

'You're getting very difficult to provoke these days,' grinned Noble. 'It's unnerving.'

'It's the new me,' retorted Brook, pouring hot water into a mug.

'Thought we were going home to get some rest.'

'I don't sleep, remember,' said Brook, picking up the phone.

Noble pulled out his cigarettes, and walked to the door,

pausing to compose his next utterance. 'I wasn't being cynical, by the way. Cooper's in your squad and on the shortlist for DS.'

'What does that have to do with anything?'

'It means don't be surprised when detectives on your team start working harder,' said Noble. 'It's because they know you'll notice and help them be better at their job.'

Brook looked up from Ostrowsky's business card. 'Isn't that what a DI is supposed to do?'

'Try telling that to Frank Ford.'

Brook's brow furrowed. 'I thought Ford was popular with his people.'

'He's popular with DCs who want to coast,' replied Noble. 'You don't get it, do you? It's no accident that Jane made DI and I'm favourite to be next. Did you think it was coincidence? Why do you think clock-punchers like Ford and Hendrickson hate you? And DI Greatorex before them.'

'Because I'm not local,' offered Brook. With a smile, he added, 'And because I'm mentally unstable.'

'With respect, that's BS!' said Noble. 'It's because you embarrass them with the quality of your work – that's why all the ambitious DCs want to work with you and why they're prepared to put in the hours. They know they're more likely to get promoted.'

In the silence that followed, Brook stared into his tea, unsure how to respond. By the time his confusion had cleared and he looked up to offer a comment, Noble had slipped out for a cigarette. Brook returned his gaze to the card with Ostrowsky's Pride Park contact details. In his head he composed a message for the answering machine, but his call was answered on the first ring.

'Warsaw Import and Export.'

Brook hesitated. 'Mr Ostrowsky?'

'Inspector Brook,' said the businessman smoothly.

'You're working late.'

'I'm waiting for a shipment,' said Ostrowsky. 'When you work for yourself, that's what you do. But you, you're a public servant with your snout in the trough. You should be at home with your family, enjoying my taxes.' Brook detected an edge in his voice, as if Ostrowsky knew he wasn't a family man. 'That's why I didn't ring as soon as I saw the news bulletin.'

'What do you mean?'

'I was gathering the documents for the van when I saw your press conference. I wish I'd known how serious this was this morning. You see, Jake Tanner was recently employed by Bar Polski to stock the place before we open for business.'

Brook smiled. *Tell me something I already know to gain my confidence.* 'We know.'

'You do? I'm impressed,' gushed Ostrowsky. 'How?' Brook was rarely prepared to explain lines of enquiry to the public, but the Polish businessman answered his own question. 'The references. Of course. Quick work.'

'And all without money changing hands.'

Ostrowsky's laughter barked short and sharp down the phone. 'I'm afraid Jake didn't show up for work this morning,' he continued. 'Now I know why. Shocking. He didn't seem the type. And his brother seemed so nice.'

'You know Nick?'

'For a few days Jake would bring him to the bar while he worked. I only met him once, but he seemed pleasant. What should I do now, Inspector?'

'I need to speak to you and your brother tomorrow,' said Brook.

'Max told me—'

'No,' said Brook firmly. 'I don't want second-hand information and I don't want it over the phone.'

'Very well. When?'

'One o'clock tomorrow afternoon. The station at St Mary's Wharf. Do you know where it is?'

'My driver will find it,' said Ostrowsky before ringing off.

Brook sipped his tea, deep in thought.

The door opened and Noble walked in. 'Someone to see you at reception.'

'At this hour?' exclaimed Brook. 'Who is it?'

'They didn't say. I was having a smoke in the car park.'

'I thought I told you to go home,' said Brook. He could smell the seductive eddy of tobacco wafting over from Noble.

'I've got my promotion to think about,' said Noble drily. He turned on his computer. 'Besides, I thought you wanted some background on Ostrowsky.'

Brook plucked his jacket from the back of the chair. 'I just put the phone down on the man. He saw the news bulletin. Jake Tanner *was* working at Bar Polski, though he didn't show up this morning. When Ostrowsky saw Jake's face on the news, he says he put it together.'

'And took the trouble to tip us off,' scoffed Noble. 'Very public-spirited.'

'My sentiments exactly.'

'We should put him down for a good citizenship award.'

Tymon watched the activity around the Milton block from the safety of the Matalan car park. There were police vehicles everywhere, mostly empty as the occupants were knocking on the doors of the flats and houses in nearby streets. Occasionally a scene-of-crime technician would walk to the scientific support van, mask down, carrying evidence or ferrying equipment, before returning to the block for the arduous climb back to the eleventh floor.

Tymon examined the photocopy of Jake's references in his pudgy hand. His boss had underlined the home address and all previous employers, as Tymon's English language skills were a work in progress. Skimming down the list, something caught his eye.

'Cream,' he said aloud, checking the address on his list against the imposing cream-coloured building on the roundabout. Police vehicles were lined up no more than fifteen yards away, although there was no activity in or around the derelict bar.

Tymon opened the car door. *A derelict building. Good place to hide.*

Twenty

24 April

Pc Anka Banach trudged along the corridor, flicking her torch into the dark corners, hunger gnawing at her stomach. Cold and damp was leeching off a concrete floor that never saw the sun's rays. It was late and she was ready to knock off and get home to a warm bed.

'Glad it's not round here,' she muttered, scanning the dank walls. The peeling paint, the crumbling permafrost concrete, the lack of lighting did not appeal as she shone the beam towards her destination. Two more flats.

Rapping her knuckles on the penultimate door, Banach stepped back. As she did so, her head swam and she stumbled forward, forced to jam a gloved hand against the door frame to steady herself. She felt like she might throw up. There was no answer to her knock, so she took a second to regain her equilibrium. A moment later, the nausea passed.

Must be hungrier than I thought.

A glance back along the dark corridor confirmed that her misstep had gone unnoticed among colleagues, so, back to business, she made a note of the flat number, put a cross beside it and prepared to move to the last door. As soon as she stepped away, the door opened and an old woman peered tentatively out at her. Banach put a tick next to the cross. 'Mrs Porter?'

'Miss,' said the white-haired woman, her opaque eyes blinking myopically.

'Sorry,' said Banach cheerily. 'Look, my love, I know it's late and we don't want to alarm you, but we're just asking a few questions about two brothers who lived on the eleventh floor. Jake and Nick Tanner.'

'So that's what all the commotion's about. Not that I can sleep, what with Annie and everything. What did they do?'

'Do you know them?'

'No, dear,' she replied sadly. 'Never been up there and I wouldn't know them to talk to. I don't get out much except next door to Annie's for a cup of tea and a natter.' She nodded sadly towards the neighbouring flat.

'You've not been up to the eleventh floor?'

'Why would I, dearie? The lift never works and the next time I get that high I'll be on my way to sit beside the baby Jesus, God willing.'

Banach smiled. 'And you don't know them by sight?'

'My eyes aren't the best,' she said, brandishing her spectacle chain between finger and thumb. 'And I don't venture out after dark at my age. You don't know who's out there.' She smiled. 'You look a bit pale, my love. Are you cold?'

'I'm fine.'

'Would you like a cup of tea to keep you going?' she said. 'Warm you up in this cold weather. It's supposed to be spring.'

'No, but thank you,' smiled Banach. 'I'll let you get back to the warm.'

'Good luck finding those boys. The streets aren't safe to walk these days. I only opened the door because I thought it might be Annie. Stupid of me.'

'All right my love, I'll say good night.' Banach headed for the neighbouring flat.

'That's Annie's flat,' called out the old woman, reaching out a claw. 'She's gone.'

A heavy footfall approached and a male voice shouted to Banach from the darkness. 'We're wanted.'

Brook arrived in reception. Cooper was there, exchanging banter with a constable he couldn't put a name to. By the glass doors, a girl stood up from her chair.

'Inspector Brook.'

'Laurie! What are you doing here?' He studied her. She looked different, her hair longer, worry lines on her brow beginning to take up residence. She'd been crying.

'Is it Caitlin?' she said, approaching him. 'On the news. In that van.' The words were an effort and her composure was on a knife edge. She seemed on the brink of collapse, and Brook stepped forward in case her legs gave way. She fell towards him, and he grabbed her shoulders to keep her upright. Her emotion couldn't be contained and she forced her head on to his chest.

Reluctantly Brook's arms began to enfold her and he rested a hand on her sobbing head as she moaned something wet and unintelligible into his shirt. He looked across at Cooper as though to tag him into the hug – Brook wasn't good at this sort of thing – but realising he was stuck, he essayed a few consoling pats on her shaking shoulder blades with his free hand.

'Okay, sir?' enquired Cooper.

Brook nodded to confirm and Cooper headed silently for the exit, laptop in hand.

'Sit down,' said Brook, unpeeling the girl from his damp shirt and leading her back to the chairs. He glanced across at the unidentified young constable looking on. 'Can you make a cup of tea, Constable? Sharpish. Plenty of sugar.'

A couple of minutes later, Laurie was able to raise her face to sip at the mug.

'It is Caitlin, isn't it?' she said after a mouthful of hot tea. 'It couldn't be anyone else.'

'We don't know that,' answered Brook truthfully.

'I know. I recognised him,' she said. 'Jake was the barman that last night. At the Flowerpot.' Brook didn't answer. 'Did *he* kill her?'

'We don't know,' repeated Brook. 'When we speak to him—'

'All these weeks I've spent wondering where she went,' continued Laurie. 'I thought of all the places she could be, the people she might be with, sunbathing on a Greek beach with a new boyfriend, living a new life.'

'She might be there yet,' answered Brook.

'Bullshit!' snapped Laurie, standing abruptly and spilling the tea. 'Don't patronise me. She's dead. She never left Derby, you said. She's not living any kind of life because that bastard man killed her.' This last was shouted and the tears began again. She gazed in horror at Brook, member of the same corrupt gender as Jake Tanner. The young constable glanced over to see if the senior detective needed assistance, but Brook reassured with a splayed hand and stood, unable to look at the girl.

'Come on, I'll take you home.'

'Why?' pleaded Laurie, shaking her head. 'Why did this happen? Kitty's life just snuffed out like that. For ever. What gave that bastard the right?'

Brook decided to abandon the soothing tone and weary platitudes. 'Nothing gave him the right, Laurie,' he said softly. 'The person who did this assumed that right with no thought for the pain of others. Whatever he wanted with Caitlin – if that *is* her lying in the mortuary – whatever he needed her to do for him or *with* him or *to* him . . .' his eyes speared into Laurie's and her mouth opened in shock and awe, 'he knew that he could never let her tell the tale, because he was so weak, his sense of self so compromised, so degraded, that he couldn't risk his deepest, darkest desires being broadcast to others, couldn't bear the disgust of ordinary people for the acts he felt compelled to commit. He didn't hate her, Laurie. He hated himself, and probably still does.'

There was silence as both took stock of the sermon, Laurie stunned and mute, Brook breathless, contemplating victims past and present. Even the young PC was rapt, unmoving at his counter, his mouth open, his Adam's apple temporarily stranded.

A few seconds later, Laurie managed movement, the rustle of her Gore-Tex coat bringing back basic sensation. She closed her eyes. 'I'd like to go home now, Inspector.'

Brook nodded, a curious half-smile deforming his lips. 'I'll take you, Laura.'

She glanced up at his face as he led the way. 'My name is Laurie.'

Brook's break of step was barely noticeable as he marched on towards the smoked-glass doors. 'That's what I said,' he mumbled over his shoulder.

* * *

PC Mitchell Ryan was tugging at the boards covering the windows of the deserted Cream Bar. They were solid.

'Looks pretty dead,' said Banach, appearing from the front of the building. 'Funny, though, the front door lock seems well oiled.'

'You tried knocking?'

'Actually, I did.'

'No sign of B and E.' Ryan saw Banach yawning. 'Come on, girl. We've done a double and we're fifteen minutes over.'

'Feels like longer.'

'That's lates for you. The next time I suggest coming off early turn for a bit of excitement, just ignore me.'

Banach's answering smile froze on her lips and she trained her eyes on the first floor.

'What?'

'I thought I saw a light – upstairs.' She gazed up at the building before marching towards the rear. 'Come on. There's an exposed window round the back and some crates we can stand on.'

'Maybe it was a car headlight reflecting,' hissed Ryan. 'Slow down, Angie.'

A moment later, Banach stood at the rear of the boarded-up building, gauging the height of the first-floor window. She looked at the pile of wooden pallets positioned against the wall. 'This is how they got in.'

'You think someone climbed up there?'

'How else?'

'You said the lock was oiled. Maybe it's legit, a keyholder or something.'

Banach raised an eyebrow. 'At this time of night? It's a derelict, Mitch.'

'You're not thinking of climbing up there.'

She turned to him with a familiar tight-lipped expression that spoke to her determination. *Just watch me.*

'We should call it in. Wait for instructions.'

Banach put her foot on the first pallet. 'Our *instructions* were to investigate, weren't they? That's what we're doing.'

'I don't think this is what the sarge meant.' Banach looked down at him from halfway up the column of pallets. 'Damn it, Angie, be careful.'

'Always,' grunted Banach, clambering up to the top pallet, where she was able to lever herself on to the ledge of the first-floor window. The glass was broken, so she felt around for a catch, being careful not to cut herself on the jagged pane. A second later, she pushed open the window and swung her legs inside, then popped her head back out to gesture at Ryan.

'Wait there for me,' he hissed at her as he began to climb, but she was already gone.

Banach flicked her torch around the bare room. The beam caught something in the adjoining room and she made her way across the corridor, stepping gingerly on the bare boards. She knelt to examine a sleeping bag. It was cleaner than might be expected. There was even a cushion for a pillow, which looked new.

'Odd.' She moved the light across the floor and found an empty sweet packet, picking it up and discarding it a second later. 'Someone's been here.'

She heard a noise behind her. 'In here, Mitch,' she called, flicking the torch briefly over her shoulder. She was standing to continue the search when a footstep crunched on a bare board directly behind her and she turned towards the source.

A heavy blow caught her on the side of the head and she gasped in shock and pain, her body crumpling on to the sleeping bag like a sack of potatoes.

Brook and Laurie drove on in silence, eyes glued to the road. A moment later, Brook became aware of Laurie's discomfort and stole a glance at her. Following the direction of her gaze, he saw they were passing the Flowerpot and would be hugging the route of Caitlin's last journey. At the lights by the A38 overpass, she spoke.

'I've not been in that pub since. I've not even seen it.'

Brook nodded, still forming questions of his own, practical questions about the case, about the hunt for a killer. He held his tongue. At this moment, any enquiry would be intrusive. But as Markeaton Park loomed large and dark on the left, he felt as though Laurie wanted to talk.

'That night,' he said. 'Did Tanner do or say anything while you and Caitlin were in the pub? Anything strange or that struck you as odd.'

'Strange?'

'Did he pay Caitlin any undue attention or give the impression . . .'

'That he was fixated on her?' She shook her head. 'Honestly, no. He served drinks like a normal barman.'

Brook pulled the BMW on to the side road and ground to a halt outside Laurie's bungalow before turning to her. 'So you noticed him, then?'

'I noticed him. Caitlin was going at it pretty hard. She hadn't had a drink for a while. I mean, she'd missed St Patrick's Day because of the pregnancy. And she's Irish.' She lowered her head. 'She was Irish.'

'Don't make assumptions until we identify the body,' insisted Brook. 'How did Tanner make himself noticed?'

'He saw that she was drinking too fast and suggested she slow down.'

'What did he say?'

'First it was just a look, kind of hesitating before filling her glass, giving her the eyes, like, *Are you sure about this? You've had plenty.* Then he said she could have another if she could read his name tag.'

'Did she?'

'Oh yes, but he knew she was bladdered.'

'But he refilled her glass anyway.'

'The customer is always right,' said Caitlin. 'Except she wasn't. And that was her last drink before she ran out to the toilet. She pretended she was fine, but I knew she was going to puke. I didn't know she would take off like that, though.' Her voice cracked as the implication hit her, but she retained her poise. 'I never saw her again.'

'Did you see Tanner after Caitlin left?'

'You mean, did he leave and go after her? I'm not sure. I think he served my boyfriend when he arrived.' She looked miserable. 'I'm sorry, I don't remember that well, I'd been drinking too . . .'

'Don't worry,' soothed Brook. 'We're pretty sure he stayed.'

'So maybe he grabbed her later,' said Laurie. 'If Caitlin was home alone, he could just as easily have gone along after his shift.'

'But unless he followed her, he wouldn't know her address,' said Brook. 'Unless he asked for ID.'

'Oh shit, yeah. I showed him my NUS card.' She squinted in confusion. 'But that only has my date of birth.'

'What about Caitlin?' asked Brook. 'Did her ID have her address on?'

'It might have. I didn't really notice.'

Brook smiled to signal the end of his questions and put a hand out to open his door.

'I don't live here any more,' muttered Laurie, looking guiltily at him. 'I couldn't. Not after . . . Sorry, I meant to say. I moved into halls.'

'Not a problem.' Brook turned the BMW round for the short drive to the main university site. 'That's what I love about Derby. Everything's five minutes away.'

The rain was starting when Brook pointed the car towards home. Either muscle memory or fatigue induced him to push in the cigarette lighter as he roared along the tight country lane to the north of Markeaton Park to take him to the A52. It was hard to focus on the wet road on so little sleep, so he eased back on the speed and opened his window on to the sweet air of a damp spring night.

At the junction, before he could swing right towards Ashbourne and the Peaks, his antiquated mobile vibrated in a pocket.

'John.' He listened for a moment. 'On my way.'

Ten minutes later, Brook parked as close to the Cream Bar as possible as an ambulance pulled away for the short journey to the Royal Derby. There were seven police vehicles in attendance, blocking off the traffic island overlooked by the dilapidated hostelry, closed in 2006 after a series of violent incidents.

Noble stepped away from a small throng of officers,

discarding a cigarette, and Brook made a beeline for him. He spotted an officer seated, head down, on the steep, weed-encrusted steps leading to the front entrance of the bar. Another officer stood adjacent, notebook in hand. The front door of the bar was wedged firmly open and the dark interior yawned.

Noble followed Brook's eyes. 'We put the ram to it. To gain ingress,' he added, a ghost of a smile disappearing as quickly as it arrived. 'Cooper was right,' he continued in more sombre vein. 'Jake must have hung on to the keys. Although we had to force the door, the lock's been maintained. It was oiled recently. Someone's been using the place.'

'The perfect spot to hide for a few days,' said Brook, looking up and down the dilapidated building. 'Talk me through it.'

'A couple of uniforms went round to check the place out and were ambushed. One's just gone off to the Royal. Possible fractured skull. We've got about sixty bodies pounding the surrounding streets. Nothing so far.'

'How serious?'

'Possible brain injury,' said Noble. Brook nodded towards the stricken officer sitting on the steps. 'PC Banach – headache and possible concussion.'

'Why hasn't she gone to hospital?'

'She insisted on staying to help.'

The officer taking notes snapped his book closed and moved aside at Brook and Noble's approach.

'What happened, Constable?' enquired Brook to the bowed head, hand clutching a wet towel to the neck. He couldn't see any blood.

Banach looked up and tried to stand, and Brook recognised

the female PC who'd been on crowd control at the *Telegraph* building. 'Sir, I . . .'

'No, stay down,' said Brook, putting out a hand. 'What can you tell us about your attacker?'

Banach shook her head and winced in pain. 'I didn't see a face, sir. Constable Ryan and myself were sent to do a reccy. I saw a light through a first-floor window. A torch, I think. We went to investigate. All the doors were locked so I climbed in through a rear window. There were some old pallets stacked up to reach the first floor and the window pane was broken . . .'

'Broken?' interrupted Brook. 'By whoever was already here?'

Banach paused. 'Unknown. It might have been smashed by vandals. It was fastened, though. I had to reach in and open it to get in.'

'Go on.'

'I turned on my torch and I could see the room was clear, so I went into the next room and that was it. I got walloped from behind. I lost consciousness, and when I came round, I went back to find Mitch and . . .' her lip wobbled and her eyes sought the floor, 'he was down too.' Her eyes glazed over at the memory of her injured colleague.

'How long?'

'No more than fifteen minutes after I was attacked before I called it in.' Her eyes filled with tears. 'The paramedic said Mitch might have brain damage.'

'We don't know that,' said Noble.

'Get PC Banach off to hospital, John,' said Brook.

'Sir, I'm fine,' interrupted Banach, struggling to her feet.

'That's heartening, but we'll take it from here.'

'I want to help . . .'

'When you've had a check-up,' said Brook, motioning Noble towards the building.

'No,' she insisted. 'I owe it to Mitch . . .'

Brook turned, irritated now. 'Stop talking, Constable,' he barked. 'If this is guilt because you messed up in some way, it's misplaced. You're no use to me in this condition. You're going to hospital and you're going now.'

'But sir . . .'

'And please accept my apologies if it sounded like a request before.' He held her gaze to confirm compliance before turning to the other officer. Surprisingly, he knew his name. 'PC Stone. You take her. While you're there, get PC Banach's uniform bagged for Forensics . . .' He rolled his eyes, not wanting to add *in case this really turns sour* in front of Banach.

'Will do, sir. Come on, Angie,' said Stone as though to a child, gently taking hold of her arm to guide her. Banach walked compliantly but her gaze was fixed malevolently on Brook, unable to form any of the sentences trying to jostle their way into her speech centre.

Brook approached a group of half a dozen uniformed officers, some fiddling with unlit cigarettes, some checking watches to see how far over their shift they were working. But all faces were set hard against the perpetrators. 'I only want two officers at the front entrance to secure the building. The rest of you I want patrolling the neighbourhood. Be vigilant. If our suspects are out there, they're on foot and desperate, so take care.

'Gardens and garages. Any lights on, knock on doors and get residents to unlock their outbuildings. Anybody walking the street at this ungodly hour, I want stopped and questioned.'

He paused for emphasis. 'I don't want unrelated arrests if someone's had a drink and backchats you; I want eyewitnesses who've seen something or I want whoever assaulted Ryan and Banach.' He waited to ensure his point was made. 'And tell everyone to be on the watch for jittery residents. A home invasion is a hostage situation, and the last thing we need is more lives under threat.'

'And for God's sake, people,' added Noble, 'two of our own are hurting, but that excuses nothing. If you hit the jackpot, don't get overenthusiastic and hand their brief the wiggle room to get them off.'

'And tell everyone over their hours that they should book it in as overtime,' said Brook finally to a low murmur of approval, and despite injuries to colleagues, smiles broke out.

'Better be careful,' said Noble as the officers dispersed quickly. 'You might become popular.'

'That'll be a great comfort when Charlton sees the dent in his budget,' replied Brook, setting off for the building's entrance. About to disappear into the interior, he was distracted by the noise of a low-flying helicopter and looked to the grey sky to follow the beam of light shining down on the surrounding streets. 'Ours?'

'I thought it best,' said Noble. 'Dog handlers on the way as well.'

Brook nodded. 'And since we're going for broke, divert more patrol cars to the area for the next few hours, then get on to traffic to throw up some roadblocks. If they haven't already, our suspects may feel the need to steal a car. All major routes until rush hour.'

'If this is Jake and Nick, they're in the big time now,' said Noble.

'Let's hope they can handle it,' said Brook. 'Or this could turn into a spree.'

With no arc lights yet in place, the two detectives had to rely on torches to examine each of the rooms in turn. The downstairs bar area was a sea of broken glass that complained at each step taken. Without a major clean-up, it was effectively uninhabitable. A toilet leading off the bar seemed to be in working order, with bowl and cistern intact and water supply still available.

'En suite,' quipped Noble, eliciting an answering grunt from Brook.

Upstairs was more hospitable, if littered with detritus. Empty cans and bottles, some of them blackened by the burning of crack cocaine, were strewn across the floor. There was a pile of dusty clothes and a pair of worn boots, twisted and covered in mildew. A metal bucket with holes punched in it had been used as a makeshift brazier, and the smell of damp ash invaded the nostrils.

In the penultimate room, a sleeping bag with a cushion for a pillow lay in the corner, both artefacts relatively unsoiled. An empty sweet packet lay on the sleeping bag. The two detectives crossed the corridor to the room with the broken window. Brook leaned out to look down on to the enclosure below, being careful not to touch the wooden frame. Adjusting his eyes to the faint moonlight, he saw a small black puddle staining the concrete.

'See the blood,' said Noble, joining him at the window. He indicated the pallets stacked below. 'And that's where Banach climbed up – quite a feat in the dark.'

'What happened to Ryan?'

'Not sure. Banach says she was attacked over by the door and knocked out. Ryan must have followed her up to the window . . .'

'And someone pushed him off,' concluded Brook.

'Looks that way,' nodded Noble.

'Yet you had to force the front door.'

'No choice. It was locked when we arrived.'

'So Banach called it in, then climbed down the way she came in to tend to Ryan.'

'That's what she said.'

'Because she couldn't unlock the door,' mumbled Brook.

Noble was curious now. 'I'm not sure she even tried, but it was locked and impossible to budge without keys.'

'Did you see Ryan?'

'Briefly. He didn't look good, but then it always looks worse when there's blood. The paramedics said there was some swelling, which could indicate internal bleeding and pressure on the brain. On the other hand, they said they'd seen worse injuries survived with a full recovery.'

'That's something,' murmured Brook. 'Get on to Cooper and give him the new timeline for any film. Alert Smee and Read. If this was the Tanners, they might make a run for transport out of the city and we need to contain them.'

'Already done,' said Noble. 'They should be easier to catch out in the open. Is there any doubt this *is* the Tanners?'

'There's always doubt until there's certainty, John,' answered Brook.

'It all points to them,' said Noble. 'They torched the van, they're on the run, they live close and Jake used to work here.'

'Sounds viable,' conceded Brook.

Noble detected a doubt. 'But?'

'Something doesn't add up. If Jake had keys and was hiding here with Nick, why attack two police officers gaining entry to the first floor when all you have to do is unlock the front door and run?'

'Maybe that's what they did *after* they attacked Banach and Ryan.'

'But why attack them at all?' said Brook. 'If they had a key, they weren't cornered and the assault makes no sense.'

'Maybe they were asleep. They were surprised and reacted. If they've killed once, an assault comes easy.'

'That's possible,' conceded Brook. 'But why attack Ryan when he's not even in the building?'

'All right, maybe they weren't surprised,' said Noble, exasperated. 'But since when did ex-cons need a reason to attack the police?'

Brook nodded, deep in thought. 'So they attack Banach and push Ryan off the pallets. Then what?'

'They run out the front door.'

'Locking it behind them,' said Brook. 'Why? The place is blown.'

Noble was stymied for a moment. 'I don't know.'

Brook poked a toe at an ancient rusted can. 'Another thing. Where are the artefacts to suggest recent occupation?'

'They can't have been here more than twenty-four hours.'

'Exactly,' replied Brook. 'If they were going to hole up here, everything they took the trouble to bring over from the flat should still be here. So where is it? Where's the canned food?'

'Maybe they hid it.'

'Where?' demanded Brook. 'And why?'

'All right, they took it with them.'

Brook pulled a face. 'Having attacked two police officers?'

'Then maybe they didn't bring cans from the flat.'

Brook shook his head. 'Jake knew they'd have a few hours' grace after setting fire to the van. They didn't have a car, and they didn't steal one as far as we know. They left in a hurry but Jake knew they couldn't make it on foot in the middle of the night. But he knows a place. It's close. So they packed what they could for a short hop before they go to ground. That means food. If they had any foodstuffs in the flat, they had to bring them. They brought the can opener, so where are the cans?'

Noble thought it through before conceding and switching to Brook's wavelength. 'And if you're discovered and seriously assault two police officers, your window of opportunity closes fast. You panic. The place might be overrun with officers at any moment . . .'

'So you leave with nothing and at great speed,' finished Brook.

'Okay. If it wasn't the Tanners, then who? Crackheads? Dossers? And if Jake and Nick weren't here, where the hell are they?'

'Maybe we should be giving the world's dumbest criminals a bit more credit,' said Brook. 'He might not have the exams to back it up, but I'm starting to think Jake Tanner's cleverer than we thought.'

'Worth processing?' queried Noble, looking around.

'There's no telling how many have flopped down here. But lock it down in case. And take the sleeping bag and cushion. They look new. We might get DNA to match to Jake.'

Noble nodded to the broken window. 'And dust around the frame. You never know.'

The pair walked silently downstairs back through the dark,

glass-strewn bar and towards the cool spring air. Brook paused to examine a bottle, not as old and blackened as the rest. It was a vodka bottle – the same brand Ostrowsky had been drinking that morning. A finger of liquid remained.

'Polish vodka.' With gloved hand, he took out an evidence bag and dropped the bottle into it, handing it off to Noble. 'Prints, please.'

'Charlton's going to be paying our wages on his credit card at this rate.'

Brook smiled. 'How pleased am I that *you* deployed the helicopter.'

A stiff wind was getting up and cold pellets of rain were blowing into their faces as they stepped outside. It was three o'clock, and both men knew that any sleep that night would be in a chair.

Twenty-One

BANACH WOKE WITH A START and the pain registered immediately. Her back ached, her head throbbed and her knuckles were clenched in anger. But the worst pain wasn't physical. An unknown assailant had attacked her partner and she had let him get away, had disgraced herself in front of her colleagues. She raised a bloodless hand to her head in self-disgust.

'Gotta get back out there.' She swung her legs off the bed.

'No you don't,' said a female voice. A practised hand guided her legs gently but firmly back on to the mattress. 'You're going nowhere. Doctor's orders.'

Banach struggled to rise. 'Where's Mitch? I want to see Mitch.'

'If Mitch is the other police officer, I gather he's going to be fine.'

Banach stopped struggling and lay back, relieved. 'Thank God.'

The doctor took out a pen light from her top pocket and, sitting on the edge of the bed, put a hand on Banach's chin to hold her head steady. She shone the torch into her right eye and ordered her to turn her gaze in various directions before repeating the same procedure in her left eye.

'Can I see him?'

'He's just out of theatre so he'll be sleeping for a few hours yet. He should be coming round when we're ready to discharge you, so get some rest now.'

'He's really going to be fine?'

'A full recovery,' smiled the doctor. 'Promise.'

Placated, Banach relaxed on to the soft pillows and contemplated the attractive white-coated woman writing on her chart, her dark hair tied up in a ponytail to show off the smooth, pale skin of her neck. On her lapel, Banach made out the name tag: 'Dr Cowell'.

A tall, middle-aged man in de rigueur white coat and stethoscope stepped through the dividing screen. His head was held high and he had a stern patrician air.

'This is Dr Fleming, Anka,' said Dr Cowell. 'He's a specialist.'

'Anka,' repeated Fleming. 'Is that Slovenian?'

'Polish on my father's side,' retorted Banach. 'But I'm English. I prefer Angie.'

Fleming's inscrutable grunt was emitted through sealed lips. 'Lift, please,' he said, nodding at her gown. Puzzled, Banach complied and Fleming's stethoscope landed on her stomach. After listening to three areas, he stood back, nodding for her to lower the gown.

'Well, *Ms* Banach,' he said officiously. 'The scan was fine and the womb is uninjured. As soon as Dr Cowell clears your head injury, you can go. The baby's in fine fettle.' He smiled at Banach, waiting for gratitude.

'And you've just got bruising to your skull – no concussion,' said Cowell. 'You'll have a headache for a day or two, and in your condition you should rest for a few days.'

'Baby,' mouthed Banach as though the word were alien. 'I'm pregnant?'

'Ah,' said Fleming, glancing over at his colleague. 'Over to you, Dr Cowell.'

'You didn't know,' nodded Cowell. 'It's not unusual this early.'

'I can't be pregnant,' muttered Banach, barely able to speak. Her mouth was dry, her heart pounding. 'It's impossible.'

'An immaculate conception?' chipped in Fleming, smiling for the first time. 'I'll call *The Times*.'

'There's no mistake,' said Cowell. 'You're about eight weeks along. Didn't you notice you were missing periods?'

'I . . . I just thought I was late. I've been so busy.' Banach stared into space. 'You're certain?'

'There's no doubt.'

'And the foetus is fine,' said Fleming. 'Though I wouldn't encourage you to tackle any more bad guys for a while.'

'But I can't have a baby,' said Banach, shaking her head. 'I just can't.'

'Many women with unplanned pregnancies feel the same way when they first hear the news,' said Cowell. 'Give yourself a few days to think about things, talk to the father . . .'

'And for busy career girls like yourself, there are always options,' added Fleming.

'This isn't the right time, Doctor,' said Cowell, her face souring. 'Angie needs a chance to come to terms with her news.'

'Please don't patronise the patients,' said Fleming. He placed a card on the side table and tapped it with a finger. 'My clinic.'

'This is not the right time . . .'

'Please,' said Banach, holding up both hands and closing her eyes. 'I'd like you both to leave me alone now.'

Fleming smiled. 'Of course. And congratulations,' he added without warmth. 'Good day.'

Cowell took a deep breath after his departure. 'Sorry about Dr Fleming. I'm afraid male consultants of a certain age have a tendency to play God.'

'It's okay,' said Banach. 'I'm a big girl. So when can I leave?'

'Just waiting for some more bloods.' Cowell picked up Fleming's card. 'Get some rest and before you know it you'll be chatting with your colleague.'

'Thanks. And Doctor,' she added as Cowell turned to go, 'I do want to know about my options.' She paused so that she was fully understood. 'All of them.'

Cowell held her eyes for a few seconds, then acknowledged with a curt nod and returned Fleming's card to the table. 'Whatever you need.'

Brook woke to the smell of coffee and lifted his head from the desk.

Noble was gnawing on a chocolate bar, a mug of coffee in his other hand. Morton was stirring sugar into his cup. He flicked the kettle back on for Brook.

'Anything?' croaked Brook, lifting himself out of his chair, grimacing as his back straightened.

'Not a sniff,' said Noble. 'Of the Tanners or anyone else.'

'We're still going door-to-door?'

Noble pushed the end of the chocolate into his mouth, chewing furiously. 'For now.' He took a long slurp of coffee. 'Still worried about a home invasion?'

'Desperate men, desperate deeds.' Brook stood to stretch. 'They're still in the neighbourhood somewhere. I'm sure of it.'

'Thought you weren't convinced the Tanners attacked Ryan and Banach.'

'I'm convinced they're on the run and potentially dangerous, *whoever* attacked our officers,' said Brook, squeezing hot water from a tea bag. A moment later, he took a life-affirming sip. 'Any news on Ryan?'

'Stone says he's unconscious but stable. They're hopeful.'

'Good,' said Brook, moving around to get the circulation going. 'Reminds me. Was I a bit hard on what's-her-name last night?'

'Banach? I don't think so,' said Noble. 'She shouldn't have gone mountaineering around like that when the cavalry was across the road. Showed a lack of judgement.'

Brook took another long sip of tea. 'But plenty of mettle.'

'Metal?' queried Morton.

'She didn't hesitate,' explained Brook. 'She was first into that building, no thought for her own safety.'

'Is that a good thing?'

'It's admirable, at least,' said Brook. 'Banach. Sounds Eastern European.'

'I think her father is Polish,' said Noble.

Brook paused mid sip. 'Is that so?'

The door opened and Charlton marched in, expression like thunder. Even before seven in the morning his uniform was crisp and his face carefully scraped. He halted in the face of superior numbers, bridling at his lack of height next to three tall detectives. 'Busy night.'

Brook smiled at Charlton's pussyfooting, tempted just to dive in and save time. 'Yes, sir.'

'Progress?'

'We're making all the moves,' said Brook. 'Nothing yet.'

'I see.' Charlton couldn't meet eyes. 'How's Ryan?'

'Still unconscious, sir,' said Brook, sombre. 'But stable.'

'Good.' Charlton hesitated, realising that the budget was not a suitable topic of conversation at that precise moment.

Brook sensed an opportunity. 'I'm afraid I took a bite out of the budget last night trying to bring the perpetrators to book. My shout, sir. Seeing our officers in that state . . .' He shook his head, his approximation of dismay hitting the right notes. Noble prepared to speak but was silenced by Brook's warning glare.

Charlton nodded, his frustration equal to Brook's. 'One of our own,' he conceded. 'Keep me informed.' He departed with an air of defeat hanging over him.

'*My shout?*' said Noble. 'You don't need to run interference for me.' Brook raised an eyebrow. 'No, I'm not American and I can justify my own decisions to the Chief Super.'

'I didn't say anything,' smiled Brook, pulling on his jacket. 'I'm not allowed.'

'Then why take the hit for the budget?'

'Because I'm in Charlton's good books, John, and no matter how uncomfortable that makes me, I'm going to draw water from that well until it's bone dry.'

'But it was my decision.'

'And you were only doing what I would have done. Come on. A bacon sandwich beckons.'

'Before the mortuary?'

'The mortuary?' said Brook. 'I get queasier talking to Charlton.'

* * *

'Brook. Sergeant Noble.' Dr Ann Petty turned from the stainless-steel sink, deep inside the Royal Derby Hospital's sprawling complex, and turned off the tap. She tore a yard of disposable hand towel from a dispenser and carefully dried her hands before squirting disinfectant gel on to her palms and rubbing it through her fingers. 'Hope you don't mind forgoing a handshake?'

'We'll survive,' said Brook absently, oblivious to the implied insult. Petty lingered over his answer and shot a fleeting look towards Noble.

'We've been on the go two days straight,' explained Noble, looking nervously past the small anteroom to the soulless post-mortem suite beyond, scanning the brushed-steel trolleys for human remains. A male cadaver lay on one, his chest flayed back like an unmade bed.

'That must be it,' said Petty, gathering her notes. 'All the fuss on the news, I take it. Glad to hear you're as overworked and underpaid as I am.'

Brook was examining the high-ceilinged window-free suite, lit by the jaundiced glow of artificial light. 'How do you survive without daylight, Doctor?'

Petty shook her dyed-blond hair free from beneath her disposable cap. 'I'm not confined in here, Inspector. I can walk out among the living between procedures. Besides, there are worse things to worry about down here than a light source.'

'I suppose.'

'And I'm pleased to see you back in the land of the living,' said Petty. 'Last I heard you were exiled to cold cases. Sentence commuted?'

'Let's just say I worked my passage,' replied Brook.

'And with one bound he was free,' grinned Petty before her

face morphed to a more serious expression. 'I'm glad it's you, Brook. A young girl brutally snatched from life just as it's about to begin. Catching this bastard will make all women sleep easier, and though we've not worked together long, I know you'll go the extra mile.'

Brook was taken aback by such appreciation and could only think to say, 'I will.'

'Pay me no attention,' said Petty. 'This line of work goes easier when you remove the emotion.'

'Some things you never get used to seeing,' concluded Brook.

'No argument here. And a developing foetus in a dead mother's womb is top of my list.'

'Foetus?' said Brook, glancing at Noble. 'The victim was pregnant?'

'That's not possible,' said Noble.

Petty looked askance at him, considering various put-downs before keeping it professional. 'Take it from me, Sergeant, the victim brought to me from your crime scene was having a child.'

'Sorry,' said a sheepish Noble. 'I didn't mean . . . It's just we know our missing person had undergone a recent termination.'

'Is this the Irish girl on the front of last night's paper?' enquired Petty. 'Caitlin . . .'

'Kinnear.'

'Right age range then,' said Petty. 'Your victim was approximately twenty years old. But if you're certain this Caitlin Kinnear wasn't pregnant, then the body next door is not hers. Sorry if that makes life harder.'

'It is what it is,' said Brook. 'With a body we start the inquiry from scratch anyway to avoid misdirection.'

'Misdirection?' said Petty.

'With a missing person, we chase shadows . . .'

'You take your information where you can find it,' said Petty, nodding. 'I see that.'

'. . . and with a body we chase the science,' said Brook. 'A murder inquiry is a time for hard facts.'

'So Caitlin's alive,' said Noble, trying not to sound relieved that another father's daughter had just taken her place.

'She's still missing, John,' said Brook. 'And she may still be dead. Sorry, Doc, we're briefing on your time.'

'Nice to know there's a process,' smiled Petty. 'Sorry to throw a spanner in the works.'

'You haven't,' said Brook. 'Sadly, we're not short of other candidates. How long had the victim been pregnant?'

'I'd say between ten and twelve weeks.'

Brook nodded. 'Cause of death? The mother, I mean.'

'The fire didn't kill her. Her blood was negative for carbon monoxide and there's no scorching or scarring in her throat and lungs. The blaze was an afterthought to burn off trace, I assume. But we have other markers.' She pulled photographs from a large brown envelope, then hesitated. 'Unless you really want to see the body . . . We photographed all the essentials. It's a bit of a stir fry.'

'And I was so looking forward to it.' Brook held out a hand for the first picture, a large colour head shot.

'The victim was badly beaten about the head,' began Petty. 'Fists to start with, then a blunt instrument – although that was possibly post mortem. No clue as to what without further analysis from EMSOU.'

'Hammer?' said Noble.

'If you recovered one from the scene, I'd say it's a good bet judging by the indentations on the skull. Special Unit can rule on that for you. Suffice to say there's plenty of damage. Blows post mortem were presumably to hide identity. You can see the ruptured nasal cartilage, which is consistent with a beating. Also the jaw. Both TMJs are dislocated, which is a classic signature for trauma to the lower face. Notice the teeth?'

'All the damage is on the right side of her mouth,' said Brook.

'Correct,' said Petty. 'Combined with the direction of the cartilage rupture and the preponderance of blows to the right side of the head, it's likely you're looking for a left-handed male.'

'Likely?'

'You can never know for certain how an assailant is going to utilise a blunt instrument,' explained Petty before shrugging. 'If it were just fists . . .'

'But definitely a man?' said Noble.

'Very high probability given the stats on violence against women plus the strength needed to inflict such damage,' said Petty. Noble nodded in a sad condemnation of his sex.

'Sexual activity?'

'None – consensual or otherwise – so no DNA from that source, I'm afraid.'

Brook shrugged. 'She wasn't raped, at least. Is it possible to determine paternity?'

'If you have DNA to match to the foetal cells,' said Petty. 'All the father's markers will be present. Do you?'

'Not yet, given that we don't know who she is,' said Brook.

'Higginbottom suggested she was strangled,' said Noble.

'He's right. The killer got on top of her, cracking three of her ribs. She may have fought back, so the beating was to subdue her. There are depression marks on her throat and her hyoid bone was broken, which closed off the airway.' She unfurled another picture, a close-up of one eye to show small blood spots.

'Petechial haemorrhaging,' said Noble.

'Broken capillaries caused by asphyxiation. There would have been blood spots and discoloration all over her face, but the fire destroyed them. I'm guessing the blaze didn't last long, otherwise the eyeballs would have boiled away completely.'

'How long dead?' asked Brook.

Petty checked her notes. 'From the rate of decomp, I'd say between sixty and seventy-two hours . . .'

'So murdered thirty-six to forty-eight hours before her body was dumped and torched,' said Noble slowly.

'Sounds right,' answered Petty.

'You said she fought,' chipped in Brook.

'Didn't mean to get your hopes up,' said Petty. 'Sitting on the chest is a classic suppression technique and it works very well. No skin under her fingernails, and any hair she might have grabbed didn't survive the fire.' She produced a plastic evidence bag. 'On the plus side, I'm fairly sure the killer wore fire-retardant gloves, because we found a couple of usable fibres in her mouth and underneath the tongue. They probably detached when he was strangling her.'

'Fire-retardant?'

'I've sent the sample off to EMSOU for confirmation. Suggests you're looking for somebody who needs heavy-duty specialist gloves – a workman, a gardener, a fireman . . .'

'Somebody with a trade like an electrician?' said Brook.

'Sounds reasonable,' nodded Petty.

'Even if we match fibres to the gloves in the van, the van was stolen,' said Noble. 'So whoever had access to it had access to the gloves.'

'True. What about fingerprints, Doctor?'

'Her prints are gone, and if I were a betting woman, I'd suggest they were burned off *before* she was set alight, because the blistering is extreme compared to the rest of her hands and arms.' She showed Brook and Noble another photograph. 'See how her right hand was partially protected from the flames but still the fingertips are incinerated.'

'Post mortem?' asked Brook, squinting.

'Undoubtedly,' nodded Petty. 'I'm guessing he had time.'

'Thorough,' said Brook.

'Cold would be a better word.'

'Blowtorch? Acid?' enquired Noble.

'You'll have to wait for more tests, but continuing the tradesman theme . . .' Petty shrugged the rest.

'Blowtorch,' said Noble, arching an eyebrow at Brook.

'I've been saving the best until last.' Petty walked them over to a computer terminal. 'The victim had a tattoo on her upper right arm. Whoever killed her must have believed it could lead to an ID, so instead of trusting the fire to get the job done, he blowtorched that as well.' She tapped a key to bring up another colour close-up of the victim's skin. 'See anything?'

'Burnt skin,' said Noble.

'Third-degree burnt skin to be precise,' said Petty.

'So it's not superficial,' said Brook.

'No. The burn extends through all layers of the dermis. However, our killer reckoned without the latest forensic toys.' Petty tapped a key for the next picture. 'This is a shot taken with a video spectral comparator.'

'I can see lines,' said Noble, pointing. 'And those are letters underneath.'

'Right.'

'I've read about this,' said Brook. 'Different pigments react differently under filtered lights.'

'And will become luminescent under different parts of the light spectrum despite superficial attempts to obscure them,' continued Petty.

'Even after the skin is blowtorched?' asked Noble.

'As long as the ink is still present in the tissue, yes. You have to fool around with the filters. Some pigments react best to infrared, some to ultraviolet . . .'

'All mod cons.'

'We aim to please. Watch.' Petty tapped another key and the image on the burned flesh changed slightly.

'It's a flag,' said Noble.

'And that's red ink, and I think that's supposed to be a white eagle,' said Petty, pointing.

'P-O-L-S-K-I,' said Brook, reading the six-letter word beneath the rectangular flag.

'Poland,' breathed Noble. 'Interpol was right.'

'Interpol?' queried Petty.

'We'd been working on a series of disappearances before this body turned up,' said Brook.

'I hope the tattoo narrows it down.'

'Not nearly enough,' sighed Brook, his mind now alive to the possibilities he'd so far managed to dismiss. The abduction and murder of young overseas females was no longer idle speculation.

'We have three missing Polish YWFs on the books,'

explained Noble. Dr Petty's head dropped, her pride at showing off her skills forgotten.

'And now an actual Polish victim,' said Brook.

'Do you have to be Polish to have the flag tattooed on your arm?' asked Noble. 'I mean, Hell's Angels walk round with the Confederate flag on their jackets. Doesn't mean they whistle Dixie.'

'He's got a point,' said Petty, pulling more photographs from the envelope. 'She could have met a Polish boy on holiday and had it done.' Brook and Noble looked at an image of the victim's inner mouth, relatively undamaged by fire. 'However, I've done dental shots for twenty years and I can usually recognise British work when I see it. And I think this is foreign.'

'Thank you,' said Brook, preparing to leave. 'You'll email your report? We might need basic physiognomy to compare against our missing girls, give us a nudge in the right direction.'

'You'll have it today.' Petty smiled sympathetically. 'You look exhausted, the pair of you. Get some rest.'

Two sets of bloodshot eyes returned the blankest of acknowledgements before Brook and Noble trudged out into the corridor.

Back in daylight, Brook squinted at his watch. 'Get a taxi back to St Mary's, John . . .'

'You're not coming?'

'Not yet. Follow up your Interpol enquiry on Ostrowsky and widen it to include his brother. They're coming in this afternoon, and if there's anything we need to know, I'd like to know it before we talk to them. Criminal and arrest records a priority. And if you get time, go over the profiles on the three missing Polish girls. See if there's any mention of tattoos; compare heights and hair colours from Dr Petty's report when it lands.'

'The profiles could pre-date the tattoo,' said Noble.

'I know,' said Brook. 'But check anyway. And get Cooper to start the ball rolling on dental records.'

'In Europe?' said Noble. 'That could take weeks.'

Brook let his expression say *I know* for him. 'Do it for all the missing women. The two Irish girls should be easier at least. That reminds me. The first Irish girl . . .'

'Bernadette Murphy?'

'Wasn't her aunt a nurse here?'

'Mary Finnegan?' said Noble. 'Three years ago, yes. What do I do about Caitlin's family? And Laurie Teague?'

'What do you mean?'

'That's not Caitlin's body in there,' said Noble. 'It's the one thing we *do* know and I think they deserve to be told.'

Brook was silent for a moment. 'Yes, they do, John. But not yet. We're entitled to wait for confirmation. We've got the Ostrowskys coming in, and if the victim's nationality *isn't* a coincidence, we don't want them on the defensive any more than they already will be.'

'So let them think we have Caitlin's body,' nodded Noble.

'Excuse me, Doctor. I'm looking for the two police officers who were brought in last night.'

The white-coated woman turned. 'And you are?'

'DI Brook, Derby CID.' Brook flashed his warrant card, dropping his eyes to her ID tag and betraying recognition. 'You're Dr Cowell. You worked at the university.'

'Do I know you?'

'Your name came up in an investigation.' The frost descended over her attractive face and Brook smiled to reassure. 'You were Daniela Cassetti's campus doctor last year.'

'Daniela Cassetti,' repeated Dr Cowell slowly. 'I remember her. What of it?'

'This is a bit off-the-cuff, but what can you tell me about her?'

Cowell glared at Brook. 'Not a thing. Haven't you heard of doctor–patient—'

'She's missing.'

'Missing? Since when?'

'We're not sure,' admitted Brook. 'But she spent two terms at Derby University and never returned for the summer term.'

'Yes, I know,' said Dr Cowell. 'She went back to Italy, I believe.'

'That may have been her intention, but according to her family, she never arrived,' said Brook. 'Interpol declared her a missing person a year later.'

'A year?' exclaimed Cowell.

Brook shrugged. 'People travelling abroad tend not to be missed straight away. So if you have any information about her health or state of mind, it would—'

'I'm sorry,' said Cowell. 'But there are rules and you'll need some kind of warrant. And even if I wanted to help, I don't have my records here.'

Brook held her eye for a moment. Pushed for time, he decided not to argue and the doctor made to walk away. 'What about my officers?'

Cowell turned and nodded beyond Brook. 'Last cubicle on the right. The head injury is out of danger and should make a full recovery.'

'One more thing. I know it's a big hospital, but you wouldn't happen to know a Nurse Finnegan, would you?'

'Mary Finnegan?'

'That's right.'

'She left two or three years ago,' said Cowell.

'You wouldn't happen to know where . . . ?'

'Right again,' said Cowell, her voice clipped, already walking away. 'I wouldn't. But feel free to speak to Personnel.'

Twenty-Two

CAITLIN WOKE TO THE SHOCK of cold water hitting her. She was lying on the rough concrete floor of the barn, being hosed down. The water was freezing and she could barely move, so tightly was she bound, but she knew she had to stop the powerful jet choking her or she might drown right there and then. She found she could get a little purchase with her feet, and managed to push her soaking body round a few degrees to take the full force on the back of her neck.

A few seconds later, the water stopped.

'Getting your head right?'

Unable to speak through the gasps for breath, she nodded as best she could. 'Getting . . .' she spluttered. The jet started again.

A few minutes later, the barrage stopped and the barn door closed on its smooth rail, taking the light with it. Every fibre of her body screamed in pain from her collision with the van. Worse, it was impossible to adjust her position to ease her aching muscles.

'Getting my head right,' she screamed.

But her head wasn't right. None of her was. Her left side

was bruised and battered, her feet were cold, her hair felt dank and itchy on her scalp and she stank to high heaven, despite her daily soaking. Not surprisingly, she'd started to sneeze, her nose running and her throat sore. Having lost all track of time, she felt alone and powerless.

At that moment, she began to wish for death. And why shouldn't she? Her God had abandoned her, had been vengeful and guided her back into the path of her abductor, and it wasn't hard to guess why.

'Kill me now,' she whispered.

Weak from hunger, her mouth and lips sealed by dehydration, Caitlin woke as usual to the shock of cold water hitting her. She peeled her lips apart and gulped at the spray to moisturise her parched mouth. But something had changed. When she tried to shield herself against the jet with her hands, she found that they moved. Her legs too.

'Stand up,' came the barked command.

With no little difficulty, caused by light-headedness and lack of exercise, she managed to comply. To her shock, she discovered she was in bra and knickers, her clothes cut off and dropped in a heap beside her. Unconscious, she'd been unbound and stripped, and now freezing water was blinding her.

She felt something hit her in the midriff and looked down to see a large tablet of soap.

'Wash!' said the man.

Caitlin reached down and picked up the rough soap and began to rub it over her body, slowly at first but then with mounting enthusiasm – her hair, her face, her sticky underarms and what her mum referred to as the *nether regions*. She tore off the grubby plaster and gingerly washed her damaged arm, then gratefully cleansed her soiled crotch with her back to the hose.

When she was finished, she faced her abductor and dropped the soap behind her, dimly aware that it might make an effective cosh if only she had a sock to swing it in.

'Turn round.'

Caitlin obliged, and a few seconds later, after a pounding between the shoulder blades, the cascade ended. A towel hit her head and she grabbed at it greedily, drying herself down, scouring her skin with the rough material. When she'd finished, she held it to her face and revelled in the fragrance of cleanliness.

She heard the door roll closed and turned to see it fastened, her captor gone. A towelling dressing gown hung on a hook on the wall, a plastic bag with it.

Caitlin pulled on the robe. There was a packet of tissues in each pocket. She tore one open, blew her nose. She emptied the plastic bag – water and more cooked chicken. She took a gulp of water, then tore the chicken apart, trying to eat delicately, knowing that days without food might result in her throwing up if she ate too fast. She finished the food and took another satisfying draught of water. Within seconds her vision began to play tricks and it seemed the world before her eyes was made of melting wax, which was being poured into a very deep, dark box.

Caitlin held up the bottle, her last sight the white residue in the bottom.

'Bastard,' she mumbled, dropping the bottle, and, head swimming, staggered towards the pens and the ease of a soft landing. She didn't make it.

* * *

Mitch lay in the bed a few feet from her chair, his head swathed in bandages, his arm attached to tubes. He seemed to be breathing rhythmically, which comforted her as much as the brief word and thumbs-up he'd given her before succumbing to the medication.

Angie Banach finished her prayer and crossed herself before resting her hands on her stomach. The thought of the young life growing in her womb overwhelmed her. She closed her eyes and released a huge sigh. *Things had been going so well.*

'That explains the dizzy spell at least,' she mumbled as she stretched.

Opening her eyes again, she was shocked to see DI Brook standing at the other side of the cubicle.

'Feeling better?'

Banach scanned his expression for any loading in the question. There didn't seem to be any hint that he knew. *I'm being stupid. Why would the doctors tell him? There's a protocol. They wouldn't give out medical information without consent.*

'A little dizzy maybe,' she replied to cover her tracks.

'But no concussion.'

'No. Sir.'

'The surgeon tells me the prognosis for Constable Ryan is good.' Brook turned his gaze on the stricken officer.

'No thanks to me. Sir.' Banach felt distinctly uncomfortable in bare feet and flimsy hospital pyjamas. Brook considered her and smiled.

'Something funny?' she demanded, remembering their battle of wills the previous evening.

Unfazed, Brook's smile widened. 'People are funny.'

'You mean me?' she replied, anger catching in her throat.

'Yes, I mean you,' replied Brook, a sharper edge to his weary voice.

'I'm glad you're getting a laugh,' she dared to reply, unable to look at him, expecting the rebuke she was earning.

'So am I.'

She fumbled for the right words. 'If this is about me climbing into that building before calling it in . . .'

'See that,' said Brook, holding out his right hand for inspection.

Banach stared at Brook's outstretched hand then back at him. 'I don't understand.'

'Skin graft,' explained Brook. 'I was laid up for five months after a car fire. You see, I thought my daughter might be inside, so I tried to get it open.'

'And was she?'

'No, thankfully. But I was injured in the line of duty nonetheless. Like you.'

'Okay,' she said uncertainly.

'But if I hadn't thought she was in that burning car, I wouldn't have gone near it. You, however, with no thought for your own safety, and no personal profit, climbed into that building.' Banach looked down at her bare feet. 'You're the thin blue line, Constable, and I'm in awe.' She looked up into the inspector's eyes. '*Huj w dupe policji*,' said Brook, grimacing at his poor impersonation of Ostrowsky's giant bodyguard.

Banach's half-smile disappeared. 'Screw the police?'

'You speak Polish,' said Brook.

'You too. Almost.'

'Just a phrase I picked up.' He looked her up and down. 'Your personnel file says you want to move over to CID – eventually.'

'Maybe.'

'When will you be ready for duty?'

'My uniform was bagged.'

'But you have civilian clothes in your locker.'

'My mum brought some in, yes.'

'Good. When are you discharged?'

'Two hours ago,' she said. 'But I wanted to be here for—'

'Constable Ryan will be fine,' said Brook. 'Gather your belongings and let's go and get a decent cup of tea.'

'Go where?'

'You're joining my squad until you're reassigned.' Brook watched for her reaction. 'If that appeals.'

She took a moment to answer. 'Okay,' she said uncertainly.

'Don't hurt yourself turning any cartwheels.'

'Sorry.' For the first time she smiled in his presence. 'I'm flattered, of course, it's just the last ten hours have been a bit . . . full on.'

'I can imagine. I hope your clothes are suitable.' Brook paused as she ran the rule over his shapeless worn suit and faded overcoat. She arched an eyebrow.

'We could always stop at an Oxfam shop on the way,' she muttered, leaving the cubicle.

'You and DS Noble will get on like a house on fire,' mumbled Brook as she passed.

'I'm bored.'

Nick's monotone gave Jake pause but he didn't look up. 'Read a book.' He was sitting with his feet up on the tasselled sofa, unable to get comfortable on the cheap foam cushions.

'I can't read.'

'You're not in school now, Nick.'

'What does that mean?'

'It means I know you *can* read when it suits you.'

'No I can't.'

Jake looked up. *I'm not going to argue with you.* 'There are magazines.'

'Yeah, about knitting and the royal family,' snapped Nick.

'Suit yourself.'

'I wanna go down the Intu, look in the shops.'

'Keep your voice down.'

'I wanna go down the Intu,' said Nick, louder. He glared at the string round Jake's neck where the door key dangled.

'You're not leaving this flat to stare at shit you don't need and can't afford,' answered Jake, patting his T-shirt and giving Nick the eyes. *And I don't want to have this conversation again.*

'I got money,' replied Nick, sour-faced.

'Yeah, and pigs shit bacon sandwiches,' muttered Jake.

Nick laughed and repeated the sentence. 'Pigs shit bacon sandwiches.' He laughed some more, his discontent temporarily forgotten. 'What you reading?'

Jake looked at the cover of his book as though unaware. 'Agatha Christie. *Death on the Nile.*'

'What's it about?'

'It's about all these rich people on a boat who don't think they're rich enough. They've been a bit dodgy so they might have to kill some richer woman to get her money and shut her up. Problem is, there's some Frog detective on the boat who's all over 'em like a rash.'

'Any good?'

'Not bad.' Jake looked off into space and smiled.

'What?'

'You wouldn't understand.'

'Tell me.'

Jake looked around at the room's austerity – the ancient lightshade, the few drab furnishings, the mildew, the yellowing wallpaper beginning to peel. 'I thought it was a recent thing, but this book was written in nineteen thirty-seven.'

'Wow. When was that?'

'A long time ago. But even then the rich pricks never knew when they had enough money.'

Nick sniggered. 'Rich pricks.'

'Yeah, you laugh,' smiled Jake. 'It's all there is to do when you see where we are.' He stared blindly at the faded carpet. 'Where we've always been.' He looked back at Nick and shook his head. 'I had plans, Nick. I'm sorry I couldn't have given you a better life.'

Nick smiled. 'Rich pricks. They the ones gonna fuck us over?' Jake laughed, which sent Nick into waves of hysteria.

'Always.'

'Rich like Mr Ost . . .' Nick tailed away, unable to find the pronunciation.

Jake's merriment dissipated rapidly. 'Yeah, just like Ostrowsky.'

'And like Max?'

Jake glared malevolently at Nick, and the younger brother bowed his head. He'd said the wrong thing. Sulkily he picked up his inert PS2 and fiddled with the buttons, glanced over at his brother, an innocent expression on his face.

'No,' said Jake, not looking up.

'I didn't say nothing.'

'You were going to ask me for the batteries.'

'No I wasn't.' A pause. 'But can I have them?'

'After tea,' said Jake.

Nick sighed in frustration. 'How come there's no telly?'

'There probably was, but someone took it.'

'Time is it?'

'You've got the watch,' said Jake.

'It's stopped.'

'Sorry. It was only cheap.'

'If we went out, we could find out the time.'

Jake took a breath. 'I've told you we can't do that. The police are looking for us.'

'We can't do nothing.'

'Anything. We can't do anything.' Jake smiled at his pouting brother. 'Why don't you read a book?'

'Can't read.'

Jake pulled a face and wandered over to the window to look through the crack in the curtain. 'They're still in and out of the Cream. Must have pulled it off my references.' He turned, shaking his head. 'Thank fuck I couldn't find those keys.'

Nick sniggered. 'Thank *fuck*.'

Jake smiled but then looked back towards the window. 'Wonder where they went.' He looked back at Nick, who suddenly picked up an old copy of *Majesty* magazine to flick through.

Brook listened to the recording one more time before closing the lid of his laptop. He gulped down the last of his cold tea, then massaged his eyes, trying to ignore the musty odour beginning to envelop him. He yearned to get home and soak in the bath for an hour but knew that rest and recreation were some way off. At least the situation hadn't escalated and turned into a spree, which was always a possibility with fleeing suspects.

He finished his questions for interview and scribbled a few notes for the afternoon briefing before settling back in his chair to look around the incident room. A sudden burst of spring sunshine illuminated the mass of dust particles hovering in the air like distant galaxies in a NASA photograph, adding to the sense of time suspended.

Cooper was busy downloading images from the post-mortem and pinning them up on the boards. Pride of place was given to the tattoo from the victim's upper arm. DC Read was chasing Daniela Cassetti's medical records from the university. Morton and Smee had brought through the display boards from the smaller incident room now that the victim's nationality had been identified and a connection to Brook and Noble's Interpol enquiry had been established.

Banach was compiling a list of Bar Polski employees with the help of the Inland Revenue database and Noble was poring over his monitor, racing against time to get what information he could from foreign police forces before the Ostrowsky brothers arrived for interview.

Considering the mayhem of the last thirty-six hours, the place was eerily quiet, as though the world had stopped on its axis for a few seconds. It seemed to Brook there was a moment like this in every investigation, where time appeared to slow and he felt the peace within the eye of the storm. It occurred after the initial flurry of activity, when the case had settled down into a bureaucratic chasing-up of all the leads. In these moments, Brook often wondered what would happen if he followed his instincts and just stepped away from the madness to go walk in the sunshine for a few hours.

A glance at the happy faces of the three Polish girls on the photo array brought him back. One of them was doomed.

'Sir.' Brook's reverie was broken by Morton brandishing a piece of paper. 'The lab boys working the van found a fingernail inside one of the workman's gloves. They're working up the DNA and trying to match it to Jake Tanner.'

'It could just as easily be Max's,' said Brook.

'Which wouldn't be much use as it's his van.'

'I know. Be nice to have his DNA on file, though. And his brother's.'

'We could ask for a sample when they get here,' said Noble.

'They're not stupid enough to volunteer,' said Brook. 'If we could arrest Max for something . . .'

'Take a drinks order when they arrive,' suggested Morton. 'Save jumping through all the hoops.'

'That's a little underhand,' said Brook. 'Did they check the gloves against the fibres in the victim's throat?'

'They're a match.'

'What about the hammer?'

'Looks likely. They found blood, which they're testing against the victim's.'

The phone disturbed Brook's train of thought. He picked up the receiver. 'Interview Three. On our way.' He replaced the receiver on its cradle. 'John.'

Noble heaved his wheeled chair away from his desk, like a kid riding a supermarket trolley. Getting to his feet, the chair still moving, he brandished his notes, stumbling over the pronunciation again.

'Grzegorz Ostrowsky. Businessman. Forty-three years old. Married in Warsaw, nineteen ninety-five. Wife and child died three years later during childbirth. Single ever since. He's been an importer/exporter for fourteen years, so you can probably guess how the authorities know him.'

'Smuggling?' offered Brook.

'Right. He used to trade in China and Hong Kong but now works exclusively in the UK, where he has three Polish minimarts – one in Derby, two in Nottingham. According to the PSTD – the Polish arm of Interpol's database network – he was arrested by the Polish national police in 2002 when a batch of heroin with a street value of two million pounds was discovered during a routine inspection of one of his containers arriving in Gdansk from Hong Kong.'

'But he got off.'

'Why do you say that?'

'If he'd served serious time, I doubt he'd be allowed to settle in the UK without his past being flagged up for us to pick over.'

'You might be overestimating the Home Office and the Borders Agency, but you're right,' said Noble. 'He was released two weeks later when an employee in his Hong Kong office confessed to illegally hiding the package in the container.'

'Convenient.'

'Very,' agreed Noble. 'The employee was sentenced to twenty years in a Hong Kong prison, though he only served half.'

'Two million pounds?'

'Not much in terms of weight,' said Noble. 'Barely fifty kilos at today's prices, and it's gotten cheaper. So in smuggling terms it's a drop in the ocean. But that's the clever bit. I had a friend on the narcotics squad in Liverpool who calculated that smugglers could fit over a billion quid's worth of gear into one container if they wanted. But they never do, partly because of the losses involved if your container gets picked out for inspection and partly because smaller batches can be made to look like the work of one or two people . . .'

'Instead of a cartel,' nodded Brook. 'Makes sense.'

'And it's more deniable in court,' said Noble. 'Easier to pass the buck on to a rogue employee trying to line his own pockets at the expense of a victimised employer.'

'You think Ostrowsky pulled the same scam?'

'Seems plausible,' said Noble.

Brook nodded towards the photographs of Nicola Serota, Valerie Gliszczynska and Adrianna Bakula. 'Any mention of people-trafficking in his record?'

'They were hardly trafficked,' said Noble. 'And we can forget Valerie and Adrianna for now,' he added, tapping his pen on the first picture. 'Nicola Serota is our new front-runner. She's the right height according to Petty's PM measurements. The other two are taller.'

'Prioritise her dental records,' said Brook. 'But if that *is* Nicola in the mortuary, it means she's been kept alive some-where for over a year.' He checked his watch as he reached for his jacket. 'We'd better not leave them sweating too long. You haven't mentioned Max.'

'A couple of arrests for drunkenness and fighting and three for sexual assault,' said Noble. 'No convictions, though.'

'Interesting.'

Angie Banach walked over in her slim-fitting black trouser suit and handed Brook a sheet of paper. 'Apart from Jake, the only other English employee is barman Ashley Devonshire. Tymon Symanski and Max Ostrowsky are the only others on the Bar Polski payroll. No female staff, officially at least.'

'Thanks,' said Brook. 'Ready?'

'I think so,' she replied, taking a deep breath.

Brook walked with her, Noble following. 'You're not a DC,

but the plain clothes will suggest it. So I'll introduce you as Constable Banner. When you get in there, don't speak or react to the interviewees or anything they say and don't take notes. Just listen and remember.'

As Brook walked on, she fell into step with Noble. 'Why Banner?'

'He doesn't want them to know you're Polish,' said Noble. 'If they say something incriminating in Polish and claim entrapment later, he can say he mispronounced your name.'

'But if we're taping it, we could just as easily get it translated,' said Banach. 'Why would they risk incriminating themselves?'

'They likely won't,' said Noble. 'But it's amazing how many people forget there's a tape rolling.'

Twenty-Three

TAKING A LONG BREATH, AS though she'd just surfaced from a deep pool, Caitlin opened her eyes. She blinked to try and see, but all was darkness. The gag was back in her mouth, held by another plaster. It took her a second to realise she was no longer cold and damp, and that the background smell of manure and straw was gone.

She was not in the barn but indoors, warm and cosseted, sitting upright on soft cushions. And she was clothed. Her left side still ached from where she had been struck by the van, but it felt better away from the cold concrete. In fact, if it weren't for her bonds, trussing her up like a chicken once more, she'd be almost comfortable, having only recently wished herself dead.

She tried to assess her situation calmly. Her hands were in front, held against her legs by stiff leather straps, firm and unyielding. Legs and feet were strapped too, unable to move more than a couple of inches, but at least she could support herself with her right elbow propped on the arm of the chair or sofa.

She tested her bonds and struggled to get more play for her legs, but the rubbing hurt her bare ankles. On her right hand was what felt like a stiff glove, which was too big for her hand. She was aware of something hard resting on her palm, but she couldn't see what it was or feel it through the material.

She could hear background noise – water in the pipes, the hum of electricity and that sealed-off stillness of being indoors. Then something struck her. Sliding an inch along the sofa, her clothing felt wrong. When she wriggled again, she felt a strange sensation along her buttocks and groin. Her crotch felt damp and sweaty. She'd been dressed in some kind of padded nappy. Somebody had removed her knickers to re-dress her in a skirt with a diaper underneath. Why? Her brain juddered and images of being undressed filled her head.

She wanted to be sick and her breathing quickened, but with a gag in her mouth she feared choking, which would only generate more panic. And to vomit could prove fatal.

Get control, girl. Get control. You might finally be about to get screwed.

Bizarrely, the possibility calmed Caitlin. At least that would normalise the pervert, show that the man was after the same thing all the other drooling wankers had ever wanted from her.

She flexed her shoulders as best she could and felt the comfort of material against her skin, the pressure of her bra. Whoever had removed her knickers hadn't wanted to see her breasts. She remembered a joke about redirecting a new boyfriend's hands from knickers up to bra. *Oi! Tits first! I'm no slag.*

The smile died a quick death and she hung her head as far as the strap holding it up would allow. She stared sightlessly at her bare legs in the darkness, feeling the cotton skirt on her thighs. Something she couldn't put her finger on tried to penetrate her consciousness.

Before she could rack her brains, a sudden vibration distracted her. It was the small object in her gloved palm. She turned her hand over. With a pant of excitement she saw the glowing display of an old-style chunky mobile phone.

Flexing her wrist, she was able to use the pale green light to illuminate her situation. It only took a second. She was sitting on a sofa in a large room. The furnishings were stripped down and basic. Wooden floor. Traditional fireplace. A large TV on one wall and what must have been a window shrouded by heavy curtains.

Her body was held by a construction of thick leather straps, her constraints enforced by traditional belt buckles only bigger. The overall effect reminded her of prisoners on death row being strapped to the electric chair. The analogy dispatched another flutter of anxiety through her when she saw the cable winding its way around her waist.

She held the phone as close as she could manage, gripping it hard as her gloved thumb searched for the keys. They weren't there. By the light of the LCD display, she could see that the bottom half of the phone was swathed in tape until any discernible contours from the keypad had been obliterated. The tape in turn attached the phone to the thick suede gardener's glove on her hand. She probed for the seam of the tape to get to the keys but it was impossible to unpick it through the heavy material.

A violent seizure stiffened every sinew as an electric current passed through her, and she bit down on the gag and her tongue. When the current ceased a split second later, she opened her watering eyes to the phone displaying a message.

Don't do that bitch or u get zapped we can staple it to ur hand if u prefer.

Her head sagged on to her chest. The phone vibrated again.

These are the rules.
1. Don't ever speak in this room. Ever. U get zapped and worse if u do.
2. When HE's there u smile. Be nice.
3. Dinner bell goes and u sit upright like U R now. This is the dinner position. Sit still and smile.
4. If he wants to kiss u or touch your tits u smile like u like it. More later. PS Nice pussy Kitty. LOL.

Caitlin closed her eyes and sobbed quietly in the dark.

'Detective Inspector Brook, Sergeant Noble and Constable Banner in the room,' said Brook. He looked up at Ostrowsky reclining on his chair, cross-legged, gazing at Banach, then up to the camera in a corner of the room. 'Please identify yourselves for the tape, gentlemen.'

Ostrowsky looked coolly back at Brook. 'Grzegorz Ostrowsky.' He glanced at his brother and, speaking briefly in Polish, nodded towards the tape.

'Makszi Ostrowsky,' said the younger man, half standing to lean into the machine. He was nervous and looked uncomfortable in a suit and white shirt, the pinkness of his blood-dappled cheeks testifying to a recent shave.

A uniformed officer arrived with a tray of hot drinks and set them down for the occupants of the room to help themselves. Both brothers eyed the cups but made no move to take one.

'Jeremy Patterson, solicitor for both parties,' said the smooth-looking man on the end chair. He opened a briefcase and took out a plastic wallet; held it out for Brook, who kept his arms folded. 'I refer Inspector Brook to the documents pertaining to Mr Ostrowsky's stolen vehicle while it was in the possession of his brother Max.' Eventually Noble took the wallet, barely examining the contents, while Brook stared between Ostrowsky and Patterson. Max was too uncomfortable to maintain eye contact.

'I'd like to hear details of the theft from Mr Ostrowsky,' said Brook.

'Max speaks poor English,' said Ostrowsky.

'If I may proceed on behalf of my client,' continued Patterson, with a critical glance at Brook. 'You'll see the subsequent insurance claim for the vehicle, which is currently pending. The log book and insurance document were unfortunately in the van, but you'll find a copy of both in the wallet plus the account of the theft given to the attending officer.'

Patterson had changed his position to engage with Noble, hoping for a more civil reception. He helped himself to a beaker of tea. 'As you can see from the police report, the vehicle was left by my client in a public street at six p.m. on the evening of April twenty-second, near his new apartment on Arboretum Street, and he didn't return to the vehicle until six thirty the following morning – a window of opportunity for the thief of over twelve hours. I'm sure I don't need to remind you that the stats concerning theft of trade vehicles reflect a much higher attrition rate than those for private vehicles.'

Brook flicked a glance towards Patterson but said nothing.

'I've also taken the liberty of noting down my clients' movements on the night in question, as a formality. Mr Ostrowsky left—'

'What happened when you discovered the van had been stolen?' Brook asked Max directly.

The younger brother gazed at Brook, slowly realising he was being addressed. '*Nie rozumiem.*' He drew out a packet of cigarettes and patted his jacket in vain for a lighter.

'He doesn't understand,' said Patterson. 'Please speak to me, Inspector . . .'

Max gestured at Noble's lighter on the desk.

'No smoking,' said Noble.

'*Nie rozumiem,*' repeated Max.

'He doesn't understand, John,' said Brook. He picked up Noble's lighter and lobbed it in a gentle arc towards Max, who flicked up his left hand to catch it, then proceeded to light his cigarette.

Grzegorz's thin smile disappeared and he snatched the lighter from his brother and plucked the cigarette from him, extinguishing it between his finger and thumb. He extracted a cigarette packet of his own and thrust in Max's cigarette, turning to his brother. '*Idiota. Zakaz palenia.*' He addressed the solicitor. 'Hurry this up, please. I've got a business to run.'

'Inspector Brook,' said Patterson, 'in your own news conference about the murdered girl, the men who stole my client's van were clearly identified.'

'One of whom was your client's employee,' said Brook.

'Ex-employee,' said Patterson.

'Not at the time of the theft,' said Brook. 'Right now I want to know what happened when your client discovered his van missing.'

'He called the police and reported the vehicle stolen,' said Patterson, impatiently.

'Before he rang his brother?'

Patterson hesitated, sensing a problem. 'That's right.'

'With his poor command of English.' No one spoke. Ostrowsky maintained eye contact with Brook. He seemed unconcerned. Brook opened his laptop and clicked on the touchpad, looking back at Ostrowsky.

'*Emergency. Which service, please?*'

'*Police*,' answered a male voice, with a distinct foreign accent. When put through to the police call centre, he answered the opening question with '*My van stolen – in Arboretum Street.*'

'*What's your name, sir?*'

'*My name is Max Ostrowsky.*'

'That proves nothing, Inspector,' interrupted Ostrowsky, still able to smile. 'I told you. Max speaks a little English. He knows his street name.'

'He can conjugate verbs,' said Brook. 'And I'm pleased to see you now know where your brother lives.'

'Inspector Brook . . .' began Patterson.

'No,' said Ostrowsky, putting a hand across the solicitor. 'Let me speak. Inspector Brook, my brother and I are immigrants. I am sorry I lied to you about Max's accommodations . . .'

'His mobile phone too,' added Noble.

'It's true,' agreed Ostrowsky. 'I was wary. My brother and I work in a foreign country and we are not wanted here. People give us filthy looks when they hear us talking. We take their jobs, they say, though I don't see many British who work as hard. And we don't know the police and how they take care of their business.' He looked at Banach standing against the side wall. She moved to the wall behind the interviewees.

'And to clear up a murder you think we'd pin it on the nearest immigrant?' said Noble.

'I don't know,' said Ostrowsky. 'But when you came to

Bar Polski, you were also not truthful with me.'

'We may not have told you what we knew, but that's normal procedure, and at least we didn't lie,' argued Noble.

'I think I'd call pretending to be a building inspector somewhat of a deception,' said Patterson.

Brook held up a pacifying hand. 'I assume the upshot of all this is that your brother can speak for himself.'

'Max will answer now,' said Ostrowsky. 'Tell them why you called the police before me.'

'Yes, I call police,' said Max.

'The call didn't come in until seven that morning,' said Noble. 'Yet you claim to have discovered the theft half an hour earlier.'

Max turned to his brother and received a quick translation. 'Yes. I try to find van. I think my brother will be crazy with me. And I worry about insurance.' He hung his head. 'I leave tools in. I should take out but I was tired.'

'There,' said Ostrowsky.

'When you parked the vehicle the previous evening, was there a dead body in the back?' asked Noble.

'Is that a serious question?' said Patterson.

Noble smiled. 'For the record.'

'No,' said Max, shaking his head. 'No body.'

'What exactly *was* in the van?'

Max threw his head back to think. 'Tools for electrician. Some petrol. Boots. Gloves.'

'A blowtorch,' said Brook.

'Yes.'

'Why does an electrician need a blowtorch?' asked Noble.

'Sometimes we put wire into wall and find old pipes,' explained Max. 'We must take out.'

'A hammer?'

Max nodded. 'Yes. In my tool bag.'

'A bunch of keys.'

Max hesitated, thinking. 'Yes.'

'And when did you tell your brother about the theft?'

'Later,' said Max. 'Don't know time.'

'I managed to contact Max that afternoon – following your visit to Bar Polski,' said Ostrowsky to Brook. 'Then Max came to the bar to speak with me.'

'So you didn't know about the van until DS Noble and I told you?'

'You know I didn't.'

'We only know you took the theft very lightly,' said Noble.

Ostrowsky shrugged. 'It's a van. Obviously I had no idea someone had been killed. Or Jake was involved. You didn't say or I wouldn't take so lightly.'

'Did you know Jake Tanner, your brother's new barman?' said Noble, addressing Max.

Max shook his head. 'Not to speak but I see. I can say hello. No more. I don't go to bar. I work hard.'

'Jake had been at Bar Polski less than two weeks. I needed an experienced man to stock the bar,' said Ostrowsky. 'Jake applied. He was smart, knew about drinks. I gave him the job.'

'Did he provide references?'

'Testimonials? Yes, some. He was presentable, well-spoken. I hired him.'

'Did he mention he had a criminal record?'

'He was in prison?' Ostrowsky's surprise seemed genuine.

'We'll take that as a no,' said Brook.

Ostrowsky shook his head. 'What did he do?'

'A minor conviction,' said Brook, unwilling to gift information to a suspect. 'A short period of custody ensued.'

'Vehicle theft, by any chance?' insinuated Patterson.

'And how was Jake doing in his new job?' asked Brook, ignoring Patterson's jibe.

'Good,' said Ostrowsky. 'He worked hard. Didn't miss a day until the morning you called.'

'He was trying to impress?'

'I suppose so.'

'Stealing Max's van can't have impressed you,' said Brook.

'*My* van,' corrected Ostrowsky. 'Max borrowed it for his work.'

'Would Jake have made that distinction?'

'Sorry?'

'Would Jake have known it was your van and not Max's?'

'Possibly, no. Possibly, yes. You'll have to ask him.'

'We intend to,' said Noble.

'Two weeks is not a lot of time to develop a grudge,' said Brook.

'Grudge?'

'Well, he stole your van to dump a body. Why would he do that?'

'Just a wild guess, Inspector, but after committing a murder, I'd suggest Mr Tanner was desperate,' said Patterson. 'He knew my clients. He might have found out where the van would be overnight and took it. Seems obvious.'

'Who knows why people do what they do?' added Ostrowsky, his cold eyes boring into Brook's. 'Maybe Jake didn't know the van belonged to me. Maybe he stole it because he saw it and he's a thief. He and his brother lived no more than three hundred metres from Arboretum Street.'

Brook looked up. 'You know where Jake and his brother live.'

'Of course my client knows,' said Patterson, haughtily. 'The address would be on all the references, and they'd need it for payroll.'

'It's one thing to have someone's address,' said Brook. 'Quite another to know where it is, especially if you're new to Derby.'

'I'm not so new, but you're right,' said Ostrowsky. 'I didn't know until last night. When I saw Jake was involved, it became my business to know, so I looked at a map.'

'So when we visited you at Bar Polski yesterday morning and you became agitated at the non-appearance of a staff member,' said Brook, 'that was Jake.' Ostrowsky nodded.

'Quite a show of temper,' said Noble. 'Did you treat him badly?'

'He was new,' shrugged Ostrowsky. 'He seemed good at his job. That's it. My show of temper is exactly that – a show. I'm a businessman, so I show my people I mean business to make them work hard for my benefit; for theirs too.' He leaned forward, wagging a finger. 'And I pay good money for good people. You can ask.'

'I believe you,' said Brook. 'I'm told you inspired great loyalty when you were trading in South-East Asia.'

Ostrowsky's expression turned to pure ice. He toyed with an answer, choosing instead to glance across to his solicitor.

'Is there any relevance to that remark, Inspector?' said Patterson. 'If you're suggesting some past impropriety, then I must strongly object. My clients are EU nationals and the fact that they're here in this country is evidence of their good character.'

'I'm heartened.'

'I really don't like your tone,' said Patterson.

'Don't leave without a complaint form,' replied Brook.

'It's okay,' said Ostrowsky, holding out a hand to Patterson. 'We're grown men. And the inspector must be under pressure to get results. Are we finished?'

'Let's talk about Jake's brother Nick,' said Noble. 'Sources have told us they were inseparable. In fact, Jake had trouble getting permanent work because he often had to take Nick with him.'

Ostrowsky nodded. 'Yes. I told your colleague last night. He seemed a pleasant young man. He was around for a day or two when Jake started work, but I didn't speak to him.'

'What about you?' said Brook, addressing Max.

Max shook his head. 'I don't go to bar. I work.'

'You're on the payroll.'

'Please?'

'Max fixed the wiring,' said Ostrowsky. 'Most of the work has been done, but he's on retainer.'

'Must be nice for you, working in a bar,' said Noble.

'What's that supposed to mean?' said Patterson.

'We understand from our Polish colleagues that Max likes a drink or two after a hard day,' said Noble.

'If you have no sensible questions to ask, we'll leave,' said Patterson.

'It's okay,' said Max, staring coldly at Noble before breaking into a huge grin. 'Sure. But I can't afford to drink Bar Polski. I go pub if I need.'

'Is that because Bar Polski doesn't employ any female staff?' asked Brook.

'Female staff?' queried Patterson.

'Girls,' said Brook drily. 'We're also given to understand that when Max has had a few drinks, he has a liking for young women.'

'Women around twenty years of age, according to the files we've seen,' added Noble, glancing at a document.

Max stared at his brother for a translation, but Ostrowsky just smiled quietly at Brook.

'May I see?' said Patterson. Noble slid the sheet across to him.

'Quick work, Inspector,' said Ostrowsky. 'But those ... situations were very minor and my brother was released without charge.'

'Lucky you were around to help,' said Brook. 'Did money change hands, by any chance?'

'That remark is uncalled for!' snapped Patterson, pushing the paper away. 'These arrests were clearly without foundation.'

'How do you know?'

'Because *neither* of my clients has a criminal record,' said Patterson. 'And frankly I find your insinuations insulting.'

'Why don't you employ female staff?' Brook asked Ostrowsky.

'Why do you ask?' said Patterson.

'I'm just curious,' said Brook. 'If you open a Polish bar and restaurant, it seems reasonable to hire Polish staff – for authenticity.'

'Bar Polski isn't open for business yet,' said Ostrowsky. 'When the kitchen is ready, we advertise for cooks and waitresses next week. Then we hire girls.'

'Don't you have cleaners?' asked Noble.

'Not yet,' said Ostrowsky.

'With all that building work going on?' said Brook. 'Must get very messy.'

'The builders are Polish, not British,' grinned Ostrowsky. 'They clean up after.'

'Perhaps Jake had a Polish girlfriend who came to visit him there,' suggested Noble.

'I didn't see Jake with any girl,' said Ostrowsky. 'Or Nick.'

'What about the building workers?'

'They work for me before and know very well not to mix business with pleasure.'

'What about you?'

'Me?'

'You're a successful businessman . . . and single,' said Brook. Ostrowsky narrowed his eyes. 'It would be perfectly natural if you sought a relationship with an attractive younger woman.'

'I don't have time,' said Ostrowsky. 'My brother and I work too hard.'

'The victim was Polish, wasn't she?' said Patterson. 'Why else all these questions about girlfriends and female staff?'

'We're exploring all angles,' said Brook.

'And the emerging picture we have of Jake and his brother seems to exclude women,' said Noble.

'So we're looking for ways Jake's path may have intersected with the opposite sex.'

'Ever thought they just plucked her off the street, Inspector?' suggested Patterson. 'Maybe that's what the van was for.'

'I'm sure that's it,' said Brook. 'Bad business, though. Did we mention the victim was pregnant?'

Max looked up and then across at his brother before

resuming his examination of the floor, while Ostrowsky sat in silent contemplation before shaking his head. 'That is tragic,' he said. 'I had no idea.' He glanced at Patterson.

'I think we've taken this about as far as we can, Inspector,' said Patterson, standing.

'One more thing,' said Brook. 'We've found genetic material in the vehicle and need a control sample to eliminate your clients from our enquiries.'

'That won't be happening,' said Patterson, fastening his briefcase. 'Certainly not on a voluntary basis after the hostile way you've conducted this interview. I suggest you test the sample against Jake Tanner's DNA that you'll have on file. In the event that it doesn't match, get a warrant.

'Mr Ostrowsky told me he made it clear to you that he doesn't drive and consequently has never set foot in any of his vans, so any request for *his* DNA is nothing short of a fishing expedition. As for Max, you'd expect his DNA to be in the vehicle, so if you find a second sample, feel free to ask again, otherwise go through channels. Good afternoon, gentlemen.'

Ostrowsky was the last to leave, and as he passed Banach, he mumbled something at her in Polish.

'Thank you for coming in, sir,' said Banach to his retreating back.

'What was that?' Brook asked her when the Ostrowskys were gone.

'He said, "Only a whore of Satan would work to harm her own people."'

'Clever,' said Brook. 'Trying to get a reaction.'

'And you played dumb,' said Noble.

'Yeah, I really had to work at it.'

'Think he knew?' asked Noble.

'I don't see how,' said Banach. 'He just took a punt. I suspect he's a bit of an old hand at this kind of stuff.'

'You wouldn't be wrong,' said Brook. 'What do you think?'

'I think Greg is ice cold,' said Noble. 'They didn't drink the tea or even touch the cups. And notice how he kept hold of Max's unlit cigarette. Smart.'

'Constable?'

'Agreed,' said Banach, surprised to be asked. 'He's charming and ruthless, but one thing he couldn't hide. When you said the victim was pregnant, his neck flushed. He was uncomfortable. They both were.'

Twenty-Four

AN HOUR LATER, THE INCIDENT ROOM fizzed with conversation, fed by the exhaustion of some of the occupants. Brook, Noble, Cooper and Morton, who'd missed two nights' sleep, were bleary-eyed but sharp of mind in that perverse way fatigue sometimes produced. Eventually the crash would come, delayed for now by caffeine, nicotine and empty stomachs. The relatively fresh Smee and Read compared notes, while Banach sat quietly in the rear gazing at the display boards containing the pictures and potted histories of the six missing women.

The incident room door swung open and in strode the squat figure of Chief Superintendent Mark Charlton, walking self-consciously towards Brook and Noble, trying to ignore the dip in noise levels.

'The Tanners?' demanded Charlton.

'We're doing all we can,' said Noble, his expression betraying the lack of progress.

'And PC Ryan?'

'Should make a full recovery,' said Brook.

'Good to know,' replied Charlton, heaving an ostentatious

sigh of relief in front of the troops. 'But that shouldn't lessen the severity of our response . . .'

'No,' said Brook mechanically.

'It's attempted murder against one of our own,' continued Charlton, practising for the evening news, when he would pontificate solemnly in front of the hospital.

Brook nodded at Noble, who dimmed the lights before flicking at a remote, and the assembled detectives fell silent. The faces of Nick and Jake Tanner stared out at them, the younger brother in school uniform, face distorted by a silly grin, the elder glassy-eyed and stern for the custody suite camera after his previous arrest.

'On the left, Jake Tanner, twenty-eight years old and unskilled, though he seems to have worked regularly through the years, mostly as a relief barman in pubs around the city centre, including the defunct Cream Bar. Nick Tanner, the younger brother, is nineteen and has never worked. He has special needs and relies completely on Jake, who is effectively his guardian. By all accounts, the pair are inseparable.'

'Should make them easier to pick up,' said Charlton.

'You'd think,' answered Noble. 'But we've not had a single sighting on the streets or at any of the transport hubs where they might be expected to head if they want to get out of Derby. Also no reports of stolen cars in the vicinity of the Milton tower block, and local cabs drew a blank.'

'So how did they get away?'

'We don't think they did,' said Brook. 'We think they've gone to ground somewhere nearby.'

'Or someone's hiding them,' suggested Charlton.

'Possible,' said Noble. 'But if so, we don't know who. They

have no family in Derby and no friends or acquaintances that we can find.'

'Then where the hell are they?'

'Unknown,' said Noble.

'Are we sure they went home after torching the van?' asked Charlton.

'Their flat was partially cleared out,' replied Noble. 'After setting the fire, they left the scene at twenty-one minutes past two yesterday morning and CCTV shows them making their way through the city centre, heading roughly in the direction of the tower block fifteen minutes later.'

'Why go back?' asked Banach. 'Having killed someone, wouldn't they have prepared their escape before dumping the body?'

'And if they've got no other transport, why didn't they take the van where they needed to go and torch it there?' asked Morton.

'Panic, maybe,' said Noble. 'Also, we don't know where they needed to go. They have no connections outside Derby and no obvious destination. Their lives are here. For that reason, we think they packed a few clothes and filled a bag with food before they ran.'

'Why pack food?' said Charlton.

'So they could have something to eat,' replied Brook, instigating a ripple of laughter. Charlton didn't join in.

'When we searched their flat, we found a receipt for twelve pounds' worth of groceries, mainly baked beans, bought the previous evening,' explained Noble. 'Yet there were no provisions in the place. They're young and fit, but even so they couldn't have been planning to go far on foot with all that. We've had DC Cooper looking for possible locations . . .'

'Hang on,' said a puzzled Charlton. 'I thought they went to the Cream Bar. Jake was working there when it closed. You said he might have had keys.'

'He did work there, and it's *possible* he had keys,' conceded Brook.

'Possible?' said Charlton. He nodded at Banach. 'Two officers were assaulted there.'

'We can't be certain that was Jake and Nick,' said Brook softly, aware that he was pulling the rug of certainty from under Charlton's feet.

'I don't understand.'

'Someone stacked pallets against the wall and climbed in through the window before Banach and Ryan,' said Brook. 'Why would the Tanners do that if Jake had keys?'

'And when we arrived, the door was locked,' added Noble. 'If they had keys, Jake and Nick would have come through the front door and left the same way. And having just attacked two coppers, you don't stop to lock the door behind you . . .'

'Then who?' demanded Charlton.

'We don't know,' said Brook.

'I can't go on the local news with that,' said Charlton. 'It's Tanner and his brother. Has to be.'

'We searched the Cream and didn't find any of the food or clothing the Tanners took from their flat.'

'They could've taken it all with them after the attack,' said Charlton.

'Would you be calm enough to do that, or would you just run?' said Brook.

'And why assault me?' asked Banach, coming to Brook's aid. 'If I'm climbing through a first-floor window, why not just run out the door?'

'Then Jake didn't have keys,' said Charlton, after a moment's thought. 'The brothers climbed in through the same window and assaulted you and Ryan because you were blocking their escape route.'

'That would mean they carried their baggage and heavy cans through a first-floor window and out again after the attack,' said Brook.

'Then that's what they did,' insisted Charlton. 'Assuming they even had bags, which I seriously doubt.' Brook was silent. 'Look, people, I can't go on *East Midlands Today* with all this . . . conjecture.'

'Would you rather go on record with facts that are wrong?' enquired Brook.

Charlton took a deep breath. 'Okay, let's leave aside the assault. Where are we on actually finding them?'

'We abandoned the roadblocks before rush hour, sir,' replied Noble. 'If they had access to a vehicle, they would have left the city by now.'

'No sign of them at Derby Midland or Morledge bus station?'

'None,' chipped in DC Smee. 'But we're keeping a presence in case they break cover.'

'We've still got dog handlers going door-to-door until this evening, but after that we're relying on the phones,' said Noble.

Charlton nodded up to the whiteboard. 'You'll need a better likeness for Nick if you want the public ringing in.'

'We're still trying to find a recent image,' said Cooper, 'but Nick's not on Facebook or social media. Nor is Jake.'

'That's unusual,' said Charlton.

'Poverty may be a factor,' said Cooper. 'And because Nick has special needs, he's never had a job or been to college. He has no mobile, no bank account and has never applied for a passport or driving licence or anything that might require a photo ID.'

'A nineteen-year-old without a mobile?' said Read. 'Weird.'

'They could have PAYG phones,' suggested Smee.

'But then we'd have no record.'

'You said no family,' pressed Charlton.

'Mother deceased,' said Cooper. 'Three arrests for soliciting. One for using. No convictions. Father unknown and no male name on either birth certificate . . .'

'Sounds like the mother didn't know the fathers either,' said Banach.

'Fathers?' said Charlton.

Banach nodded at the screen. 'They don't look much alike. In her profession and with the age gap, different fathers seem likely.'

'Jake must have work colleagues at least,' insisted Charlton.

'He's a relief barman,' said Cooper. 'He doesn't stay in a job long enough for people to get to know him. Being full-time guardian to Nick can't help.'

'Social Services?'

'Minimal involvement.'

'What about prison?'

'Same story,' said Cooper. 'No known associates either on Jake's file or behavioural reports. He kept to himself and the warden gave him a spotless record.'

'What was he in for?'

'GBH. Sentenced to six months, out in three. It was a serious attack but a first offence so he got off lightly. Until the GBH, he was a Category D poster boy – a few cautions as a teenager and a fine for shoplifting.'

'Do we have background on the assault?' asked Brook.

'The file says it was an argument in the street that escalated,' said Cooper. 'The victim was a thirty-three-year-old civil servant, Aaron Robertson. Respectable. No priors. But Robertson is gay and there were suggestions that it was a hate crime, though Tanner's brief managed to fight that off or the sentence could've been a lot worse.'

'No shared history with the victim?'

'None,' said Cooper. 'It was a random attack.'

'Something else that doesn't add up,' said Brook. 'But it means we have his DNA at least.'

'To test against what?' demanded Charlton.

'We have DNA from a pair of gloves in the van,' said Brook. 'If it's not Tanner's, it could be the van owner's, or more likely his brother Max, who used the van, but we don't have a control sample yet.'

Charlton shook his head. 'The Tanners don't strike me as very bright. How the hell can they still be at large?'

'Their options are limited,' said Noble. 'With no friends or family, we're looking for a lock-up or an allotment. Failing that, our best bet is derelict buildings and squats. So far, nothing.'

'You've considered a home invasion,' said Charlton.

'We haven't ruled it out,' said Noble, 'but we've been all over it with door-to-door and not a single resident gave off the vibe.'

'I'm not convinced those two could control a family,' suggested Read.

'Not convinced?' exclaimed Charlton. 'The Tanners murdered a girl and burned her body. Or am I dealing in the *wrong* facts?'

Brook hunched forward, talking to the floor. 'We can tie them to the van, no question. We have film and a witness.'

'Then what more do you need?' demanded Charlton. 'When you confirm Caitlin Kinnear as the victim, it's a slam-dunk.'

Brook tagged in Noble with a weary glance.

'The post-mortem ruled out Caitlin Kinnear,' said Noble. 'She wasn't the victim.'

'Not the victim?' said Charlton. 'I thought you connected Jake Tanner to Caitlin on the night she disappeared?'

'We did,' said Noble. 'The victim is the right age, but Caitlin Kinnear had an abortion a few weeks ago and the dead girl was between ten and twelve weeks pregnant.'

Brook's eye was drawn by Banach, her head bowed in sympathy, her hands moving from forehead to chest, circumnavigating her crucifix – the instinctive response of a Polish Catholic to the death of an unborn child. His eye strayed to the photographs of the missing girls.

'An unborn child,' repeated Charlton, pained. 'God bless. Do we have ID on the mother?'

'Unknown for the moment,' said Noble. He pointed the remote, zipping through several crime-scene photographs showing various angles of the melting plastic sheets containing the charred and disfigured corpse. 'Her fingerprints were destroyed so we're working on dental. But that won't be straightforward.'

'How so?'

'Because of this.' Noble flicked through the slides of the victim's scorched arm, looking for the best shot.

'It's a tattoo of the Polish flag,' said Banach, her mouth dropping open.

'The dead girl was Polish?' asked Charlton.

'It seems likely,' said Noble. He glanced across at Brook, but he was transfixed by the pictures of Daniela Cassetti, Caitlin and the others.

'Any candidates from Missing Persons?' asked Charlton.

'Several possibilities, sir,' said Noble. He flicked again at the remote to load another photograph. 'But this is the current favourite because she's the closest match to the dead girl's specs. Nicola Serota. Polish national from Poznan . . .'

'I remember her,' said DC Read. 'I made enquiries. She was visiting her sister in Derby when she disappeared . . .' He clicked his fingers.

Noble obliged. 'Veronika.'

'Veronika, that's right,' said Read. 'But . . .'

'But what?' demanded Charlton, when Read hesitated.

'She disappeared . . . must be eighteen months ago,' answered Read.

'Not that long,' said Noble, before adding quietly, 'January third, twenty-fourteen.'

'Sixteen months!' exclaimed Charlton. 'Is this one of the young women Interpol enquired about?' Noble nodded, looking at Brook for help, but he seemed lost in thought. 'You're telling me this Nicola Serota was abducted sixteen months ago and kept alive until she turned up dead the other night.'

'I'm not telling you that because we don't know, sir,' said Noble. 'But she left her sister's flat in Derby on that date and hasn't been seen since. She's Polish, she's the right height—'

'Why don't I know more about the disappearance?' demanded Charlton.

'You said it when we took this on, sir,' said Brook, rejoining the fray 'She's a foreign national. Her movements were always going to be tough to follow. And even then her disappearance could turn out to be completely innocent.'

'And I suppose her family had no idea she was missing until months later,' conceded Charlton.

'Exactly,' said Noble. 'They thought she was travelling until it was too late to pick up her trail.'

'It was months before she crossed my desk,' said Read. 'She hadn't been in touch with home since leaving Poland, yet her parents had no idea there was a problem. With no sightings, all I could do was check her plane ticket from East Midlands – it was unused.'

'And?'

'That was it, sir,' replied Read. 'She'd only been in Britain a week. I did a risk assessment and passed her file on to the Missing Persons Bureau. Normal procedure.'

'So let me get this straight,' said Charlton. 'We have a pair of fugitives connected to Caitlin Kinnear, who *is* missing, killing and dumping a corpse that *isn't* Caitlin's in a stolen van.'

'Except we don't have direct evidence that they committed the murder, just the body dump.'

'God forbid we'd have a stone-cold fact,' snarled Charlton.

'It gets more complicated,' said Brook. 'Jake recently took up a position at a new bar that's opening in Friargate – Bar Polski.'

Charlton narrowed his eyes. 'Sounds Polish.'

Brook managed an acknowledging smile. 'The stolen van belonged to the owner, Grzegorz Ostrowsky, a Polish businessman with a murky past in the Far East.'

'How murky?'

'Drug smuggling,' said Noble. 'Though it didn't stick.'

'Any connection with this . . . ?' Charlton waved a hand towards Nicola Serota's image.

'None that we can see, but without a definitive ID, we haven't asked him yet.'

'You've spoken to him?'

'We're feeling each other out,' said Brook. 'His brother Max is an electrician and used the stolen van for his work. He'd just moved into a flat in Arboretum Street a stone's throw from Jake and Nick's tower block, and that's where the van was reported stolen.'

'So maybe the victim was connected to these brothers,' said Charlton.

'It's possible.'

'But if Jake worked for this Ostrowsky, that would connect him to the victim as well,' said Charlton, looking pleased with himself.

'That's true,' admitted Brook.

'The plot thickens.' Charlton glanced at his watch. 'So what can I tell the media?'

'That we're looking for Jake and Nick Tanner.'

'What about Caitlin?'

Brook shook his head. 'We'd prefer the family didn't get it from the media, even though it's qualified good news.'

'Qualified?'

'She's still missing.'

'I can mention Nicola Serota, right?'

Brook sighed. 'Not until we're sure. Her biog made no mention of a tattoo. It may not be her.'

'Then we need to put the tattoo out there from the off,' said Charlton.

'At this stage, best we hold that back for confirmation, sir,' said Noble.

Charlton nodded. 'I suppose.' Wearily he stood to leave. 'I'm going to look like a right chump.' He glared across at Brook, finally managing a smile. 'But at least you'll be sitting next to me.'

'Something tells me you just flushed your goodwill down the toilet,' said Noble, looking after Charlton.

'Back in my comfort zone, then.'

'So what now?' asked Noble.

Brook glanced at Banach and beckoned her over. 'I've had an idea. I want a warrant for the Rutherford Clinic, John. We need to go through their records. Constable, you're a Catholic.'

Banach grinned. 'I'm Polish – it's the most Catholic country in Europe.'

'More than Italy or Ireland?'

'Absolutely – nearly ninety per cent of the population.'

'Is this relevant?' asked Noble.

'And what can Catholic girls from those countries get in England that they can't access so easily in Poland, Ireland and Italy?' persisted Brook.

While Noble floundered, Banach's eyes widened in sudden realisation. 'Oh my God.'

Twenty-Five

HARSH LIGHT FLOODED THE ROOM. Unused to the brightness, Caitlin kept her eyes closed for a moment to make the adjustment. Then the music came, the sort of stuff her gran listened to on a sleepy Sunday afternoon after the Gaelic football had finished – non-threatening, easy-listening instrumentals. It sent a shudder down her spine. The phone buzzed in her hand.

Rule 5. If spoken to u can say how was your day darling? Nod if u understand.

Caitlin nodded, the fear rising in her.

Over the lush strings she heard a door close behind her and strained to see an elderly man walk in front of her, his eyes lighting up when he saw her, wrinkling in the effort of a smile.

Caitlin stared in horror at his face, one side of which had slipped away, as though his head was a painting that had been partially left out in the rain until the right flank sagged like the stump of a used candle. When smiling, the left half of his mouth turned up while the right sank further towards his jaw, his tongue waving amidst the wreckage, peeping uncontrolled from the damp twist of his lips.

He had thick white hair swept back over his head and huge

unkempt eyebrows. He was wearing a dark-green velvet dinner jacket over a white shirt with a green bow tie, and carried a dinner tray in his liver-spotted hands. The tray looked like it might fall from his quivering grasp at any moment as he approached her, dragging his right foot slightly. Caitlin guessed he'd suffered some kind of stroke.

He plopped the tray on her lap as gently as he could manage, moving in close to smell Caitlin's hair. She in turn could smell the sharp aftershave splashed on the clean side of his face. The right side was shaggy and unshaven, though someone – she doubted it could have been the old man – had made an attempt to trim the patchy beard with scissors.

As she eased away from his sniffing nostrils, Caitlin's gaze was fixed on the food and her own nostrils began to quiver. It looked like chicken breast in some kind of cream sauce with mashed potatoes and green beans – her dry mouth filled with saliva and she realised she was starving.

The man let go of the tray and the full aroma of hot food hit Caitlin, making her light-headed, almost nauseous. She'd read somewhere that when the Americans had first stumbled upon a concentration camp during the Second World War, they were forbidden to feed the skeletal inmates, fearing the damage solid food might do to their insides.

The old man shook out a blood-red napkin and shuffled behind her, humming along to the music as well as his disfigured mouth would allow, the chords translated into a series of gasps.

He moved out of her sight and Caitlin's pulse quickened when she felt his breath on her neck. She shivered and closed her eyes as he tucked the napkin down the front of her shirt, lingering too long at the top curve of her breasts. Close to her ear, the old man tried to configure a couple of words, and she could feel his breath on her neck as he spoke. She couldn't be sure but it sounded like 'Our song,' and she trembled from the combined effects of his words and the splash of spit on her skin.

She opened her eyes and fixed them on the food, tried to concentrate on the meal to come and swallowed a large gob of drool at the prospect.

When the man finished fixing the cloth around her neck, Caitlin felt his rough hands on her skin. They were trembling, though probably through infirmity rather than fear. As his fingers dragged across her soft skin, his nails hard as diamonds, he noticed her goose bumps and she shivered again, her breath quickening.

'You're cold,' he gasped – barely coherent – into her ear. He gave her lobe a light peck, the tip of his dry tongue touching the skin, then drew his gnarled talons through her hair. She could feel him running strands between finger and thumb like the nit doctor her mam had told her about in school.

'Darling?' The man left a pause for her to answer. Caitlin tried to ask him about his day but the words wouldn't come. Instead the old man continued. 'You changed your hair.'

My hair? Realisation flooded into Caitlin's fevered mind. *Jesus! I'm not the first.* She could stand it no more and shook off the man's hand, then tried to lever herself upright but in so doing propelled the dinner tray to earth with a crash of plates and cutlery.

The old man began to howl like a smacked child and covered his uncooperative mouth with shaking hands. 'No-oooo,' he wailed, though Caitlin failed to register that or anything else except the current flowing quick and hot through her body. And as she lost consciousness, she felt comforting warmth spread through her diaper.

Banach sat in the back seat of Brook's BMW, her unease growing as he pulled into the small car park at the side of the Rutherford Clinic. She still had the clinic's card, given her by Dr Fleming, nestling in her pocket, and if she encountered him in Brook's company, beans might be spilled that could damage her career. If anyone at St Mary's got to know about her pregnancy, then the whole station would know soon after. That was just how it was. Keeping secrets from colleagues you might rely upon in a life-threatening situation was frowned upon and the station's gossip mill did all it could to enforce the policy.

Brook drew alongside a gleaming new Audi – private number plate TOP DR01 – which nestled in a bay reserved for Dr Fleming. A sign sported not just the doctor's name but two lines of medical qualifications.

The detectives disgorged and were greeted by the sight and sound of around twenty people blocking the tarmac path to the main double doors of the clinic. The crowd were cheering and jeering as a tearful waif of a girl in a tracksuit hurried away from their taunts. As they approached, a portly nurse left the slab of a building and advanced from the other direction to remonstrate with the mob.

'Father O'Toole, you know you have no right to be on this path,' she shouted to answering heckles.

'We have a right of lawful assembly,' replied the priest, his dog collar hidden beneath a woollen scarf. A chorus of 'Amen' greeted his riposte.

'Is there a problem, Father?' asked Brook. All heads turned to him.

'Not any more,' said Father O'Toole, glancing beatifically at the heavens. 'A sinner repents and the Lord's will be done.' More muttered Amens.

'I'll be the judge,' said the nurse, folding her arms.

'I asked if there was a problem,' said Brook, holding up his warrant card.

'No problem, Inspector Brook,' said the priest, squinting at his ID and holding out a hand to shake. Taken unawares, Brook accepted the grip on a reflex. The old man's hand was cold and clammy, his fingers bony. He pressed his thumb down on Brook's knuckle, a gleam in his eye. 'We're doing God's work protesting the taking of innocent lives.'

'You're abusing that right, Father, and you know it,' said the nurse. 'You've no right to block the path to the clinic to intimidate patients.'

'Patients, you call them,' snarled an elderly woman bedecked in expensive furs, stepping forward. Her American accent drew Brook's attention. 'They're not patients. Ain't a thing wrong with them that opening their hearts to the Lord wouldn't up and cure.'

'Amen,' mumbled the rest of the group as one voice.

The priest beamed up at Brook, still holding the handshake. 'I should mention that I'm a close friend of Chief Superintendent Charlton. We sometimes pray together and I'm always keen to support the division in my parish newsletter.'

Brook withdrew his hand, returning an icy smile. 'I'm so pleased you mentioned that, Father. Constable, escort these good people away from this thoroughfare to an appropriate safe distance.'

'Happy to,' replied Banach.

'Thank you, Inspector,' said the nurse, turning to glare triumphantly at the priest. Brook saw the name Moran on an ID badge on her chest.

'You'll burn in hell for this,' snarled the American woman at Brook.

'Already booked in,' replied Brook. 'But if you get there first, reserve me a room with a view, will you?'

'Who in God's name do you think you're talking to?'

'Mrs Trastevere, let me deal with this,' said the priest. 'Inspector, I don't think you understand—'

'No, you're the one who doesn't understand,' said Brook. 'The patients and staff at this clinic have the right to go about their business free from molestation, and all the Masonic handshakes in the world won't undermine that right.'

'We obey higher laws,' spat Mrs Trastevere. 'Make a note of the inspector's name.' The old woman glared malevolently at Brook as a young man took out an iPad. Brook watched him tap the keys and gestured to Banach who slipped behind the knot of protesters.

'You're making a mistake, Inspector,' said Father O'Toole, his face pinching in judgement.

'It wouldn't be the first,' said Brook. 'Constable, take names and arrest anyone who resists. Call a wagon if you have to.'

'Sir.' Banach whipped the device from the young man's gloved hands.

'Hey, give that back,' he ordered.

Banach held out an arm to show him the direction of travel. 'Step this way, please.'

The burly young man seemed prepared to make a lunge for

his iPad, but the elderly woman laid a gloved hand on his arm. 'Turn the other cheek, Gabriel.'

'If you wouldn't mind turning it over in that direction,' said Banach, gesturing at a pair of benches off to one side. 'I'll return your shit list when you're off the path.' There was silence and nobody moved.

Father O'Toole smiled into Brook's tired eyes. 'Well, perhaps our mission is accomplished for the evening, brethren.' He gestured compliance and the throng moved off the path.

'My iPad,' growled the burly young man, holding out a hand.

Banach depressed the off button and held it out to the young man who opened his mouth to complain further, but Mrs Trastevere squeezed his bicep again. 'I'll pray for your soul, officer . . .' she prompted with a raised eyebrow.

Banach's smile disappeared. 'Thank you.'

'Much appreciated, Inspector,' said Nurse Moran, preceding Brook and Noble through the automatic doors. 'Lucky you were passing.'

'We're not passing,' said Noble. 'We're here to see Dr Fleming.'

'This would be about poor Caitlin, would it?' said Moran, her face grim.

'You remember her?' said Brook.

'When I saw her picture in the papers . . . terrible,' answered Moran in her soft Irish brogue. 'A young girl like that, her whole life ahead of her.'

'You'd notice the Irish girls, I suppose,' said Brook.

'I do, and it was only recently she was here,' said Moran. 'We get a fair sprinkling of desperate women from Dublin, as you can imagine, what with the direct flights to East Midlands and all.'

'Caitlin's from Belfast,' said Noble. Moran looked puzzled at his use of the present tense.

'She *was* from Belfast, Sergeant,' corrected Brook, deciding deception was easier than explanation.

'So she was,' nodded Moran. 'But a Catholic nonetheless. And she certainly stood out from the crowd.'

'Really? How?'

Moran considered. 'Caitlin wasn't like a lot of the girls who pass through our doors. Even the more mature ladies that come for a termination are at least a little . . .'

'Conflicted?' suggested Brook.

'Conflicted,' agreed Moran. 'But not Caitlin. She was very sure of herself for one so young. Said she wasn't going to waste her life *pushing out babies*. That's how she put it. Some might have called her hard-faced, but honestly, I prefer that to the awful vulnerability most of them carry. Sure it was probably a bit of an act, but it showed strength of character.' Moran smiled. 'Gave those fanatics out there a taste of their own medicine, I can tell you – the language on her.' Her smile disappeared. 'I had no idea the poor girl was even missing.'

'No one did,' said Noble.

'We may need to interview you further,' said Brook.

'Tonight?' said Moran.

Brook registered Noble's expression of exhausted dismay. 'We'll be in touch.'

'You know where I am,' said Moran, approaching the reception desk to address the thin-lipped woman behind. 'Sally, is he free?'

* * *

Tymon looked around to check he was unobserved. He examined the door before pulling on bright yellow washing-up gloves from a black holdall, then drew out the keys he'd used at the building's entrance. He turned a Yale in the flimsy lock, pushed open the door and reached for a light. Once illuminated, he scanned the apartment, a small and functional one-room studio that aped the characteristics of its tenant. The pungent smell of death hung like a shroud in the air, and Tymon placed the holdall on the floor and quickly opened the high skylight on the sloping roof to freshen the atmosphere. Then he extracted two bottles of cleaning fluid, a large bottle of strong bleach and a pack of J Cloths.

Having located a plug-in air freshener, he tore off the packaging and pushed the device into a socket before moving quietly round the room removing anything that might carry fingerprints or DNA – a bottle of cheap perfume, a clean ashtray full of cheap earrings, a picture frame showing a young girl flanked by her parents, the mother an older version of her and the proud father in full camouflage gear. Tymon recognised the insignia of the Polish Special Forces but barely paused before tossing the frame into the holdall.

He spun the cap off a half-finished bottle of vodka on a cabinet and took a long swig, examining the label as the fiery liquid burned its way down his throat. There was a blood spot on the white label. He resealed the bottle and placed it carefully in the bag.

Next he emptied the waste baskets into a carrier bag, not bothering to examine the contents, and after tying them up, threw those into the holdall as well. He shook out a large plastic refuse sack and rolled up the bloodstained bedding, bagging the duvet, sheet and pillow cases before setting the sack by the door. Into another refuse sack he emptied the wardrobe of the few items of clothing and shoes, then threw the toiletries next to the sink and shower on top.

Finally he went to work with the cleaning fluids on surfaces, light switches and door handles to remove prints and any obvious blood spatter. It would be as though Kassia Proch had never set foot in the place.

'As I said, there were no complications, Inspector Brook. Everything went smoothly and Ms Kinnear spent the night with us before leaving the next morning.' Dr Fleming smiled as he returned Brook's warrant card.

'Something funny?'

'You've not heard of Brook Advisory Centres?' said Fleming. 'They provide advice and information on a range of sexual health matters.'

'Now you mention it,' answered Brook, unmoved.

'Did Caitlin have any visitors while she was here?' asked Noble.

Fleming raised his chained glasses to his nose to glare at the monitor. 'It's not always recorded, but according to this, a young lady called Laurie Teague paid her a visit.'

'No men?'

'None.' Fleming shrugged. 'That's normal. Even supportive male partners are uncomfortable in the clinic.'

'What was Caitlin's mood while she was here?' asked Noble.

'I can't be expected to remember every patient I treat, Sergeant,' said Fleming. 'I've got a job to do and my patients wouldn't thank me for worrying about how they're feeling. And depending on length of pregnancy, patients are often anaesthetised – some local, some general, depending on the stage of the pregnancy – so even when conscious, their mood can be altered by the drugs.'

'Isn't there an initial appointment to interview the patient before the procedure?' said Brook.

'Of course,' retorted Fleming. 'But a lot of that work is beneath my skills. We do a blood test for anaemia and check for STIs, have them sign the consent form. And sometimes a vaginal examination or an ultrasound is required so it's preferable to have a female nurse run the appointment. The patients are often young and uncomfortable about their bodies being probed by a man other than their sexual partner.' His eyes creased in thin amusement.

'Does the clinic do any counselling?' asked Noble.

'Again, yes but that's not my strong suit, I'll freely admit,' said Fleming. 'My nurses are experienced and sympathetic enough to take the patient through her options and counsel accordingly.'

'And you're not?'

'I'm a surgeon, Inspector,' replied Fleming with a hint of irritation. 'And a bloody good one. That's what I do. One mistake and people die, so I keep the emotion out of it because the buck stops right here.'

'Nurse Moran says Caitlin was very sure of herself,' said Noble. 'She thought it unusual.'

'I didn't notice, but if she told you that, I'd say she's right,' said Fleming. 'Most patients are, at best, reflective. To be expected.'

'Especially for a Catholic,' said Brook.

'Indeed.'

'You knew Caitlin was Catholic?'

Fleming pondered for a second before nodding at the monitor. 'It says here on her record.'

'Is it policy to record religious affiliations?'

'We ask for denomination so that it might inform our counselling,' replied Fleming. 'The fact that she was a Catholic is neither here nor there when it comes to *my* role.'

'Was?' said Noble.

Fleming was confused. 'It said in the papers that she died. In that van by the river.'

'We haven't formally identified the victim,' said Brook.

'These things take time, I'm sure,' said Fleming. He held out his hands to draw a line. 'Well. I'm sorry I can't be more help.'

'Don't be sorry, we're not finished yet,' said Brook, glancing across at Noble. 'We have other names.'

'I don't understand,' said Fleming. 'What other names?'

'Did you have occasion to operate on someone called Daniela Cassetti?' asked Noble. 'It would be about a year ago.'

Fleming stared between Noble and Brook. 'What's going on?' he asked, leaning forward in his chair.

'She's missing,' explained Brook, leaving the rest unsaid.

Fleming's brow creased as he felt his way around the implication. 'Are you suggesting there's a link between the Rutherford and the disappearances of Caitlin Kinnear and this . . . ?'

'Daniela Cassetti,' repeated Noble. 'And we're not suggesting, we're asking.'

'That's monstrous,' brayed Fleming. He stood aggressively, shooting his leather chair from under him. 'I'd like you both to leave.' Neither detective reacted. 'Did you hear me, Inspector?'

Brook couldn't prevent a smile. It was a default reaction to suspects and witnesses trying too hard to exert control over a situation that was getting away from them. Control that Brook had. Control the other party wanted.

He spoke softly, feeling no need to wield the big stick. 'Do you think we're here for our health, Doctor? I'm investigating a murder. I'm also looking for several young women who have disappeared in the last three years, all of them Catholics, from countries where access to the service you offer is either limited or non-existent. At the moment it's just a theory and one that you can blow out of the water by checking your records. So I'd appreciate a bit less drama and a lot more cooperation, for which – let me remind you – we have a warrant.'

Fleming stared at him, defiant at first until defeat began to register and he pulled his chair back under his legs, drawing the keyboard towards him. 'Daniela . . . ?'

'Cassetti.'

A moment later Fleming stared saucer-eyed at the monitor. 'Oh Lord.' Lowering his gaze, he slapped the screen round towards them, and Brook and Noble sat forward to read details. Noble took out his Bar Polski pen and jotted down the essentials on a fresh page of his notebook.

'It says here she was a private patient, but there's no mention of further charges.'

Fleming flipped the monitor back round. 'Right,' he sighed. 'She paid a small deposit and came for the initial exam and blood test and to set up a schedule for the procedure but never came back.'

'Why?'

'Who knows?' retorted Fleming, on safer ground now. 'We don't enquire. It happens. Girls change their minds, or are persuaded from their course. Especially Catholic girls, I imagine.'

'And I guess being forced to cross a picket line doesn't help,' said Brook.

'No, it doesn't,' retorted Fleming fiercely. 'We've put up with that mob for far too long and I've complained often enough to your superiors. They've cost me a small fortune.' He hesitated, realising he'd prioritised poorly. 'And of course the patients who decide to proceed can be very upset by it.'

'As you're being so obliging, Dr Fleming,' smiled Brook, 'remind me to show you a special handshake that might help you with that.'

Fleming returned a tight smile before nodding at Noble. 'I hesitate to ask, but you mentioned other names.'

Noble glanced at his notes. 'Nicola Serota?'

The receptionist held out the appointment card and information leaflet but they remained uncollected while Banach looked furtively around for the return of her colleagues.

'Miss Banach,' said the woman, waggling the papers at her.

Banach turned, almost snatching them and stuffing them hurriedly into a pocket.

'Your first appointment will be a preliminary interview with a nurse,' announced the receptionist.

'Yes, thank you,' replied Banach, keen to be away.

'The leaflet will inform you of what will be discussed, what information we require and suitable clothes to wear on the day.'

'I understand,' said Banach, already backing away towards the double doors. She heard a door open on the corridor containing Dr Fleming's office. Nurse Moran emerged, pulling on a coat.

'Your colleagues are just finishing up, officer.'

'Thank you.' The mechanism on the double doors was triggered before Banach reached the sensor and she peered out into the gloom in time to see an indistinct figure in a hoodie, face hidden behind a smartphone. A second later, the camera flashed and the figure turned to run away from the building.

'Oi,' shouted Banach, briefly setting off in pursuit before halting outside the doors, straining to identify the photographer, now almost out of sight. Moran appeared, also looking after the mystery photographer, a hand shielding her eyes. She stared into the distance, then smiled uncertainly and cut across the grassy bank towards the car park.

Banach followed to wait by Brook's car, pleased now that the appointment was made and colleagues were none the wiser. She glanced across to where she'd moved the protesters. The gathering had dispersed for the night. She felt light-headed and moved a hand to her mouth in a rush of sudden nausea. After steadying herself, she felt beneath her blouse for her crucifix and held it briefly between her fingers.

Brook and Noble walked briskly through the clinic's brightly lit reception, Noble clutching a folder of still-warm printouts.

'What now?'

Brook glanced at a clock on a pastel-coloured wall. 'Now I'm going to babysit the Chief Super through the media briefing, make sure he says as little as possible. You're going to find as much information on the new girl as you can.'

'Kassia Proch?' said Noble, peering at a printout.

'Right. Check out the address she gave the clinic, and if it's not a fake, get a team round there and get it processed. I'll join you as soon as I can. If this is our victim, there's a decent chance that's where she died.'

'Thank Christ for that,' said Noble, with a tired grin. 'I was worried I might have to go home for a shower and a sleep.'

'No stamina,' quipped Brook. 'You'll be mentioning food next.'

'Forget food,' said Noble. 'Another day in this shirt and they're going to have to sandblast it off my body.' His mobile rang and he held it to his ear.

Leaving through the double doors, Brook spied Banach standing by the car, a hand held across her mouth. 'You okay?' he asked as they drew near.

'Never liked that hospital smell.' She smiled to reassure.

'What happened to the priest and his merry band?'

'Showed them my forked tail,' replied Banach.

'I don't suppose you took any names?' asked Brook.

'Didn't have to,' replied Banach. 'Why?'

'In retrospect, it might have been useful,' said Brook. Banach cocked her head. 'We have our connection. The clinic is the common bond between the missing girls. We're going to be doing background on all the staff.'

'And you want names of demonstrators too,' she concluded. 'What do you want me to do?'

'Get back to the incident room and give Cooper these staff and patient lists to photocopy for briefing tomorrow morning, then rustle up contact details for Father O'Toole and the old woman . . .'

'Mrs Trastevere,' said Banach.

'Hopefully they can give us a list of parishioners and assorted activists who've taken part in pickets.'

'I wouldn't bank on it after tonight,' smiled Banach.

Noble rang off. 'That was Rob. The DNA in the glove doesn't match Jake Tanner's.'

'Get the paperwork started for Max Ostrowsky's DNA,' said Brook. 'I want a warrant in front of a magistrate as soon as possible.'

Brook emerged from the briefing unscathed. Brian Burton was still on holiday, so he hadn't had to face his sly criticisms dressed up as journalistic interest. Besides, Charlton had fielded most of the enquiries and had kept to the script, urging the public to be on the lookout for Jake and Nick Tanner and glossing over officially identifying the body as Caitlin Kinnear *until the victim's family have been informed.*

'The prayer group are meeting tonight if you want to join us, Brook?' said Charlton, after the briefing. 'I don't know about you, but I could use a bit of inspiration.'

Brook's mobile vibrated and he pulled a face so devastated he feared he might have overdone it. 'Sergeant Noble,' he mouthed over his hand. 'What is it, John?'

'I'm in Kassia Proch's flat on Vernon Street. It's in the centre of town, just off Friargate.'

'Convenient for Bar Polski. Tell me you've found a connection.'

'No connection to the bar, but it's her place all right. I just got off the phone with the managing agent.'

'Was she killed there?'

'I think so,' said Noble. 'SOCO are here and picked up blood spatter on the wall behind the bed, but other than that, the place has been stripped and cleaned from top to bottom. All surfaces. They needed luminol to find the blood. Bed linen has been taken and there are no clothes or any personals. If we didn't know this was her place we'd be hard pressed to say she was ever here.'

'Excellent news, John,' said Brook loudly. 'What's the address?'

'Number thirty-six,' replied Noble. 'But don't bother. I'll leave the SOCO team but I doubt they'll find anything else. The rest will keep. I'm going home to sleep.'

'Right. On my way,' answered Brook, ringing off before Noble could question his hearing.

'Developments?' said Charlton.

Brook walked away backwards at a brisk pace. 'We might have an ID on our victim.' He mimed his impatience to be away.

'Yes, yes,' said Charlton. 'Go.'

Brook looked around Kassia Proch's apartment, watching the scene-of-crime officers doing their work. Noble was right. There was little to see with the naked eye. The blood spatter had been wiped clean but chemicals had reanimated its journey on to the wall behind the bed, clear indication that the victim had been struck forcibly, several times, while lying on it.

After exchanging a few words with the lead SOCO, Brook descended the steps, knocking on all the doors in turn. He paused at the entrance lobby and scanned the list of occupants, each announced on a sliver of card taped to a buzzer. Apart from the victim, at the top of the house, the other tenants were small businesses – a printer, a literary agent and a games designer – and they'd all departed for the day. It was possible that Kassia Proch was also running a business from her apartment, but there was no sign of anything except professional cleaning. No artefacts, and so far, no fingerprints or DNA. Even the shower trap had been removed and cleaned with bleach.

Forty minutes later, Brook stood under his own shower at home in Hartington, letting the hot water soothe away the tensions of the last forty-eight hours. Later he sat with a cup of tea in front of the glowing woodburner, mulling over his brief visit to Vernon Street.

The Tanner brothers didn't clean Kassia's flat, he'd texted Noble from the scene. *Too thorough. Remember their place?*

Who then? replied Noble. *Ostrowsky?*

That would be my guess. She's Polish. Connected somehow. Suspect Max killed her and Greg's covering for him again.

He's got history of violence okay. Thought you were going home to rest ☹

'That'll be the day,' Brook muttered under his breath before going through to his office to spend a couple of hours trawling around various pro-life websites.

'These people really mean it,' he said, logging off finally. He returned to the dying embers of his fire and tapped out another text to Noble. *Priority on picture and dental of KP.*

His head sagged and his eyelids closed. The vibration of Noble's reply stirred him. *Ye-sssssssss. Now leave me alone.*

Brook lay on the sofa to compose further thoughts for the morning but failed to commit them to the digital ether before collapsing into a deep sleep.

Twenty-Six

25 April

JAKE WOKE WITH A GROAN. He had read long into the night, unable to rest on the spongy foam cushions. The fetid draught being sucked under the ill-fitting front door had given him a stiff neck, though it was preferable to the reek of old woman – decay and cheap perfume – stuck in his throat.

No doubt Nick was sleeping like a baby in the next room: he could get a full night's kip on a bed of nails. Knowing this, he had offered Jake first dibs on the soft bed, but Jake had let him have it, certain that the old woman had died on that mattress. Even ten years after his stint at the hospital laundry, he knew the smell of death. The way he'd known his mother was gone almost before he'd opened her bedroom door that last morning. The pungent, vinegary odour of burnt crack overwhelmed by the faecal smell of uncontrolled bowel and bladder, the first casualties of the dead brain's inability to direct muscle function.

He dragged himself upright, wondering why he couldn't hear Nick moving about like a kid on Christmas morning. Every morning. Always out like a light, then first to rise, chivvying for breakfast or a PlayStation opponent. As Jake swung a foot to the floor, he felt the string fall away from his neck. It had been cut, and the key was gone.

'Nick!'

With one bound he was at the front door. It was unlocked, the key on the inside. He opened the door and popped out a wary head. The corridor, with its slick of permanent damp, was deserted. He stepped back into the flat and closed the door, then ran to the bedroom to confirm what he already knew. Nick was gone.

He dressed, his mind racing. Where? The answer wasn't long in coming – the Intu Centre. Nick loved it there. The bustle. The bright, colourful shops where he could window-lick, panting at all the things he couldn't afford because his brother was a relief barman who wouldn't even do the lottery.

Jake zipped his top and pulled the hood in tight, a scarf covering his mouth. He stepped outside into the cool morning for the first time in days, locking the door behind him, and passed the neighbouring flat in time to see the door close on an old woman's frightened gaze.

Nick finished the large chocolate chip cookie, unaware of the brown glaze smeared around his mouth. As he walked, he gazed happily at the shops, smiling at the well-scrubbed faces rushing by, pleased that he could take time while others hurried.

He passed the mobile phone store for the third time, trying not to look. Technology was calling but Nick had to resist temptation or a telling-off beckoned. He had enough money – he'd checked his stash inside Mr Ted – but Jake would be suspicious, and would demand to know how Nick had managed to afford a new phone.

Fucked over, Nick remembered with glee from previous reprimands, shaking his head in wonder at the pleasure bestowed by a handful of harsh consonants.

He wandered on past WH Smith towards the escalator for the first floor and the food court, aware of more than one person staring at him as they passed. He stepped smartly on to the moving steps and turned to see a woman following his progress.

Nick pulled up his parka hood, mood darkening. *Jake said we couldn't go out. He's gonna be real mad.* He put his hand in his pocket to feel the comforting crinkle of the notes stuffed into his teddy, and smiled, his disquiet forgotten. Time for a burger.

Noble and Brook finished explaining the background to their search for the missing girls to the packed incident room.

'So now you're saying the girl in the van wasn't Caitlin Kinnear *or* Nicola Serota,' said DC Smee.

'The dead girl was pregnant,' said Noble. 'We confirmed last night that Caitlin had recently had an abortion. We haven't ruled out Nicola Serota yet but we have a new front-runner.' Noble flicked at the remote and the Interpol girls disappeared, to be replaced by a single new face. 'This is Kassia Proch. She's from Warsaw and has been in the UK for about a year, according to Immigration . . .'

'Interpol again?' said Charlton.

'Actually we generated this lead ourselves,' replied Brook. 'John.'

'Kassia has been renting a small flat in Vernon Street for six months. We spoke to the agent who showed her round the place. Kassia paid her deposit in cash, which leads us to believe she's been earning regularly, but we've found nothing on the books.'

'She's not PAYE.'

'No.'

'Prostitute?'

'All things are possible.'

'Benefits?' queried Charlton.

'Not claimed a penny,' said Noble.

'Cash-in-hand work,' concluded Charlton through pursed lips. 'This is why they come here. The black economy. Too many cracks to fall through—'

'Sir,' interrupted Brook. Charlton fell silent.

'The agent remembers that Kassia had a tattoo of the Polish flag on her upper arm,' continued Noble. 'It's not definitive and we're waiting on dental records and blood tests for final confirmation, but . . .' He shrugged the rest.

'How long on dental?'

'It'll take time, but at least we have a name.'

'Killed in her flat?' asked Charlton.

'She was,' said Brook. 'SOCO found extensive blood spatter, though the place had been thoroughly cleaned. Sheets and fabrics have been removed, every surface wiped, scrubbed and bleached, where necessary. No prints or usable DNA yet. The SOCO team are still working it, and we're canvassing, but the timeline's a little vague and we've had nothing from neighbours so far.'

'Nothing?'

'It's not a residential building,' said Noble. 'Most of the units are small businesses and empty after six if not before, so she'd have the building to herself in the evenings.'

'If she was a prostitute, maybe the Tanners were customers,' speculated Charlton.

'Again possible.'

'CCTV?' prompted Charlton.

'Not installed and no record of visitors, though there is an entryphone system,' said Cooper. 'There are dozens of prints but we'll keep trying to isolate anything useful.'

'What about cameras?'

'Vernon Street is off the main drag so no cameras pointing at the building. DC Cooper is looking for the stolen van travelling on nearby streets, but it's a needle in a haystack without a time.'

'Then assuming Kassia Proch is the girl in the van,' Charlton continued carefully, 'why brief us about Caitlin and the Interpol girls?'

'Because we've found a link,' said Brook.

Charlton closed his eyes briefly. 'A serial killer?'

'As we only have one body, that's overstating it at this point,' said Brook.

'Two bodies if you count the foetus,' retorted Charlton.

Brook lowered his head in agreement. 'I put it together in the briefing when I mentioned the victim was pregnant. Constable Banach touched her crucifix and I knew. Bernadette Murphy is Irish, Daniela Cassetti is Italian and the other three girls are Polish. They're all from devout Catholic countries where family planning is frowned upon and access to abortions is either restricted or non-existent.'

'Caitlin Kinnear is Northern Irish,' argued Read.

'But she's from the Catholic community.'

'So you think these girls were abortion tourists?' said Charlton.

'Not all of them came to Britain exclusively for that purpose,' said Noble. 'Valerie Gliszczynska was in the country for eighteen months before she disappeared.'

'Then how . . . ?'

'We paid a visit to the Rutherford Clinic last night,' said Noble. 'Spoke to a Dr Fleming. Four girls from the original Interpol inquiry were on record at the clinic. Caitlin Kinnear and Kassia Proch make six. They'd all made an appointment to arrange a termination. Some became pregnant while they were here, like Valerie and Caitlin, some journeyed to England with the sole objective of getting an abortion.'

'Nicola Serota,' said Read.

'Right,' agreed Noble. 'She was only here for two days before she visited the clinic for an appointment.'

'Why didn't her sister tell me she was pregnant?' asked Read.

'Likely she wouldn't have known,' said Banach. 'Unplanned pregnancies in Poland are kept secret. If the news gets out, I've heard about girls being sent to another part of the country to stay with relatives – sometimes never to return. Nicola's safest option was to tell no one.'

'I agree,' said Brook. 'To that end, all the girls found the money to pay for a no-frills private abortion so fewer people would know about their condition.'

'But if Kassia Proch wasn't on Interpol's list,' said Charlton, 'how did you find her?'

'As you pointed out, Nicola Serota disappeared sixteen months ago,' said Brook. 'That's a long time in captivity, so I asked Fleming about young women from Catholic countries who'd registered recently but hadn't gone through with the termination. Kassia Proch's name came up.'

'She visited the clinic thirty-six hours before we found her body,' said Noble. 'She was due to undergo the procedure that evening but pulled out. Apparently she had a change of heart, quite common in Catholic women.'

Charlton was thoughtful. 'And you think someone at this clinic is targeting these girls on religious grounds?'

'Might be racial,' suggested Morton. 'Nobody likes a health tourist.'

'We're ruling that out,' said Brook. 'All the girls on the clinic's books, apart from Kassia, were willing to put up the money to ensure discretion.'

'So race isn't significant?' queried Charlton.

'Only insofar as whoever's targeting these girls knows that foreigners are less likely to be missed until it's too late to pick up their scent.'

'And we think it's somebody with a connection to the clinic?'

'Either one of the staff or someone on the picket line,' said Noble.

'Picket line?'

'Every girl who visits the clinic has to run the gauntlet of pro-life protesters persuading them to think again.'

'Something they have every right to do,' retorted Charlton.

'As they're not striking miners, yes,' said Brook. Charlton shot him a glance. He sometimes forgot Brook's past growing up near the Barnsley coalfields. 'But when we visited, persuasion had spilled over into intimidation, which Dr Fleming complained was a daily ritual for staff *and* patients. We had to step in.'

Charlton sought the right words. 'Some people find it hard to condone the taking of a human life.'

'And some find the responsibility for another human life too much to contemplate when their own is spinning out of control,' replied Brook.

'Then these women should take care not to get pregnant.'

'I'll be sure to mention that on our next battered baby call.'

There was silence in the room and the assembled detectives looked between Brook and Charlton like a crowd at a tennis match.

Cooper's face contorted in calculation. 'Hang on. I make that seven missing girls in total – we're missing one.'

Brook nodded at Noble, who reloaded the picture of the original girls. 'We've eliminated the first girl, Bernadette Murphy. She wasn't on the Rutherford database.'

'Meaning?'

'She didn't have a termination and may be a separate case,' said Brook.

'So she might actually have gone off on her travels after all,' said Charlton.

'It's possible.'

'So what now?'

'We've put together a list of staff at the clinic, from the director down to the cleaners,' said Noble. 'This includes staff members who have since left but were in post when Valerie Gliszczynska disappeared two years ago. I've divided the names up. We're looking for anything that jumps out – extreme religious views, criminal record; the usual drill. But these are the caring professions, so we may have to dig deeper for other skeletons.'

'What sort of skeletons?' asked Smee.

Brook shrugged. 'People with moral and religious objections

to the clinic's work are unlikely to be working there, but there might be somebody who, for instance, has lost a child and, religious or not, might take a dim view of destroying a healthy foetus.'

'But with that mindset you're unlikely to murder a pregnant woman,' said Banach.

'That's true,' admitted Brook. 'So Kassia may also be a separate case. But according to Dr Fleming, she changed her mind and cancelled the termination at the last minute.'

'So maybe the killer didn't know that,' said Banach.

'Who knows, but we're groping in the dark here.'

'Are we checking names against the Sex Offenders Register?' asked Smee.

'None of the staff are on the register,' said Brook. 'John and I already discussed the possibility of a pair of rapists operating, but we don't think these crimes are sexual in nature. Kassia hadn't engaged in sexual activity before her death.'

'A pair?' said Charlton.

'It was a line of enquiry on Caitlin and Valerie,' explained Brook. 'Abduction is a lot easier with two pairs of hands.'

'You mean like the Tanner brothers,' observed Charlton drily. Brook prepared a reply but thought better of it.

Banach said, 'I don't have a staff list.'

'No,' said Brook. 'I want you and Rob back to the clinic to check out the protesters. They may not be keen to cooperate, but do your best. We want a list of regular pickets, and when you get names, feed them back to Dave to run background.'

'We have a pregnant murder victim,' said Banach to Morton. 'We can use that.'

'Good idea,' said Brook. 'Start with Father O'Toole. He's likely to know everyone and seemed to be in charge.'

'Father Patrick O'Toole?' exclaimed Charlton.

Brook eyed him. 'He mentioned he knew you.'

Charlton nodded. 'We've . . . met.'

'Then you'll know where can we find him,' said Brook. 'Sir.'

Charlton spent a few seconds hunting for offence in Brook's tone. 'I'll get my address book when we're done.'

'One final thing, something we need to bear in mind,' said Noble, his tone sombre. 'We have one body so far.'

'Two,' insisted Charlton, stern at this second omission.

'That's the complication,' said Brook softly. 'Not all the girls were abducted at the same time.'

Charlton stared at Brook. 'I can see that from the timeline.'

'What Inspector Brook means is that apart from Caitlin, the three Polish girls and Daniela Cassetti were all abducted *before* their terminations took place,' said Noble.

'So?'

'So if those women were abducted by pro-lifers . . .' said Banach, leaving the rest unsaid.

Charlton took a second to grasp the full implication. 'My God. You think these women . . .'

'It's possible that one or all of them may have been forcibly brought to term, yes,' concluded Brook. 'In which case we could be looking for at least four children as well.'

'Coerced childbirth?' said Read.

'It's unheard of,' said Charlton.

'It's unusual but there have been cases in the US,' said Brook.

'That wouldn't be an easy operation to keep under wraps,' said Read. 'They'd need plenty of privacy and lots of room.'

'Not if the mothers were killed after the birth and the babies trafficked,' said Cooper. All heads turned to him. 'They *were* taken one at a time.' Expressions registered objections but no one was able to challenge his logic. 'Just saying.'

The incident room door burst open and the portly figure of Sergeant Grey popped his head round. 'There's been a sighting of Nick Tanner. Thought you should know.'

'Where?'

'Wandering round the Intu like he's Christmas shopping,' grinned Grey. 'Three units on the way. I've alerted Intu security, for what it's worth.'

Brook nodded at Noble, who rushed out of the incident room, beckoning Smee and Read to join him.

Nick wiped his hands on several tissues and threw them into the empty burger box. He burped happily and slid out from the banquette to make his way to the escalator. He'd bought some cookies for Jake in case he came looking for him. *Then maybe he won't be so narked.*

He came to a halt as he turned the corner at Starbucks, a familiar figure standing in front of him. Nick smiled and raised a hand in greeting.

'Hiya, Max.'

Max took a moment to consider before returning the smile.

Twenty-Seven

CAITLIN WOKE TO THE SOUND of blood throbbing in her eardrums. Everything was black. She took a breath, inhaled cloth, and after a brief moment of panic snatched a thick bag from her head and sucked in oxygen.

She examined the black cotton bag. There was a scrap of paper attached. *New rule. Bag on head when u r moved. 3 knocks to warn u. Don't forget bitch.*

'Bastards,' spat Caitlin, looking around her cramped and gloomy new cell. She was on her back, her legs bent and knees up to her chin, head and neck contorted by lack of space, cheek jammed up against something cold. Her hands were cuffed in front by the kind of plastic restraints she'd seen in movies, but the rest of her fetters were off, including the heavy glove with phone attached.

Slowly she stretched her aching legs to the cold tile wall and pushed herself upright until she reclined against another wall, wedged tight between it and cold, hard china. She was in a cramped toilet closet with an old-fashioned toilet bowl and could hear the trickle of the cistern high on the wall.

She flexed her legs like a newborn foal. On the ground was a small plastic food bag smeared with a creamy substance. She examined it with distaste before realising it was the chicken breast from her abortive meal with the deformed old man.

She tore open the plastic. The chicken was covered in carpet fibres, but Caitlin didn't care and, after picking off the worst of the debris, tore the meat apart, devouring it in seconds before running a finger around the bag to lick up the creamy sauce.

In the faint light, she saw the box jammed into the space on the other side of the toilet. On top was a small bottle of water. She twisted off the cap and drank down the entire bottle with no thought of rationing. When it was empty, she retained it for a refill and read the writing on the box.

Belted Diapers for Incontinent Seniors.

'Jesus.'

At the same time, she registered the squelch of human waste in her own diaper and her eyes filled with tears, which she quickly blinked away.

'No,' she spat. 'I've cried enough,' she added quietly, taking calming breaths. 'You perverts don't get the satisfaction.'

She stood with as much dignity as she could muster and reached under her dress to remove her soiled diaper. With bound hands it was fiddly work, but eventually she released the garment with an unholy squelch and scrunched it tightly to incarcerate the fumes before flushing it away.

She sat on the cold white china of the toilet bowl, leaving the seat up, and stared down at the water. It seemed fresh. With a grimace, she set about washing herself as best she could, reaching back under herself with her bound hands. Eventually she was satisfied she'd done her best and dabbed herself dry with toilet paper which at least was soft.

After flushing, she knelt over the bowl to rinse her hands as thoroughly as possible. The crucifix-shaped burn on her forearm began to sting, so she bathed her arm in the fresh water. This time she didn't dry off. Then she reached reluctantly into the box and took out a fresh diaper.

In the dim light she read the leaflet from the nappy box. 'Suitable for both urinal and faecal incontinence. No mention of electric shock therapy. Maybe I should sue.' She threw the flyer and diaper back into the box. 'Going commando,' she mumbled.

Gazing down at her dress, her expression contorted with confusion. 'I was wearing jeans in the barn. This dress was in my rucksack, in my room,' she said slowly. Her eyes widened. 'So if my rucksack is here . . . Shit! I'm not even missing. People will think I'm in Belfast and Mairead will think I'm in Derby.'

She hung her head. 'Kitty. They knew my name, where I lived. Jesus. They came for me. They wanted *me*.' Her lip wobbled but the tears refused to flow. She remembered the old man stroking her hair. 'I'm not the first.' She raised her face to the sky to shout. 'Laurie! They get you too? Are you here? Can you hear me?' No answer. 'Looks like you're on your own, girl.'

She slumped on to the toilet seat and looked up the high whitewashed walls. Small rays of sunshine were illuminating the rusting metal cistern through a ventilation grille embedded high in the wall. It was an old-fashioned duct, built into the brickwork, and through it she could hear the sound of distant birdsong, which ignited a sudden pining to be outside.

She clambered on to the toilet seat, but even standing, she couldn't get close to the grille. Cocking an ear, she fancied she could pick up the noise of traffic. Not the all-pervasive drone of the city but the intermittent roar of a car hurtling along at speed. The farm must be near a main road.

I ran away from the road. Why didn't I turn left? Jeez, if the Devil had sat at the Lord's right hand, I might have made it.

She lifted her face towards the distant grille.

'Help!' she shouted, holding the word as long as her breath allowed. 'Can anyone hear me?'

After ten minutes of increasingly desperate shouting, she jumped down, her mouth set, tamping down her despair. 'You're a rat in a trap, Kitty. Deal with it.'

She turned her attention to the solid wooden door and pushed, shoved and probed at it methodically, seeking weakness. It didn't budge an inch and there was nothing to get hold of on her side to give her any play – no handle, no latch, nothing.

In fact the only weakness was a missing knot of wood leaving a hole, but something had been wedged over it from the other side so she couldn't see out. In a rush of sudden anger, she banged and kicked at the door, screaming for help, feeling and hearing her voice crack under the strain. After two minutes of fruitless violence with feet and bound hands, she sat down again, appraising the walls of her prison.

It was like a public convenience, though Caitlin was sure it wasn't cold enough to be in a separate outhouse and she didn't remember being carried outside. Then again, she'd been unconscious. She winced at the memory of the electricity coursing through her, ran her teeth over the self-inflicted bite on her tongue.

'Wait till I hook you up to a socket, cocksuckers. There won't be enough juice left in the grid to boil a kettle.'

She slouched on the toilet, glancing resentfully up at the

door. An eye blinked back at her through the peephole and Caitlin's smile froze. Holding back her anger, she sneered towards her jailer. 'See anything you like, needledick?' She'd slipped back into her broadest Irish accent, knowing that some people found it intimidating.

She stood, lifting her bound hands under her breasts, and hefted them towards the peephole. 'Nice tits as well, you pervert. Hey, freakshow!' she screamed, jumping up to crash her bound hands against the door. 'Try the internet. You can see the lot for free and you don't need to jack off standing up.'

'You scared my dad, bitch,' shouted a male voice from the other side of the door.

Caitlin leaned into the wood. 'You've got to be fucking kidding me. What about me?'

'What about you, you tramp? You give yourself to men for free like the baby-killing whore you are while my dad's all alone.'

'*I'm* all alone,' snarled Caitlin.

'Then you're made for each other,' retorted the man. 'And he wouldn't have used you like those other men. A bit of hand-holding and a kiss on the cheek. Then maybe later see what develops. Was that too much to ask?'

'See what develops?' Caitlin's mind was racing. 'You fucking kidnapped me. You tortured me. And you think I'm gonna fall in love with your dad. You think we're gonna have sex.'

'Not sex,' said the man. 'Love.'

'Love?' screamed Caitlin. 'He's a fucking gargoyle.'

'You baby-killing bitch. By the time I've finished with you, you'll be begging to spend time with my dad.' The eye withdrew and the peephole closed.

'Wait. Where are you going? Give me another chance.' No reply. 'Are you there? Please. Give me another chance.'

Caitlin woke and stretched out stiffly on the cold floor. Sunlight poured through the grille set high in the wall. It must be morning. After flexing her neck she began to agitate. She needed food and she needed exercise. She devised some simple stretches to keep herself occupied, which wasn't easy as she could touch all four walls of the cubicle from the toilet seat. And, of course, any physical activity created a keener sense of hunger after she'd finished.

'Hey, how about some food in here?' She kicked out at the door in frustration.

Eventually she sat down panting, staring at her surroundings, searching for weaknesses in her cell. There had once been a bolt on the inside of the door – she could see the pilot holes for screws. There'd also been an old-fashioned round light switch but this had also been removed, judging by the circle of different-coloured paint, which continued in a line to the ceiling, suggesting an absent cable. The distant ceiling rose was still in place but was too high to reach and contained no bulb.

Caitlin clambered on to the toilet seat and stood on tiptoes to examine the flush as best she could. Instead of a traditional handle and chain, a durable length of nylon rope hung down from the unreachable cistern, and she wondered how she might put it to use if she were able to detach it from the lofty handle. She grabbed the rope and tried to pull herself up but stopped immediately. If the cord couldn't bear her weight, she might break the cistern, and if she damaged the flush before she had a plan, she might have no access to clean water.

Instead she felt along the old lead pipe hugging the wall to the bulky cistern. It was embedded in the plaster with no way to get purchase or her hands round it. However, as she prepared to jump to the floor, her fingers alighted on something metallic that had been jammed between the wall and the pipe. It was a rusty nail. It wasn't part of the pipe's support structure so must have been forced into position for some reason. Maybe someone had hidden it there, though Caitlin couldn't think why. Nevertheless, she prised it from behind the pipe and examined it.

The nail was rusty apart from the point, which seemed a lot shinier, as though it had been used regularly. For what? Manoeuvring her cuffed wrists, she tried to force it into her plastic hand ties, but it was too difficult to get purchase and she gave up, replacing the nail behind the pipe until she could think of a better use for it. Frustrated, she jumped down from the seat, lost her balance and fell back against the wooden toilet-roll holder, which broke away from the wall bringing a pair of white tiles with it.

'Shit.'

She sank to her knees to pick up one of the tiles. It was broken in two and the white glaze felt sharp to the touch. She sucked her grazed finger, then picked up the broken tile and set to work, holding it between her knees and forcing her bound hands across the serrated edge.

After a few misfires, the plastic cuffs fell apart and, feeling a mixture of elation and relief, Caitlin knelt to cool her sore wrists in the clean water of the toilet. As she soothed her bruises, she glanced across at the gap left by the tiles. A series of marks was gouged into the plaster in the manner of a Stone Age calendar – the sort of primitive timekeeping that prisoners might use to document captivity.

'The nail.'

She totted up twenty counting gates – six small vertical scratches in the plaster scored through with one diagonal. Her heart sank. If one counting gate equalled one week, someone had recorded twenty weeks of confinement in this tiny cubicle.

Twenty weeks. Five months! She pressed herself closer to the makeshift calendar, flattening her palms against the wall, feeling for further scratches. She gritted her teeth and prised away another tile, relieved to see that there were no more counting gates. But there was something just as depressing. Letters. Now Caitlin could put a name to the previous inmate. She traced each letter with a forefinger to be sure.

D-A-N-I-E-L-A.

'Daniela.' Caitlin was sombre. 'What did the bastards do to you, girl?' She looked up at the faint sunbeams, a yearning to be outside in the light overwhelming her.

'Count your blessings, Kitty,' she said, setting her jaw. 'Daniela survived in here for five months. And if she could, so can I. And I promise you this, girl. If I get the chance, I'm going to hurt these cocksuckers real bad.'

Nick wouldn't linger in a store that sold old people's clothes, so Jake walked quickly through Marks & Spencer at the corner of the Intu mall, not wanting to lower his hood but realising that to keep his head covered would arouse suspicion. Already a security guard had registered his presence and was following at a discreet distance, speaking into a radio on his epaulette.

Jake hurried out of M&S into the anonymity of the crowded walkways, where hordes of Saturday shoppers wandered aimlessly, and made a beeline for likelier venues. There was no sign of Nick at any mobile phone stores, so he headed for Eat

Central, where his brother would gorge himself for hours whenever Jake had money. No sign.

He was about to head into a sports store when he saw two familiar figures outside on the pavement. One was holding open the door of an idling black Mercedes, sleek and long, while the other dipped into the cabin clutching a bag of cookies, a happy grin on his face.

'Nick!' shouted Jake, setting off at a lick towards the smoked-glass doors that drowned his appeal. 'Nick!' he repeated at the car already pulling away. He sprinted outside and towards the vehicle, which slammed on its brakes. The driver's door opened and a man jumped out.

Jake recognised Ostrowsky's bodyguard grinning at him, and stared back, frozen. He glanced at Nick, happily munching away in the back seat, took a deep breath, then jogged reluctantly towards the waiting car.

At that moment, a police car pulled up behind the Mercedes and four uniformed officers poured out and headed towards him. Jake stopped cold and turned on his heel back towards the mall, pulling his hood tighter as he marched away, listening for signs he'd been recognised.

Tymon's smile faded as he calmly got back into the driver's seat and pulled away at low speed until subsumed into the cover of other slow-moving cars crawling along Traffic Street towards Pride Park.

'That was Jake,' said Nick from the back seat through a mouthful of cookie.

'Yes, it was,' said Ostrowsky beside him. He relaxed on to the tan leather to contemplate Nick.

'Why didn't he get in?'

'Maybe he doesn't want a lift home,' smiled the businessman.

'Well it's not far . . .' Nick stopped, realising he'd said too much.

'Not far?' demanded Max gruffly from the front seat. 'Where do you live now, Nick?'

'I can't tell,' said Nick, a little puzzled. 'Jake says we might get *fucked over*.' He grinned at the sound in his throat and looked round for approval. Ostrowsky smiled his encouragement.

'He's right,' growled Max, reaching an arm over the seat to grab at Nick.

His wrist was caught by his brother and held in a vice-like grip. 'Calm down, little brother,' said Ostrowsky. He smiled, but there was flint in his eye. He barked an order at Tymon, then let go of Max with an accompanying flick, addressing him in Polish. 'We're civilised men, Max. Violence is a last resort.'

'We must get to Jake before the police do,' retorted Max. 'We don't know what he'll say to them.'

'On the contrary, I know exactly what he's going to tell the police,' said Ostrowsky.

Max turned to stare at his brother. 'You do?'

Ostrowsky gazed back inscrutably. 'I sometimes wonder if we're from the same family, *braciszek*.'

Charlton handed DS Morton a note. 'That's his home address. It's next to Our Lady of Lourdes.' Morton accepted the paper and gestured Banach to the door. 'Sergeant!' said Charlton, halting the detectives in their tracks. 'He's a man of the cloth. Tread lightly.' Morton glanced across at Brook, who didn't countermand.

'A member of the station prayer group?' asked Brook, when Morton and Banach had left.

'No,' replied Charlton, testily. 'But then you wouldn't know, would you, never having attended?'

'Would that I could,' said Brook.

'I'll bet,' sneered Charlton. 'You know you should cross your fingers that whoever's behind these abductions *is* religious.'

'Why's that?'

'Because when you have faith in the Lord, you value human life,' said Charlton, making his way to the door. Brook decided against cataloguing all the wars fought to defend or impose a faith. 'Under any other scenario,' continued Charlton, pompously, 'I'd expect these babies to turn up dead.'

Brook turned to the photograph, the dead girl's smile still beaming hopefully from the whiteboard. 'Then why is Kassia Proch's baby dead?'

'I don't know,' retorted Charlton. 'Do you?'

'Let me talk to him,' said Max. 'I know him better than you.'

'I thought you only knew him to say hello,' said Ostrowsky, lighting a cigarette.

'That's more than you.'

After brief consideration, Ostrowsky shook his head. 'No.' He turned to Tymon. 'I'm expecting a container. Keep an eye.' Tymon pushed through the heavy-duty plastic sheeting out on to the delivery concourse, itself set apart from the small suite of offices and, beyond, the warehouse. Ostrowsky tossed the pack of cigarettes to Max. 'Both of you.' Max stood his ground, turning to follow only when his elder brother raised an impatient eyebrow. Tymon held the plastic door until Max preceded him out towards the loading bay.

Ostrowsky went into the unlocked office. Nick was seated at the computer terminal absorbed in an online game of pool. 'Boom,' he yelled as he pocketed a ball.

'You like games, Nick.'

'Love 'em,' said Nick, barely shifting his gaze from the monitor. 'Especially on a high-res machine like this.'

Ostrowsky smiled. 'Do you have a phone, Nick? I want to let Jake know you're okay.'

'Not allowed phones,' said Nick. He lined up another shot.

Ostrowsky considered Nick, deciding he was telling the truth. The boy was like a child and deceit didn't come easy. Trying a different tack, he produced his wallet and pulled out a fifty-pound note, held it in front of Nick, who finally managed to turn his head from the monitor. 'Then why don't I order a taxi for you? Give me your address and take this to pay for it.'

'That's too much,' said Nick cautiously, eyeing the note, thinking of the dwindling funds inside his teddy.

'That's okay,' smiled Ostrowsky. 'Treat yourself.'

Nick held out a hand and took the money. He nodded before looking around the office. 'Have you got a cushion?'

Brook worked through his list of Rutherford Clinic staff but could find no compelling background that required a more in-depth examination. Only he and Cooper remained in the incident room, checking through names against various databases. As the resident IT expert, Cooper had been given a longer list, with the most prominent names; from the silence behind Cooper's monitor, Brook knew that nobody had yet caught his eye.

On his way to the kettle, Cooper handed over his labours

on Dr Fleming. The shake of the head hadn't lifted Brook's spirits.

Brook read the information. Rafe Fleming was a wealthy surgeon and consultant, and on top of his high earnings and brilliant reputation he was one of the pillars of the county's social elite, judging from his frequent appearances in *Derbyshire Life*'s society pages. Married to a woman twenty years his junior, he enjoyed the good things in life, living in a large house on the edge of Ashbourne, when he wasn't holidaying in his Provençal villa. His two teenage sons studied at Queen Elizabeth's Grammar School, one of the county's top schools. If Fleming had a motive for abducting his patients, neither Cooper nor Brook could come up with it.

For something to do, Brook clicked on one of the icons on his toolbar to look again at the home page of the last pro-life group he'd loaded. The night before, he had pored over dozens of sites for organisations across the world, some extreme, some less so. One article in particular had caught his eye. An American religious group called Abolish All Abortions were advocating the kidnapping of 'abortion-minded women', who would be held while being lectured about the sin they were contemplating. After a suitable period for re-education, they would be released and dropped off at a local church.

After making a cup of tea, Brook loaded his email account and was reading the results of forensic examinations when his mobile vibrated on the desk.

'John.'

'We missed him,' said Noble. 'Apparently he was eating at Burger King and wandering around like he didn't have a care in the world.'

'Maybe he hasn't,' replied Brook. 'Any sign of Jake?'

'None. The brothers seem to have separated.'

'What about security?'

'They were keeping an eye. They noticed some guy in a hoodie behaving suspiciously in M and S but they lost him.'

'Inspector Gadget would be appalled,' said Brook. 'Get them to send over film. It could give us an up-to-date likeness at least. By the way, EMSOU confirms the hammer as the blunt instrument, used post mortem.'

'DNA?'

'They tested Tanner's DNA against the foetus. No match and no sign of his DNA on the gloves.'

'That doesn't prove he didn't wear them to kill Kassia Proch,' said Noble.

'But we've only got Max Ostrowsky's DNA in the glove.'

'Which we can't confirm unless he agrees to a sample.'

'I know,' sighed Brook. 'How soon for that warrant?'

'I can hurry it up, but even if we prove it's Max's DNA, his brief will say it's where it's supposed to be. In his glove, in his van. We need a matching sample from Kassia's flat or the body.'

'There's nothing on the body and the flat's clean. What about the vodka bottle?'

'From the Cream Bar?' said Noble. 'It wasn't prioritised. No telling how long it was there or who put it—'

'Have you ever seen that brand of vodka before?'

'Only at Bar Polski.'

'Then maybe it's their exclusive brand and somebody connected to Ostrowsky left it there.'

'That's a bit of a stretch,' said Noble.

'Test it anyway, John. If either Max or Ostrowsky's

bodyguard was there, we'd have a line on who attacked Banach and Ryan.'

'Max or the bodyguard? In other words, you haven't a clue,' said Noble. 'Charlton's going to love you when he gets the bill.'

Brook had no answer and rang off. 'In *Max's* glove,' he mumbled. 'In *Max's* van.' He scrabbled around his desktop, locating the paper he required and scanning down the list. 'Bag of tools, bunch of keys. In Max's van.' At Noble's desk, he rummaged through drawers in the hope his sergeant hadn't had time to book all the minor exhibits into evidence.

He drew out the sealed plastic bag containing the large bunch of keys, blackened by smoke and silver-grey fingerprint powder but still recognisable.

He pulled on his jacket, gesturing at Cooper. 'If anyone wants me, I'm nipping out to a bar, and then I'm off to see a man about a God.'

Ostrowsky emerged on to the loading bay, shaking out a cigarette and lighting up. His face was severe. 'Tymon, get Ashley into the office to look after the boy. He's to keep him here but he's not a prisoner, make it understood. Keep him happy. Let him play on the computer and give him what he wants from the vending machines. We go back to Bar Polski to wait.'

'What did he say?' asked Max as Tymon lumbered away.

Ostrowsky examined the blood-red sky, darkening by the moment. 'Nothing.' He smiled at Max to reassure. 'He's just a child.'

'Let me talk to him,' said Max, already on his way.

Ostrowsky caught his brother's arm. 'No need. We have

him and Jake knows we have him.' He reached a hand behind Max's head to hold his attention. 'And if he behaves anything like an elder brother should, we'll see him very soon.'

Max nodded. 'I need a drink.'

Ostrowsky smiled at him, but as usual his eyes had trouble joining in. He walked over to an opened carton and withdrew a full bottle of vodka. 'Here, *braciszek*.'

'*Dzieki*,' grinned Max, cracking the seal.

Ostrowsky put a hand over the bottleneck. 'No. It's for the journey.'

'Journey? Where am I going?'

'Home to Poland,' answered Ostrowsky. Max made to protest, but Ostrowsky talked over him. 'Just until things calm down and this dead girl is forgotten. There's a ferry leaving from Harwich tonight. Tymon will drive you.'

'How long?'

'A month, maybe two.'

Max nodded. 'If you think it's best, brother.'

'I do. Go home and pack. Wait for Tymon to pick you up. I'll see you in a month.' Max turned away. 'Little brother,' said Ostrowsky, his arms extended. Max moved in for a hug and Ostrowsky held him tight, then pushed him away to look affectionately into his eyes.

Jake hurried past Matalan without breaking into an attention-seeking run, but only breathed freely when under the damp pall cast by the tower block. It had taken a lot of serious walking and doubling back to get out of the Intu, which was now crawling with uniformed police. Fortunately there were plenty of exits, and Jake had been able to depart the complex on East Street, the farthest point from Milton Flats. Once out of the bright mall and on to the teeming streets, he had gradually begun to feel invisible again.

He unlocked the door of the ground-floor flat and headed for the sofa, where he sat in silence for what seemed like hours, barely moving, breathing shallow. Finally he slid a hand under the foam cushion to extract a mobile phone. He pulled the SIM card from his pocket and recommissioned the phone before turning it on and scrolling down for the number, then depressed a thumb on to the speed dial and held it to his ear.

A gruff foreign accent greeted his ears. 'Bar Polski.'

'It's Jake.'

No reply for a second as the phone was passed along, then a familiar voice. 'Jake. How are you?'

'Where's Nick?'

'Safe,' said Ostrowsky.

'Where?'

'Don't waste his time or mine,' said Ostrowsky. 'The clock moves round. What time shall I expect you?'

Jake took a deep breath to make the calculation.

Brook extracted the bunch of keys from the clear plastic bag and examined them against the mortise lock of the Cream Bar's front entrance. The door had been forced open the night Banach and Ryan had been assaulted, smashing the strike plate on the door jamb. However, Brook could see no reason why the locking mechanism shouldn't work.

He selected a key and tried to insert it into the lock, but it wouldn't fit. Trying a thinner key, he managed to get it into the lock but it wouldn't turn. His third selection worked, and the rectangular metal block emerged from the housing. Just to be sure, he walked into the building and tried other keys on other doors. They all worked.

'Have a drink, Jake,' said Ostrowsky, solicitously pouring vodka into two shot glasses without waiting for a reply. 'You look like you need one. And this time you won't have to steal it.' He handed the glass to Jake and sat down opposite him, reclining, the epitome of self-assurance, rolling vodka around his mouth.

'I don't steal drinks from employers,' replied Jake, hunching forward on the edge of his seat, clutching the untouched vodka in a rigid hand, the occasional glance round at Tymon standing out of his eyeline increasing his unease. Outside the large windows of Bar Polski's unopened first-floor bar, the darkness had gathered.

'You know, I'm inclined to believe you,' said Ostrowsky. 'So, drink.'

Jake sniffed at the glass, his hand shaking. He took a minute sip, then gasped at the heat and slumped back in something approaching relief. What he feared had arrived. No more waiting. He was even able to joke about his situation, albeit nervously. 'Is this about the twenty quid?'

Ostrowsky chuckled softly. He looked up at Tymon to translate and the big man grinned in appreciation. Ostrowsky finished his vodka and poured himself another from the bottle next to his chair. 'You joke. That's good. Relax, feel comfortable.' His smile disappeared. 'Then tell me why you stole my van.'

'Where's Nick?'

'Safe.'

'Here?'

'Somewhere.'

'I want to see him.'

Ostrowsky shot an impatient glance up at Tymon, muttered something in Polish.

'If I don't see him—' Before Jake could finish the sentence, he fell to the floor clutching a hand to his back, writhing in agony and unable to catch his breath.

Ostrowsky watched impassively, then bent down to pick up Jake's spilled glass and refilled it. A moment later he nodded at Tymon, who reached a hand down to Jake and yanked him back up on to the padded chair, where he continued his recovery, rubbing his back and drying his watering eyes.

'Drink,' said Ostrowsky, holding out the glass.

Jake took it, and this time, eyes closed, drained its contents, finishing with a rough cough before regaining his breath. Finally he looked up at Ostrowsky. 'I didn't know it was yours. I thought it was just a random van . . .' Ostrowsky glanced at Tymon, who drew back a fist. 'All right, all right,' shouted Jake. 'I thought it belonged to Max, not you. I found his address in the office and I went to his place to smash up the van.'

'Why would you wish to damage my brother's van?' Ostrowsky's voice was flat, devoid of curiosity.

'To piss him off.'

'Why?'

'You're his brother,' said Jake with a disbelieving sneer. 'Don't you know?'

Tymon raised an arm in anticipation but Ostrowsky shook his head. The big man lowered the fat fist to his side.

For the first time it was Ostrowsky's gaze that fell, and he nodded quietly. 'But instead you stole it.'

'Only because the dozy bastard hadn't locked it.' Ostrowsky

glanced at Tymon. 'I thought I'd run a few speed traps, dent a few parked cars. Drop him right in it.'

Ostrowsky's expression was severe. 'And you took Nick with you to steal my van? What kind of example is that for an elder brother to set?'

Jake was surprised. 'I couldn't leave him in the flat all day and night. Not on his own. You've seen him. He's just a kid.'

'Then you should lock him in to protect him.'

'Is that what you do with Max?' said Jake.

Ostrowsky flicked his eyes at Tymon and another blow caught Jake in the kidneys. Ostrowsky took a sip of vodka, waiting for the spluttering and panting to be over. 'And the girl?'

Jake recalled the disfigured face, the broken body, but could barely speak. 'What about her?' he finally squeezed out.

'Who was it?'

'It was Kassia.'

'Kassia?'

'Your cleaner.'

'You're sure?'

Jake nodded. 'She was badly beaten about the face. But I think so.'

Ostrowsky downed his drink and refilled his glass. 'Why did you kill her?'

'What?'

'Why did you kill her? I need to know.'

'I didn't kill her. Max did.'

'Why do you say that?'

'It was his van, wasn't it?'

Ostrowsky studied him before taking another large gulp of vodka. 'It was my van. Now I want the truth. Let's start again.'

'This is a waste of time.'

'Then why did you come?'

'To get my brother.'

'Then give me a reason I can believe. For Nick's sake.'

Jake laughed bitterly. 'Think I don't know how this ends? Just kill me and get it over with.'

'Kill you?' laughed Ostrowsky. His mirth subsided quickly, his brilliant eyes boring into Jake. 'I'm not going to kill you.'

'I don't believe you.'

'It's true.' Ostrowsky shrugged. 'I won't insult you by saying I value your life, but I'm not going to kill you.'

Jake stared. 'Why?'

'Because I don't need to. But I'm curious. You expect to die, yet you say nothing. I have to cause you pain to get answers. Most people would talk for hours and say *anything* to delay that. But not you.'

'Step into my life for a week,' said Jake. 'Then tell me it's worth the living.'

'Ah, you persuade me that you welcome death so I don't kill you,' said Ostrowsky appreciatively. 'Very clever. But it won't work. When you are young, life is good. I know this. Yes, you are poor, but I have been where you are.'

'You forget the police are hunting me for a murder.'

'Yet you are here. Either the police are stupid or you are clever.'

'Clever?' Jake laughed without mirth. 'If I was clever, I wouldn't be living with a brother . . .'

'Continue.'

'Forget it.'

'I understand. You don't wish to speak ill of Nick because he's a child. But all the same he is your brother. And it's difficult. I understand very well. I have such a brother – a brother who causes me great concern. And sometimes, in your frustration with him, you do and say the wrong thing. But never forget you are acting out of love.'

'Just kill me,' said Jake. 'You'd be doing me a favour.'

'It is a mortal sin to wish your life at an end before God is ready,' said Ostrowsky, wagging a finger.

'There is no God.'

'How can you say that?' said Ostrowsky, shocked. 'He is everywhere, helping us, guiding us.' He fondled the crucifix at his neck. 'You must open your heart to him.'

'Why?'

'Because he loves you.'

'Does he love Max?' demanded Jake. 'Because that's not a God I'm gonna like.'

Ostrowsky sighed. 'You are an intelligent man. I wish the circumstances were different, but time presses.' He stood with a glance at Tymon, who yanked Jake to his feet. 'You leave me no choice.'

Jake cowered. 'What are you going to do?'

Ostrowsky nodded in satisfaction. 'You were keen to die. Not so easy when the moment arrives, is it?'

'No,' admitted Jake, barely audible.

Ostrowsky paused for effect, then, 'You know the way out. You're free to go.' Walking away, he gestured at Tymon to release his bear-like grip on Jake's shoulders.

'Wait!' shouted Jake. 'Where are you going? What about Nick?'

'What about him?'

'He doesn't know anything,' pleaded Jake. 'You don't need to hurt him.'

'Need? It's been a long time since I've done anything from need. But you've changed that, Jake, because now I need *you*.' Ostrowsky puckered his lips as though considering something that had just occurred to him. 'Your brother, on the other hand, I don't need. So if I kill anyone to get what I want, I will kill him.'

'Mr Ostrowsky, please.' Jake's breath began to quicken. 'I don't know what I can say to change your mind.'

'Yes you do,' smiled Ostrowsky. 'Tell me exactly what I want to know and you both live.' He paused, waiting for Jake's refusal. When it didn't materialise, he returned to his seat. 'Good. Start with why you killed the girl.'

Twenty-Eight

A LOUD KNOCK WOKE CAITLIN FROM her catnap, followed by two more.

I'm being moved.

She looked to the door. An unblinking eye scanned her, unable to see her unfettered hands between her legs. She moved in front of her captor's vision, holding her wrists as if still bound.

'Please, I'm hungry,' she said in a submissive tone. The three knocks sounded again. 'Bag on head,' said Caitlin. 'Right, sorry.' She pulled the black cotton bag over her head, being careful to keep the nail pressed into her palm, then sat primly on the toilet lid, hands between her thighs.

She heard two bolts slide back and quickly leant down to pick up the broken tile, placing it on the seat behind her. The door creaked open. She could see nothing through the thick bag so she waited, poised like a big cat, for a footstep or the touch of a hand on her shoulder, manoeuvring the nail to protrude between her middle and forefinger and covering it with her left hand.

'I'm ready,' she said through the bag. 'And sorry about last time. I just want another chance.' Still no commands, but Caitlin could smell that unmistakable musk of unenthusiastic washing in front of her.

'Up,' said a male voice.

She sprang to her feet and leapt towards the sound, swinging her fist with the nail gripped as tightly as possible in her hand. She felt contact as the head of the nail pushed back against her palm and heard the satisfying yelp of pain and surprise from her captor.

A second later, rough hands grabbed at her throat. She swung again and on the downswing yanked at the bag covering her face, pulling it off to see a fist being drawn back, a thickset face behind it. She ducked to avoid the punch, managing a small sidestep that left the man grasping at thin air as he toppled towards the toilet bowl. She threw out a hand to grab the jagged tile.

'Bitch,' spat the man, kicking out at Caitlin as she jinked past him and made for the door.

She stumbled and fell over his leg, banging her head on the jamb. The man righted himself, his face puce with anger, a small puncture wound on his chin weeping blood on to his neck. He clenched his fists, puffing himself up as he loomed over her, but she sprang at him and slashed the tile across his cheek, a line of blood confirming her success.

The man screamed, and while he was on the back foot, Caitlin flung her head into his spongy midriff, forcing him down on to the toilet, levering herself back through the doorway in the same move. She slammed the door shut, feeling frantically for the bolts. It felt like a lifetime before she pushed the top one into place, but before it was fully home, the door shuddered and she was knocked backwards. Another shove and the catch plate buckled, a powerful hand pushing through the small gap.

Caitlin flung herself off her feet at the door, slamming the wood into the groping hand with a sickening crack. The man howled in pain but was unable to withdraw his trapped hand, so she eased back on the door, slashing across the knuckles with the tile.

More screaming but she didn't hesitate, forcing home the damaged bolt when the hand disappeared then stooping to do the same at the base. She flopped back against the wood, panting.

'You fucking bitch,' screamed the man, flinging his full weight against the door. It shuddered but held. 'You're fucking dead. You hear me? Dead.'

Caitlin flipped the cover away from the eyehole and, still panting, called out, 'Rule one, numb nuts. Don't mess with a Kinnear.'

She closed the peephole and looked around to get her bearings. A gloomy corridor seemed to lead back into the house, so she turned instead to a heavy door that must have been on the same external wall as the toilet grille. She pulled bolts and lifted latches but it wouldn't budge, despite her best efforts. She saw the sturdy lock, but there was no key and nothing hung anywhere in sight.

'Where are the keys to this door?' she screamed towards the toilet door.

'Fuck you,' was the muffled reply, the tone betraying his injuries. 'In here – come and get 'em.'

'Shit.' Caitlin had little option but to penetrate deeper into the house, so she inched her way carefully along the dark corridor with its cold stone flags. Before long she came to a door, not fully closed.

Pushing it open, she entered a bright kitchen. A pan of something brown and meaty simmered gently on the hob, scum frothing on the top. She was shocked to see the old man sitting in a corner chair, his hands on his lap. His disfigured head turned slowly towards her and he made a weak attempt to stand.

'Stay down, Grandad,' ordered Caitlin, brandishing the bloodied tile. The man relaxed back into the chair, his expression blank. 'Where am I?' she barked. No reaction.

She marched to the heavy kitchen door, drew back the two barrel bolts and seized the handle to wrench it open, but again it wouldn't budge. The door was locked and the window over the sink was barred and padlocked. She cast around for keys but none were visible.

'How do I get out of here?' No answer. She advanced aggressively towards the old man to loosen his tongue, but he didn't seem to register the threat or even understand what was going on. In fact he seemed to be smiling, if that were possible.

He croaked out a pair of indistinct syllables, which Caitlin deciphered as *nice hair*. A trembling hand reaching out to her head seemed to confirm this. It was then that she saw the column of tablets assembled on a small table beside the armchair. She halted, looked the old man in his vacant black eyes and lowered the tile.

'These locks aren't just for me, are they? You're ill. How do I get out of here?' she asked, gesturing at the bars. He started humming the tune from their abortive dinner.

Caitlin gave up. A folded newspaper sat on the table and she pounced on it, glancing at the date.

'April twenty-fifth,' she said. 'So little time. Feels like a lifetime.' She skimmed through for any mention of her disappearance. Nothing.

Tossing the paper aside, she proceeded to pull out kitchen drawers, emptying them on to the stone floor in her search for keys. The old man began to whimper at the noise of crashing cutlery but she ignored him, picking fruitlessly through the piles of silverware. Frustrated, she stomped over to the window, peering outside at a walled courtyard where a white panel van was parked. All was quiet. She was so close. A noise from the floor above drew her attention and she rounded on the old man.

'Who's up there?'

He moaned at her aggression, lowering his eyes in confusion. Caitlin darted an eye to an internal door set above a wooden step. She pulled it open and swayed back in case of attack. It revealed a polished wooden stairwell that turned left and wound out of sight. She stood for a moment considering her options, glanced at the fading daylight through the window then turned to the tangle of silverware and plucked out a butcher's knife before making her way to the bottom of the darkened staircase.

She peeked hesitantly round the corner, and in the dim light saw her rucksack in the stairwell, leaning against the wall. Gripping the knife tightly, she tiptoed up to it, wincing at the creaking of the carpet-free steps. It was still packed with her gear, and she pulled out socks, trainers and knickers and put them on quickly. The trainers felt wonderfully alien on her feet. She left the rucksack where she'd found it and continued towards faint daylight at the top of the stairs, every wooden board marking her progress with a groan.

On the landing she was faced with four doors, all of them

closed. At the far end, late-evening sunlight danced through a lace-curtained window. She hurried towards it and yanked the curtain aside. The window was locked but at least there were no bars. She looked out at freedom below. The ground was churned and muddy and she saw that it was part of a pen full of fat pigs nuzzling around. Beyond, a large metal barn bookended the property and in the distance the cover of trees was bisected by a rough drive.

She looked around for something to smash the window with, but the corridor was bare except for a worn carpet, so she tried the nearest door. It opened on to a pleasant, if ordinary, double bedroom. It was clean and simple, with a large walk-in wardrobe on one wall. Caitlin ran a hand through the clothes – male and female. With a jolt she saw one of her sweatshirts on a hanger; she grabbed it and pulled it quickly over her head. She closed the door behind her when she left.

The next room was a complete shock. It was like a hospital room, with an adjustable bed made up with spotless starched sheets and pillows. There was a dinner tray on wheels – the kind that could be positioned over a bed to feed immobile patients – a bedside cabinet with an empty fruit bowl and a water jug and glass.

Attached to each side of the bed were sets of leather straps with small adjustable collars at the end. Some form of restraints for unwilling patients, no doubt. *Weird.* She saw a sink beneath the barred window and next to that a toilet. On one wall was another rail of clothes, mainly cardigans and nightwear. She left, closing the door softly.

To open the next room, Caitlin had to draw back a bolt. She instinctively tightened her grip on the knife as she prodded open the door. Unlike the previous rooms, this one was in darkness because the curtains were drawn, but their rippling suggested an open window and a way out. On a mattress on the floor a shapeless form covered by a blanket was wheezing the harsh rhythm of sleep. A knot of straggly black hair peeped from beneath the blanket.

Caitlin walked to the window and drew the curtain aside. The window was barred, though the small top part was open. Knife held in front of her, she turned back to the mattress and with a magician's flick pulled the blanket away from the sleeping body. She stepped back in revulsion. The girl on the mattress was naked except for knickers and a tiny negligee, which rode up above her stomach to her breasts. She was thin, and her skin had the pale, sickly sheen of jaundice. On her ankle bones and heels were lesions that Caitlin assumed were bedsores. Worse, the leather tether on her left ankle had turned the flesh dark purple with the constant friction. On her wrists were further wounds that Caitlin recognised from her own struggle against the plastic handcuffs.

'Daniela?' enquired Caitlin, realising. She edged closer. 'Daniela!'

The sleeping form, tucked into the foetal position, stirred, and eyes began to blink awake. 'Adrianna,' groaned the girl, barely able to part her dry lips. She rolled on to her back as though heavily sedated. 'Is that you?' Her Italian accent was pronounced.

Caitlin dropped to her knees and placed a hand on the girl's bare shoulder. 'Daniela.'

The girl's face registered confusion as dazed dark eyes tried to focus on Caitlin. When she'd processed the question, she replied with a faint nod. 'Si, Daniela.'

'You're Italian,' said Caitlin.

'*Si*. Yes. Who are you?'

'I'm Caitlin.'

'You must go, Caitlin.'

'That's the plan. Can you sit up?' Caitlin grabbed the girl's frail hands. Her skin was like paper and Daniela winced at her touch. 'This could hurt.'

'No,' said the girl, pulling her bruised hands away. 'You can't let them find you here. You must go.'

'Them? How many are there?'

'*Tre*. Three. An old man, a younger man and a woman.'

'A woman? Where is she?'

'I don't know.'

'Never mind, we've wasted enough time. We're leaving.'

'If they find you . . .'

'Listen,' hissed Caitlin. 'Do you want to stay here?' Daniela's only answer was to lower her eyes, so Caitlin cut the leg tether with the knife and examined the lesions on her wrists and ankles. 'Can you stand?'

'I don't know,' replied Daniela.

Holding her thin arms, Caitlin helped her to her feet, trying to take a sympathetic grip. Daniela was unsteady and held on to her.

'Take a step.' Caitlin winced with Daniela when she made to put her weight on her skinless heel. Daniela nodded to reassure but gazed around as though she had vertigo.

Caitlin gingerly withdrew her support and stepped backwards, watching the pathetic creature in front of her attempt to stabilise herself. 'Wait there,' she ordered superfluously and dashed out of the room. Daniela reached a hand out in terror and stumbled forward with a gasp of pain, but Caitlin ignored her and made for the bottom of the stairs, snatching up her rucksack on the way.

She poked her head into the kitchen to satisfy herself that the old man was where she'd left him. He was asleep in the chair. Her eye alighted on a solid-looking weight behind the kitchen door, used to wedge it open when unlocked. It was hard to lift, but she gathered it up and lumbered back up the stairs.

She left the weight outside the room, then flung the rucksack down and helped the stricken Daniela, encouraging her into a painful step. Then another and another until Caitlin was confident in her ability to stay upright while she emptied her rucksack. She pulled out a pair of jeans but realised the material would chafe too much. Instead she opted for khaki shorts and helped Daniela into them, the Italian girl's thin arm around her neck. They were a little baggy, but there was a belt attached and Caitlin fastened it on the tightest notch for her.

Next she found a tube of Canestan in her toiletries bag – better than nothing. She dabbed some on Daniela's heels and ankles, ignoring her moans of agony, before delicately cladding her feet in a pair of light cotton socks and plimsolls, tying them tight to prevent rubbing. She tossed a T-shirt at Daniela, who looked helplessly back. She saw the bedsores on Daniela's elbow so cut the cheap nylon negligee off with the butcher's knife and helped her drag the T-shirt painfully over her head.

'Let's go.'

Daniela took a tentative step, then another, emerging into the corridor, where she leant against a wall, panting. She smiled and shook her head, putting a hand to her mouth. 'I won't make it. I'm sick. Dizzy.'

'You can't stay here.'

'Then go. Bring help.'

Caitlin lowered her head, accepting the inevitable. Picking up the doorstop, she advanced on the end window and hurled the weight through the glass, then ran back to the room to scoop up the blanket, returning to knock out as much glass as possible before draping it across the ledge. She lifted her leg over the sill, looking back at Daniela holding on to the wall. The exhausted girl raised a wasted arm, gesturing for Caitlin to leave. Caitlin swung her other leg over the sill and looked down from the ledge.

At that moment, a baby's cries rent the air and Daniela staggered towards the only unopened door. 'My baby!' She lost her footing and fell to her knees, clawing at the door.

'Your baby?' exclaimed Caitlin, jumping back through the window. 'Daniela. Wait.'

But Daniela scrabbled at the handle and pushed open the final door, forcing herself back to her feet and tottering into the room.

'Daniela!' Caitlin halted at the entrance, dumbstruck. The room was beautifully decorated in pale pink with a soft, luxuriant carpet and embroidered curtains. A young blond-haired boy, two or three years old, stared curiously at the pair of them from the security of a playpen. He was light-skinned with bright eyes and held one of the many toys from the pen up to his mouth. His tiny shorts and T-shirt were clean and of good quality.

Daniela ignored the boy and stumbled her way towards a lace-covered crib in the middle of the room, bursting into tears as she fell to her knees. She cooed at the olive-skinned child in Italian and reached in to pluck the infant from its swaddling, setting off a further volley of terrified screaming, deafening after the heavy silence of Caitlin's captivity.

'Take my baby,' urged Daniela, holding out the child.

'What the fuck is going on here?' said Caitlin, glancing down at a shock of black hair poking out of a wrap. She sought a delicate way to break the bad news to Daniela, but failed. 'Leave the baby, Daniela,' she said. 'It'll be safe. Someone's looking after it.'

It. She had said the word twice and felt a pang of guilt. That was how she'd objectified her own offspring, the seed that had taken root inside her body, before destroying it – the only way to rationalise, the only way to get through.

'Take my baby,' pleaded Daniela, her eyes feasting on the child as she gathered it to her chest. 'Please.' She turned, beseeching Caitlin, her hollow cheeks determined. Then her mouth dropped open in horror.

Caitlin turned to follow Daniela's gaze, briefly registering a mop of red hair before her head was yanked back and a blade pulled across her throat.

Brook walked down the centre aisle of the church, his footsteps booming like cannon fire in the tiny brick-built building with its functional square nave and cramped pews. To Brook it felt more like an electricity substation than a house of God.

From a side room a priest carrying a stack of hymnals appeared, his cropped salt-and-pepper head elevated to accommodate the books under his chin. 'Damen,' he grunted, levering the books on to the front pew.

'Father Christopher.' Brook shook the outstretched hand.

'Come for confession?'

'I don't have time.'

'I can do the express service, if you'd like,' said Christopher. 'Absolve you on the main bullet points.'

'Funny,' retorted Brook, trying not to smile.

'Then what do you want?'

'I need to pick your brains. Father Patrick O'Toole.'

Father Christopher sighed. 'What's he done now?'

'Nothing yet,' said Brook, mildly surprised. 'I'm looking into the protest group picketing the Rutherford Clinic, and he organises it.'

'Important work,' said Christopher. 'Promoting the sanctity of human life.'

'Can you tell me about the group?'

'Why don't you ask Father O'Toole?'

'We will.'

'But you expect him to lie.'

Brook hesitated. 'I expect him to accentuate the positive.'

'I saw you on the news,' said Christopher. 'Is this to do with the girl in the burning van?'

'I can't answer that,' said Brook, in a tone that told its own story. 'But I can say we have a string of missing young women from Catholic countries, all exercising their rights under the law to terminate a pregnancy and all patients at the Rutherford.'

'And you think they've been targeted by Patrick's band of religious zealots.'

'It's an angle we're exploring.'

'You're a Catholic fifty years and more,' said Christopher. 'Surely you can fill in the blanks.'

'I'm a long way from First Communion,' replied Brook. 'And I get lost around aspects of Church doctrine that are more . . .' He paused, for once the right word evading him.

'Crackpot?' suggested Father Christopher drily.

'I was going to say extreme,' conceded Brook. 'But let's agree on passionate.'

Father Christopher beckoned him to sit on a pew beside him. 'My only role is to advise you if there's a conflict between your job and your faith.'

'I have little faith, Father,' answered Brook.

'Then why come to me?'

'We have laws . . .'

'Those are men's laws, Damen, not God's.'

'God maketh the men,' said Brook.

'You know the Church's position on free will. Our faith makes clear—'

'It was a mistake coming here,' said Brook, standing abruptly. 'I shouldn't have put you in this position. I'm sorry.' He headed for the door.

'Constance Trastevere,' said Christopher at Brook's retreating frame.

Brook turned. 'I know her. She told me I'll burn in hell.'

'She might be right,' retorted Christopher, only half joking. 'She's a wealthy woman, Italian-American from Arizona, widowed, I'm given to understand. Trastevere is her family name – it's a suburb of Rome. She bankrolls the group and has contacts in the US bible belt. They're called CRI. Citizens Resisting Infanticide. Her politics are extreme even by the Church's standards – anti-contraception, anti-homosexual . . .'

'How is that different to the Church?'

'The Pope doesn't advocate chemical castration for gays and confinement for single mothers, Damen.' The priest looked around the church as though God was about to join the debate. He beckoned Brook into a tiny side chapel, a statue of

St Francis beaming down at them, dusty woodland animals arranged around his bare feet.

'I warned Patrick but he wouldn't hear a word said against her. She's hard as nails. There's not an ounce of compassion in the woman and she walks all over him.'

'How did she make her money?'

'She married it and inherited from her third husband, Oliver Portland. He was English. She met him in the States and moved to Derbyshire when they married, though she kept her name for business reasons. He'd already amassed a fortune in property around the county and had a portfolio as far down as London, I believe. Left her a big house in Duffield and too much time on her hands, you ask me. That's all I know.'

'Thank you, Father.'

'You can thank me by going easy on Patrick,' said Christopher. 'His sister-in-law had a difficult pregnancy and bled to death during childbirth, so he's not posturing for a bishopric – he feels it personally.'

'Pity she couldn't have opted for a termination,' said Brook.

'She had the choice,' said Christopher. 'Abortion was legal. It's just that some of us have principles and understand the need for personal sacrifice.'

'Let me guess. Father O'Toole had the principles and his sister-in-law made the sacrifice,' said Brook, making for the exit.

Christopher called after him. 'Make time for your soul, Damen, or you'll never know peace.'

Brook raised a hand in acknowledgement even as he extracted his mobile and a piece of paper. He dialled a number and threw the paper away. Much as it pained him, he knew he'd have to add DS Morton's number to his speed dial.

'Rob,' he opened. 'Constance Trastevere.'

'We're en route,' answered Morton, hiding his shock at a direct call from the inspector.

'Ask her about CRI – Citizens Resisting Infanticide,' said Brook. 'It's a pro-life group she's heavily involved with. Get Cooper to try and rustle up a membership or mailing list, but get as much background from the horse's mouth as you can. Father O'Toole may be more open.'

'Already spoken to him and CRI was the first thing he mentioned,' said Morton. 'He's very proud of their work. He said Mrs Tras . . . whatever puts up the money and they run it jointly. I asked him about other members but he clammed up.'

'So not that proud, then.' Brook rang off but the phone vibrated straight away. 'John.'

'You better get back here. It's Jake Tanner,' said Noble on the other end of the line. Brook listened and walked quickly to his car.

Constance Trastevere ushered Banach and Morton into her living room, boarded on four walls by dark, almost black oak. The contrast with the chintzy tasselled furnishings was marked – a man's room furnished by an elderly woman in an expensive floral dress. The only light came from an ornate standard lamp behind one armchair.

'Would you like to sit?' asked Mrs Trastevere, standing in front of the lamp, which cast its ethereal glow over her stern countenance. When the two officers declined, she remained upright, her hands clasped loosely in front of her.

'We've come—' began Morton.

'Father O'Toole called me,' she smiled, her eyes not leaving

Banach's face. 'You could've saved yourselves the trip, officers. Like Father O'Toole, I'm immensely proud of our work but I won't reveal the names of any supporters or give you access to our mailing lists.'

'Sounds more like guilt than pride,' remarked Banach.

It hardly seemed possible but Mrs Trastevere's expression became even frostier. 'And the little whore speaks.'

'Excuse me?' said Banach.

'You heard me,' retorted the old woman.

'Mrs Trastevere,' said Morton. 'We—'

'You've got a nerve coming here after your performance at the clinic, lady, I'll grant you that,' said Mrs Trastevere to Banach.

'Just doing my job,' retorted Banach.

'And is your job more important than the life growing inside you?' snapped the old woman.

Banach's mouth opened in shock and Morton turned to gaze at his stunned colleague. Trastevere laughed. 'My dear girl, what do you think our organisation is for? CRI is not involved in an industrial dispute. We're not a debating society. We're involved in a struggle between life and death. The fight against abortion is a war against evil, and knowledge is power. Intelligence, if you will.'

Banach caught Morton staring at her. 'I don't know who told you I was pregnant, but they're sorely mistaken.'

'Then make a liar out of me, Constable,' snarled Trastevere. 'Empty your pockets. If you don't have a leaflet about your prelim about your person, I'll apologise.'

Banach lowered her head. 'How . . . ?'

'How do I know? You told me, Constable Banach, the moment you arranged an appointment at the clinic.'

Banach had a memory of the camera flashing in the reception area. 'Someone photographed me.'

'One of our supporters photographs every murdering bitch that crosses our picket,' said Mrs Trastevere. 'Do you think we just shrug our shoulders and wring our hands when one of you whores decides to kill a child? That's not how you win a war.'

Banach couldn't look at Trastevere any more. She felt faint. The old woman's words, each one like a bullet, seemed to be launched at her with increasing venom, every syllable exploding in her brain.

'And before you left the building, Anka Banach, we knew who you were. We sent your picture to our sympathisers, and members of your own parish identified you,' she continued, taking pleasure in the assault. 'And you a Polish Catholic, to contemplate the murder of your child – shameful. But then shame is something you know all about.'

'Shut up,' mumbled Banach.

'You're even ashamed of your heritage,' continued Trastevere. 'Unwilling to use the name your father gave you at baptism. I pity you. And I pity your family when our newsletter comes out.'

'I need to leave,' said Banach, putting a hand up to her head.

'Are you all right, Angie?' said Morton.

'Course she's not all right, Sergeant,' laughed Trastevere. 'She's carrying a child she doesn't want because her life is so much richer without it.'

Outside, Banach threw up long and loud while Morton stood by pulling on a cigarette. 'Morning sickness?' he ventured, trying his hand at a little humour. The quip froze on his face under Banach's Medusa stare.

'Give me some of that,' she ordered, nodding at the cigarette.

'Are you sure you should?'

'Oh, fuck off,' she said, snatching it from his grasp, taking a deep draw and exhaling smoke with her eyes closed.

'You know I outrank you, right, Ange?' said Morton, trying to get a smile out of her.

She handed the cigarette back but Morton gestured her to throw it away. 'So I guess ordering you to keep quiet isn't going to cut it?'

Morton laughed but knew he couldn't answer. What Mrs Trastevere had revealed might be relevant to the inquiry.

'Thought not.'

'Come on, Angie, I'll take you home.'

'No,' said Banach. 'Drop me at my car. I need time to think.'

Back at St Mary's Wharf fifteen minutes later, Banach got out of Morton's car without a word. She slid into her dark blue Peugeot and roared out of the car park.

Twenty-Nine

'ZEKE. YOU IN THERE?' shouted the girl.

The young man jumped to his feet and banged on the toilet door with his undamaged hand. 'I'm here. Get the bolts, Red. My hand's broken.'

The sound of stiff bolts sliding back presaged the door opening.

'Shit,' said Red, seeing blood on his face. 'What happened to you?'

'Bitch slashed me,' said Zeke, pushing past her, holding his left hand in his right. 'We gotta find her . . .'

'I cut her,' said Red, showing him the bloodied knife in her hand, unsure what his reaction would be. 'I think I killed her.'

'You killed her?'

'I'm not sure. She was getting away, Zeke. They were taking my baby.'

'Where?'

'She's just a murdering whore, after all,' said Red, deploying her final argument.

'Where?' he shouted. She raised her eyes to the ceiling. Zeke nodded and placed a hand on her shoulder. 'Don't worry, Red. You did good.'

* * *

Daniela crouched over Caitlin's rasping body and tried to drag her into the corridor but gave up at the door, instead kneeling to comfort her. Caitlin's chest was moving but her throat was awash with blood. Bubbles burst from the laceration in her windpipe as she struggled to inflate her lungs. But it was the shocked expression on her face that brought tears even to Daniela's chronically dehydrated eyes.

'*Mi dispiace*,' said Daniela, squeezing Caitlin's hand and staring at the panic in the stricken girl's eyes. '*Mi dispiace*.'

She grabbed Caitlin's butcher's knife and picked up the baby, then scuttled painfully over to the smashed window. Hearing pounding on the stairs behind her, she tried to lift her injured heel but failed to get her foot as high as the sill.

'Where you going, bitch?' shouted Zeke, Red in his slipstream. They paused at Caitlin's prostrate form bleeding over the threadbare landing carpet. 'Sheesh, what a mess.' Zeke stepped over the expanding pool of blood towards Daniela, who raised the knife in self-defence, her teeth clamped in determination.

'She's got my baby, Zeke,' shouted Red. 'Do something.'

'No,' shouted Daniela, the violence of her emotion belying the frailty of her body. 'He's mine.'

'You don't deserve him, you whore,' snarled Red. 'You were gonna kill him.'

Zeke held an arm out to quiet her. 'Where are you going to go, Daniela?' His voice tried to soothe, his steps small but inexorable. 'There's nowhere to run.'

Daniela's resolve gave way to fear. She darted an eye out of the window, then back at Zeke.

'You jump, you could kill the child,' implored Zeke, inching forward. 'You don't want that, do you?'

The baby wriggled in Daniela's arms and her face softened into a smile. Zeke was only five yards away.

'Give me the baby,' he said, holding out his arms for the child.

Daniela's smile vanished and she lifted the knife to the baby's throat. 'Go back,' she shouted, nodding to the stairs.

Red lunged towards mother and child. 'My baby.'

'Red!' Zeke stood across her path. 'Let me handle this.' He smiled at Daniela, splaying his empty hands to signal good intentions. 'You're not going to kill your child, Daniela. We didn't let you before and we're not about to start now.'

'Back!' ordered Daniela.

Zeke halted but didn't step back. 'You won't do it. The Lord gave him to you. To us. He put love in your heart for the child. We're a family.'

Daniela looked helplessly round at the window, out to the gathering darkness, resignation flooding into her. She turned back towards Zeke, a bitter smile playing around her chapped lips, then she raised the baby to her face and kissed him on the forehead.

'*Ti voglio molto bene*,' she said, tears rolling down her face. '*Molte bene*.' She took a shuddering breath and placed the wrapped child on the floor, then before Zeke could react, she sliced deeply across the vein of her left wrist. Blood gushed from the wound but it didn't stop her transferring the knife to cut her other wrist, though she only had strength for a shallow slash before slithering down the wall.

Zeke stepped over the baby and kicked the knife away as Red pounced on the child and held him to her chest, tears in her eyes. As she hurried him away to the nursery, Zeke lowered himself to sit beside Daniela and examined her wounds. He placed an arm round her. Her head was bowed – resigned – her breathing shallow, but she opened her eyes at the embrace, a bloody hand feeling for the absent crucifix around her neck.

'Here,' said Zeke, unhooking his own necklace to place in her hands, which tightened briefly around the cross. 'Shush now. Your work is done. You didn't kill your child. You will sit beside the Lord. He forgives you.'

Red emerged empty-handed from the nursery. 'How is she?'

Zeke shook his head. 'There's no fixing that wound.'

Red began to sing. '*Amazing grace, how sweet the sound.*'

'Go to him,' whispered Zeke in Daniela's ear. 'He's waiting.'

'*That saved a wretch like me.*'

Zeke disentangled himself from Daniela's ebbing life force, taking up the song.

'*I once was lost, but now am found.*' He tensed his arms around her neck, shushing her as he got the best grip he could with his damaged hand.

'*Was blind but now I see.*'

He wrenched her neck sharply round until it snapped before standing up, head bowed in brief prayer. 'She's gone.'

'What now?' asked Red.

Zeke opened his eyes and shrugged at her. 'Now she's just meat.'

'The unit?'

'The unit,' agreed Zeke. 'I'll get her processed and in the pig trough tomorrow.'

'She's barely enough for a starter,' said Red.

Zeke grabbed Daniela's flayed heels and began dragging the emaciated body along the corridor. When he came level with Caitlin, he gestured towards the Irish girl.

'Well if Kitty here doesn't pull through, they'll have a main course to follow.'

Zeke pounded back up the stairs from the barn. 'Take her legs, Red,' he ordered, putting his broken hand gingerly under Caitlin's armpit. 'This one's got more meat on her.'

'She's still breathing.'

'Maybe, but she's not gonna make it.'

'Maybe God wants her alive,' said Red. 'We should do something.'

Zeke grinned. 'Should I call an ambulance?'

'Be serious.'

'What then?'

'Get her to the barn,' said Red. 'I've got an idea.'

Zeke lifted Caitlin's shoulders. 'Is it worth it? You saw the way she reacted to Dad. We should never have taken her. If my uncle finds out . . .'

'He won't find out,' replied Red. 'Besides, she's a baby-killing whore, right?'

'So?'

'So the longer she lives, the more she suffers. And if, by God's grace, we can get your Dad to seed her, there's nothing your uncle *can* say.'

Zeke blew her a kiss. 'Love you, Red.'

They carried Caitlin's blood-spattered body down the stairs, through the house and out into the moonlit night. As they approached the pig pen, a loud squealing was taken up and several of the fat animals threw themselves at the sturdy fence, chewing aggressively at the posts, scrabbling over each other to get closer to Caitlin's blood trail.

'The boys are getting hungry.'

The bright moon disappeared behind a drifting cloud. At the barn, Red flicked a switch and the large building was flooded with pale light. They laid Caitlin next to Daniela. Zeke examined his hand and probed his bloodied cheek.

'Heat the branding iron,' said Red.

'What for?'

She nodded at Caitlin. 'I'm going to cauterise the wound.'

Noble handed hot drinks to Jake Tanner and Janet Gillstrap, the duty solicitor, while Brook listed those present for the tape.

'You've had a chance to confer with counsel,' said Brook. Tanner nodded. 'Say yes or no for the tape, please.'

'Yes,' said Tanner, leaning towards the recorder, an attempt at flippancy in his voice.

'A young girl is dead,' said Brook.

Shamed, Tanner lowered his head to stare off into space. Brook glanced at Noble, who acknowledged with a lift of the eyebrows. This was not the detached expression of a hardened killer potentially responsible for the deaths of six young women. A single death, perhaps. Everyone was capable of taking a life under enough pressure.

'And I killed her,' said Tanner.

'I knew you'd crack eventually,' replied Brook.

Tanner shrugged. 'I want this over.'

'Murder's quite a leap for someone with a single assault to his name.'

Tanner resurrected a little aggression. 'Maybe I've been offing people all along without you noticing.'

'Does your client understand the gravity of his situation?' Brook asked Gillstrap, noting her tired expression.

'Mr Tanner, we've been over this,' she said with a sigh. 'If Inspector Brook asks you a question, unless I advise against, you may answer. But don't follow the inspector around the houses making comments that aren't required and which may prove detrimental to your defence.'

'I don't need a defence,' said Tanner. 'I killed her. What more can I say?'

'Why, where and how would be useful,' said Noble.

'And you can start by confirming the victim's name,' added Brook.

'Don't answer that,' said Gillstrap.

Tanner was surprised. 'You don't know who she is?'

'We have an idea,' said Brook. 'And we'll confirm soon enough with or without your help.'

'Without suits best,' said Gillstrap. 'My client isn't here to do your job, Inspector.'

'Her name was Kassia,' said Tanner softly. Gillstrap sighed in frustration.

'Surname?'

'I only met her that night. She's from Poland. Was.' He seemed about to say more but thought better of it, smiling instead. 'Do I win a prize?'

'A lifetime's holiday at Her Majesty's pleasure for starters,' said Gillstrap.

Tanner sneered. 'I told you I killed her. What do you care?'

Gillstrap crossed her arms, confirming his analysis.

'Why?' asked Noble.

'She was fit and I fancied her.' He shrugged. 'It turned out she was a pro and I wasn't about to pay for it.'

'She was a prostitute?'

'S'right.'

'So you killed her. Where?'

'In her flat.' Brook prompted him with an eyebrow. 'On Vernon Street.' When Brook and Noble stared at him for more, Tanner said, 'She took me back there. I don't know the number. Big house, top room.'

'But you had sex with her before you stabbed her, right?' said Brook.

'No,' said Tanner quietly, his gaze steady. 'I didn't stab her and we didn't have sex.'

'Why not?'

'I haven't got a knife so I strangled her.'

'No, why didn't you have sex with her?' said Noble. 'I thought you fancied her . . .'

'I wasn't gonna pay.'

'Who's talking about paying?' said Brook.

'Once you've smacked her about, you can take what you want by force,' added Noble. 'It seems a natural progression.' Tanner didn't answer.

'Where did you meet her?'

'In a bar.'

'Bar Polski?'

'No.'

'But that's where you worked, isn't it?'

'I did. I was stocking the bar.'

'So you met her there.'

'No, Bar Polski's not open yet. How would I meet her there?'

'She worked there too.'

'She didn't,' exclaimed Tanner. 'I think I'd remember.'

'But we spoke to your employer and he said Kassia worked there,' continued Noble.

'You're lying.'

'It's academic,' said Brook. 'We're getting a warrant to check the security cameras.'

'Good luck,' said Tanner. 'The system's not installed yet. I worked there, remember.'

Brook nodded. 'You've thought of everything. Or someone has.'

Gillstrap turned to take an interest again. 'What's going on here, Inspector? Who is this *someone*?'

'Kassia wasn't really a prostitute, was she?' continued Brook, ignoring the solicitor. 'There were no needle marks on her arms, no signs of alcohol abuse, no clothing appropriate to prostitution in her wardrobe.' He waited, the trap set. Someone had cleared and cleaned Kassia's flat and removed all her clothes in case they'd picked up traces of DNA. If Jake Tanner had killed her, he'd have to know that.

'That's because I cleaned the place from top to bottom, then took all her clothes and stuff plus the sheets off her bed. Happy now?'

'What did you do with them?'

'Binned them.'

'Where?'

'A skip somewhere. I forget.'

'You're lying,' said Noble.

'It's the truth.'

'We're police officers, Jake,' said Brook. 'Everyone lies. So where did you meet Kassia?'

'In a bar. We had a few drinks and things went on from there.'

'Did she pay for her own drinks?'

Tanner hesitated. 'No, I paid.'

'Living in that fleapit you shared with Nick,' scoffed Noble. 'You don't have two pennies to rub together and you expect us to believe you stood for Kassia's drinks and paid for sex . . .'

'I didn't pay for sex, that's the point. And I had an advance on my wages – enough for drinks.'

'Which bar?' demanded Brook.

'I don't remember.'

'Convenient.'

Tanner didn't rise to the sarcasm. 'One of those student pubs off Ashbourne Road. They do cheap drinks, right. I can't remember which one because I'd never been there before. Shouldn't I be signing something?'

'Somewhere to be?' enquired Noble. Tanner closed his eyes in frustration. 'Thought not.'

'When did you leave the pub?'

'Closing. We staggered back to her place and she started warming me up.'

'And that's when she asked for money.'

'Right.' He leered at Brook. 'And I'm not about to pay for it – leastways until I'm your age.'

Brook raised an eyebrow at Noble's sudden smile. 'What happened when she asked for money?'

Tanner concentrated hard. 'I . . . I was shocked. I thought she liked me. Then she laughed at me and I blew my stack. I was drunk. The next thing I knew, I had my hands round her throat.'

'So you strangled her.'

'Eventually,' said Tanner. He licked his lips nervously. 'I smacked her around a bit first.'

'A bit?'

'Punched her a few times,' said Tanner, unable to meet eyes.

'How many times?' said Noble.

'Until she stopped moving. Then I strangled her to make sure.' He looked up finally.

'Did that give you an erection?' snarled Noble.

Tanner's face soured. 'You're disgusting.'

'Look who's talking.'

'Where was the body?' said Brook.

'On the bed.'

'Clothes on?'

'Some of them.'

'Hands.' Brook gestured at Tanner, who held them out for inspection.

'I can't see any damage,' said Noble.

'I wore gloves to do her,' said Tanner.

'Gloves?' said Brook. 'In her flat?'

'We'd only just arrived. After a couple of knee-tremblers she asked for the money.'

'How long were you in the flat before you started strangling her?'

'About five minutes.'

'How much did she ask for?'

'Fifty notes.'

'Nice round number,' sneered Noble. 'Easy to remember.'

'It's the truth.'

'What kind of gloves did you wear?' asked Brook.

'Leather.'

'Are you right- or left-handed?'

'Right.'

'Where are the gloves now?'

'River,' answered Tanner. 'They had blood on them.'

'The river,' said Brook drily. 'Because the skip where you were forced to dump her clothes after spending five whole minutes in her flat was full, yes?' He contemplated Tanner, drained his cup and looked across at Noble, who raised a splayed hand. Brook acknowledged with an imperceptible dip of the head. The fibres found in Kassia's throat weren't leather but fire-retardant suede from the workman's gloves in the van.

'And the van?'

'I nicked it to move the body.'

'Why?'

'I just said.'

'No, why move the body at all?' demanded Brook. 'You kill an unattached foreign national in a bedsit in an empty house – a girl with no family and few ties to Derby.'

'What's your point?'

'My point is she could have lain undiscovered for days, even weeks in that flat. Why not just leave her where you killed her? All the offices were closed. No one would have seen you enter or leave. Instead you take an unnecessary risk.'

Tanner took a while to reply. 'I thought about leaving her in the flat but I couldn't risk it. In case I left evidence. I've got form.'

'But you were wearing gloves,' chipped in Noble.

'I may have left other traces. Hair or something. From the struggle.' Tanner found his stride again. 'You've got my DNA on record.'

'So is that why you took a shower before you left?' asked Noble. 'To wash off blood and DNA?'

'I didn't shower,' said Tanner. 'I was too freaked.'

Brook and Noble exchanged another glance. 'Why Max Ostrowsky's van?'

'Because I knew Max from the bar. He's the owner's brother. I knew his address. I knew the van would be there. I didn't know there was a blowtorch, but that came in handy to burn off her fingerprints.'

'Just her prints?'

'No. She had a tattoo as well. Polish flag. I burnt that off too.'

'Anything else?'

'I took a hammer to her face. So you couldn't identify her.'

'Why would it matter if we identified her?' said Brook. 'You claim Kassia was a stranger with no connection to you.' He stared at Tanner's bowed head. 'No answer?'

'Did you know Kassia was pregnant?' asked Noble.

Tanner couldn't keep the shock from his features. 'No,' he eventually croaked.

'Don't worry,' said Noble. 'You're not the father. We checked.'

'I wouldn't be,' muttered Tanner. 'I'd just met her.'

Tanner was concentrating hard when answers fell outside his prepared story and it was taking its toll. He'd barely moved a muscle during the interview, so hard was he trying to remember details that were foreign to him. Cognitive overload it was called. The more you lie, the less you move, to avoid distraction and keep the brain on task.

'What happened after you disfigured her?'

'I put her in the van and drove down by the *Telegraph* building and torched it. There was a billycan of petrol in the back.'

357

'Then why put her clothes in some random skip when you can burn them in the van?' asked Noble.

'I didn't think.'

'Where did you pick up the cleaning materials?' asked Brook.

'They were in the flat.'

'For someone claiming they'd just blown their stack, you sound pretty calm,' observed Brook. 'On the one hand you claim you were drunk and can't remember details, on the other you're able to strip and clean the place. Then you walk across town to Arboretum Street to steal Max's van and pick up your brother to help you load the body before dumping it. That sound calm to you, John?'

'Icy,' confirmed Noble.

'Say what you like, I was shaking like a leaf,' rejoined Tanner. 'But you're half right, Inspector. After I killed her, I panicked, didn't know what to do. So I snatched the door keys from her bag, locked up and somehow got myself home. Next morning I saw what I had to do and then everything you said happened just the way you said.' He stared coldly into Brook's eyes. 'Except it happened a day later.'

'So you killed her on the twenty-first,' said Noble. 'What day was that?'

Tanner looked up, confused by the simplicity of the question. 'I . . . Tuesday,' he said after a pause to work it out.

'And dumped her the next night, the twenty-second.'

'That's right,' nodded Tanner. 'Though it was well past midnight so I guess it was early on the twenty-third.'

'And how did Nick help?'

'He wasn't involved. He sat in the van the whole time playing with the radio while I cleaned up and fetched the body.

I only took him because I can't leave him alone at night. He gets scared.'

'I'm not surprised. What time did you pick him up?'

'We left my flat just after midnight to go to Arboretum Street. It's only five minutes' walk.'

'So late?'

'I'd been at work,' said Tanner.

'In Kassia's flat, where did you clean?'

'I washed off all the blood I could see, hoovered the carpet . . .'

'The shower?'

'I cleaned that too.'

Brook's smile was thin. 'Why? If you hadn't taken a shower.'

Realising his mistake, Tanner stared at his hands. 'I just did.'

'Did it never occur to you that stealing Max's van and dumping it with a corpse inside would automatically direct the police to Bar Polski?' asked Gillstrap. 'Where you worked?'

'I'm not very smart,' explained Tanner.

'Smart enough to elude a city-wide manhunt,' said Noble. Tanner shrugged. *Just lucky*. 'Where *have* you been hiding, out of interest? The Cream Bar? We know you had keys.'

'How?' asked Tanner, surprised.

'We're trained detectives, Jake.'

Tanner shrugged again. 'I was a keyholder when the place closed. What of it? I lost them.'

'You'll be glad to know we found them,' said Brook, aware of Noble's puzzled glance in his direction. There hadn't been time to tell him.

'Where?' demanded Tanner. 'They weren't in our flat, 'cos I looked.'

'Stop lying,' said Noble. 'After you dumped Kassia's body, you used them to get into the Cream before assaulting two police officers.'

'What?' exclaimed Tanner. 'No way.'

'You had keys,' insisted Noble. 'We know you were there.'

'I wasn't.'

'He's confessing to a murder, Sergeant,' said Gillstrap. 'Why would he deny an assault?'

'Exactly,' answered Tanner. 'I wasn't there. I haven't been inside the place for years. If I hadn't lost the keys, then yes, I might have tried to hide there.'

'If you want us to believe you, tell me where you *were* hiding,' said Brook. Tanner was tight-lipped. 'Is Nick there now?'

'No.'

'Then why not tell us? You're not going back there, are you?'

'Jake,' coaxed Gillstrap.

'Flat three,' answered Tanner finally. 'Ground floor of our building.'

'Impossible,' said Noble. 'We checked every apartment.'

'Not the old woman's flat, you didn't. Annie something.'

Noble stood off the wall. 'Is she okay?'

'No, she's dead,' said Tanner.

The two detectives bristled. 'You killed her?'

'Course not. She died two weeks ago,' said Tanner. 'And you can check. I saw her being carted off. When we had to leg it, I knew it was still empty so I broke in.'

'And took your luggage?' asked Brook.

'Yes.'

'And your beans,' added Noble.

Tanner puzzled over this but saw no reason to withhold. 'Yes.'

'You say Nick's not there.'

'Would I be blowing the gaff if he was?'

Noble stared inquisitively at his colleague. 'Send a car,' said Brook. Noble left the room.

'The old girl's key is with my stuff,' Tanner shouted after him. 'No sense busting the door down,' he explained to Brook.

Brook recorded Noble's exit for the tape. 'So all the time Ostrowsky and the police were looking for you—'

'Mr Ostrowsky's got nothing to do with this,' insisted Tanner. 'I was hiding from you lot.'

'Sure,' said Brook. 'Ruthless businessmen like Ostrowsky don't get upset when insignificant nobodies steal from them, especially when that theft brings them to our attention.'

'I was hiding because I killed the girl,' insisted Tanner. 'Why won't you believe me?'

'Because after evading hundreds of police officers for days, you stroll into St Mary's Wharf and confess to murder,' said Brook. 'So what changed?'

'Nothing.'

'It's Nick, isn't it?' said Brook, realising. 'Ostrowsky grabbed him.'

'This is nothing to do with Mr Ostrowsky,' repeated Tanner.

'We know your brother was wandering around the Intu. What happened? Did he go stir crazy? He couldn't stand it any more so he snuck out. Ostrowsky's people got to hear about it and gathered him up.' No rebuttal from Tanner. 'And once he had Nick, Ostrowsky made you an offer you couldn't refuse. Confess to the girl's murder and Nick can go free.'

'No. I killed Kassia. I've told you.'

'I don't think so,' countered Brook. 'You've been coerced into a confession to draw attention from the brothers. Max killed Kassia. It's his van, his hammer, his blowtorch – he's got a history of drunkenness and sexual violence . . .'

'I killed her, I tell you.'

'Then where's Nick?' demanded Brook. 'Tell me where he is and I'll write out your confession for you.'

'Nick has nothing to do with this,' said Tanner, beginning to sag in his chair. 'He's just a child.'

'A child? We have a witness and film of *both* of you dumping the victim's body before setting fire to the van.'

Tanner was sullen. 'Nick didn't know there was a body inside.'

'Come on.'

'He *didn't* know.'

'He ran away from the crime scene pretty smartly. So where is he?'

'I don't know.'

'Did Ostrowsky stash him away somewhere until you're charged?'

'No.'

'Jake, I think Inspector Brook is trying to help you,' said Gillstrap finally. 'He's giving you a chance to do yourself some good.'

'Then let me sign a confession,' demanded Tanner. 'I killed Kassia. I don't know where my brother is and I don't care. He's over eighteen. He can go where he likes. Now give me a pen. I want to put this behind me and get some sleep.'

Brook glanced up at the red dot of the camera on the ceiling. This was going to be tough to sell to Charlton, doubtless squirming in front of the monitor next door. Brook had half expected him to charge in and stop the interview. Asking his boss to believe that Tanner's confession was false would go against the grain.

'Interview suspended at twenty-two forty.' He leaned into the machine to stop the recording. 'Jake, I'm going to make you an offer and I want you to think about it very seriously. Assuming Ostrowsky is holding your brother—'

'He isn't.'

'Let me finish. If Nick is being held, that tells me you didn't kill Kassia. If you confirm that verbally, I'll put out a statement that you've been arrested and charged and you'll be held in a cell until we find your brother safe and well. What do you say?'

'Jake?' said Gillstrap. 'If DI Brook is right, speak now.'

Tanner gazed at Brook. 'I want to sign a confession and I want to do it now.'

In the incident room, Brook made a beeline for DC Cooper. 'Anything?'

Cooper clicked his mouse three times. 'See for yourself.' Noble walked in and Brook beckoned him over. They watched Nick Tanner stroll through the Intu Centre on Cooper's monitor, accompanied by a bulky, dishevelled man in dusty overalls. Nick didn't appear to be under duress as the pair moved towards the exit.

'The camera's some distance away—' began Cooper.

'That's Max Ostrowsky,' interrupted Brook, glancing at Noble.

'I think you're right.'

'Get a car round to his flat and arrest him for kidnap.'

Noble picked up a phone. 'DNA?'

'First order of business. Where did they go after leaving the Intu, Dave?'

'Brook. Are you out of your mind?' Charlton was striding across the room. 'I've already arranged a press conference for tomorrow morning. This is a good closure.'

'He didn't do it.'

'You forget I was watching,' said Charlton. 'Jake Tanner confessed – no matter how hard you tried to talk him out of it.'

'Sir . . .'

'We have film of him dumping the body,' said Charlton, counting on his fingers. 'We have a witness who saw them run and we have a confession. That's what we call a result around here, so when are you going to charge him?'

'His brother's missing and Jake's been coerced into a confession,' said Brook. 'There are inconsistencies in his statement . . .'

'Coerced by whom?'

'Grzegorz Ostrowsky.'

'The bar owner?'

'Ostrowsky's protecting his brother. I think Max killed Kassia. He has a history of violence and sexual assault in Poland.'

'By history, you mean convictions,' said Charlton, pouncing on Brook's choice of words.

Brook hesitated. 'Some arrests.'

'I see. Can you prove that Max Ostrowsky killed Kassia Proch?'

'Not yet,' said Brook softly.

'I'll take that as a no.'

'Sir, Nick Tanner is dependent on Jake for everything. They

were together when they torched the van. They wouldn't have split up.'

'Maybe he's hiding in that flat they broke into,' said Charlton, sarcastically.

'I just got the call,' said Noble, rejoining Brook. 'It's empty.'

'They were there?'

Noble looked hesitantly at Brook. 'It looks that way.'

Charlton's demeanour darkened. 'So how the hell was *that* missed?' he barked. 'The same bloody tower block.' Silence broke out and all heads in the room turned to see blood spill.

'My fault,' replied Brook coldly. 'I relied on uniform to do the legwork.' If a pin dropped, nobody heard it, and the silence crackled with unspoken anger. But far from taking the wind out of Charlton's sails, a volcanic rage seemed to bubble up through him and he jabbed a finger into Brook's chest.

'We have a confession; I want Tanner charged. Now! Get him in front of the magistrates first thing in the morning and stick one in the win column. Then we question him about Caitlin and the others. Understood?'

Brook stared back at Charlton's animated expression, aware that he had nothing but a theory to void a signed confession. 'There's *no* connection between Kassia Proch's murder and the other missing girls. I should've realised sooner.'

'You don't know that,' scoffed Charlton.

'I know Tanner was in prison when Valerie Gliszczynska disappeared.'

Charlton was on the back foot for a second before clambering on to safer ground. 'You haven't answered my question. Will you charge Tanner, or do I need to do it?'

Brook's gaze fell. 'I'll do it,' he said quietly, though by this time Charlton, anticipating victory, was already storming away. When the incident room door slammed, Brook looked uneasily round at his team, their faces turned to him for a reaction. 'That went well.' The assembled detectives laughed before returning to their work, the hubbub of normality restored.

Cooper sidled up. 'Nick got into a black Mercedes outside the Traffic Street entrance. It belongs to Ostrowsky. No sign of coercion. I'm working on a route.'

Thirty

26 April

BANACH FELT A HAND GENTLY touch her shoulder to rouse her.

'Are you okay, Angie?' said Helen Cowell.

Banach yawned and stretched in the chair. 'Good, thanks.'

'You've been crying.'

Banach reached up to feel the dry tackiness on her cheeks. 'Just tired.' She stood to get feeling back into her legs, looking down at Mitch sleeping peacefully. The drip had been removed and only a fresh bandage around his skull was evidence of injury. 'Been a hard week.'

Cowell smiled. 'It's after two. You should go.'

'I'd like to stay a while longer,' said Banach. 'I can't face going home.' Cowell submitted with a sigh. 'Thank you.'

'How's . . . everything?'

Banach laughed. 'You should've been a diplomat. No decision yet.'

'Have you spoken to the father?'

Banach rolled her eyes towards the sleeping policeman. 'He doesn't know yet. But I made an appointment at the Rutherford.'

'I see,' said Cowell. 'Constable Ryan will be discharged in the morning, if that helps.'

'Doctor . . .'

Cowell smiled. 'You want to tell him yourself. I understand. Mum's the word.'

'Interesting choice of words,' said Banach.

Brook and Noble's footsteps echoed on the exposed floor-boards. It took them only a minute to confirm that Max Ostrowsky had left his three-room flat in a hurry.

'I thought Tanner's flat was bare,' said Noble, looking around. The main room contained only an armchair – no carpet or curtains – and the floor was littered with half-eaten takeaway cartons, full ashtrays, crushed cigarette packets and empty vodka bottles. The bedroom contained only a single sleeping bag, though this time the detritus was confined to teeming ashtrays and Styrofoam cups.

'It's an identical sleeping bag to the one in the Cream,' said Brook, examining a label.

'At least DNA shouldn't be a problem.'

A uniformed constable appeared at the door, ushering a whiskered old man in front of him.

'You have information about Max?' said Noble.

'Is that his name?' said the old man, moving his eyes around the room. 'Fuck me! What a shithole. You wouldn't think he'd know someone with a Merc.'

'Did you see him leave?'

'Aye, carrying a holdall.'

'And he got into a Mercedes.'

'With some bald bloke big as a brick shithouse. I kept my door closed, I can tell you.'

'When was this?'

'Few hours ago. Maybe six.'

Brook beckoned Noble outside on to Arboretum Street, where the squad car lights were still flashing. 'Forget local and house-to-house, John. If Ostrowsky's got any sense, he'll get Max out of the country. It's the smart move.'

'Ports and airports,' nodded Noble.

Zeke put an ear to Caitlin's mouth. 'She's still breathing.'

'Good.' Red withdrew the white-hot iron from the blow-torch flame. 'Hold her head.'

Zeke held Caitlin's skull to the ground while Red moved the hot iron closer to the bubbling wound. With a quick move-ment she touched the iron against the damaged tissue and held it for a few seconds, ignoring the sizzle of evaporating blood and burning flesh.

'There,' she said, tossing the iron on to the concrete. 'It's in God's hands now.'

The distant sound of a phone ringing distracted them.

'At this hour?'

Red ran to the house while Zeke plunged his broken hand into a bucket of icy water and splashed his bloody cheek clean. Then he opened the steel door leading off the main barn and pulled on the handle of a circuit breaker. Dormant machinery inside the unit began to hum. With his good hand, he gripped Daniela's long hair and dragged her body towards the darkened room.

He didn't notice Caitlin's eyes open briefly at the noise of

Daniela's body being hauled away, instead setting to work with the unit's high-powered machinery.

He reappeared a few minutes later in a bloodstained rubber apron, steaming faintly in the cold night air. He carried a large steel pan covered with a lid.

'That was the Doc,' shouted Red. 'Get cleaned up. We've got a new girl.'

Zeke grinned. 'The Lord will provide. When?'

'Now.'

'Now?' said Zeke, setting down the pan and removing his apron. 'But we haven't scoped her out. Who is it?'

'Unknown, but the Doc has a line on her and says it's an emergency.'

'I don't like it.'

'Neither do I, but with a baby to save, we do as we're told, right?' said Red.

'What about the pick-up spot?'

'The Doc says it's perfect. No one knows she's there.'

'Where?'

'Tell you on the way.'

'Sorry, boys.' Zeke called across to the pen. 'You'll have to make do with pig nuts until tomorrow.'

'It's full of holes,' said Noble, reading through a copy of Tanner's confession.

Wearily Brook turned a page of the original. 'You should go home before you lose another night's sleep, John.'

'I'll follow you out for a change,' replied Noble, not looking up from Tanner's statement. 'Jake knows just enough to convict himself – the cleaning, the cause of death. Is it possible he did it?'

'He was coached,' said Brook. 'He didn't take a shower, so why clean the trap and why risk moving the body? The moment he stole Max's van, he put himself in our sights. It doesn't make sense.'

'So you think . . .'

'I think he stole the van not realising the body was already in there.'

Noble concentrated hard. 'Okay. But here's what I don't understand. If Max did kill Kassia . . . in her flat . . . why would *he* move the body? Surely it makes just as much sense for him to leave Kassia where she is.'

'That is a very good question.'

'I've got a better one. Having taken the decision to move the body, why the hell would he leave it in his van?'

Brook flicked through Tanner's statement. A few moments later, he covered his face with his hands. 'Christ! What an idiot.'

'Who?'

'Me! Listen to this. "The van was unlocked so I got in. The key for the ignition was on the floor in front of the driver's seat. I signalled Nick to get in and we drove away."'

'Max didn't lock the van?'

Brook slumped forward to rub his eyes. He took a minute to think it through. 'I've been so blind. He's been at least two steps ahead all the way.'

'Who?'

'You're right,' said Brook. 'Max wouldn't kill Kassia and leave the body outside his flat in an unlocked van – nobody's that stupid.'

'So if Max didn't move the body . . .'

'. . . then he didn't kill her.'

'So all that business with the hammer and the blowtorch?' said Noble.

'Same objection I made to Jake,' said Brook. 'Why go to all that trouble to burn off her tattoo and prints and disfigure her when she's already invisible?'

'It wasn't done to hide her identity?'

Brook shook his head. 'It was done to *suggest* an identity – the killer's.'

'Max.'

'Exactly. Max's blowtorch and hammer, the van too – all used to implicate him. And the victim was stripped to make it look like a sex crime to point to Max's history.'

'But Kassia hadn't had sex.'

'Because it wasn't *about* sex, John. It was a crime of passion – her head injuries tell us that. But it wasn't passion for Kassia.'

'What then?'

'It was passion for what she carried.'

'The baby?'

'The baby,' repeated Brook. 'Damn it, I should have realised when we checked the Rutherford staff for anyone who'd lost a child.'

'Ostrowsky's wife and baby died in childbirth,' suggested Noble.

'And he never remarried,' said Brook.

'He's single, good-looking and successful,' continued Noble, nodding. 'He met Kassia somehow and she fell for him. Why wouldn't she, living in a poky flat a long way from home? They had an affair.'

'Hardly an affair, John. I suspect their relationship was largely sexual. But when Kassia became pregnant, Ostrowsky fell in love with the idea of replacing the child he'd lost . . .'

'But Kassia decides to have an abortion.'

'When she tells him her plans, she doesn't realise the anguish it causes him,' said Brook. 'To lose a second child after the death of a first. It's against his religion and his instinct to father a child at last.'

'He would have tried to change her mind . . .'

'No doubt. Maybe he even threatened her, but Kassia must've realised he didn't love her. She refused, and when she left the clinic the night she was scheduled to have the procedure, he killed her.'

'But she didn't abort the child,' argued Noble.

'But he doesn't know that,' said Brook. 'Either she doesn't tell him or, blinded by rage, he doesn't give her a chance to speak.'

'Killing his own child,' said Noble, shaking his head. 'You could almost feel sorry for him.'

'Don't. He was smart enough to wait until she arrived back at the flat and cold enough to disfigure her corpse and frame his brother.'

'But he couldn't cover his shock when we told him Kassia was pregnant,' said Noble.

'Under the circumstances, I'm surprised he held it together that well.'

'It all makes sense. But why would he implicate his own brother?'

'Because Max is a sexual predator.'

'We don't know that,' said Noble. 'He's never been charged.'

'Only because Greg's been covering for him over the years.'

'Then why stop now?'

'Ostrowsky thinks himself a religious man,' said Brook.

'And to a religious man, Max's recent behaviour is not just an embarrassment but an affront to God.'

'Recent behaviour?'

'Max is bisexual.'

'What? Are you sure?'

'Pretty sure. Ironic that what was happening between Nick and Max was the final straw for both Ostrowsky *and* Jake.'

'Nick and Max?' repeated Noble.

'Remember when Jake started at Bar Polski, he took Nick along while he worked. I'm guessing Max started grooming Nick the minute he saw him. With special needs, Nick would've been flattered by the attention, and maybe even by money and gifts. Who knows? I suspect he is suggestible; he'll do things he doesn't understand because it makes him feel popular.'

'And Jake starts to suspect and stops taking his brother to work,' said Noble.

'And starts thinking of how to send Max a message.'

'By stealing his van.'

'I doubt there was a set plan, but once he finds the van unlocked, it's hard not to steal it,' said Brook. 'What Jake doesn't know is that he's blundered into Ostrowsky's plan to frame his degenerate brother. It's all there in Jake's past. The assault on a homosexual that landed him in prison – the only violent act on his record – a reaction in defence of a brother unable to understand consent, unable to comprehend what some people might want from an attractive young boy. Remember the sleeping bag at the Cream Bar . . .'

'Max's?'

Brook nodded. 'The vodka, too.'

'But how did Max get his stuff into the Cream Bar?' said Noble.

'I found the keys. There wasn't time to tell you.'

'Where?'

'In your desk. You hadn't booked them into evidence.'

'The keys from the burnt-out van?' Noble was confused. 'So Jake dropped them when he stole the van.'

'SOCO found them in the *back* of the van, John.' Brook arched an eyebrow. 'Max's van. If Jake mislaid them during the theft, they'd be near the driver's seat. Max had the keys.'

'How?'

'Probably Nick took them and gave them to him so they could have somewhere to meet and have sex.'

'But if the keys were in the burnt-out van, Jake couldn't have been in the Cream.'

'No.'

'Unless he climbed in.'

'Admit to murder but deny an assault? No. He was telling the truth.'

'Then who assaulted Ryan and Banach? Max?'

'Why would he?' asked Brook.

'Maybe he went there looking for Nick.'

'But Max knew the keys to the Cream were in his van, which by then was in the police pound. And there was someone with a more compelling reason for finding Jake and Nick.'

'Ostrowsky,' nodded Noble.

'And when the news conference told him that Jake and Nick had stolen his van, he set his people on their trail. His bodyguard . . .' Brook clicked his fingers.

'Tymon.'

'Tymon went to the Cream looking for Jake,' said Brook.

'And it was Tymon who went to Arboretum Street to take the van after Max had parked up for the night. Ostrowsky owns it; he'd have spare keys. So if Tymon's challenged, it's not even stealing. Then he drives to Kassia's flat and takes Max's hammer and blowtorch from the van to disfigure the body. He wraps her body in a plastic sheet . . .'

'Why not just use the bed sheets?'

'They're not transparent, John. With plastic, anybody investigating the van will see immediately that there's a body. It's a frame-up, remember. That's why Tymon replaces the tools in the van and drives back to Arboretum Street with Kassia's body. He leaves the van unlocked and sometime later returns to the flat to clean up.'

'So when Kassia's flat was cleaned, it was to cover up *Ostrowsky*'s presence.'

'His DNA would be everywhere. The shower, her clothes . . .'

'You've got to hand it to Ostrowsky. It's brilliant.'

'He must have got the shock of his life when we turned up to tell him his van had been stolen. His plan was in ruins and he needed a new one, and quickly. Fortunately for him, he has Jake – a convicted criminal and the perfect fall-guy. All he needed was leverage.'

'Nick,' nodded Noble. 'Where do you think they're holding him?'

'The warehouse in Pride Park has got to be favourite.'

'We should—'

'Charlton would never sign off on a raid,' said Brook. 'And even if we find Nick there, we still wouldn't have enough to touch Ostrowsky.'

'We'd have Nick at least,' said Noble. 'Then Jake might

cooperate, testify that Ostrowsky coached him.'

'All that gets us is proof that he's protecting Max,' said Brook.

'Catching Ostrowsky in a lie would be a start, at least. And with Jake's testimony we could link Kassia to Bar Polski . . .'

'Which just ties her closer to Max or Jake,' said Brook. 'We need Max and Tymon.'

'Which is why Ostrowsky wants them out of the country,' said Noble. 'Wait. Why do we need evidence that Ostrowsky killed Kassia when we could put him away for kidnapping Nick?'

'Always assuming Nick knows he's been kidnapped.'

'Jake knows.'

'But Jake's not telling. He seems to have another agenda.'

'He's afraid for his brother.'

'Maybe. But when I offered to charge him until we found Nick, he still refused to come clean. There's something else going on there.' Brook stood in the darkened office and pulled on his jacket.

'So that's it? We go home and leave Nick to Ostrowsky's mercy?'

'That's the one blessing about Jake's confession. If Ostrowsky harms Nick, Jake is free to retract – at least until the trial.'

'I suppose.' Noble gathered a pile of papers under his arm to follow.

Brook nodded at them. 'Where are you going with all that?'

'I didn't get a chance to go through the clinic's list.'

'Go home and get a couple of hours' sleep, John.'

'You first,' said Noble, pulling out his cigarettes. Brook stepped out of the office and they walked to the stairs. 'One thing.' Brook turned a bleary eye towards him. 'I get that Tymon leaves the van unlocked to make it easier to discover Kassia's body.'

'Right.'

'But how can he be sure it won't be Max that finds her?'

Brook stopped in his tracks and stared at Noble. A second later he sprinted back to the office and leafed furiously through Tanner's statement. 'After midnight. After midnight.' He tossed the sheaf of papers down. 'Where's the stolen vehicle report?'

Noble took a plastic wallet from his desk. Brook snatched the wallet and pulled out all the documents, reading frantically. A big smile broke out on his face.

'John. You're a genius.'

Banach pulled on her coat and left the ward, her footfall echoing around the deserted corridors of the hospital. She paid for her parking ticket and trudged across the access road that ringed the hospital, towards the car park. The bright moon bestowed an undeserved lustre on the pale concrete walls of the new hospital, and the ground shimmered as she walked.

She passed a top-of-the-range Audi that looked familiar. At the same moment she noticed a figure hidden beneath a black hoodie trying the handle of her Peugeot, parked in splendid isolation by the bushes.

Cheeky sod. Banach hurried her step, quietly slipping her hand into her bag for the Mace and reaching for the handcuffs on her belt. The thief didn't look much taller than her, but Banach was taking no chances. A growing number of car thieves were drug addicts, looking to fund their habit by plundering the cars of medical staff, on the ridiculous assumption that the boot would be chock full of narcotics. While such offenders might be deluded, they were also desperate and often violent.

When Banach was only a few yards away, the thief knelt down to peer into the car, continuing to work at the door, half a tennis ball in hand, trying to create enough suction to force up the old-fashioned lock.

As Banach approached, she caught sight of her reflection in the driver's window and realised the thief would see it too. Sure enough, the diminutive figure dropped the mangled tennis ball and pivoted to face her, arms raised in self-defence. Although police work had taught her to expect the unexpected, Banach was shocked to see it was a young woman.

'Police officer. Face the car, hands on the roof,' she ordered, bristling with all the aggression her training had bestowed. 'Face the car!' she barked again.

The young woman's face, framed by the oval hood, was contorted with hate, eyes blazing. She seemed far removed from the run-of-the-mill drug addict or twoccer.

'Last chance,' said Banach, brandishing the Mace. After a beat, the girl turned and placed her palms on the car. Banach stepped forward and tapped the inside of the girl's ankle with her toe to make her spread her legs, before giving her a quick frisk. Then she pulled the girl's right arm behind her back and snapped on a cuff before doing the same to her left.

Then she pulled out her mobile and swivelled her round. 'Tough luck, soldier. You picked the wrong car to boost.'

'You can say that again, copper.'

Banach gazed at the young woman's freckled face, a memory gnawing at her. 'I know you.' She reached out a hand to pull

379

down the hood, and long red hair cascaded on to the girl's shoulders. 'My God. You're Bernadette Murphy.'

The prisoner stared back malevolently. 'Well aren't you the clever one, Constable Banach.'

'You know me?' Banach's peripheral vision registered a darkening shadow in the driver's window behind her, but she reacted too late to avoid the blow from behind. Her legs buckled and twitched before turning to jelly, and she fell into the waiting arms.

'She's a copper, Zeke,' hissed Bernadette.

'What?' he answered, holding Banach upright.

'You heard me. She was at the clinic the other night. I took her picture for the newsletter.'

'Shit. What do we do?'

The girl considered for a few seconds. 'Not much we can do. She knows me.'

'You're not suggesting . . .'

'She's got a child inside her, hasn't she? Get the keys and get these off.'

Zeke picked up the keys from the ground and unlocked the handcuffs before hoisting the police officer over his shoulder. Unfettered, Bernadette ran to open the van doors, then took Banach's car keys from her handbag before throwing cuffs and bag in the van. Zeke lowered Banach carefully in after them and closed the double doors.

'Plenty of cameras,' he said, nodding at a nearby building.

'Yeah, but if no one knows she was here, they've no reason to look at the film,' said Bernadette. 'You take the van. I'll follow in the car.'

* * *

Brook got home in the early hours and dragged his exhausted body to the shower to wash away the trials of the day. He slept for an hour before a grumbling stomach woke him. He couldn't remember the last time he'd eaten but knew he had to take fuel on board, so he trotted downstairs at five o'clock and ate four slices of toast.

Sipping on his mug of tea, he heard the muffled buzz from his coat pocket. It was a text from Noble, sent half an hour before.

Ring me urgent when you get up.

'Would it kill you to use good grammar?' he mumbled, suspecting that Noble did it deliberately to annoy. He dialled and Noble picked up immediately. 'What?'

'I found something going over the Rutherford's staff list. Every missing girl had the same nurse.'

'What do you mean?'

'Just that. A senior nurse runs the preliminary appointment for all prospective patients. And if the patient proceeds, she's assigned that nurse until discharge.'

'Makes sense.'

'For continuity, right,' answered Noble. 'That's just it. All the missing girls were seen by the same nurse. Even Kassia Proch.'

'Who?'

'Mary Moran. We met her the other night, complaining about the picket . . .'

'I remember,' said Brook. He took another sip of tea. 'How many nurses run the appointments?'

'Four.'

'Could be coincidence.'

'I'd agree, but there's something else,' said Noble. 'I looked up Moran's address on the staff list. She lives in Statham Street.'

'And?'

'Mary Finnegan, the nurse who used to work at the Royal – Bernadette Murphy's aunt . . .'

'The first girl to vanish,' said Brook.

'Right. Shortly after Bernadette fell off the radar, the Finnegans split up and Mary went to live in Statham Street. Mary Finnegan *is* Mary Moran.'

'Only now she's working at the Rutherford Clinic under her maiden name,' said Brook. 'Interesting.'

'It is, but it doesn't make sense after looking at the Rutherford's patient database. There's no mention of Bernadette, or of her ever being pregnant. If Bernadette had a termination, she didn't have it there.'

'That may be precisely the point, John.'

Two hours later, Brook and Noble were driving through Derby as the rain fell softly from a grey sky. Rush hour hadn't started in earnest and traffic was light. The two detectives were silent until Noble loosed off a huge yawn.

'Trouble sleeping?' asked Brook, amused.

'You're the expert,' said Noble. 'Anything from the control room?'

'They're emailing a copy of the call. What about Max?'

'No news. He may be in the wind.' Noble pulled the car into Statham Street to park outside Mary Finnegan/Moran's house. 'Maybe we *should* be looking locally.'

'No. Ostrowsky sent him back to Poland.'

'How do you know?'

'Because Max is a liability – he's the only one with a stake in

contradicting Ostrowsky's narrative about Kassia's murder.'
Brook indicated a car parking in front of them, and opened the
door. 'There's Jane.'

'Morning,' said Gadd, sleepy-eyed. 'I'd forgotten the early
starts on your team.'

Brook smiled. 'Thanks for this.'

'As you said, it's my case,' replied Gadd. 'How do you want
to play it?'

'She'll be suspicious when she sees you, so drop in Caitlin's
name as soon as you can,' said Brook. 'Might throw her off the
scent for a while.'

Mary Moran pulled her thick towelling dressing gown tight
across her chest to cover the half-inch of neck still visible.
'Couldn't it wait,' she said, repeating her complaint for the
third time. 'I was on shift until midnight.' She lifted the hastily
brewed mug of coffee to her lips and glared at the three
detectives in turn, registering the well-grooved regret on their
faces.

Sorry for your loss . . . of sleep.

'Apologies again,' soothed Jane Gadd. 'We wouldn't be
here if it wasn't important, Mrs Finnegan . . .'

'Moran,' snapped the portly woman. 'I'm separated from
my husband.'

'But not divorced,' chipped in Brook.

'I'm Catholic,' she replied, as though this was explanation enough. 'What did you want to ask me about poor
Caitlin?'

'What can you tell us about her time at the clinic?' said
Gadd.

'You'll need to be more specific.'

'We'd like to know if there was anything unusual about her procedure,' said Brook.

'Her termination was routine,' said Moran. 'I said all this the other night. Caitlin took it in her stride, which was unusual in itself. There's always some upset somewhere along the line. It's an emotional rollercoaster for most of the girls, even if they're not religious. For the Catholic ones, it's ten times worse.' She drained her mug. 'Are you sure I can't make you a cup?'

'We're fine,' said Noble. 'Did Caitlin say anything unconnected to clinical matters?'

'She talked about that gobshite of a boyfriend of hers. Ronald, was it?'

'Roland,' corrected Noble.

'Spitting feathers every time she mentioned his name, she was, but it was more annoyance than anger. Said she was going to make him pay. When I asked her what she meant, she said, "Literally that. I'm going to make him pay." I assumed she was talking about money.'

'What did she think of Dr Fleming?' asked Noble.

'I don't think she had an opinion one way or the other,' answered Moran, glancing thoughtfully at Gadd.

'And you?' said Brook.

Moran smiled. 'How many surgeons do you know? Let me tell you, they have one vice above all others.'

'Vanity?'

She grinned. 'He doesn't hide it very well, does he? Dr Fleming's got ice in his veins. And when it comes to dealing with staff and patients, his social skills aren't the best.' She lowered her voice. 'But when you're lying unconscious on that table, those are the people you want working on you, believe me.'

There was an awkward silence beyond the absorption of Moran's opinions. Brook raised an eyebrow at Gadd, but Moran caught it and stared at her.

'Can we talk a little about Bernadette?' asked Gadd.

Moran looked at Brook and Noble, and back at Gadd. 'What's happened? Have you found her?'

'Nothing like that,' said Gadd. 'We'd like to go over details from the last time you saw her before she disappeared.'

'I've been over all that too,' said Moran.

'Please,' coaxed Gadd. 'For the benefit of my colleagues.' Moran's head turned to Brook and Noble. 'They want to help.'

After a moment's thought, 'There's nothing new to say. Bernie came to stay for a while. One morning she was there. By the evening she'd packed her bags and left. That was the fourth of July, near three years ago.'

'Why so sudden?' said Gadd. 'And why leave without saying goodbye?'

Moran stared into space. 'You asked me that at the time and I still don't know. Why would the answer have changed?'

'Because three years have passed and Bernadette's still missing,' said Brook. 'And now you might think the argument you had with her carries more significance than you thought at the time.'

Moran glared at him fiercely, her lips pursed in anger. She stared blankly into her empty cup. 'Bernie's my niece,' she said softly. 'We were on good terms.'

'That's a phrase I might use about my bank manager,' observed Brook. 'Not a relative.'

'She's a relative on my husband's side,' said Moran. 'Barry's blood, not mine.'

'And Barry's side of the family see things differently to you.'

Steven Dunne

'I have to get ready for work,' said Moran.

'Do you have access to the patient database at the clinic?' asked Noble.

'What does that mean?' snapped Moran. 'Of course I have access. I'm amending and creating records all the time. Why?'

'So if you wanted, you could delete a patient's records?' said Brook.

'What are you talking about?'

'For example, if a female relative became pregnant and not only wanted a private termination but all records of the pregnancy and procedure expunged.'

Moran jumped to her feet, her face contorted with anger. 'What are you suggesting? Why are you here?'

'Please sit down, Mary,' said Gadd.

Moran ignored her, panting in anger. 'How dare you suggest I might tamper with records.'

'We know these are tough questions,' continued Gadd. 'But we're hunting a killer of young women and we have to follow lines of enquiry.'

'Please,' said Brook, indicating the chair. He nodded at Noble, who extracted a stack of photographs and placed them on a coffee table in front of the distraught nurse. The newly acquired photograph of Kassia Proch was first. Portraits of Caitlin Kinnear, Daniela Cassetti, Adrianna Bakula and the others followed. Moran put a hand over her mouth and her eyes began to fill with tears when Bernadette Murphy's cheerful face stared out from the final snap. She began to shake.

'Now that both families have been informed, I can tell you that the identity of the dead girl in the papers is Kassia Proch,' said Brook, tapping a finger on her likeness.

Moran let out a whimper of recognition and a tear rolled

down her cheek. 'Kassia. The poor little thing.'

'The clinic's records show she had a preliminary appointment with you to set up a termination a few days before she
died,' said Noble.

Moran nodded, unable to take her tear-filled eyes from
Kassia's face. 'Yes, but the night she was supposed to have the
procedure, she changed her mind.'

'We know,' said Brook, lowering his head.

Moran averted her eyes for a moment, before dropping her
gaze on to Caitlin's picture. 'So Caitlin . . .'

'May still be alive, yes.' Brook saw her eyes drift across the
row of pictures. 'You recognise these other women?' Moran
nodded, her expression asking the question. 'They're all
missing. Including your niece.'

'Sweet Jesus,' she breathed.

'Mary, you're the common denominator between all these
women,' said Gadd. 'You examined them all, all except
Bernadette. According to the records.'

'But records can lie,' said Noble.

'Or be tampered with,' added Gadd.

'Am I a suspect?' said Moran.

'Until you tell us what happened between you and
Bernadette, yes.' Brook waited. The silence would be all the
pressure required.

Eventually Moran nodded. 'You're right.'

'You doctored her records?'

Moran looked incredulous. 'No. Not about that. I would
never do that.' She paused to compose herself. 'But the night
before she left, we had a terrible row. She was spouting off
some nonsense about the abortion laws in this country and I
made the mistake of challenging her, telling her some actual

facts.' She laughed without humour. 'Big mistake. Barry's family are feckin' medieval, and facts cut no ice with their brand of religious dogma, I can tell you.'

'So Bernadette disapproved of your work at the Rutherford.'

'I was still working at the Royal then. It had just opened and I'd moved from the City Hospital three months previous. But something had happened the month before Bernie arrived to stay and I'd already applied for a job at the Rutherford.'

'What?'

'There was a patient,' said Moran. 'Clare. Thirteen years old, skinny, barely into puberty, and so innocent. Not the kind of girl you expect to be ten weeks pregnant.' She took a deep breath. 'She'd been admitted with internal haemorrhaging and I found out later she was being sexually abused by her elder brother. The father – of the family, I mean – was a strict Catholic. He'd decreed the baby would come to term and that was the end of the matter. With no thought for Clare or the baby's future, the parents concocted some story about Clare's loose morals to be told when the time came. And, of course, they threatened her with hell and damnation if she didn't keep quiet.'

'And did she keep quiet?'

'She didn't tell a living soul about what her family had done to her – I had to drag it out of her. How she became pregnant and quickly realised she was on her own. She decided to induce a miscarriage.' Moran looked at the floor. When she resumed, she was barely audible. 'A friend at school had told her it was done with knitting needles.' She shook her head and another tear rolled down a cheek. 'We saved her with the help of several blood transfusions. But she'll never be able to conceive a child born of love. The day after we discharged her, I applied to the Rutherford.'

'And you told Bernadette about Clare.'

'Just to put her straight on some of the shite her family had poured into her. When that didn't work, I told her I was applying to work at the clinic, yes. I might as well have said I'd crucified Jesus personally. Barry's family were always so intense, so uncompromising. I still felt terrible when she left. Our last words were exchanged in anger.'

'You did nothing wrong,' said Gadd.

'I know. But during the argument Bernie told me she couldn't have children – some infection when she was younger – and she'd have to adopt . . . And she loved children. That's why she trained as a teacher.'

'What do you think happened to her?'

Moran looked down at her lap. 'I don't know. But recently I thought I saw her, or someone who looked very much like her.'

'Where?'

'It was dark. I can't be sure . . .'

'Where?' insisted Brook.

'A few nights ago. She was at the clinic. The night you were there. She was taking a photograph of a young woman making an appointment . . .'

Thirty-One

NOBLE SPED INTO ST MARY'S Wharf car park and screeched to a halt in the nearest bay, glancing over at Brook, his ear glued to the phone. Brook returned the look and shook his head before ringing off.

'Try Rob,' said Noble. He leapt out of the car and jogged over to the doors of main reception, Brook trailing in his wake. 'Wait. There he is.'

'Glad I found you, sir,' said Morton.

'Where's Banach?' said Brook quickly.

'She's probably on her way.'

'Her mobile's unattainable,' said Brook. 'Do you have her landline?'

'I don't.' Morton hesitated. 'Sir, she didn't want me to say anything, but I think she might be pulling a sickie for a day or two. You see—'

'We know about the pregnancy,' interrupted Brook. 'Get on to Personnel and get her landline. Then text her mum's address to DI Gadd. She's on her way to Banach's flat. Did you drop her at home last night?'

'No, at her car,' said Morton. 'What's going on?'

'We know how the missing girls were targeted,' said Noble. 'And we think Angie may be next.'

'How did you find out about the pregnancy?' said Brook, seeing Charlton walking along the corridor towards them.

'The Trastevere woman knew all about it,' said Morton.

'Did she now?' nodded Brook, his expression hardening. 'How did Banach take it?'

'Badly. She swore me to secrecy.'

'Well the cat's out of the bag now,' said Brook. 'But that might be the least of her problems. Get Cooper to circulate her vehicle details to Traffic. Hurry.' Morton headed off. 'John, send a couple of cars to pick up Constance Trastevere and Father O'Toole and get search warrants for all their property in the pipeline. And I mean all. Trastevere has extensive interests so get Cooper on to the Land Registry for a comprehensive list and make sure they all fall under the warrant. Go.'

'Ready for the press conference, Brook?' said Charlton, perplexed, as first Morton then Noble nodded a curt greeting as they ran past. 'Something wrong?'

Banach registered birdsong and her eyes flickered into life. Immediately she noticed the whitewashed ceiling and was puzzled by its unfamiliarity. Her head was pounding and she tried to move her hands to feel it but they wouldn't obey.

She looked down to see that she was in bed, a clean white sheet pulled up to her throat. Using her teeth, she pulled the sheet aside to reveal a pair of leather straps binding both wrists to the bed. Try as she might, she couldn't move her arms, and she kicked out to be sure her legs were unfettered. They were bare, which struck her as odd, but at least she could move them. Somebody had removed her trouser suit and dressed her in a stiff white cotton nightdress.

'What the hell. Where am I?'

She shouted a hello into the spacious room, but no one came running. It was sparse but spotless and had bars on the window. On one wall was a rack of assorted women's clothes on hangers. Her suit was neatly hung on the end. Shelves on the far wall were filled with laundered white towels and bedlinen. On the external wall, under the window, was a sink and, bizarrely, a toilet set back in the corner. From the marks on wall and ceiling, it appeared that someone had knocked through to the stall to create a rough and ready en suite. Apart from that there was just the bed and a bedside cabinet. A bible lay on the cabinet next to a carafe of water and a bowl of apples and oranges, none of which she could reach.

Hospital or prison?

'Then where is she?' demanded Brook.

'Unknown,' said Noble. 'She's not at home or her mum's, and no sightings of her car as yet.'

'She looked pretty shook up after last night,' said Morton. 'Maybe she went away for a couple of days to clear her head.'

'And maybe she's been abducted like the others,' argued Noble. 'She was targeted when she made an appointment at the Rutherford, Rob.'

Morton shook his head. 'What about her father? Is he around?'

Noble shook his head. 'Divorced ten years ago. He moved back to Poland.'

'Father,' said Brook softly.

'What is it?'

'The baby's father,' continued Brook, deep in thought. 'Maybe Constable Ryan . . .'

'The Royal,' said Noble, running for the door.

Ninety minutes later, Brook stood in front of the display of missing girls. Before him, the assembled detectives were sombre and hushed. Charlton was looking on anxiously, having cancelled the press conference to announce the charging of Jake Tanner.

Brook wasted no time. 'In the course of enquiries, DS Noble and I have come to believe that two people are responsible for the abductions of six women – Valerie Gliszczynska, Nicola Serota, Adrianna Bakula, Daniela Cassetti, Caitlin Kinnear . . .' Brook pointed to each likeness in turn before pausing to face colleagues. 'And now Constable Anka Banach.'

A murmur rippled round the room as Morton hit the lights. Cooper flicked at his mouse and the packed incident room watched CCTV images of Banach's abduction at the Royal Derby Hospital in the early hours of the morning as she returned to her car. After she'd been attacked by two assailants and bundled into a white van, both vehicles were driven away.

'Do you know where they went?' said Charlton when the lights came up.

'Short answer, no,' said Cooper. 'Long answer, we're working on it.'

'See that you are. And commit any and all resources if need be.'

'Thank you, sir.'

'You didn't mention Kassia Proch.'

'Kassia Proch isn't part of the series,' said Brook.

'Young, foreign, transient . . .' persisted Charlton.

393

'She fits the profile in all but the most vital aspect of this case, which Constable Banach herself pointed out,' replied Brook. 'Kassia Proch was pregnant when she was murdered. Significantly, the other women who sought to terminate their pregnancies at the Rutherford Clinic weren't killed. They were targeted and abducted *because* they were pregnant.'

'And held against their will until their babies were born,' said Charlton. 'You're serious?'

'Deadly serious,' replied Brook. 'Kassia decided to keep her baby. And according to her nurse, Mary Moran, the pro-life group CRI, who I believe are targeting these women, were made aware of that. For that reason, she was no longer of interest to them.'

'Whoa,' shouted Charlton. 'You're not suggesting Father O'Toole's organisation is responsible for these kidnappings?'

'Not the entire group,' conceded Brook. 'But someone connected to CRI is using its legitimate protests as a cover for drawing up a list of pregnant women to target and abduct. Constable Banach recently made an appointment at the clinic and put herself on that list.'

Charlton huffed. 'You need to be very careful about wild allegations like—'

'We only found out last night that Constable Banach is pregnant,' interrupted Brook. 'But Nurse Moran already knew because she saw Banach arrange a prelim at the clinic. She also saw someone take a picture of Banach. That's how the girls were targeted. Rob.'

'Last night Angie and I interviewed a Mrs Trastevere, who bankrolls this CRI mob,' said Morton. 'She admitted that her group takes pictures of all the pregnant girls visiting the clinic so they can ID them. They then put pressure on them by shopping them to their parents and priests. Mrs Trastevere knew Angie was pregnant and said the whole Polish community would be hearing about it the next day. Angie was in a state afterwards, as you can imagine.'

'After that interview, Banach drove to the Royal to sit at PC Ryan's bedside,' said Brook. 'When she left, she was attacked by the two assailants, one of them unknown, as you saw.'

'We know one of them?' said DC Read.

Brook held up a photograph. 'Bernadette Murphy.'

There was another murmur of excited conversation.

'One of your missing girls?' said Charlton. 'Are you sure?'

'Not a hundred per cent,' replied Brook. 'But she may have been seen on the pro-life picket at the Rutherford by Nurse Moran. She's Bernadette's aunt.'

'So it's not a coincidence, Bernadette targeting Rutherford patients,' said Cooper.

'Far from it,' replied Brook. 'The night before she dropped out of circulation, Bernadette and her aunt had a blazing row about abortion because Moran had applied to work at the clinic. And all the girls targeted were Moran's patients. I'm guessing that was payback, though how Bernadette knew which patients were assigned to her aunt, I don't yet know.'

'Maybe the aunt's in on it,' said Morton.

'We haven't ruled it out.'

'Bit young, isn't she?' said DC Smee. 'Bernadette, I mean – not the profile of your run-of-the-mill religious fanatic.' Brook shrugged.

'But Caitlin Kinnear wasn't pregnant when she disappeared, so how can she be part of the series?' queried Charlton.

'In Caitlin's case, I think priorities had changed, though I don't know why or how,' said Brook. 'Maybe she didn't look guilty enough when she walked past the pickets, and I gather she gave them a piece of her mind, I don't know. But these are fanatics and that's their weakness. They think they're doing God's work and that makes them untouchable. It's the kind of arrogance that allows them to kidnap a police officer even after their leader admits they took Angie's picture to out her to her community.'

'Maybe they're punishing Caitlin for her sins,' suggested Morton.

'Possible,' said Brook. 'And if so, Caitlin's in the most danger.'

'Because she's not pregnant,' suggested Smee.

'Exactly,' said Brook. 'She's expendable.'

'You think Banach is safe as long as she's pregnant,' said Gadd.

'I'd say so,' replied Brook. 'But that doesn't mean we have time to waste.'

'No sign of Trastevere at home,' called out Noble, entering the incident room. 'Father O'Toole's in Interview One.'

'Something to share, Brook?' demanded Charlton.

'DC Cooper was drawing up a list of target properties for warrants . . .'

'Warrants?' said Charlton.

'Father O'Toole founded CRI with Connie Trastevere's money,' said Brook. 'She's a widow with ties to militant pro-life groups in the US. She also inherited extensive properties . . .'

'What has that got to do with anything?'

'It's likely that whoever abducted these girls is going to need space and privacy,' said Noble.

'That is speculative at best.'

'It's not speculation that we have an officer in danger, sir,' said Noble.

'You have no evidence of an indictable offence against anyone connected with CRI, Sergeant,' said Charlton. 'No magistrate will issue a search warrant for a fishing expedition like that.'

'Then we'll go in without one,' snapped Noble. 'Would you like to see the abduction again, sir?' he demanded, the aggression in his voice giving Charlton pause.

For once Brook was the peacemaker. 'Sir,' he said, stepping in front of Noble. 'Perhaps you can use your influence with Father O'Toole, get him to cooperate.'

'He's under arrest?'

'Here at our invitation, sir.'

'Do you realise how insane that sounds?' protested Father O'Toole. 'Kidnapping young women and holding them until they deliver their babies.'

'We do, Patrick,' said Charlton.

'Citizens Resisting Infanticide is a legitimate charity,' continued O'Toole.

'We have to ask,' continued Charlton. 'One of our colleagues was abducted last night. A Constable Banach. I believe you met her.'

Brook and Noble exchanged a despairing look.

'Good Lord,' said O'Toole, genuinely surprised. 'Are you serious? That nice young policewoman abducted?'

'We haven't confirmed it,' said Brook. 'And putting aside how insane it sounds, can you tell us whether Mrs Trastevere ever mentioned such a tactic, even in passing?' Brook saw O'Toole hesitate. 'Father?'

'I really don't think talking about something means you believe in it,' said O'Toole.

'If you have something to say, spit it out, Patrick,' implored Charlton.

There was silence while O'Toole wrangled with himself. Charlton was about to speak again but Brook caught his eye with a minute shake of the head.

A moment later, O'Toole's expression betrayed a mind made up.

'Well?' said Brook.

'She once told me about a group in America she was connected with years ago. Children of the Lord Jesus Christ, they were called. They used to abduct women going into the clinic. But it wasn't really kidnapping, Inspector – more of an intervention. You see, a lot of these girls feel pressured into having abortions by friends, parents, even a society that holds motherhood in contempt—'

'Patrick!'

O'Toole took a deep breath. 'Connie said they would . . . intercept the girl for a few hours, take her to a secret location and talk through the relevant scriptures with her. They'd pray with her until she saw the error of her ways.' He looked down. 'Or not. Then they'd take her home or to a church.'

'Did Connie approve?' said Charlton. O'Toole's lips were firmly sealed. 'Patrick.'

'Broadly, yes, but that doesn't mean . . .'

'Where is she now?' asked Noble.

'If she's not at home, I don't know,' replied O'Toole.

'Do you know anything about Mrs Trastevere's property interests?'

'I know she has them,' said O'Toole. 'Nothing more.'

'But you're not familiar with anywhere specific she likes to spend time. Somewhere out in the country, away from it all.'

'As far as I know, she spends her time in her Duffield home. It's semi-rural, nice area – very pleasant garden. All her other properties are tenanted.'

'Do *you* own any property, Father?' asked Noble.

'No.'

'Not even a place to live.'

'The parish provides accommodation,' said O'Toole. 'A small house in Littleover behind the church. It meets my needs.'

'Does the church own property around the county to which you have access?' asked Brook.

'I really don't see the relevance, Brook,' said Charlton. Brook's glare spoke volumes.

'Father,' prompted Brook, turning back to the priest.

'There's a small hall in the church grounds,' said O'Toole. 'We use it for the youth club.'

'Nothing further afield,' continued Brook. 'Something larger, more remote.'

'No.'

Brook glanced at Noble, who placed a photograph of Bernadette Murphy on the table. 'Do you know this young woman?'

O'Toole looked at the photograph. 'Should I?'

'Her name is Bernadette Murphy,' said Charlton. Brook put a hand over his face while Noble stared at Charlton open-mouthed. 'We're fairly certain that she was involved—'

'Sir,' snapped Brook. 'Can I have a word?' He stopped the tape and ushered Charlton through the door.

'Yes?' enquired Charlton when he was outside.

Brook closed the door behind him but held on to the handle. 'Please wait here.'

'Pardon.'

'Or go to your office,' said Brook. 'But don't come back in.' He turned back to the interview room but was halted by Charlton's indignation.

'Would you care to explain that remark?'

Brook faced Charlton, choosing his words with care. 'It's my fault, sir. Sergeant Noble and I are trained detectives. You're not. I should never have let you sit in.' Charlton went red and Brook sensed a tantrum was only seconds away so continued in his most reasonable voice. 'When we interview witnesses or suspects, we ask for information. We don't give out the information we have because that might influence what we get back.'

'I was just asking if he knew her,' said Charlton.

'No, you were just telling him that we knew her. And now Father O'Toole knows that he has no reason to lie.'

'Lie?' exclaimed Charlton. 'He's a priest. Why would he lie?'

'Everybody lies,' said Brook. 'And what's more, we encourage it because when we catch them in that lie, we have them.'

'Are you suggesting Father O'Toole is a suspect?'

'I don't have to suggest it. He clearly is.'

'I don't understand.'

'I know,' replied Brook. 'That's why you should leave this to us.' He slipped quickly back into the room.

'I recognise the face, yes,' said O'Toole. 'I've seen her at demonstrations from time to time but never spoken to her. What did you say her name was?' Brook turned off the recording of O'Toole's disembodied voice and looked across at Noble.

'The Chief Super teed him up nicely,' said Noble.

'He did.'

'What did you say to Charlton?' asked Noble with a grin.

'Essentially to stay out of the interview room while the professionals did their work.'

'Ouch.'

'Ouch is right,' said Brook. 'I suspect my reservoir of goodwill is now a dust bowl.' He looked at Noble. 'Put someone on Father O'Toole, John.'

'Follow him?' Noble raised an eyebrow. 'You know he's a priest.'

'Don't you start! O'Toole lied to us. He knows where Trastevere is so there's a chance he might lead us to her.'

'Okay,' said Cooper, clicking on the mouse. Brook and Noble watched the abduction of Banach again. The young officer approached her car, creeping up on the hooded figure seemingly intent on theft.

'She did everything right,' said Noble.

'She should have called for back-up,' said Brook.

'Would you stand and watch some scumbag nick your car?' enquired Noble. 'Would anyone?'

Brook conceded with a shrug. 'Wait. Freeze it, Dave.'

'I haven't got to the van yet,' said Cooper.

'Go back,' said Brook. Cooper obliged. 'There.' Brook moved his head closer to the monitor. 'Another car.'

'Part of one,' said Noble, also straining to make it out. 'Looks like an Audi. Dr Fleming?'

'Dr Fleming,' agreed Brook. 'That's his personalised plate.'

'To be fair, he does work there.'

'That's a pay-and-display, John. Fleming's a consultant. He'd have his own parking space.'

Cooper restarted the film and they watched the burlier of the two assailants give Banach a fireman's lift to the large white van while the slighter figure sprinted ahead to open the rear doors. A minute later the van roared away round the hospital ring road to the main entrance, followed by Banach's Peugeot in hot pursuit.

'Tell me you know where they went,' said Brook.

'I know roughly,' said Cooper. 'They drove north up the A38 and took the A52 towards Ashbourne. We can't be sure but I don't think they go past Ashbourne. The traffic flow cameras tracked them beyond Shirley. The bad news is the camera before Ashbourne is on the blink . . .'

'Where's that?'

'Osmaston. But the good news is I checked the cameras on all exit routes from Ashbourne on that timeline and there's nothing matching the van and the car driving through.'

'So their destination was somewhere this side of Ashbourne.'

'That's still a big area,' said Noble. 'They could even be holed up in Ashbourne.'

'Van plates?' ventured Brook.

'Fakes,' said Cooper.

'What about Mrs Trastevere's properties?' asked Brook.

'She doesn't own anything in the area,' replied Cooper.

'Damn.'

'There was one thing,' said Cooper. 'I said *she* doesn't own anything.'

'Meaning.'

'CRI is a charity, right?'

'So Father O'Toole claims.'

'Well, he's right,' said Cooper. 'He's a trustee. The thing is, when you register as a charity, you have to demonstrate public benefit.'

'Go on.'

'To do that, Mrs Trastevere handed ownership of a small-holding near Rodsley over to the charity . . .'

'Just off the A52,' said Noble. 'That could be it.'

'What is it?'

'According to the records, it used to be a farm, but it's being converted into some kind of retreat,' said Cooper. 'Do you want an address?'

'We do,' said Brook, looking at Noble.

'Wagons roll,' said Noble, plucking his jacket from the back of the chair. 'Not coming?' he asked when Brook didn't move.

'Take Charlton.'

'You're joking.'

'Far from it. It doesn't need both of us and he needs a win for all our sakes.'

'But . . .'

'It'll be good for him,' said Brook. 'And the division. I'm going for Fleming.' Noble tried and failed to compose a further objection, nodded reluctantly and left the incident room, gathering up a pair of radios charging on a rack.

'Dr Fleming, please,' said Brook, speaking into his mobile.

'He's out of the clinic at the moment,' replied the receptionist at the Rutherford. 'Can I put you through to Dr Simons?'

'Don't worry. I'll catch him at the Royal.'

'You won't,' said the receptionist. 'He's taking a couple of days off to go walking in the Peaks.'

'Whereabouts in the Peaks?'

'I'm afraid I can't give out that information, sir.'

'This is DI Brook, Derby CID.'

'I have strict instructions . . .'

'And I'm investigating a murder.'

A pause at the other end. 'I'll have to clear it with—'

Brook rang off and tapped out a text to Noble. *Fleming may be in Rodsley. Good luck.* 'Tell me more about CRI, Dave.'

'There's not a lot to tell,' said Cooper. 'Founded in 2012 . . .'

'The year Bernadette disappeared. How many trustees?'

'Just three. O'Toole, Constance Trastevere and a Dr Cowell.'

Brook stared at him. 'Helen Cowell?'

Brook ran down the corridor on to Cowell's ward. He fumbled for his warrant card and thrust it into the nearest nurse's eyeline. 'Dr Cowell. Where is she?'

'You just missed her, I'm afraid,' said the nurse. 'She left about fifteen minutes ago.'

'What car does she drive?'

'I don't know if I should—'

'It's a matter of life and death,' said Brook.

'Her car broke down last week,' shouted another nurse. 'She's borrowed Dr Fleming's car for a few days while he's away. It's an Audi . . .'

Brook sprinted out towards the car park, grappling with his mobile. 'Any joy, Dave?' he barked when Cooper picked up.

'The response car says Cowell's not at her home.'

'Tell them to stay there. Meantime get details to Traffic.

She's driving a high-end Audi belonging to Fleming; you know the registration. And find out if she has other property.'

'I checked. She's only got the house in Ockbrook.'

'What about O'Toole?'

'He's on the electoral register but not as a homeowner and doesn't own any property in his name.'

A thought occurred. Brook thumped the roof his car. 'Sister-in-law,' he mumbled.

'What's that?' said Cooper.

'Father O'Toole's sister-in-law died in childbirth.'

'So?'

'So he must have had a brother at some time.'

'Samuel O'Toole,' said Cooper, reading from his monitor a minute later. 'Still alive and living in Derbyshire.'

'Do you have an address?'

Thirty-Two

AT THE SOUND OF BOLTS BEING drawn back, Banach turned her head. Bernadette Murphy appeared, carrying a tray. She laid it down on the trolley and pushed it over the bed, smiling brightly. 'How's the patient?'

'How do you think?'

'Excited, I imagine,' said the redhead. She pulled back the sheet and, with no little difficulty, unfastened one of the stiff buckles binding the leather straps to Banach's left wrist.

Banach moved her freed hand to feel the bump on the back of her head.

'Zeke overdid it, didn't he? Sorry about that. He's a love but he doesn't know his own strength.'

'You need to let me go. I'm a police officer.'

Bernadette smiled. 'Not going to happen. It'll take time to adjust, but you will. I hope you're ready for some lunch.' She put an extra pillow behind Banach's back and removed the metal cover from the plate with a flourish. 'There. T-bone steak today – in honour of your arrival. Good protein.' Banach looked down at the steak, already cut into bite-size pieces. 'We've got mashed potatoes, peas and gravy to go with, and a glass of apple juice to wash it all down.'

'How about a glass of wine?'

Bernadette raised an eyebrow. 'No more alcohol from now on, Anka. You've got responsibilities.'

'Why are you doing this, Bernadette?'

'I can't believe you know who I am. Are they honestly still looking for me?'

'Disappeared fourth of July, twenty-twelve.'

'I suppose I should be flattered,' said Bernadette. 'The Garda would be shrugging shoulders in the pub after a week.'

'What the hell happened to you?'

'I met Zeke and chose a different path. Now I follow the Lord.'

'Don't you care that your family is worried? Your aunt . . .'

'My aunt is a murdering cunt!' spat Bernadette. 'She kills babies for money. Understand? *That's* what happened to me. When my aunt decided to become a killer at an abortion clinic, I knew I had to do something.'

'Your aunt works at the Rutherford?'

Bernadette smiled. 'Didn't know that, did you? You met her. In fact I saw you with her.'

Banach paused to think. 'Nurse Moran?'

'Moran!' sneered Bernadette. 'The bitch wouldn't even keep her married name. Another sacred promise to God betrayed.'

'She's only doing her job.'

'And Zeke and me are doing ours. God before family. Work that the Lord means for us to do. Saving babies.'

'You mean saving my baby?'

'You're welcome. Now eat while it's hot.'

'This is too much food,' said Banach.

'Not any more.'

'I see. Eating for two,' nodded Banach. 'What if I don't want this baby?'

Bernadette's face hardened. 'Luckily for your child, that's not an option.'

'But I have a career.'

'Fuck your career,' said Bernadette. 'God has given you a gift, and you don't snub the Lord in this house.'

'But—'

'But nothing,' said Bernadette. 'Be glad you're pregnant, lady, because if you weren't, I guarantee you'd be cast down like the Whore of Babylon and your life wouldn't be worth the living.'

Banach stared. 'Like Caitlin Kinnear?'

Bernadette looked away. 'Caitlin was a mistake.'

'A mistake?'

'Forget it. Eat your food.'

'No.'

'Eat your food,' snarled Bernadette.

'Or what?' said Banach. 'You'll beat me. Kill me.' She saw the doubt on Bernadette's face. 'Course you won't. Not while I carry a child.'

'We could force-feed you.'

'I've got a better idea,' said Banach. 'Tell me about Caitlin. Then I'll eat. After all, I'm not going anywhere, so what harm can it do?' She picked up the fork and lifted a mouthful of mashed potato to her mouth. 'Smells good.'

Bernadette stared sullenly before her eyes dropped. 'Very well. Zeke's dad lost his wife giving birth to him. The poor man couldn't cope with the loneliness and grief and had a stroke. It was all very sad.' She hesitated, staring at the fork in Banach's hand.

Banach put the food in her mouth and began to eat. 'Mmmm, yum yum.'

'A few months ago, Zeke was joking around, saying we should find his dad a girl to keep him company – someone who didn't care who she gave her body to, someone who wasn't pregnant and could be a proper wife.' Bernadette grinned, then whispered as though blowing a kiss, 'Physically.'

'So you picked Caitlin,' said Banach, biting down on her revulsion.

'No, the bitch picked us.' Bernadette looked at the plate and Banach forced herself to spear a piece of steak into her mouth. 'Zeke was on the picket at the Rutherford one night . . .'

'Taking pictures of future victims?'

'You worked it out. Clever you. Well if you spent any time there, you'd know that every girl who walks in or out of that godforsaken place carries the guilt with her. Even you. Don't bother to deny it. But when Zeke and the others confronted the Kinnear girl, they encountered someone with no shame about the crime she was about to commit. Worse, she had a mouthful of obscenities about God and our work.'

'Maybe she had some blasphemous notion that her body was hers to control.'

'Then she should have controlled it before she got pregnant.'

'You believe in contraception, then?'

'Of course,' exclaimed Bernadette. 'We're not fanatics. Use whatever you want to lead a selfish life. But don't get pregnant, because once that seed starts to grow in your belly, that life belongs to God. Not you.'

'So you abducted Caitlin even though she wasn't pregnant.'

'Zeke wanted a companion for his dad. And to teach her a lesson in humility. We tried with one of the other girls . . .'

'Other girls?'

'One of the mothers . . . but she screamed every time he went near her. I can't say I blame her.'

'And now the other girl's dead,' said Banach.

'No, of course she's not dead.'

'Then where is she? *Cast down like the Whore of Babylon.*'

'She's on her way to a new life in America.'

Banach managed to laugh. 'Fuck off.'

'It's true. We have the resources. A rich patron.'

'You mean Mrs Trastevere?' said Banach. Bernadette raised an eyebrow. 'And the other girls? Daniela, Adrianna, Nicola, Valerie.'

Bernadette stared at her open-mouthed. 'You're good.'

'Answer me.'

'They're all in America. Some took their babies with them. Others gave them up for adoption to rich childless couples for a cut of the fee. That's how we raise our money.'

'And that's what I'll be offered?'

'It is.'

Banach grinned. 'You actually think I'm going to swallow that bullshit. I know a scam when I see one.'

'It's not . . .'

'I'm a police officer, Bernadette. We both know you can't risk letting me go.'

'Trust me,' said Bernadette, busying herself with a little sheet-straightening. 'Everything changes when we put your baby in your arms. Until then we care for you like a goddess. The best food, the best treatment . . .'

'Treatment?' scoffed Banach.

'We have a doctor on the team,' said Bernadette, looking at her watch. 'Someone else you've met.' Her smile was teasing. 'Though not at the Rutherford.' Banach cocked her head in confusion. 'Worked there as a locum for a few weeks, of course, and saw the horror for herself. She left but kept her password, which got us access to the records of all the girls we wanted . . .'

'Her?' exclaimed Banach. 'Dr Cowell?'

'She'll be here soon. See! We take no chances with your baby.'

'My God.'

'Amen to that, sister.'

'But we took a printout of Rutherford employees,' said Banach, confused. 'Dr Cowell wasn't in the records.'

'That's the beauty of access,' said Bernadette. 'You can delete your own record.' She leered malevolently. 'While making sure you only abduct the patients of your murdering bitch of an aunt.'

'Neat.' Banach darted a glance at her. 'Why are you telling me about Dr Cowell?'

'Because you're family now,' said Bernadette. 'We trust each other.'

'Then undo these straps.'

'One day at a time, Anka – as soon as you come to understand the value of our work. And on the slim chance you can't . . . appreciate your child, he or she will be offered to a couple who desperately want a baby to love.' Bernadette made an involuntary grab for her own stomach.

'Like you?'

Bernadette's smile disappeared. 'Your meal's getting cold.'

Banach gazed forlornly at the barred window. 'Scream all you want.'

'How did you know?'

'That's what they all do. At first. But the room's sound-proofed, so save your breath. Ain't no one gonna hear you that ain't in here.'

Banach stared unhappily down at the tray. Realising that she might need all her strength to get out of there, she speared another piece of steak.

A phone rang somewhere deep in the house and Bernadette left the room. Seconds later the bolts were drawn across, and Banach dropped the fork, picked up the T-bone from the plate and tore at the meat with her teeth.

Driving through a sudden shower, Brook turned left at the Mackworth roundabout on to the A52 towards Ashbourne, making the same journey that Noble and Charlton – with Read, Morton and DI Gadd in tow – had taken earlier that afternoon once the warrant had been swiftly issued.

The skies were dark and brooding and the roads wet. Brook looked across at his mobile, cursing his failure to grab a radio handset from the incident room. Having set out to go to the hospital, he had thought his phone would be sufficient, but once in the countryside, he realised his mistake when the mobile signal became sketchy.

Five minutes later, the car in front turned off and Brook found himself behind an Audi. He realised with a jolt that it was Fleming's car. The personalised plate left no room for doubt. He plucked his mobile from the passenger seat – still no signal.

'Damn. On your way to Rodsley, I hope,' he said.

Ten minutes later, Fleming's Audi ignored the first turn-off to the village of Shirley that would have fed into Rodsley. When Cowell also failed to take the second road, Brook realised there was a third option. He held the directions to Jobs Wood Farm up to his face.

'Next right, Doctor?'

Sure enough, the Audi turned on to a tight little road called Rough Lane. Brook slowed to make the turn and drove unhurriedly to let the Audi put some distance between them. If Cowell was heading for Samuel O'Toole's farm, she'd be there when Brook arrived, and he didn't want to frighten her away.

Bernadette watched as Zeke took the lid from the steaming pan. The water had cooled sufficiently for him to manoeuvre a large slotted spoon under the head and lift it from the milky liquid before dropping it in a bucket. He repeated the procedure with two hands and two feet.

'Errrrr,' said a voice from behind him.

Zeke turned to smile at the gargoyle in the corner chair, with his twist of pink tongue. 'No, it's for the pigs, Dad.' He winked at Bernadette. 'Italian pig feed.'

'Very funny,' she replied, without mirth. 'What have you done with the pluck?'

'I put all the chopped innards and organs in the trough this morning. You should have heard the noise. Hog heaven.' He nodded at the bucket. 'Now these are softened up, they'll go in the grinder with the legs and trunk.'

'Good. Make sure it all goes in the trough by tomorrow.'

'No problem,' replied Zeke, keeping his eyes trained on her. 'What's occurring, hun?'

'That was Mrs T on the phone. The police have been to see her and she thinks we need to have a clear-out.'

'The police?'

Bernadette flattened her hands on the kitchen table. 'We took a copper, Zeke.'

'I know, but how did they connect her to Mrs T?'

'Seems they've been working it for a while,' said Bernadette. She nodded to the ceiling. 'Clever clogs knows who I am, and about some of the other girls too.'

Zeke grabbed her hands in his. 'It wasn't your fault, Red. Cowell should never have selected her.'

'Unfortunately, that changes nothing. The police won't rest until they find her.'

'Let them try,' said Zeke, pulling her towards him. 'We have God's shield around us.'

She rested her head on his shoulder and a tear fell on to her cheek. 'That's not all. Mrs T says she's taking the boys.'

'Our boys?'

'They're not our boys, Zeke.'

'But she said we could have them.'

Bernadette managed a watery smile. 'I know. But they're evidence.' It was Zeke's turn to stifle a tear. She rubbed his arms until he looked at her. 'When this dies down, we'll be together again. The boys too.'

'A new life in America?' Bernadette laughed and Zeke managed a sad smile.

She touched his scarred cheek. 'Come on. Finish up and then you need to process the Kinnear whore. She deserves no better.'

'What do we do about . . . ?' He left the sentence unfinished, content to nod to the upper floor.

'To be decided.'

'She carries part of God's plan in her womb.'

'I know.' Bernadette was distracted by a car pulling into the farmyard and strained to see out of the barred window. She beckoned Zeke over anxiously. 'Do you know that car?'

Zeke shook his head. 'It's an Audi.'

'See who it is.' He unlocked and unbolted the kitchen door and was about to step out. 'Zeke!' Bernadette nodded towards the bucket. Zeke covered it with a tea towel.

'It's the Doc,' he called from the yard.

Bernadette saw a fingernail floating in the pan of steaming water and placed the lid over it.

'How's the patient?' said a disembodied voice.

'Good,' said Zeke, stepping back over the threshold. Helen Cowell followed him into the kitchen.

'New car?' said Bernadette.

'Did I worry you?' said a smiling Cowell.

'Yes, frankly,' replied Bernadette, withholding a return smile. 'Seeing as we abducted a police officer last night.'

'Car trouble. Had to borrow a colleague's.'

'Did you hear what I said?'

Cowell opened her doctor's bag. 'Usual room?'

'Did you know she was a copper?' insisted Bernadette. 'The new girl.'

Cowell looked absently across at her. 'I knew.'

'Jesus. What the hell were you thinking?'

'I was thinking she was going to have an abortion,' said Cowell, sounding out each word as though talking to an idiot.

'That's no reason to deviate from the process.'

'What are we trying to do here but save innocent lives?'

'Yeah, great,' sneered Bernadette. 'You give us the green

415

light and now the shit's hitting the fan. Mrs T's already been on the phone.'

'What did she say?'

'She went ballistic when I told her.'

'Anything else?'

Bernadette exchanged gimlet glances with Zeke. 'She told us to be careful.'

'Good advice,' said Cowell, making for the stairs.

'Another thing,' said Bernadette. 'She's British.'

'So what?'

'So it's one thing convincing foreigners they'll be leaving the country after the birth, quite another to persuade a Brit. She's got it into her head that once we have the baby, we'll kill her.'

'I'll talk to her,' said Cowell, disappearing up the stairwell. Zeke gave Bernadette the eyes and she hurried after the doctor. 'It's okay. I know the way.'

'I need to collect her food tray.'

'Got her eating already,' smiled Cowell. 'I'm impressed. Thought she'd be more stubborn.' From the top of the stairs, she surveyed the corridor – the boarded window, the bare floor. 'What happened to the carpet?'

'It got a bit grubby,' said Bernadette, pulling back the bolts on Banach's door.

'And the window?'

'Passing kids,' answered Bernadette, not meeting her eyes. She shrugged when Cowell raised a disbelieving eyebrow. 'Boredom.'

'So much for the rural idyll,' quipped Cowell, stepping through the door.

* * *

Coming to a junction, Brook made a right turn before heading over a crossroads. It was getting dark, so he turned on the headlights. The trees of Jobs Wood loomed on the right, and after passing a small pond, Brook came to a halt beside a rotting wooden sign – Jobs Wood Farm. He extinguished the headlights and pulled the car off the road into trees and on to a dirt track, rattling over a cattle grid and through a small stream.

He caught sight of the farmhouse through the trees. It was a good size, though not as large as the modern barn beyond. Both buildings were on higher ground, sitting above the surrounding fields with a clear view of cars approaching along the rough track.

Brook halted before the car broke cover and tried his mobile again, but three times the call failed. 'Damn it,' he muttered. The protocol was to wait for back-up, but he felt a paternal responsibility towards Banach after recruiting her to his squad. He put the car in first gear but stopped when he saw the lights of another car coming along the lane. He quickly reversed off the track and under the cover of a lush clump of overhanging ferns, turning off the engine and slipping out of the driver's door in one movement.

He hurried back to the track and crouched behind bushes in time to see a sleek black Land Rover make short work of the uneven track and power up to the house. A familiar figure was behind the wheel.

'You're taking it well, Angie,' said Cowell, cleaning her hands with an antibacterial wipe. Banach didn't reply.

'Anka is the name God gave her,' said Bernadette.

'So it is,' said Cowell. 'Sorry about the head, Anka, but we can't risk chemicals in your condition.' Banach sat perfectly still on the bed, her eyes following Cowell around the room.

'Quite an appetite,' said Bernadette, removing the dinner tray. Banach watched her take the plate, hoping she wouldn't realise something was missing amidst the leftover steak gristle. She laid her hand obligingly over the open buckle to distract her captor and Bernadette abandoned the tray to fasten the strap around her wrist.

'Isn't one hand enough?' asked Banach.

'No,' replied Bernadette.

'She's right,' said Cowell. 'We've been over this. You have to let the patient move around for the sake of circulation. She can't get out and it'll save you coming in all the time to let her use the toilet.'

Bernadette yanked the strap as tight as she could until Banach winced. 'She's a police officer, remember.'

'What did I just say?' said Cowell, approaching the bed. 'You'll cut off her blood.'

'You worry about my circulation,' said Banach, through gritted teeth, 'but in six months, after I deliver your cash cow, you'll let these fanatics butcher me.'

'Shut up, you whore,' snapped Bernadette.

'Anka,' said Cowell, shaking her head and shooting a fierce glance at Bernadette. 'That's not what this is about. Once we have your child safe and well, we offer you a new life. Mrs Trastevere is a wealthy woman and you can go anywhere . . .'

'Bullshit,' said Banach. 'That fairy story might have worked with Caitlin and some of the others, but I'm a police officer. How naive do you think I am?'

Cowell's face registered confusion. 'Caitlin? That was the girl in the burned-out van, wasn't it?'

'Aaah.' Banach smiled her understanding. 'Need-to-know basis. Caitlin wasn't pregnant so you didn't need to know.'

'What are you talking about?'

'I'm talking about your group abducting Caitlin Kinnear,' said Banach.

'Are you finished in here, Doc?' said Bernadette. 'I've got work to do.'

'Better do as Bernadette says, Doc,' said Banach. 'Before you learn something.'

'Let's go,' ordered Bernadette.

'Or stay and ask me about Caitlin and how they took her to be a surrogate wife to Zeke's dad.' Banach's fierce eye issued her challenge.

Cowell turned to Bernadette. 'What's she talking about, Bernie?'

Bernadette hesitated. 'She's a cop. She's playing you.'

'Ask her what they did with her,' said Banach.

'I don't need to,' said Cowell. 'Caitlin Kinnear burned to death in a van in Derby. Two brothers kidnapped her and set fire to her. It was on the news and in all the papers.'

'That's what everyone assumed,' said Banach. 'But that was a young Polish girl called Kassia. Meanwhile Caitlin was abducted by this nutter and her psycho boyfriend and kept here as a concubine for his crippled father.'

'That's enough,' ordered Bernadette, marching round to pull harder on the strap.

'Seems she doled out a bit of lip at the clinic to God's warriors,' grimaced Banach through the pain.

'I'm telling you to shut up, bitch.'

'Bernie, stop.' Cowell tried to pull the wiry redhead away.

'You'll damage her.' Bernadette shoved her off and forced the prong into its tightest setting.

'That hurts,' cried Banach.

A powerful car roared up to the house and Bernadette ran to the window to look down into the gloomy cobbled yard. Father O'Toole and Mrs Trastevere climbed out of the Land Rover. Bernadette's face fell.

She turned to see Helen Cowell unfastening the strap round Banach's wrist.

'Leave that!' she ordered, marching back to the bed, pushing Cowell aside. 'She's a copper, you idiot.'

She bent back over the loose strap to refasten it, but quick as a flash, Banach produced the jagged T-bone in her fist and drove it ferociously into Bernadette's eye. The shards of bone, broken and sharpened by Banach's teeth, plunged into the socket and Bernadette let out an unholy howl of pain and staggered backwards clutching at her face.

Screaming, she lurched back towards the bed, where Banach flicked up her unbound legs and wrapped them around Bernadette's neck, pulling her down against the bed and squeezing as hard as she could.

Cowell ran to pull Bernadette away, but Banach's grip was too tight. Instead she fell on Banach, who dropped the T-bone and grabbed the doctor by her hair, twisting as hard as she could and ignoring the feeble connection from the doctor's flailing fists. Soon Cowell was screaming as well, but Banach only twisted harder, feeling the satisfaction of Cowell's roots giving way in her grip.

Cowell finally jerked her head from Banach's grasp and lurched towards her bag, leaving a fistful of shiny black hair behind. Still bound by her right hand, Banach continued to squeeze the weakening redhead's neck with her thighs; at the same time, no longer fighting off Cowell, she was able to claw at the strap restraining her right arm. It was stiff but hadn't been fastened as tightly as her left, and as Cowell advanced on her with a hypodermic, she wrenched her stronger arm free and swung viciously at the doctor's chin.

Banach could hear the snap of the jaw, and Cowell stood for a moment, frozen, before her arms dropped to her sides, her eyes rolled back and she fell like a demolished building. Banach jumped to her feet, releasing Bernadette to the floor, then fell on her with a fist brought from way behind her head.

Both women lay still, Banach's heavy breathing the only noise. Barefoot, she stepped over Bernadette and plucked the hypodermic from Cowell's hand, pumping half into the doctor's neck with an unceremonious plunge of the fist. She withdrew the syringe and emptied it into Bernadette's neck.

'Sleep tight, girls,' she panted.

In just her nightgown and underwear, she tiptoed to the window, seeing the priest and Mrs Trastevere disappear into the house. With little time to think, she rustled through Cowell's bag for her phone, but if the doctor had one, she must have left it in the car.

Banach ran into the corridor, closed the door and eased the bolts across. She opened each door on the upper floor but was relieved to find them unoccupied, until the last one.

It was a playroom and contained two children, one little older than a baby. It was clear they'd been conceived by different mothers.

'Hello,' said the little boy from his playpen.

'Hello,' said Banach. 'What's your name?'

'Sean.'

'I'm Angie,' said Banach. She took a step towards the pen but stopped before reversing for the door, smiling. *No way will I make it with kids in tow. And these kids are loved.* 'I'll see you later.'

'Bye, Angie,' said Sean, waving.

Softly closing the door, Banach headed to the top of the stairs. She could hear voices from the room below and looked around for an escape route. Making her way to the boarded window at the far end of the corridor, she pulled away the panel and gazed out into the gathering night through the broken window.

Thirty-Three

BROOK WATCHED THE LAND ROVER power up the hill and stepped into the clearing to follow. He'd be at the house in two minutes and without the car would at least have the advantage of surprise. A second later he stopped, a thought gripping him. He sprinted back over the cattle grid to the lane.

Fifty yards away DC Smee sat in an unmarked car, window open, talking on his radio.

Seeing Brook approach, he jumped out. 'Sir, I was just trying to reach you.'

'Pull off the road here and block the farm track,' said Brook, sliding into the passenger seat. 'No lights.'

Smee got back into the car, drove on to the track and killed the engine.

'Get hold of DS Noble and the Chief Super and get them here. They might still be in Rodsley. And contact Ashbourne station too. All hands.' He opened the passenger door. 'Better get a couple of ambulances while you're at it.'

'We should wait for back-up, sir.'

'Make sure you do. Don't let anyone leave, and when the

423

cavalry gets here, come hard and heavy.' He turned and jogged towards the farmhouse.

'Mrs T, Uncle Pat,' said Zeke, eying the bucket, the tea towel still hiding its contents. 'I was just going to feed the pigs.'

'Zeke,' said O'Toole. The priest turned to his disfigured brother seated in his corner chair. 'How are you, Sam?' Sam stood and approached for a hug, his tongue swaying inertly amidst the broken grin. 'Hat tree.' *Patrick*.

'Are the children ready?' said Mrs Trastevere.

'Red must be sorting them out,' said Zeke, his expression darkening. 'Listen . . .'

'We've been over this, Ezekiel,' said Trastevere. 'You knew this day might come.'

'But they're our kids now,' protested Zeke. 'You said we could have them.'

'They are *not* your kids,' said Trastevere, her features stern.

'We love them.'

'Bring them down!' barked Trastevere.

Defeated, Zeke shouted up the stairwell. 'Red!'

The drop wasn't too bad and the ground looked muddy and soft. Banach could see the reason. She'd be landing in the pig pen and the animals were feeding in the far corner, fighting for space around the trough. She squeezed out of the broken window, ignoring the tear of broken glass along her bare thigh, and launched herself, landing awkwardly. Feeling her ankle wrench, she let out a yelp of agony and stood, gingerly testing her weight on her injured foot.

'Shit.' She cursed at the pain shooting through her leg, and half hobbled, half hopped towards the fence, a trickle of blood dripping down her calf.

She could hear the pigs clearly now, and a terrible racket they were making, clambering over each other to get to the feed, screeching when obstructed from their meal. A second later, an even louder squeal drew her attention and she turned to see two very large pigs, unable to get their snouts in the trough, walking towards her. The larger of the two broke into a porcine gallop and the other followed, pounding at the ground.

With a tic of horror, she looked down at the rivulet of blood rolling past her ankle bone to pool in the mud. The fence was only yards away, but a quick glance over her shoulder told her the pigs were almost on her. Gritting her teeth, she drove her twisted ankle into the ground, biting down on the shard of pain, and launched herself at the stout wooden barrier.

She felt the heavy animals strike the fence a second after she had pulled herself over, and the collision dropped her in a heap on the other side. Her face was inches from a gap in the rails, and a second later, a hairy pink head shuddered into the opening, snout and teeth snapping and straining to get to her.

The pig bit down on a strand of her hair and Banach screamed as she felt herself being dragged towards the gap in the fence. Panic-stricken, she lashed out at its small pink eyes and the pig loosened its grip, allowing her to break free and roll to a safe distance. She lay on her back for a few seconds, panting hard.

A moment later, she hauled herself to her feet and approached the fence as the pigs wandered off, snuffling over the blood trail. 'If I get out of this, I'm personally coming back to turn you fuckers into bacon sandwiches and a huge vat of *bigos*,' she promised. The pigs turned to stare as she hobbled away.

Father O'Toole guided his brother on to the sofa. 'There you go, Sam.' His eye was drawn to the set of interlocking leather straps hanging from a wing of the sofa. He lifted the thick leather to examine them, eyebrows raised at the exposed wires glued to the inside of several of the straps.

'Dear Lord.'

He returned them to the sofa and made to leave.

'Hat tree,' said Sam, restraining him with a grasping hand.

O'Toole gripped his brother, managing to hold his eye to the ugliness, and patted the back of his hand. 'Get some rest, Sam. I'll see you soon.' He resisted the urge to explore further and marched purposefully back to the kitchen as Mrs Trastevere replaced the tea towel over a large bucket.

'I don't know what the hell's been going on,' he said, 'but I don't like what I'm seeing. This is supposed to be an intervention, not a torture chamber.'

The elderly woman turned to him, her face set. 'If you're making an omelette, Patrick, you're gonna break some eggs.'

'What does that mean?'

'We're abducting young women against their will. They're not all gonna play ball.'

'Are you going to ask him about the Kinnear girl?' demanded O'Toole.

'Me? He's your nephew.'

O'Toole had no comeback. He nodded. 'Very well. I'll do it.'

'It hardly matters.'

O'Toole was incredulous. 'We're talking about a human life. If they took her without telling us, God knows what else they've been up to.'

'Save your sympathy for someone who deserves it,' snarled Trastevere. 'We're talking about a slut who destroyed her child.'

'And what about abducting a police officer?'

'Cowell overreached herself. I blame myself. I should have stayed on top of things.'

'Constance . . .'

Zeke emerged from the stairwell carrying the two children draped along either arm. He reached the little boy down to the floor and handed a holdall to Mrs Trastevere while still juggling the baby up and down.

'Are we going for a walk, Daddy?' asked Sean.

Zeke's eyes filled with tears, his voice hoarse. 'No, Sean. You're going on a trip. It'll be fun. You'll see.'

'Where's Bernadette?' said Trastevere.

Zeke shook his head. 'Thought she was in with the new girl, but the bolts are drawn.' He gulped back more tears. 'She must have gone to the barn.' He glared at Trastevere. 'Can't face losing another child.'

'About the new girl . . .'

Zeke put up a hand. 'We didn't know she was a copper. Cowell picked her out. She . . .' His eyes narrowed.

'What is it?' demanded Trastevere.

'Cowell was in with the new girl as well.' He thrust the baby into O'Toole's arms and ran up the stairs.

'Put the children in the car,' Trastevere barked.

'I need to ask about the Kinnear girl,' said O'Toole.

'Do it!' she shouted, following Zeke up the stairs.

* * *

O'Toole unlocked the Land Rover and helped Sean up into the back seat before placing the carrycot on the seat next to him. 'Look after your brother, Sean. I won't be long.' He opened the window an inch to ensure fresh air and closed the door.

His hand was still on the door handle when a cuff was roughly clipped on to his wrist from behind. Then his left arm was yanked behind his back and wrist attached to wrist. The car keys were stripped from his inert hand.

'Children of the damned, Father?' said Brook, spinning him round.

'Inspector Brook! I—'

'Shut up.' Brook grabbed his forearm and frogmarched him to the rear of the vehicle, flicking at the key fob. The boot opened. 'Didn't anyone tell you not to leave children in a car without supervision?' He heaved the priest into the boot and slammed it closed before locking the vehicle.

'They're alive,' said Zeke, his fingers registering the pulse in first Bernadette, then Dr Cowell. 'Jesus, baby,' he said, staring at the blood around Bernadette's eye. 'What did she do to you?'

'Never mind that now, your patient's gone,' said Mrs Trastevere. 'You bloody fool. Find her!'

'Oh I'll find her,' growled Zeke, heading to the door. 'And when I do . . .' As he passed, Mrs Trastevere caught his arm, surprising him with her strength.

'Anything else you want to tell me?' she said. Zeke lowered his head. 'So you did take the Kinnear girl.'

'You heard the way she spoke to us. Like we were in the wrong.'

'And you wanted to punish her.' Trastevere shook her head. 'We don't have time to argue. Where is she?'

'In the barn – what's left of her.'

She let go of Zeke's arm and pushed him out of the maternity room. In the corridor, Zeke turned at the noise of the old woman shooting the bolts across.

'What are you doing?'

'When the police get here, they can't find any evidence. No bodies. Nothing.' She nodded at the door. 'That includes the good doctor. Understood?'

'What about the copper?' said Zeke.

'Sacrifices have to be made for the greater good, Ezekiel.'

'But she's pregnant.'

'The Lord will understand,' said Trastevere. 'As he understands the contents of the bucket downstairs.' Zeke looked away, but Trastevere grabbed his shirt and shook him. 'Find Banach. She can't have got far. Our work must continue, Ezekiel. Whatever it takes. The Lord's will must prevail.'

Zeke nodded, his face set hard. 'Amen.'

Banach hobbled to the large barn and flattened herself against the metal wall, thinking hard. She had little chance on one leg, especially with her feet sore and bloodied. At least there were no dogs.

She hobbled round to the barn's entrance – a large sliding door – and dropped on to her stomach to peer through the tiny gap between door and concrete floor, hoping to find at least a bicycle. She was horrified to see a body laid out on the concrete. She lifted the lever and slipped inside.

'Caitlin,' she hissed, recognising the missing student despite the blood caked on her face and neck. She dropped to her knees and held her up by the shoulders. 'Caitlin! Can you hear me?'

There was a blackened scar in the shape of a crucifix on Caitlin's neck, another on her forearm. An air bubble of blood inflated through the scarring. Leaning closer, Banach could smell burned meat, then spotted the cross-shaped branding iron lying on the floor nearby. It looked like Caitlin's throat had been slashed and someone had tried to cauterise the wound with the red-hot iron.

Having failed to rouse her, Banach placed Caitlin's shoulders back on the floor and grabbed her wrist to find a pulse. It was very faint.

'Caitlin,' she said, through gritted teeth. 'Don't you die on me. Not in here.' She lifted up the girl's sweatshirt, tore open the dress beneath and tried to administer CPR, a mixture of chest compressions and the kiss of life. Blood bubbled through the wound in her windpipe but there was no sign of Caitlin inflating her own lungs.

With shame pulling on her stomach, Banach scrambled down to Caitlin's feet. Same size. As she flipped off one of her training shoes, she heard a whisper.

She crouched over the girl's face. 'Caitlin?'

Caitlin's eyes opened to a slit. Her right hand moved and Banach watched it pointing to a heavy stainless-steel door. She whispered again and Banach had to put an ear to her mouth to catch the words.

'Daniela,' breathed Caitlin. 'Help her.'

Banach stared at Caitlin, then hurried to the steel door.

'Angie,' said Brook at the kitchen door. 'Are you there?' He picked his way quietly across the stone floor to the stairwell and peered up into the gloom of the staircase. A noise behind distracted him and he turned to see Mrs Trastevere flying out of the darkness towards him, a large butcher's knife glinting above her head.

'You devil!' she screamed. He tried to move aside but had nowhere to go; raising an arm in self-protection, he felt the knife tear through his coat into the soft flesh above his elbow. He let out a yell, more surprise than pain, but as he went down he was able to pull her with him to limit her scope for another strike.

Surprisingly powerful, she managed to lever herself back to her feet and fell on him again, the knife this time heading for his eyes. Brook jerked his head out of the blade's path and the knife connected with the stone floor, sending up a brief spark. Before she could draw back for another blow, he grabbed her knife hand, but she wriggled free and his palm closed around the blade.

He shouted in shock at the jagged pain and sudden dampness in his palm but couldn't attend to the damage as she threw herself malevolently at him again. Rocking back, Brook bent both legs in the air and planted his feet in her bony chest to absorb her momentum while holding the knife arm away from his face. Then, straightening his legs with all his power, he launched her violently across the room into the wall with a clatter of dislodged pans.

He clambered to his feet and was upright just in time as Trastevere flew at him again. As she thrust the knife at him, Brook grabbed a warm pan lid from the hob and swung it into the old woman's face as might a gladiator brandishing his shield in a Roman arena.

The old woman stopped in her tracks, a low moan of shock

emanating from her pinched, wrinkled mouth, but she didn't go down. Brook swung twice more with escalating fury until the knife fell, point first, from her hand and he could kick it away. Her knees buckled and blood flowed from her left eye, but though she sagged to her knees, her torso remained upright as if in prayer. Panting heavily, Brook staggered over to her stricken form.

'You're. Under. Arrest. Anything . . .' Fumbling for handcuffs, he realised he'd already used them. 'Damn.' He planted his feet wide and swung the pan lid mightily across the side of Mrs Trastevere's head one last time, and she finally obliged by slumping face first to the ground.

Brook dropped the lid, still breathless. With uncomprehending eyes he glimpsed the fingernail floating in the scummy water of the pan, and beyond, the bleached body parts scattered across the floor from the spilled bucket. He closed his eyes in horror.

A second later, he jerked back into life. Wrapping a tea towel around his bleeding hand, he stumbled up the stairs. 'Angie!'

He hurtled into three unlocked rooms and out again, then pulled back the bolts on the fourth and charged in. Cowell and Bernadette Murphy were unconscious on the floor. He refastened the door and stood to think.

He felt the breeze from the broken window and raced over to it. A posse of excited pigs looked up at him. Beyond, Brook saw the open door of the barn.

Zeke saw the barn door off the latch and touched the cattle prod to it, withdrawing it amid a shower of sparks. 'I know you're in there, copper.' He heaved the door open and saw

Caitlin's inert body on the concrete where he'd left it. Beyond, the steel door of the unit stood ajar. Zeke grinned. 'Thank you, officer – saved me the trouble of dragging your sorry carcass in for butchering.'

Cattle prod to the fore, he hurried through the darkened barn. Pulling the steel door back, he was hit by the cool air from the refrigeration unit, sweetened by the scent of old blood and bleached intestines. He never tired of it.

'Come out, come out, wherever you are.' He leaned into the darkness and flicked on the light switch, blinking at brightness amplified by stark white tiles and whitewashed ceiling. 'Dumb place to hide from the Lord's wrath, you godless bitch,' he said with a relish of pleasures to come. 'In case you haven't worked it out, the next time you leave this room, you'll be a wheelie bin of guts and ground meat. And two or three days after that, you'll be manure coating the ground in the pig pen.'

He stepped across the threshold, eyes flicking between possible hiding places – whitewashed brick columns, the scalding vat, the stainless-steel meat grinders, half a dozen fibre-glass wheelie bins for collecting blood and intestines from a freshly butchered carcass or minced meat from the grinder.

He glanced at the headless trunk maturing upside down on a chain over a drainage gutter and inched forward, his grin ever-present. 'See your predecessor here,' he shouted. 'That's how you're gonna look in a few hours, bitch.' He ducked behind a column, but Banach wasn't there. 'I'm gonna cut you into little pieces then boil your head, hands and feet before grinding you into a paste and feeding you to the pigs.

'But first order of business, I'm gonna hack out that beautiful child you've been trying to murder. Might even let

433

you watch.' Another column. No Banach. 'It'll break my heart to do it, but you can rest assured that that child will have a Christian burial – unlike you. Hey, if you've got a name in mind, I might even get my uncle to conduct a baptism.' He advanced slowly, methodically. 'Your baby will bathe in God's light while what's left of you will be crapped out of a pig's arse.'

He leapt behind one of the grinders, cattle prod at the ready, but to no avail. 'Tell you what . . . Anka. Is that your name? Stop wasting time and step out now. I'll kill you quick.' He stood on his toes and spotted the cloth from a hospital gown over an inert arm. She was laying low in the farthest wheelie bin by the wall and he crept towards her, cupping a hand to throw his voice in the opposite direction. 'That way we don't stress the meat. Don't want you all tough and stringy when I come to process you.

'Something I meant to ask,' he continued, creeping closer. 'Food labelling laws are a bitch. Just in case we get a call from DEFRA about our feed . . . are you Polish or English?'

He jumped up to confront Banach cowering in the wheelie bin, face hidden by an arm, her nightgown barely covering her bare legs. She made no move to run or beg for mercy, and Zeke relaxed. As his gaze wandered across to her bare arm, he caught sight of the crucifix brand mark burned into it, and for a split second confusion creased his forehead.

'Caitlin?' His grin froze, but he turned too late.

Banach brought the branding iron crashing down on Zeke's head. He groaned before flopping forward like a rag doll on to the wheelie bin, then down on to the damp concrete floor, his limbs flailing. Banach pushed the bin away with her foot and struck him again, this time on the temple, and a wound like a pot of fresh warm jam opened.

'What are you going to do now, bitch?' she screamed, and struck him again. 'What are you going to do now?'

The distant sound of sirens turned her round and her eye was drawn again to the human remains hanging from the meat rack. She ran and unravelled one of the hoists connected to the overhead skinning rack and wrapped it round Zeke's ankle, clipping it into place before hauling his motionless body along the cold ground and into the air. He swung a gentle arc through the air as blood dripped copiously on to the tiled floor from head wounds front and back. Securing the chain, Banach walked to a butcher's block to pick up a cleaver before advancing on Zeke.

'Angie!' shouted Brook from the door.

Banach became a statue, though her face turned to Brook, eyes pleading. She noticed the blood dripping from his hand. 'Sir.'

'You don't need that,' said Brook. She looked down at the cleaver in her hand almost in surprise. 'Angie.' Brook saw the stricken student in the wheelie bin. 'Is Caitlin alive?'

'Barely. Take her.'

'We go together,' said Brook. 'Help me get her to the ambulance.'

Banach began to shake and her body seemed to shrink in on itself. 'Please.' She tried to express a thought, but it was so incoherent she could only wave a hand at Daniela's remains to make her point. 'Do you see?'

Brook walked slowly across to her. 'I see.'

Getting her voice under control through the rising emotion, she managed, 'He deserves to die.'

'No doubt,' said Brook softly. 'But you don't deserve to live with killing him.'

She stared at him through desperate eyes filling with tears, wiping them away with the sleeve of Caitlin's bloodied sweatshirt.

Brook held out his hand for the cleaver. 'Think of your career.'

'Fuck my career,' she said, strengthening her grip on the tool.

The sound of running feet drew nearer, and Banach recognised Noble's voice.

'Okay, Angie,' said Brook, stepping back. 'You want him dead? Do it. But be prepared to live with it every single day and every single night.'

She stared at him as though he was speaking in a foreign tongue. Then a light went out in her eyes and she dropped the cleaver at her feet.

'In here, John,' shouted Brook, putting his good hand on the wheelie bin and pushing it towards the door. He gathered in Banach with his wounded arm and held her against the bin until she raised her hands to push with him.

Thirty-Four

Three hours later, Brook watched the boiled head, hands and feet being photographed and then bagged. 'There's a fingernail in the pan.'

'We know,' said the SOCO without annoyance at Brook's micromanagement. He raised the camera to take a final shot of the large pan before nodding to a colleague, who dipped a rubber glove into the filmy water to dredge up the fingernail. He held it for a couple of shots then dropped it in a bag. 'We can manage.'

'I know you can, Col.'

The SOCO registered his surprise from behind a face mask but said nothing. He pulled down the mask and indicated the fresh bandages on Brook's hand and arm. 'Go home, Inspector. You've done your bit.' He raised the camera to his face before lowering it again. 'And more.'

Brook trudged to the kitchen door, exhausted now the adrenalin of the chase was spent. 'If they're boiling body parts, there may not be much left.'

'Understood.'

437

'We're looking at multiple victims, so you're hunting for nails, teeth and hair.'

'On it,' said Col.

'Make the pig pen a priority.'

'Inspector . . .' began Col, closing his eyes to keep patience. He smiled when he had control. 'We will.'

Brook stepped outside, barely able to raise his feet. The lights of the second ambulance retreated towards the dark lane. Caitlin Kinnear and Banach had been rushed to hospital in the first ambulance, and Ezekiel O'Toole and Constance Trastevere were in the second, accompanied by three burly constables. A bloodied Bernadette Murphy and Helen Cowell, both groggy from the tranquilliser, sat in the back of a squad car. Cowell was in floods of tears after being marched in cuffs past the body parts on the kitchen floor. Noble banged on the roof and the car set off.

They'd discovered Samuel O'Toole sleeping happily on a sofa in the farmhouse and taken him into custody until mental competence and the extent of his involvement in events at the farm could be determined. Finally a social worker had arrived to take the two youngsters into temporary care. Brook was happy to see that the older boy was oblivious to the horrors being uncovered about them.

Brook made it across the courtyard to where Charlton and Noble were conversing in disbelieving low tones, organising a stream of scientific support officers walking back and forth to the barn. Several dog handlers had also arrived to begin scouring the premises with eager Alsatians, but it was clear to Brook that they'd need more sophisticated equipment to help in the search for human remains.

Chief Superintendent Charlton didn't often experience the

sharp end of man's inhumanity to man from behind his desk, and Brook was pleased to see that his face was devoid of colour after witnessing horrors usually reserved for his detectives. He turned at Brook's approach.

'You should be in hospital.'

'I've had painkillers, and the paramedics gave me a tetanus shot,' said Brook.

'Will you be okay to drive?' asked Noble. Brook had that vacant look he'd seen before at the end of an exhausting case.

'Fine.'

'Then go home,' said Noble.

'Make that an order,' added Charlton, severely. 'And for once, obey it.'

'DC Banach, Angie, said the pigs—'

'We know,' said Charlton and Noble in unison.

'They'll be slaughtered tomorrow and off to the labs the day after,' said Noble. 'Go home, for God's sake. We're on top of this.'

Brook nodded and gathered his bloodied jacket from the bonnet of Dr Fleming's Audi. He glanced at the open door of the Land Rover. O'Toole – he'd completely forgotten about him. At the rear of the vehicle, he heard a distressed cry.

'*I can't breathe.*'

He yanked the boot open with no thought for his injured hand. 'What did you say?' he demanded, as O'Toole sat up to suck in the night air. But before the priest could regain his breath to answer, Brook hauled him from the boot and dragged him along the muddied ground to the farmhouse. 'What did you say?'

'Please, I . . .'

'What did you say?' shouted Brook.

'Can't breathe,' the priest panted.

Noble and Charlton turned in astonishment and ran towards the pair, O'Toole unable still to find his feet as Brook shoved him through the kitchen door. 'Can't breathe, did you say? Can't breathe. Wrong. *She's* the one who can't breathe,' bellowed Brook.

O'Toole tried to look away, but Brook roughly grabbed his ears, forcing him to face the body parts on the floor. The SOCOs looked round. 'Her name was Daniela.' O'Toole tried to break away, but Brook twisted his ears, eliciting a yell of pain. 'Look upon your works, ye mighty, and despair. Look, I said.'

'Please. I didn't know.'

'She was the mother of the baby, wasn't she?' He shook his captive violently. 'Wasn't she?'

'Yes,' sobbed O'Toole.

Noble arrived and prised the wriggling priest from Brook's white knuckles, shoving him in the direction of Charlton, who passed him on to a nearby constable.

'Are you all right, Brook?' barked Charlton.

'Never better,' he mumbled.

'Go home! That's an order.'

Brook staggered out into the night, head resolutely down, stumbling along the dirt track towards his car. Twenty minutes later, he was home, though he remembered nothing of the journey. Slumped at the kitchen table, he poured himself a huge glass of Bruichladdich and drank it down in several large gulps before closing his eyes and resting his head on the table.

Brook slept what was left of the night and well into the evening, rising from his bed only when the pain from his hand and arm forced him to consciousness. He took two painkillers and made a flask of tea, then drove into Derby, stopping off at Jobs Wood Farm along the way.

The farm was lit up with arc lights as the shadows lengthened. Seeing no CID officers, Brook took a cursory look around the farmhouse, then left the army of scene-of-crime officers to do their work. On the way back to the main road, he passed a refrigerated truck bearing the livery of a local slaughterman.

Charlton blew out his cheeks and shook his head for the umpteenth time as he read the latest updates from the farm. Brook sat saucer-eyed, staring into space. Only Noble seemed to be operating normally.

'There's no doubt?'

'None,' said Noble. 'The butchered carcass and head belonged to Daniela Cassetti. She had dental treatment while at the university and records confirmed. And we've found more remains, which we should be able to match to other missing women when we get dentals.'

'I thought they fed everything to the pigs,' said Charlton.

'Flesh and organs, yes,' said Noble. 'But teeth, nails and hair are indigestible.'

'Christ.'

Brook made as if to speak but remained silent.

'On the positive side,' continued Noble, 'we've found no infant remains so far, so it seems the offspring were all removed.'

'Where?'

'Settled with families in North America, from what little sense I can get out of Dr Cowell.'

'Can we trace them?'

'Given time,' said Noble. 'And if we can follow the money. The only one who's speaking doesn't know about that side of things.'

'Cowell?'

'She says she was only involved in identifying potential mothers. Apparently she had access to the Rutherford's patient database, having worked there briefly. Claims she did it on principle and not for money. She thought the mothers were being resettled in America with their babies.'

'Do we believe her?' asked Charlton, glancing over at Brook for signs of life.

'When we showed her a picture of Daniela Cassetti's remains, she threw up,' said Noble.

'What about the couple?'

'Bernadette Murphy and Ezekiel O'Toole haven't said a single word or shown any sign of remorse.'

'And Patrick . . . Father O'Toole?' said Charlton.

'Not a word to us,' said Noble. 'Though he's mumbling to God plenty.'

Charlton's face tightened, preparing to protest, but he thought better of it.

'Confession,' said Brook, not looking up.

Both heads turned. 'What was that?'

Brook looked up, thinking about what he'd said. 'You need to put him with another priest. He's confused right now and needs someone to tell him what God wants him to do. And without his confession, we'll struggle to get murder convictions for anyone but Bernadette and her boyfriend.'

'Anyone in mind, Inspector?'

Brook nodded minutely. 'I'll see to it.'

'We can't let Trastevere get away with it,' said Noble. 'She's the brains behind this.'

'We can charge her with attempted murder at least,' said Brook, brandishing a bandaged hand.

'How's Constable Banach?' said Charlton.

Brook looked up. 'As well as can be expected.'

'And Caitlin Kinnear?'

Noble smiled. 'She'll live.'

'Thanks to your tenacity, John,' said Brook. 'And Banach's quick thinking.'

'You look done in,' said Noble, once they were outside Charlton's office. Brook returned a weak smile. 'Are you sending in your priest friend against O'Toole?'

'Father Christopher.'

'If he can get O'Toole to play ball, it'll give the CPS a slam-dunk against the others.'

Brook was uncertain what Noble had said for a moment. Then, 'Are you American, John?'

'I knew you were in there somewhere,' crowed Noble.

'You found me.'

'By the way,' said Noble. 'You were right.'

'Right?'

'We got the DNA results back. A hair on that sleeping bag matched the DNA in the gloves. Max Ostrowsky was in the Cream and both are a match to samples from his flat.'

'Any news?' said Brook.

'Max and Tymon took the Harwich-to-Amsterdam ferry that same night. They're gone.'

'Then the DNA hardly matters. Max will be safely in Poland at least until the trial is over.'

Steven Dunne

'So you don't want to know about the paternity test.'

'Tell me.'

'Max's DNA wasn't a match to Kassia's foetus, but it's close enough to suggest that a near relative is the father. Greg.'

Brook nodded. 'Nice to know we were on the right lines. If only it were proof of something. If we could just speak to Jake . . .'

'Forget it. He's on remand and his solicitor says he's refusing all requests for interviews. We'd have to go through Charlton . . .'

'And we know how that ends.'

'Anything else to eat, Inspector?' said Mrs Banach, standing attentively over the laden table.

'I'm stuffed, Mum,' said Banach.

'This is plenty, Mrs Banach,' said Brook, indicating his untouched plate of *piernik*, *makowiec* and *paczki*.

'Julianna, please,' said Banach's mother.

Brook nodded and drained his tea. Mrs Banach gathered the cups on to a tray. 'You need to eat more, Inspector.'

'I had a big breakfast,' Brook lied.

'Then I'll put these in a bag for later.'

'How's Caitlin?' said Banach, when her mother had scuttled towards the patio doors.

'She'll need some rehab and plastic surgery, but she should make a full recovery. Physically, at least.'

'Poor girl,' said Banach. 'What an ordeal.'

'She's alive thanks to you and John,' said Brook. 'The pair of you saved her life.' Banach looked away modestly but Brook could see she was pleased. 'How are you?'

'If that's a half-assed way of asking if I'm keeping my child,

444

the answer is yes.'

'It wasn't,' said Brook. 'But I'm happy for you.'

'You don't get off that easy.'

'Oh?'

'I'm naming you the godfather, if that's okay.'

'Do I have to do anything?'

'No.'

'Then I'm honoured.'

'I've sent off the forms,' said Banach. 'I'll be taking my CID exams on maternity. And if . . . when I pass, I'll be looking to join a team on probation, if you know anyone who'll have me.'

Brook put a hand to his chin, implying concentration. 'I'll certainly put the word out. There must be plenty of SIOs who'll put up with Americanisms like *half-assed* from their squad members. I'll let you know.'

Banach stared at him, waiting for some clue, but his expression remained blank. 'Will you now?' she said.

'Depend on it,' said Brook, rising from his patio chair, still keeping a straight face.

'Inspector.' Brook arched an eyebrow as Banach sought the right words. 'I wanted to ask. In that barn, when I was ready to . . .'

'Yes?'

'You asked me if I was prepared to live with taking a life. Do you remember?' Brook said nothing. 'The thing is, you said it as though you knew what that was like.'

Brook stared into her eyes for a moment, then smiled. 'No.'

'No what?'

'I don't remember.'

Thirty-Five

Three months later

BROOK SAT ON THE HARD witness bench waiting to be called. He flexed his hand, examining the fading scar on his palm, enjoying the peace and majesty of the court building. On a bench opposite, a man sat reading a national newspaper; Brook caught the headline – ANIMAL FARM – and recognised several of the head shots of young women that dominated the front page. His heart sank at the infamy the world's press would be visiting on his adopted county in the coming months.

The door to Court One opened and a man around Brook's age walked out, closing the door behind him. He had cropped silver hair, was a good foot taller than Brook and deported his lean frame with a lithe self-confidence. He wore a black suit and carried an overcoat over one arm. To Brook's surprise, he stared straight at him before walking over to his bench.

'Detective Inspector Brook, yes?' enquired the man.

'That's right,' replied Brook. The man held his hand out to shake, then produced a business card, which Brook accepted, staring at the name while the man continued to talk.

'I wanted to thank you, Inspector. For your prompt action.'

Brook managed to lift his eyes to engage the man, unable to think what to say.

'Anything?'

Brook was startled out of his reverie and pocketed the stranger's card. 'Not yet.'

'Who was that?' said Noble.

Brook followed the direction of Noble's eyes towards the tall stranger striding towards the main entrance. 'A friend.'

Noble slumped on to the bench beside him. 'You know if Jake pleads guilty we won't be called.'

'I know,' said Brook. 'So we'll have to be quick. Ready?'

Noble patted at a breast pocket. 'Right here. You saw the email from Crown Prosecution?'

'I saw it,' replied Brook, glancing back at the newspaper.

'Abduction, false imprisonment, child cruelty,' scoffed Noble. 'You believe that?'

'Without a ransom, it's not kidnapping,' said Brook.

'But it means only Zeke, Bernadette and Mrs Trastevere will be facing murder charges.'

'Is that a problem?'

'Yes, it's a problem,' retorted Noble. 'I can believe Dr Cowell was naive enough not to know what was going on. But O'Toole . . .'

'Without his testimony they wouldn't be able to convict Trastevere. Bernadette and her boyfriend refuse to implicate her, so there was nothing else the CPS could do. And don't forget, with no cooperation from Trastevere, they'll need O'Toole to track down the children.'

'I suppose.'

'O'Toole's been defrocked and Cowell struck off.'

'How is that punishment?'

'Their lives are over, John. Worse, when you invest that heavily in self-righteousness, such an instant and public fall from grace wipes out not only your future but the life already lived.'

'You have been to university, haven't you?' mocked Noble. 'Maybe we should let them walk free.'

'Strange as it may seem, for them, if not the victims' families, that would be the worst punishment.'

'After nine murders?'

'Confining them is a leg-up to redemption, John. It limits their scope for self-loathing.'

Noble shook his head. 'Thank God you won't be the judge.'

'Seconded.' Brook grinned. 'Put your trust in the vengeance of the establishment. They'll be doing serious time.'

The courtroom door opened and a flood of people began to emerge, Charlton first out, his face like thunder.

'Twenty years,' he snarled, shaking his head. 'Twenty bloody years. Tanner could be out in half that. And I thought Judge Belvedere was a hanger and flogger.'

Brook gestured at Noble, who excused himself and hurried away. 'That's still a long time for an innocent man.'

'I don't want to hear it, Brook,' said Charlton. 'He confessed. Pure and simple. And don't think I don't know about you trying to get in to see him.'

'His brief wouldn't let me near,' said Brook.

'I know that too, or I would have warned you off myself,' replied Charlton.

Brook kept half an eye on the emptying courtroom. Ostrowsky emerged accompanied by Jake's barrister and a handsome, fresh-faced young man in a snug-fitting designer suit flicking at a tablet. Brook excused himself from Charlton and made a beeline towards them.

'Brook,' called Charlton. 'If I see any unattributed quotes about the verdict in the local rag, I'll know it was you. You'll be finished.'

Brook paused, considering various career-ending ripostes. He settled for the uncontroversial 'Since when have I been on speaking terms with the *Telegraph*?' and stalked away.

'Just see that you don't,' Charlton retorted sourly.

The barrister shook Ostrowsky's hand and departed.

'Mr Ostrowsky,' said Brook, staring inquisitively at the smartly dressed young man. It was Nick Tanner.

'Inspector,' said Ostrowsky, indicating Jake's brother, absorbed by his tablet. 'Have you met Nicholas?'

'Briefly,' said Brook. 'Your solicitor brought him in to tell us how Nicholas was Jake's unwitting accomplice on the night of the murder.'

'Ah, yes,' said Ostrowsky. 'Stupid of me.'

'Stupid? You?' Brook turned to Nick. 'I'm sorry about your brother.'

'Nicholas, what do we do when we meet people?'

Nick lowered the tablet and held out a hand to shake Brook's. 'Hello, sir,' he said like an actor remembering lines. 'How are you?'

'I'm fine, Nick. How are you?'

'I'm good,' he replied.

Brook declined to ask if he was American. 'Have you spoken to Jake since his arrest?'

'We went to see him at the . . .' Nick looked round at Ostrowsky for a prompt.

'Remand centre,' said Ostrowsky.

Nick repeated the words carefully. 'Not a very nice place.'

'Neither is prison,' said Brook. 'And Jake's going to be there for a long time.'

Nick's expression darkened. 'I thought if he was nice to people, he'd be home in . . .' Again he sought Ostrowsky's input.

'Ten years,' said the businessman. 'God willing, he will.'

'Why did Jake kill Kassia, Nick?' asked Brook, watching Ostrowsky's reaction. He hadn't expected him to smile.

'Kassia?' asked Nick, turning to Ostrowsky.

'It was a long time ago, Nicholas,' said the businessman, still smiling at Brook. 'But your tutor is helping you with your memory skills, isn't he?'

'I can do all the way up to my twelve times table,' said Nick proudly. 'Would you like to hear?'

'The inspector's a busy man, Nicholas. He doesn't have time. Do you?'

Brook smiled into Ostrowsky's cold blue eyes, accepting another defeat. 'No.'

'Nick, go and wait with Tymon.'

'Can I . . . ?' said Nick, waggling the tablet.

Ostrowsky smiled his assent, watching Nick go. 'A good kid.'

'You seem to have adopted him.'

'He's over eighteen.'

'But so like a child,' continued Brook. 'Did you never have children of your own?'

Ostrowsky's amused countenance turned to stone. After a second, when Brook thought he might meet the same fate, the Pole crossed himself. 'I've never been so blessed.'

'Perhaps God has chosen a different path for you.'

'Perhaps. But Nick gives me a purpose apart from business. I can give him everything he could ever want, including the best possible education. So important in this competitive world.'

'How true,' replied Brook. 'I heard about Max. I can't tell you how sorry I am.'

Ostrowsky's eyes clouded over. 'Thank you – a tragic accident.'

'What happened?'

'He was on the ferry to Amsterdam, travelling back to Warsaw. He drank a bottle of vodka and fell overboard.' Ostrowsky bowed his head for a moment. 'Max was always a big drinker.'

'And now you have a brother to make you proud,' said Brook, nodding at Nick.

'What do you mean?'

'It can't have been easy,' said Brook. 'A man with your religious convictions, brother to a man with Max's . . . urges.'

'We are all sinners, Inspector.'

'Was Max alone on the ferry?'

'My assistant Tymon was with him,' said Ostrowsky carefully. 'He raised the alarm.'

'So conscientious,' smiled Brook. 'That kind of loyalty just can't be bought. But then you too are loyal, aren't you?'

'In what way?'

'Well, to employ someone who once used your shipping container to smuggle drugs. That's very understanding of you.'

'Tymon made a mistake,' said Ostrowsky. 'And there's a saying about forgiving those who make mistakes.'

'To err is human, to forgive divine.'

'You're a clever man, Inspector Brook,' smiled the business-man. He fished in his pocket for a card. 'Come tomorrow. Bar Polski opening night.'

'I thought that was weeks ago.'

'If not for British workers,' he grinned. 'Bring as many friends as you like, and it's on the house. Do me this courtesy. As a friend of Nick.'

Brook accepted his second business card of the day and followed Ostrowsky out into the summer sunshine, Nick and Tymon preceding him, the latter flashing a smile of porcine malevolence. A slim figure stepped out of the cabin of a dark Mercedes to open doors. It was Ashley Devonshire, Jake Tanner's former colleague at Bar Polski.

Once Ostrowsky was settled on the plush leather seat, Ashley slipped back behind the wheel and pulled the Mercedes into traffic. Another car drew out of the court building's car park. From the passenger seat, DS Morton acknowledged Brook with a raised hand as they set off in pursuit.

Brook hurried down to the holding cells to find Noble remonstrating with the Serco driver assigned to transport Tanner to prison.

'Listen Inspector Gadget, we've got proper police work to do,' said Noble. 'Your schedule will have to wait, so trot off and sit in your van, make sure kids don't nick it.'

The driver muttered something unrepeatable and slouched towards the courtyard door.

'Well?'

'Better than we thought,' said Brook. 'Ashley was with him.'

A minute later Brook flashed his warrant card at the court guard outside Jake Tanner's cell. 'Can we have a minute?'

* * *

Tanner prepared to object when he saw them, but Brook and Noble were already through the door. 'I told my solicitor I don't—'

'Max Ostrowsky is dead,' said Brook. Tanner didn't react. 'You lied to protect him from a murder charge. Now you don't have to.' No reply. 'And I've just seen Nick.'

Tanner smiled now. 'Me too. I barely recognised him.'

'It's not too late,' said Brook. 'We're following Ostrowsky. We can protect Nick. Tell me you want to retract your confession and I'll speak to your solicitor. She can lodge an appeal.'

Tanner's smile showed no signs of abating. 'He was wearing a suit. My brother Nick in a suit.'

'Are you listening?' said Noble. 'Max is dead. He drowned.'

'Max didn't kill Kassia, Jake,' said Brook. 'It was Ostrowsky. He was the father of Kassia's child and we can prove it. He needed your confession to take the heat off Max because Max was a threat, but now he's dead.'

'His bodyguard fed him vodka, then threw him off a ferry into the North Sea. His own brother.'

Tanner was impassive, unmoved.

'There's more.' Brook nodded at Noble, who extracted a small recorder and pressed the play button.

'*Hello, police. I live in Arboretum Street. There's someone outside trying the doors on a white van. I think they're trying to nick it.*'

'*Can you tell me your name, please?*'

'*Never mind my name. The registration is BD62 XZP. Tell 'em to get a shift on.*'

When the recording was turned off, Tanner looked up into Brook's eyes.

'Recognise that voice?' asked Noble. Tanner folded his arms.

'No?' said Brook. 'That was Ashley Devonshire.'

'Your co-worker at Bar Polski,' added Noble. 'We only heard his voice once, but we recognised him.'

'What was that?' said Tanner.

'It was a recording of a phone call to police the night you stole Max's van,' said Brook. 'It came in at eleven twenty-one p.m.' No reaction.

'At the time, it was assumed to be one of Max's neighbours who'd spotted you checking out the van before stealing it,' said Noble.

'But you told us you didn't leave your flat until after midnight,' said Brook. 'It didn't make sense until we listened to the call. It was all a set-up, Jake.'

'That call was to draw police attention to Max's van – the van in which Ostrowsky's bodyguard put Kassia's body after his boss killed her,' said Noble.

'A man like Ostrowsky wouldn't want his voice on a police tape. He probably slipped Ashley a few pounds, told him there was a call he had to make but his English wasn't good enough.'

'The van was unlocked, Jake,' said Noble. 'The keys were inside. Did you never wonder about that? They were making it easy for the police to look inside when they arrived. They'd try the doors and find the body. In Max's van. With Max's hammer, which they'd used on Kassia's face; Max's blowtorch, which they'd used to burn off her prints and tattoo. They put fibres from Max's gloves in her mouth. Everything left for us to find.'

'And with Max's history of sexual violence . . . don't you see? Max was supposed to be where you are now. If the police hadn't been delayed, you couldn't have stolen the van. It would have been swarming with officers.'

'But you did steal it, and ruined everything.'

'Instead of getting his brother off the streets, Ostrowsky had to kill him.'

Tanner took a deep breath. 'It makes no difference.'

'You're not listening,' insisted Brook. 'Max is dead.'

'You said that already.'

'Then talk to us. After what he did to Nick . . .'

For the first time, Tanner reacted. 'What about Nick?'

'We can prove Max spent time at the Cream Bar and we know he had the keys. Nick took them from your flat and gave them to him.'

'Why would he do that?'

'Because when Max found out you had them, he told Nick to take them,' said Brook. 'Max needed somewhere private, somewhere he could take a sleeping bag and a bottle of vodka and take his time doing the things he liked to do. With Nick.'

Tanner's eyes blazed. 'Nick's not a fucking rent boy . . .'

'I know that,' said Brook. 'He didn't know what he was being asked to do. He's not competent to give consent . . .'

'That's enough.'

'But he likes money, doesn't he?' continued Brook. 'Money for phones, the latest games. Especially as he lives with a brother who doesn't provide . . .'

'Shut up.'

'Max had money to exchange for sexual favours . . .'

'I don't have to listen to this,' said Tanner, walking to the door of the cell and banging on it. 'Guard!'

'Must've been frustrating,' continued Brook. 'You land a plum job at Bar Polski, a job that will let you take Nick along so you can look after him. No more part-time work. No more scraping along. You've landed on your feet. But then a sexual predator like Max sees Nick and starts filling his head with all the stuff he could buy if only he'll let Max do things to him. Things Nick doesn't understand. But he does them anyway.'

'I'm not listening.'

'And it's good that he doesn't understand,' said Noble. 'He can't feel the shame that others might.'

'But he knew enough not to tell you,' said Brook. 'Knew not to flash cash around or you'd want to know where he got it.'

Tanner stared into the distance, his eyes watering.

'But Nick didn't have to tell you, did he? Because this has happened before, and you knew.'

'Only Max was no civil servant,' said Noble. 'He was the brother of your employer, and the job you craved started to turn sour. You can't take Nick to the bar and leave him in the cloakroom with a couple of comics. Not with Max hanging around.'

'I mean it. Shut up.'

'And you can't trust him at home alone,' said Brook. 'You'll worry that Max might be meeting him at the Cream. You'd like to tell the boss, but you can't be sure of his reaction – you might be out of a job again.'

'Please . . .'

'You had to do *something*,' persisted Brook. 'You couldn't let Max prey on your little brother without payback, so you stole his van.'

'But when you drove it away, you realised there was a body in the back,' said Noble. 'It would be starting to smell after two days.'

Tanner shook his head, face tight. 'I killed her. Okay.'

'You knew you were in trouble, driving around in the dead

of night in a stolen van with a murdered girl in the back – an ex-con, your prints everywhere.'

'You have to dump the van before you're caught,' said Noble.

'But then you remembered that small lane next to the *Telegraph* building, near the pub where you used to work.'

'You can torch the van, burn off all the trace and still be home in fifteen minutes.'

Tanner was unmoved. 'Finished?'

'You know the real irony here,' said Brook. 'If you'd denounced Max's sexual debauchery to his brother, he would have listened. Ostrowsky fancies himself a religious man. He's had years cleaning up after his brother, listening to his excuses.'

'But he's also a ruthless killer who will do anything to get his way.'

'And we mean to stop him, Jake.'

'Good luck with that.'

'We're following Ostrowsky's car right this minute,' said Noble. 'Give the word and we pull them over. Nick will be safe.'

Tanner shook his head. 'I'm not retracting. I got a good deal. I could be out in ten years.'

'You could be out in ten days if we arrest Ostrowsky,' said Brook.

'It would be my word against his.'

'Not any more,' said Brook. 'Ashley's driving the Mercedes. We take him into protective custody and he testifies about the emergency call.'

Tanner shook his head. 'You think Ashley will survive until a trial?'

'We can protect him,' insisted Brook. 'Nick too.'

There was silence as Noble and Brook stared at Tanner, breath held, waiting for the word. What happened next surprised both men.

Jake Tanner broke into a huge grin. 'I couldn't protect Nick from Max. And you can't protect Ashley from Ostrowsky. Not for ever. But there's no need. I changed all that. I made a deal and now Nick's protected. Christ, he's untouchable. You saw him in court. He was wearing a suit. Don't you get it?' He spoke slowly, spelling it out. 'Stealing that van was the best thing I've ever done, and now Nick is exactly where I want him to be.'

After a moment of silence, Brook stood and gestured Noble to his feet. 'You were right, Jake. You got a very good deal.'

'I don't understand,' said Noble.

'You're clever, Brook,' said Tanner. 'It was a good try.'

'I'm far from clever. You and Ostrowsky were ahead of us every step of the way. Was Max your idea or his?'

Tanner hesitated. 'Max was a pervert. He got justice.'

'And Kassia?'

'I'm sorry for Kassia and her family, I really am, but she's dead and nothing I do or say will bring her back.'

'Confession in exchange for Max's life,' said Brook to Noble. 'The police stop looking for Kassia's killer and Max dies in a tragic accident before he drags the family name further into the gutter.'

Tanner allowed himself a little laugh. 'Oh, it's so much more than that. Have you read *Of Mice and Men*, Inspector?'

'Steinbeck.' said Brook.

'I studied it at school.'

Brook nodded. 'You think you and your brother are George and Lennie.'

458

'We *were* George and Lennie,' said Tanner.

'George tried to protect Lennie, but he couldn't.'

'And in the end he has to shoot him to save him from a lynch mob,' said Tanner. 'But . . .'

'You changed the ending,' said Brook.

'I had to. I couldn't save Nick from Max and I knew there'd be others yet to come. So I rewrote the ending, Inspector, courtesy of Mr O. He saw how the story should end before I did; he's had similar problems with Max, and for a lot longer.'

'And now Nick has the elder brother he needs and Ostrowsky the protégé he's always wanted,' said Brook softly. 'Someone who'll look up to him as a role model.' He was sombre. 'Just a shame you had to sacrifice your life to achieve it, Jake.'

'I haven't sacrificed my life, Brook. I didn't have one. Because of Nick, I couldn't work, couldn't go anywhere or do anything. He depended on me eighteen hours a day, seven days a week. Always bored. Always hungry.

'I was nine when Nick was born,' he continued. 'It's been twenty years – the length of my sentence. There's your fucking irony. I'd get home from school and spend every second looking after him while my mother drank and whored her way round Derby. And when school finished, that became a full-time job – the only one I've ever had. I wanted to go to college but I couldn't. I had dreams . . .'

'The best-laid plans of mice and men?'

'You said it,' nodded Tanner. 'I loved that book until I left school and realised I was living it – except nobody was going to put a bullet in Nick's head and set me free. But when I smacked that faggot and got sent down . . . Jesus, what a revelation. I didn't know such freedom was possible in prison. You getting the irony yet?'

'You won't be gardening in Sudbury Open, Jake.'

'And I won't be woken up by Nick whining for baked beans or a mobile phone or a PS2 *every single day*, yet not be free to earn the money to pay for them. A life spent babysitting. Can't go out, can't face staying in. No girlfriend, no wife, no family of my own. For once, just once, this is all about me. I've found peace.'

The Serco van driver reappeared with the court officer.

Brook found it hard to break away until roused with a nudge. 'We're done here,' said Noble, reaching for his phone. 'I'm calling Morton off. Let's go.'

Brook sat in front of the chessboard when he got home to Hartington. He wrote down his latest move on a scrap of paper, followed by *Mate in four moves*, and sealed it in an envelope before writing the prison's address.

After stamping the envelope, he withdrew the two business cards he'd received separately earlier in the day, looking at first one, then the other, before picking up his phone.

Game over.

Thirty-Six

NOBLE TOOK A PULL ON his third bottle of Zywiec and looked around the elegant restaurant on the upper floor of Bar Polski. 'They've done a good job.'

Brook took a sip of his water. 'How was the food?'

'Good,' said Noble. 'You should have eaten.'

'It wouldn't feel right, accepting Ostrowsky's hospitality.'

'Then why are we here? This was your idea.'

Brook stood briefly when Banach returned from the toilets with Laurie and Caitlin. 'Any more drinks, anyone?'

'No thanks,' said Caitlin. Her voice was scratchy and strained. 'I've had a lovely time, though.' She looked at Laurie.

'We ought to be going,' said Laurie. 'Caitlin's not supposed to overdo it.'

'We understand,' said Banach, glancing again at Caitlin's healing throat. 'It's looking so much better.'

'Thank you, Angie.'

Laurie dipped a hand into her bag. 'What do we owe . . . ?'

'Don't you dare,' said Brook with a gravity that stayed her hand at once.

'But after all you've done,' she implored. Brook wouldn't

461

have it, so the two girls shook hands with Brook and Noble, then Caitlin hugged Banach before putting a hand on her bump.

'How long?' she croaked.

'Four months.' Banach and Caitlin shared a bittersweet smile before the two students headed down the stairs.

'Good to see Caitlin looking so well,' said Banach. 'Laurie said she's much quieter than she used to be. Scared of her own shadow almost.'

'These things take time,' said Brook, with no great confidence.

Banach drained her sparkling water. 'Well, I'm on early turn tomorrow.'

'Can you drop John off?' said Brook, gesturing at the waitress for the bill. 'I want to finish my water.'

Noble drained his beer glass. 'You drag us along here, you don't eat or drink and now you can't tear yourself away. What are you up to?'

Brook raised his arms in a gesture of innocence. Banach and Noble said their goodbyes and left, Noble fixing him with a suspicious eye all the way to the stairs.

Brook did a quick calculation, counted out ten twenties and put them on the table, then pushed through the double doors to the back stairs of Bar Polski. In the basement, the huge Tymon stood impassively in front of another door. Brook approached, flashing his warrant card, but Tymon was unmoved.

'*Huj w dupe policji,*' he said.

'No, screw you, you big ape,' said Brook, smiling politely and moving to pass. Tymon slung an arm across his path and said something else in Polish. Brook grabbed the bodyguard's arm. A second later, his back hit the opposite wall, winding him. He recovered quickly and strode purposefully back to the office door.

'You already put two of my officers in hospital,' he said, not even sure he was understood. 'If you make it three, I'll make sure you go to prison.'

Tymon smiled and flexed his neck. As soon as Brook was in range, he raised an arm to swat him again.

'Tymon!' Ostrowsky stood at the open door. He barked out more orders and Tymon stared spitefully at Brook before climbing the stairs towards the bar. 'Inspector, come in.'

Brook entered the office. Apart from a small pool of light from a desk lamp, the room was unlit.

'Forgive Tymon, Inspector. His zeal is sometimes excessive. Sit.' Ostrowsky returned to his desk, his white shirt open, silver crucifix hanging round his tanned throat. 'Have you come to complain about the food?'

'I'm told the food was good.'

'You didn't eat?'

'I wasn't hungry,' said Brook. 'It's dark in here.'

'I like the *tenebrae*,' said Ostrowsky. Brook raised an eyebrow. 'Forgive me. It is Latin; it means—'

'Shadows,' said Brook. 'The Tenebrae is a Catholic service in which candles are extinguished one by one until no light remains. The last candle is hidden, and, after a hymnal is slammed shut, retrieved. It represents the light of Christ returning to the world.'

Ostrowsky smiled. 'My sources told me you were Catholic. I'm impressed.'

'Don't be,' said Brook. 'I'm as conflicted as poor dead Kassia.'

Ostrowsky's expression of amused curiosity hardened into something more dangerous for a second. 'Thanks to you, her killer is now in prison.'

'We both know that's not true,' said Brook quietly. 'Jake doesn't have it in him. Poor as I've been on this case, that much I saw right away. I then thought Max had killed her and you were covering for him. When I finally got my head out of the sand and worked out what you were doing, it was too late. You were the father of Kassia's child.'

'You think *I* killed this girl?' exclaimed Ostrowsky. 'Your accusation pains me . . .'

'You'll get over it.'

'The Lord said *Thou shalt not kill*.'

'Then to my knowledge that's three times you've angered your God,' said Brook.

Ostrowsky lit a cigarette, appraising Brook. 'You can prove I am the father?'

'For what it's worth. It gets me no closer to arresting you.'

Ostrowsky placed his cigarette in the ashtray, blue-brown poison swaying lazily in the triangle of light. He fixed his cold eyes on Brook. 'Three times?'

'Kassia and her child,' said Brook. 'Your brother makes three.'

'Max's death was an accident.'

'No more games,' said Brook. 'Jake told me about your arrangement. And I know all about Max's habits. Drink, prostitutes . . .' He paused for effect. 'Boys.' He watched the lineaments of Ostrowsky's face tighten in instinctive revulsion. *'There is no greater sin than when a man lies with a man as with a woman; they shall both be put to death.'*

'Leviticus,' nodded Ostrowsky.

'You knew?'

'I offered Nick money to pay for a cab. He asked for a cushion. He thought I wanted . . .' Ostrowsky took a final drag of his cigarette, stubbed it out and pulled a bottle of vodka and a shot glass from a drawer. He waggled the bottle at Brook, who shook his head, then poured himself a drink, downing it in one before refilling. 'Nick told me everything and I was determined . . . to get Max the help he needed. That's why he was on his way back to Poland when God intervened.'

Brook smiled. 'How? By inventing vodka?'

Ostrowsky's blue eyes hardened. 'What is your purpose here, Inspector?'

Brook took out the recorder and played the emergency call. 'You recognise Ashley Devonshire's voice,' he said when it finished.

'No.'

'Yes, you do.'

'I recognise that it's not my voice.'

'Nevertheless the call was placed on your instruction – to bring Max's van to our attention. It's the evidence that puts you away for murder.'

'The recording proves nothing on its own.' Ostrowsky seemed amused, confident.

'But with Ashley's testimony it does.'

'Then I will try to locate him for you so I may clear my name,' said Ostrowsky. 'Unfortunately he left my employ yesterday.'

'He can't stay hidden forever,' said Brook. 'And when we find him, you're finished.'

* * *

Ostrowsky poured a glass of vodka, threw his jacket on the floor and slumped on to the plush sofa to kick off his Italian shoes. He stared through the window towards the dark garden of his palatial home stretching into the distance.

Tymon appeared from a side room. 'You want some food, boss?' he asked in Polish, finishing a mouthful of his own.

'No. Fetch them.'

Ostrowsky had downed most of the vodka when Nick and Ashley appeared and sat together on another sofa. 'Nicholas, how was your day?'

'Wicked, Uncle Greg,' said Nick. 'Been playing AC4 Black Flag with Ashley and I'm up to—'

'What about your studies?'

Nick took a deep breath. 'I wrote a story this morning. And after lunch I learned about different chemicals.'

'Tell me one thing you learned about chemicals, Nicholas.'

Nick concentrated hard. 'Well, did you know that water contains one oxygen . . .'

'Atom,' prompted Ashley.

'Atom,' repeated Nick. 'And two atoms of hydrogen.'

'I did know that,' said Ostrowsky.

Nick grinned. 'Thing is, if water contains oxygen, why can't we breathe at the bottom of the swimming pool?'

'A good question, Nicholas. You start to think with logic.' Ostrowsky looked at his watch. 'It's late.' Nick leapt from the sofa. 'Wait, I forgot to tell you. I have to go to Poland tomorrow night, on urgent business.'

'Poland?'

'My home country,' said Ostrowsky. 'Would you like to stay here and study or would you like to come with me? We'll be sailing overnight across the sea to Amsterdam. If you want to come, I can book cabins, otherwise Tymon and I will snooze in chairs.'

'The sea?' said Nick. 'I've never seen the sea.'

'You've never seen the sea?' smiled Ostrowsky. 'Then you shall see it tomorrow.'

'Can Ashley come?'

'Well maybe Ashley has other plans, Nicholas. We shouldn't presume he wants to spend all his time with you.'

'Will you come, Ashley?' pleaded Nick. 'Will you?'

'Never been to Poland,' said Ashley sheepishly. 'Sounds great.'

'You're sure?' said Ostrowsky. 'Then I shall book two outside cabins and you can look at the sea until you fall asleep.' Nick clenched a fist in triumph. 'On condition you get a good night's sleep. Then it won't matter if you stay awake tomorrow.'

Ashley and Nick set off for their rooms and Ostrowsky drained his drink.

'Business, boss?'

Ostrowsky's steel-blue eyes burned fiercely into Ashley's back. He turned his gaze on his loyal bodyguard until Tymon nodded his understanding.

'He's asleep,' said Ashley.

Ostrowsky smiled. 'It's all the excitement. He will see the sea on the return journey.' He gestured at Tymon, waiting in the narrow corridor. 'Ashley, can you help Tymon bring something back from the car? It was too heavy for me.'

'Sure, Mr O.' Ashley closed the cabin door behind him.

'This way,' said Tymon.

The pair emerged from the well-lit walkway into the wide-open spaces of the main boutique and bar area. At two in the morning, few people were around, and those that were were slumped in their seats trying to sleep. Tymon pressed the button for the lift, and on entering hit the Deck Nine button.

'That's not the car deck,' said Ashley.

'Sorry.' Tymon fired an imaginary gun at his own forehead before pressing the car deck button. '*Idiota.*'

The doors opened on Deck Nine at the top of the ship and Tymon put a hand to his mouth. 'Seasick.' He stepped out and scuttled for the external door into the cool cloudy night, running across to the rail to lean over.

'Seasick?' gloated Ashley, looking out over the North Sea stretching flat as a mirror, then back at Tymon's huge bulk. 'It's like a sodding millpond.'

The burly figure pushed himself back to his full height and turned to Ashley with a malicious gleam in his eye. 'You right. I better.' He grinned. 'But you not look so good.'

Ashley pulled a face. 'Yeah, whatever, mate. Come on. Let's get a shift on.'

Tymon's hand was on Ashley's throat in a split second, belying his cumbersome frame. As the big Pole walked the lightly built young man back to the rail, he moaned and gasped for breath, his tongue protruding and his eyes beginning to bulge.

At the rail, Tymon loosened his grip, but before Ashley could get his breath, he swung his forearm sharply across the younger man's cheek. Ashley crumpled like a cheap umbrella, held upright only by Tymon's pudgy hand wedging him against the handrail.

Tymon took a precautionary look round, then hoisted the unconscious figure above the height of the safety rail.

'Goodbye, Ashley.'

* * *

Tymon's smile warped at a strange pain in his spine, and he turned to see a tall, powerful man at his back. A second later, Ashley crashed to the deck as the big man's arms and legs gave way and he slumped forward, his fat head now jammed against the handrail. Paralysed, he was powerless to resist as the man, dressed head to toe in black, wrenched the knuckle knife around ninety degrees before withdrawing it from his spinal column. If Tymon could have controlled his vocal cords at that moment, he would have screamed in agony.

The assailant dragged Ashley's unconscious body to the safety of the vibrating bulkhead, returning to haul Tymon's unresponsive carcass up the rail. He lifted the big man, not without difficulty, and held him against the barrier, feeling him beginning to spasm.

'You carry too much weight, my friend,' he grunted in Polish, as he forced Tymon's upper torso over the chest-high metal. He bent to the ankles, lifted them up and flipped Tymon over the side. 'May I suggest a fish diet?'

A soft knock on the door signalled job done. Ostrowsky unscrewed the cap on a fresh bottle of vodka. 'Come and have a drink, old friend,' he said as he poured two large measures. He looked up to see a tall man dressed in black trousers, gloves, sweater, shoes and woollen hat pointing a gun at him. He paused briefly before resealing the bottle. 'You're just in time.'

The man in black pulled off his hat and screwed a silencer on to the end of the gun barrel before sitting on the bunk opposite Ostrowsky, out of arm's reach.

'Drink?' said Ostrowsky. The man in black shook his head.

'Mind if I finish mine?' Again a head shake. For obvious reasons, Ostrowsky took a more conservative sip than usual and studied his uninvited guest. 'I know you,' he said, breaking into a smile of recognition. 'The photograph she kept by her bed. Special forces, right? Major . . .'

'*Colonel* Marius Proch,' said the man in the interests of clarity.

'Colonel,' repeated Ostrowsky. 'She was very proud of you.'

'And I of her.'

Ostrowsky wagged an admonishing finger. 'I made her promise not to mention me to her parents.'

Proch smiled. 'Kassia was a good girl. She kept her promise.'

Ostrowsky puzzled over this for a second before arriving at a solution. 'Brook.'

Proch didn't confirm or deny. 'Drink your vodka.'

Ostrowsky drained his glass before placing it on the floor. He straightened his tie. 'Would you allow me to pray first?'

'Did you allow my Kassia to pray?' said Proch. Ostrowsky hesitated. A bullet smashed into his heart and he crashed back on to the mattress, dead instantly. 'That's what I thought.'

Proch searched Ostrowsky and removed car keys, wallet and telephone before opening the window. He lifted Ostrowsky's head and shoulders through the gap and pushed him incrementally until gravity did its work and the body splashed into the black water below. He dismantled the gun and flung both parts into the North Sea after Ostrowsky. He did the same with the businessman's smartphone, the bullet casing and his gloves, stained with Tymon's blood.

Using his handkerchief, he opened the cabin next door and placed the car keys and wallet quietly on the floor. Ashley was still unconscious on his bunk, but Nick was snoring for

England. Proch closed the door, wiped the handle and returned to the outdoor deck, where he took out a pre-paid mobile phone and rang the only number on the speed dial.

'Hello,' said the voice on the other end.

Proch paused for a second. 'Sorry, I have dialled incorrectly.' He rang off and dropped the phone over the side, then returned to his cabin for the rest of the journey.

Brook put down his mobile and sat on his bench watching the moon emerge from behind a dense cloud. Tigerbob sat on his lap asleep, and Brook was reluctant to move, despite his thirst for tea.

An hour later, he texted Noble to set up a meeting with Jake Tanner and his solicitor at the earliest opportunity.

'Sorry, Jake,' he said aloud, a tight smile forming around his mouth. 'If justice is to prevail, there can be no peace.'

About Steven Dunne

Steven Dunne was born in Bradford, Yorkshire but moved to London after attending Kent University and St Mary's College in Twickenham. He became a freelance journalist writing for *The Times* and the *Independent* and, after co-writing a comedy pilot, wrote the book for The Latchmere Theatre's award-winning pantomime Hansel and Gretel.

He lives and works in Derby and has written five highly acclaimed thrillers, including THE UNQUIET GRAVE and DEITY, all featuring DI Brook of Derby CID.